Passions igni...
wed...

The Millionaire's Club: Jacob, Logan & Marc

Three arrogant and seductive heroes you'll never forget from three favourite authors!

In July 2010 Mills & Boon bring you four classic collections, each featuring three favourite romances by our bestselling authors

THE PRINCES' BRIDES
by Sandra Marton
The Italian Prince's Pregnant Bride
The Greek Prince's Chosen Wife
The Spanish Prince's Virgin Bride

TYCOON'S CHOICE
Kept by the Tycoon by Lee Wilkinson
Taken by the Tycoon by Kathryn Ross
The Tycoon's Proposal by Leigh Michaels

THE MILLIONAIRE'S CLUB: JACOB, LOGAN & MARC
Black-Tie Seduction by Cindy Gerard
Less-Than-Innocent Invitation by Shirley Rogers
Strictly Confidential Attraction by Brenda Jackson

SAYING 'YES!' TO THE BOSS
Having Her Boss's Baby by Susan Mallery
Business or Pleasure? by Julie Hogan
Business Affairs by Shirley Rogers

The Millionaire's Club: Jacob, Logan & Marc

CINDY GERARD

SHIRLEY ROGERS

BRENDA JACKSON

First published in Great Britain 2010
Harlequin Mills & Boon Limited,
Eton House, 18-24 Paradise Road, Richmond, Surrey TW9 1SR

THE MILLIONAIRE'S CLUB: JACOB, LOGAN & MARC
© by Harlequin Enterprises II B.V./S.à.r.l 2010

Black-Tie Seduction, Less-than-Innocent Invitation and *Strictly Confidential Attraction* were first published in Great Britain by Harlequin Mills & Boon Limited in separate, single volumes.

Black-Tie Seduction © Harlequin Books S.A. 2005
Less-than-Innocent Invitation © Harlequin Books S.A. 2005
Strictly Confidential Attraction © Harlequin Books S.A. 2005

Special thanks and acknowledgement are given to Cindy Gerard, Shirley Rogers and Brenda Jackson for their contribution to THE MILLIONAIRE'S CLUB series.

ISBN: 978 0 263 88040 3

05-0710

Printed and bound in Spain
by Litografia Rosés S.A., Barcelona

BLACK-TIE SEDUCTION

BY
CINDY GERARD

Cindy Gerard has repeatedly made appearances on several bestseller lists, including *USA TODAY*.

With numerous industry awards to her credit – among them the Romance Writers of America's RITA® Award and the National Reader's Choice Award – this former Golden Heart finalist and repeat *Romantic Times* nominee is the real deal. As one book reviewer put it, "Cindy Gerard provides everything romance readers want in a love story, passion, gut-wrenching emotion, intriguing characters and a captivating plot. This storyteller extraordinaire delivers all of this and more!"

Cindy and her husband, Tom, live in the Midwest on a mini-farm with quarter horses, cats and two very spoiled dogs. When she's not writing, she enjoys reading, travelling and spending time at their cabin in northern Minnesota unwinding with family and friends.

Cindy loves to hear from her readers and invites you to visit her website at www.cindygerard.com.

This book is dedicated to the fabulous women who
worked so hard to make this new segment of THE
MILLIONAIRE'S CLUB saga the best yet!
Shirley Rogers, Brenda Jackson, Michelle Celmer,
Sara Orwig and Kristi Gold.
Ladies, it's been my great pleasure!

Prologue

From the diary of Jessamine Golden
July 4, 1905

Dear Diary,
Today my life changed. It came out of the blue. Like a lightning strike in the midst of a sunset storm or the fireworks lighting up the sky during tonight's celebration of our country's independence. I'm not sure how else to describe what happened to me when I first set eyes on Brad Webster—or how to describe the clash of wills when he drew me aside and told me how things were going to be.

"I run a clean town," he said. "I don't want any trouble from you."

He looked stern and angry and so very serious when he talked to me. And yet he didn't arrest me, this man who walks on the opposite path that fate has set for me.

Sheriff Brad Webster. Just writing his name makes my heart kick around inside my chest like a string of wild ponies. Saying it out loud makes my fingers tremble and my face flush hot and sends strange warm flames licking through my belly. You'd think I'd been smoking locoweed. And it is *loco* for me to be so obsessed by him.

But despite his anger at me, he is the most beautiful man…if a man can be called beautiful. I remember some years ago Daddy and I were riding strays and we came upon this herd of wild mustangs. The stallion was big and ink-black and, oh, he was the prettiest thing I'd ever seen. Sleek and muscled, tall and strong. One look in that big guy's eyes and you knew he was proud and brave.

That's what I thought when I saw the sheriff. Like that wild stallion, he is proud and brave. His hair is ink-black. His eyes are the most fascinating Texas-sky-blue. And tall. Lordy, is that man tall. But he's no beanpole. Oh, no. He's got the build of a working man. And he's a man who believes in duty.

Duty. His duty is why I must stop carrying on

about him so. Brad Webster wears a badge that says he's the law. And everything about the way he carries himself says he is as loyal to the law as I am loyal to the cause that has taken me on the wrong side of it.

Dear, dear diary. Is there anything in life that is fair? Why does everything have to be so hard? I have met a man who makes me want to forget what drove me to a life of crime. But I can't forget. I can't. Just as I can't forget that this amazing, beautiful man may be forced, by duty, to end my very life. Even worse, I may be forced to end his.

One

One man's trash. Another man's treasure.

The old cliché wound around inside Christine Travers's head like a coil of barbwire as she stared, disbelieving, at the treasure she'd just discovered.

The good folks of Royal, Texas, had dug deep into their basements and attics to come up with items to donate to tonight's auction. There were antique crystal pieces. Complete china sets. Magazines that dated back to the early nineteenth century. Furniture and painstakingly hand-stitched quilts. And then there was this box.

Her breath stalled. Her heart beat so fast and so hard, she was afraid she might pass out. Right here. Right smack in the middle of this crowd of upper-crust residents, including a large contingent of Texas Cattleman's Club members—the infamous and elite philanthropic organization that had staged tonight's fund-raising auction to benefit Royal's upcoming one hundred and twenty-fifth anniversary celebration.

So, no. Passing out would not be good form any way you sliced it. And the last thing she would ever want to do was bring attention to herself—for any reason.

Okay, Christine. Settle down. Take a deep breath. Another.

Steadier now, with her fingers only marginally tingling, she glanced around the auction house to see if anyone was watching her with an odd expression—a sure sign she'd either screamed out loud, jumped up and down or done something equally ridiculous and brought unwanted attention to herself. And to her amazing find.

A relieved sigh eddied out when no one seemed to notice her excitement. Almost everyone who had turned out was busy browsing. Well, almost everyone.

Some of the Cattleman's Club members, including Jacob Thorne, she'd noticed with dismay, were laughing and joking by the bar across the room.

Why did he have to be here?

Christine made it a point to avoid Jacob Thorne. If he spotted her tonight, she had no doubt that, true to form, he'd make it his personal mission to give her ten different kinds of grief. What she'd ever done to deserve his teasing and goading—other than help save his miserable life—was beyond her.

Well, she wasn't going to think about him tonight. She had another meatier, much more exciting matter to attend to. Rows and rows of tables were filled with items that would soon be up for bid. Among those items Christine had found buried treasure—or the next best thing to it. The contents of this box, according to the notation, came from the late Jonathan Devlin's attic.

Oh. My. God.

"Is it hot in here?" Christine asked her friend, Alison Lind, as she fussed with her plain white blouse that she'd buttoned all the way up to her neck.

"It's Texas. It's July," Alison said, deadpan. Her dark eyes sparkled in her pretty chocolate-brown face. While Christine was usually cautious about opening herself up to someone, she'd sensed a kindred spirit in Alison. They'd met at a self-defense class a few months ago and had been fast friends since.

"Okay. Rhetorical question," Christine conceded. "It just seemed extra warm there for a minute."

Alison gave her friend a look and an "Uh-huh," then walked on ahead of Christine toward a bolt of red satin.

"All right," Christine whispered to herself and wiped damp palms on her tailored navy slacks. "Get a grip."

Act cool. Don't let on that you may have just discovered what must have appeared to be nothing more than an old, musty-smelling saddlebag to the late Jonathan Devlin's family. Nothing more than a novelty item someone might want to bid on to decorate a bar or a tack room—instead of a major historical find.

Well, they could bid, she thought fiercely, but she was going to leave here with the contents of this box. That's because she knew something no one else did. She was ninety-nine-point-nine percent certain that she knew who the saddlebag had once belonged to.

"What's got you so fidgety?" Alison asked, wandering back to Christine's side. She tried to peek into the box.

Christine quickly flipped the lid shut.

"Can you keep a secret?" Christine whispered, cutting a covert glance around her.

Alison frowned. "If the secret is that you're having a minor manic episode, no, I don't think so. The paramedics who treat you will need details."

Ignoring her friend's sarcasm, Christine gripped Alison's arm and pulled her close. She lifted the lid on the box. The smell of old leather and dust seeped into the air. "See this saddlebag?"

"Oh—I get to look inside now?"

Christine pulled a face. "Yes, you get to look inside." Still acting wary, Alison did.

"Notice the rose tooled on the cover flap?"

From Alison she got a slow, skeptical nod.

"The rose is what drew my attention. So I checked inside the bag," Christine confided in a low voice, "and found a pair of six-shooters. *Old* six-shooters, with roses carved into the ivory handles."

"And..." Alison said in a leading tone as Christine cast more worried looks around them.

"And there's also a delicate little purse. Again—old.

Rose-colored—with what appear to be rose petals inside. Plus—" she huddled up with Alison and whispered "—there's a map."

She snatched Alison's hand back with an apologetic look when Alison started to reach inside the saddlebag. "A map with hearts and roses twining around the edge."

"Okay. I'll play along," Alison said, still frowning as though she thought Christine had blown a circuit. "I'm guessing there's some major significance to all these roses?"

"You don't know the half of it," Christine said. "I'm positive these things once belonged to Jessamine Golden."

When Alison made a "who?" face, Christine closed the box, then tugged Alison away from the table and hustled her into the line of people waiting to acquire bidding numbers.

"Jessamine Golden is a legend in Royal," she explained in a low voice so no one would overhear. "She was an outlaw a hundred years ago who not only stole the heart of the town sheriff, Brad Webster, but legend has it that she also stole a huge gold shipment and hid the treasure somewhere in the Royal area. And she *loved* roses.

"Thanks," she said absently when the clerk gave her a paddle with a number on it. She walked Alison to the row of seats lined up in front of the podium where the bidding was already under way.

"Anyway, the rest of the story is that the mayor of Royal back then was Edgar Halifax—"

"Halifax?" Alison interrupted. "Any relation to Gretchen Halifax, our illustrious city councilwoman?"

Gretchen Halifax wasn't an *illustrious* anything except in her own mind, and both women knew it, but Christine didn't want to get sidetracked with talk about Gretchen. She'd had to deal with Gretchen on the new Edgar Halifax display at the museum and that had been more than enough exposure to the woman. Christine always was willing to give people the benefit of the doubt, but in this case the stories about Gretchen appeared to be true. The councilwoman was pompous and self-important and on more than one occasion had been very condescending toward Christine.

"Yes, I think Gretchen is some distant relative, but the point is Edgar Halifax and his men were supposedly killed by Jessamine Golden over the stolen gold. There's also speculation that Jessamine killed the sheriff, too, because when she disappeared, neither one of them was ever heard from again. And the gold was never found."

Christine tugged Alison down on the chair beside her, facing the auctioneer. "I think the map in those saddlebags is a map to where Jess hid the gold!" she whispered fiercely.

Alison searched her friend's face. "All right. Did you eat an entire bag of chocolate before you came here?"

The look on Alison's face coupled with her silly question finally made Christine laugh. "No," she assured her friend, "I did *not* eat any chocolate, and will you quit looking at me like I'm an alien? I'm serious.

You know that I volunteer time at the Royal Historical Society when I'm not pulling double shifts at the hospital. I do a lot of research there, and Jess Golden's story caught my attention. And, Alison, I swear those have to be Jess's things in that box that came out of Jonathan Devlin's attic."

"Out of Jonathan Devlin's attic?" Alison shook her head. "Boy, the Devlins didn't waste any time clearing out old Jonathan's house. He only died a few days ago—they haven't even buried him yet, have they?"

"Not yet, no. But you know his sister Opal? A month ago, when Jonathan went into a coma, it was expected that he'd never recover. I guess from the start there was no brain activity. Anyway, Opal had been going through his house for weeks in anticipation of his death, setting aside things to put up for auction."

"Gives me warm fuzzies all over thinking about her sorrow over the loss of her brother."

Christine smiled. "Tell me about it. Opal's a sentimental and sympathetic soul all right," she said, matching Alison's sarcasm. "But back to the topic at hand. One of the reasons I'm so convinced these are Jess Golden's things is that for a very brief time—around 1910 or so—she lived in Jonathan Devlin's house."

"Okay," Alison said carefully but looking as if she was a little more on board, "let's say you're right. Let's say those are Jess Golden's things because she left them in the house when she skedaddled out of town after she did her dastardly deed. What then?"

"Then I'm going to buy them," Christine stated emphatically. "For the Historical Society to put on display in the museum. That box contains priceless historical artifacts—not to mention, it might lead to the gold. What a find it would be for the town."

"Well, you'd better get your paddle ready, Miss Supersleuth. They just brought the box to the podium. It's the next item up for bid."

Jake Thorne wasn't sure what it was about Chrissie Travers that lit his fire, but every time he showed up someplace and she was there, it was as though some kinetic energy source set all his senses on supercharge and he homed in on her like a bear scenting honey.

He propped an elbow on the bar where he stood at the side of the room and got comfortable. Then he just enjoyed the hell out of watching her in typical Prissy Chrissie mode, all stiff and proper and tense, while his mind—already shifting into autopilot—started hatching plots to irritate her. Just a little. Because, man, she was some fun when she was riled.

And he ought to know. He'd spent a month in the Royal hospital five years ago after an oil-well fire had knocked him on his ass. The burns hadn't been the worst of his injuries. The smoke and fire inhalation and the resulting damage to his lungs had been. Chrissie had been his respiratory therapist, and once he'd felt human again, he'd found a hundred hot buttons to push on the uptight, serious and tolerate-no-nonsense Chrissie Travers. He was pleased to say that he'd personally pushed at least ninety-nine of them at some time or another.

Her bidding paddle shot up in the air. *Whoa. What have we here?* he wondered when she lifted it above her head. Straight up. No hesitation. As high as she could raise her arm.

Seemed the lady aimed to buy something. Judging by her body language, she meant to have it at any cost.

He watched both Chrissie and the bidding with interest. She cast a flurry of darting looks around her, those big hazel eyes warning off anyone who even looked as if they wanted to raise their paddle. Interesting. The bidding was slow and it looked as though she was going to get the box of, hell, box of rocks for all he knew, for a song.

Or is she? he asked himself and felt the beginnings of an ornery grin. Just as the auctioneer was about to start a "Going, going, gone," with Chrissie as the high bidder, Jake's paddle seemed to sort of pop up in the air, all of its own accord.

Hmm. Looked as though he was in the bidding now, too.

Chrissie's head whipped around, her fine blond hair flying around her face, her big hazel eyes snapping with smoke and hellfire as she searched the room for the culprit who dared to enter the bidding at this late hour.

When her gaze finally landed on him and he acknowledged with a grin and a friendly wave of his paddle that, yeah, he was the one who'd jumped in and spoiled her party, he swore to God lightning zapped out of her ears and shot twin puffs of smoke in its wake.

And when after a fierce flurry of bidding action between them ended with a gavel rap and a resounding, "Sold!" and Jake was the lucky owner of a cardboard box containing he had no idea what, the look she sent him could have set a forest ablaze.

He touched his fingertips to the brim of his tan Resistol, smiled sweetly and swore he heard a word come out of her mouth that he figured prissy Miss Chrissie had never even heard before, let alone used.

Oh, boy. We're gonna have some fun now.

Christine glared at the man sauntering toward her. Jacob Thorne was wearing what he probably thought was an aren't-I-just-as-sexy-as-sin rogue grin that tugged up one corner of his full, mobile lips and dented his incredible dimples. He thought he was something—looking at her as if he was God's greatest gift. As if her heart ought to go pit-a-pat and she ought to get hot all over basking in the glow of his company, as half the women in town did every time he sliced one of his poster-boy smiles their way.

Well, she was hot all right. Bonfire hot. And her heart was pounding. Not some loopy, goofy stutter step but a jackhammer, piston-pumping, so-mad-she-could-hear-each-staccato-beat-in-her-ears-and-feel-it-pulse-all-the-way-to-her-toes pounding. And in that moment she understood why it sometimes became part of the human condition to react to anger with physical violence.

Not that she'd ever stoop that low. She'd experienced enough physical violence in her life. But it didn't hurt to think about exactly how deep she could bury the tip of her boot into Jacob Thorne-in-her-side's shin. And to imagine his grunt of pain, the swelling and the black-and-blue marks when she did.

"Hey, Chrissie," he said, all sweet and sugary, with that sexy, sandpapery voice of his. "You're looking mighty fine tonight. Got a little color in your cheeks for a change. Did you finally take some time for yourself and get out in the sun a bit?"

She tilted her head to the side and glared at him. And he had the nerve to try to be cute. Again.

"Oh. *Not* sun." He made a big show of acting surprised. "You're miffed at me, right? *That's* what put that pretty pink in your cheeks."

For whatever reason, ever since she'd been his respiratory therapist, he seemed to make it his personal mission to tease her unmercifully. Like a big, overgrown bully. He needed to grow up, that's what he needed to do. In the meantime she'd treat him like the kid he was.

"You are *so* not funny. And you are *so* not charming."

She reached out and grabbed Alison's arm, holding her still when she sensed that her friend was about to slink away and avoid certain fireworks.

"Now, how much do you want for it?" she asked

with a clipped nod toward the box he'd tucked under his arm. The box that contained Jessamine Golden's saddlebag and its treasure trove of goodies. The box that had almost been hers for fifty-five bucks until he'd chimed in with his big money and stolen it from her.

He glanced from her to the box. "What's in here that's got you so excited?"

She blinked. Then, outraged, blinked again. "You didn't even know what you were bidding on?"

"Well, no," he said, lifting a shoulder. "I was just trying to make some extra money for the benefit."

"You know what?" Alison said, squirming uneasily and apparently sensing a major showdown. "I think I'll just be going now."

Christine wrapped her fingers tighter around Alison's upper arm and held her where she was. "So why didn't you bid against Ralph Schindler when he was bidding on an antique typewriter? Or Mel Grazier when he bid on a boom box? They've got buckets of moldy money. Why did you have to bid against me?"

"Well," he said, then paused and absently scratched his jaw. "Maybe I figured if you wanted it, it must be something worth having."

She snorted. "Try again."

"No, really. I've always known you to have excellent taste."

"So…that's supposed to be an explanation?"

"More like a compliment."

"More like a crock. You did it just to tick me off."

"Well—" his dark eyes danced in a tan, handsome face "—there is that."

The sound that came out of her could only be described as a growl.

"I've really got to go," Alison said, making another break for it.

This time Christine let her go. It wasn't fair to Alison to make her a party to what could in all probability turn out to be a homicide.

"How much do you want for it?" she repeated only after she was certain she could talk without screeching.

"You want it bad, don't you, Chrissie?"

Oh, he'd just love to see her rise to *that* bait. She was not going to give him the satisfaction of acknowledging the sexual innuendo he'd managed to thread through his seemingly innocent question punctuated with a wicked smile.

"How much?"

"Tell you what," he said, looking if not smug, at least pleased by whatever idea was brewing in his thick head. "How about we cut us a little deal?"

Cut a deal? She'd trust any deal he made about as far as she could shot-put his beefy carcass after she killed him but before they hauled her off to jail. Justifiable homicide would be the worst possible charge they could level.

"I can just about imagine any deal you'd initiate. You haven't changed a bit, have you?"

"Aw, Chrissie. You don't still hold a grudge after all this time, do you?"

Oh, yeah. She held a grudge all right. He made it easy.

"Tell you what, just to show you I'm not so awful," he said, working hard at sounding wounded, "since you want this stuff that badly, I'll just give it to you."

She eyed him with unconcealed suspicion. All six-plus lean feet of him. She couldn't help but notice the way his long brown hair curled slightly at the edges, giving him a sexy boyish appeal. Couldn't help but try to read the thoughts going on behind those summer-blue eyes that were always laughing, always teasing, always making her wonder what made him tick.

Well. Not *always* because she didn't spend that much time thinking about him. At least, she didn't do it intentionally. He sort of sneaked into her thoughts sometimes when she least expected it and caught her off guard.

Like now. Damn, all those wonder-boy good looks had sidetracked her again. Made her forget—if only for a second there—that she was mad and he was the reason.

"Okay. What's the catch?" Skepticism oozed in each word.

"What makes you think there's a catch?"

"Because I wasn't born yesterday?"

"There ya go. You're just as smart as you are pretty."

"Oh, for Pete's sake, save the sugar for someone with a sweet tooth."

He considered her for a moment as if he were thinking about how badly he wanted to embarrass her. Then he very coolly said, "You can have the box of stuff on one condition. Be my date for the anniversary ball."

It took a moment for Christine to process his words. When she finally realized what he was suggesting, her mouth dropped open. Nothing came out.

If he'd told her the condition was to strip and then run through the streets proclaiming she was madly in love with him, she would have been less surprised than she was right now.

And the chances of her agreeing to either condition were exactly the same.

"Boy, that got you thinking," he said, his lean cheeks dimpling. "So, what do you say? How about it?"

He wasn't serious. He couldn't be. Never in a million years would Jake Thorne—Texas Cattleman's Club member and one of the most sought-after bachelors in Royal—waste his time with her, not at something as big as the anniversary ball. Not when all the eligible socialites and darlings of society were lined up like Miss America candidates waiting for him to select one of them as his date for the biggest social event in recent Royal history. Beautiful, wealthy, socially adept women who ran in his circle and would look good on his arm—unlike her, who would look more like a lump of coal than a diamond.

Even though she didn't want it to, it stung that he'd play with her this way when they both knew good and well that, unless he thought he could find some perverse pleasure humiliating her, he'd never in a million years include her on his list of possible dates.

This was just too cruel. And she'd had enough of his goading for one night.

"How about you take your condition and put it where the sun don't shine?"

Then, hating herself for letting him get to her, she turned on her heel and stomped away while his highly amused "Was it something I said?" trailed her across the room.

Two

"I don't get it," Alison said the night after the auction as they waited at the back of the room for their self-defense class to start. "What's the problem with going to the anniversary ball with Jake Thorne? It's not like you already have a date. And good grief, girl, the man is a hottie of the major-flame variety. No pun intended."

But it was a pun regardless since Jacob Thorne's stock-in-trade was fighting oil-well fires. Or at least, it used to be his stock-in-trade to fight them until the accident. Everything had changed for him then. He still ran his own company, but from a desk now instead of on the actual site of the fires.

Christine sat down on the mat and fussed with the

laces of her tennis shoes, shoving thoughts of the trauma he'd gone through from her mind.

"He's a hottie all right. Of the inflammatory variety."

"Well, he sure seems to have incited a riot in you."

"We have a history," Christine finally admitted in a weak moment as she pulled her straight shoulder-length hair into a ponytail and clipped it at her nape.

"*No*. I never would have guessed," Alison said, clearly having guessed exactly that.

Christine grinned at her friend's staged surprise.

"What did he do, dump you?"

"No," she said sobering. "He did *not* dump me. We've never even dated."

"Ah. So *that's* the problem. You want to date him."

"Yeah, right," Christine said maybe a little too emphatically.

This time Alison didn't say a word. She just raised an eyebrow and waited.

Christine expelled a weary sigh and rose to her feet. "Okay. The problem," she sputtered, using Alison's words, "is that he's just making fun of me by inviting me to the dance. He's always making fun of me. He taunts and teases and plays on the fact that I had a little crush on him once—a *looonnnggg* time ago—and he keeps exploiting it. You saw how he was at the auction. He didn't want that box for any reason other than because I wanted it. And he didn't ask me to the ball for any other reason than to mock me."

She tugged down her T-shirt, then forked her fingers

through her ponytail, getting mad all over again just thinking about it. "He just loves to push my buttons. I'm getting tired of it."

"I think it's kind of cute," Alison said, then laughed when Christine threw her a disbelieving look. "Well, I do. Because it's all in fun and what it really means is that he has a thing for you."

Christine grunted. "It means that he's childish and sophomoric. And he doesn't have a *thing* for me. I mean, look at me—I'm as far from his type as a male stripper is from mine. He's just...ornery. The man doesn't have a sincere bone in his body. Everything's a joke with him."

"Everything?"

She thought for a moment. "Okay. For instance—he got hurt badly in an oil-well fire five years ago. Smoke and fire inhalation did some heavy-duty damage to his lungs and he spent over a month in the hospital. I was the unlucky one on duty the night they brought him in and I ended up spending a lot of time with him over the course of his recovery."

When some other class members walked in, Christine lowered her voice because she didn't want them to overhear her. And she really didn't want to relive those days in a play-by-play for Alison.

That didn't stop her from thinking about it, though. Jacob Thorne had been one sick puppy. She'd been so worried for him, while he'd been brave and determined to recover and joked his way through the pain and the fear of his prognosis. She'd admired him for it...then formed that unfortunate crush.

She did *not* admire him for it now. Neither did she have a crush on him. Not anymore.

"Anyway, a couple of weeks into his treatment his twin brother, Connor, came to visit him. His *identical* twin," she added to make sure Alison understood. "Long story short, they pulled a switch on me so Jacob—the evil twin— could sneak out of the hospital and go down to the Cattleman's Club for a beer. The end result was that I actually gave a respiratory therapy session to the wrong man!"

She got angry all over again just thinking about it. "He could have caused himself a serious setback pulling a reckless stunt like that."

Alison looked at her as if she was waiting for the punch line. Finally she said, "That's it? That's why you don't like him? The poor guy had been stuck in a hospital bed, sick as a dog. A cold beer and some male company sounded good to him so he pulled a fast one on you to indulge in a tiny little creature comfort?"

"I don't like him," Christine restated, not liking that she felt defensive again, "because he doesn't get it. He doesn't get it that life is not one big lark. Life is serious. Life is real. It's not a game, and you can't just play your way through it the way he does."

For the first time Alison looked at her with no trace of humor. And it was then that Christine realized tears had pooled in her eyes. Embarrassed, she quickly blinked them back.

"Oh, sweetie." Alison reached out, touched her hand. "What happened to you?"

Instantly on edge, Christine pulled her hand away. She wasn't comfortable with touching, even though Alison's touch held compassion and concern—something entirely different than the hard hands that had touched her in anger when she was a child. "I—I don't know what you mean."

"I mean, what happened to you that made you decide life had to be all about work and duty with no room for fun?" Alison pressed gently.

Fortunately for Christina, Mark Hartman, Alison's boss—who was also the self-defense class's instructor and another Texas Cattleman's Club member like Jacob—entered the room at that very moment.

His appearance and the necessity to get down to business saved Christine from opening up like a faucet and spilling out her sordid history to this woman whose insight and empathy had almost broken through defenses she'd kept shored up her entire life.

Christine was appalled with herself when she realized her eyes still stung with tears. She blinked them back and, giving Alison an apologetic look, moved away from her and onto her spot on the practice mat. Christine wished she could talk to her friend about her past. But she couldn't. Not yet.

For the rest of the class she went through the self-defense positions like an automaton, knowing the moves as well as she knew the secret she'd kept from anyone who had ever gotten too close.

She had good reason to know that life was not fun and games. Life was a father who had beaten her and her mother and a mother who drank to escape the pain. Christine hadn't had any escape—only fear—until she'd turned eighteen and finally had been able to run. She'd run as far away as she could from that horrible existence and the memories that sometimes still woke her, trembling, in the night.

That's what had happened to her, she thought as she showered in the locker room later. That's why she sometimes worked double shifts at the hospital, why she took her job as a respiratory therapist so seriously and why she also volunteered to work for the Historical Society. She never wanted to have to depend on anyone but herself. Her work at the hospital gave her that self-sufficiency. Her volunteer work at the Historical Society gave her a sense of community.

Both also gave her something else—something she hadn't expected and hadn't known she'd needed—respectability. Acceptance. A place to belong.

She protected those hard-earned parts of her life. Held them close—held herself aloof to make sure no one got close enough to discover that inside her, there were still strong echoes of a lost and helpless little girl who had always thought she wasn't good enough for her own father to love her. For her own mother to protect her.

She never wanted to feel that sense of helplessness or hopelessness again. Respectability, security and safety. She'd needed them most as a child but had never received them. As an adult, she'd earned them and she never took them for granted.

Life was work. Life was hard. How many times had her father driven that point home? Often enough that she'd absorbed it along with the blows from the back of his hand.

Yeah, she thought pragmatically. Life was hard. But life was also precious.

And that's why she didn't like Jake Thorne, with his life-is-a-lark attitude and his damn-the-torpedoes grin. He took everything for granted. So much so that it puzzled her how someone like him had gotten invited to join the Cattleman's Club—a club that was about duty and honor and public service. And if some of the rumors were to be believed, it was also a club where the members were covertly active in thwarting any number of horrible situations. In fact, she'd heard specific rumors that the club had been instrumental in breaking up a black-market baby network and once had prevented a bloody overthrow of a small European principality. Jacob Thorne just didn't seem to fit the Cattleman's profile.

Fun and games. That seemed to be as deep as he got. She didn't know how to react around someone who was always smiling and joking. The way he'd joked with her the other night.

"Him and his condition," she sputtered under her breath, remembering how he'd told her she could have the saddlebags if she met his condition.

Nothing had changed there, she admitted, as with a

brief hug she begged off Alison's offer to stop at the Royal Diner for a diet soda that was really a ruse to get her to talk. Christine wasn't ready to confide that part of her life with Alison, although she'd come as close to telling her as she had anyone.

Instead she went home. She still wanted the box with Jess Golden's things for the Historical Society. And because this was serious business, she knew what she'd known from the beginning and simply hadn't wanted to admit.

She'd have to give in to Thorne's condition. Eat some crow and call him. Tell him she'd reconsidered. She'd go to his damn ball—so he could have some fun at her expense.

She undressed, brushed and flossed, then slipped into a white cotton nightie. She plopped down on her back in bed and stared at the ceiling in the dark.

First thing tomorrow she'd call him.

Oh, joy. Something to look forward to. A conference with the evil twin.

Two days after the auction, Jake waded through a dozen voice mails at his office at Hellfire, International, hating it that he wasn't on-site with his men.

"You get caught up in another fire," his doctor had warned him before he'd released him from the hospital after his accident, "and the next time you won't walk away. The damage to your lungs is just too extensive to risk it. They can't take another hit."

Sidelined. Jake hated it. To take his mind off the reality that ate at him every day, he started thinking about the auction again. He wasn't sure why he'd done it. Not just that he'd gotten ornery and outbid Chrissie Travers for the box of junk, but why he'd told her he'd give her the stuff if she'd go with him to the ball.

Now, where in the name of anything sane had that come from? Okay. Sanity probably hadn't had anything to do with it. Sheer impulse had.

Still, that didn't explain why he'd asked her. Probably because he'd figured she'd do exactly what she'd done—stick that little nose of hers high in the air and turn him down flat.

He glanced at the box he'd brought to work and set on the floor in the corner. It was as closed up and secretive as the prickly Ms. Travers.

"Let's just call it a testosterone moment," he muttered grimly and leaned back in his leather chair. For some inexplicable reason, the woman was always messing with his hormones. And that in itself was a major puzzle.

She was so not his type. Uppity little tight-ass. That's what she was. He'd always gone more for the party girls who wanted to have a good time, knew how to have a good time and didn't beat themselves up the next morning after they'd had a good time. Prissy Chrissie wouldn't know a good time if it sneaked up and bit her on her cute, curvy butt.

So why did he find himself grinning at the prospect

of seeing her again? And why did he have this recurring fantasy of biting the cute little butt in question?

Uncomfortable with his turn of thoughts, he sobered and stood abruptly, tucking the tips of his fingers into the back pockets of his jeans. He walked to the window of his fourth-floor office and stared down at the street.

Well, well, well, he thought, feeling a little too much pleasure when he saw who was walking down the street. Speak of the devil—or in this case, the saint. There she was. Little Miss Priss, in all her starched-panties glory.

He leaned a shoulder against the window frame, crossed his arms over his chest and looked his fill as she marched down the sidewalk toward his building. All she needed was a uniform and she could be captain of a drill team.

What made a woman, he wondered and reached up to scratch his jaw, who was put together in a package like a sweet little china doll think she had to go through life like a caricature of a turn-of-the-century, stiff-backed, prim and proper suffragette?

Hell, he bet she *did* starch her panties. And they were probably white. Most likely cotton. With days of the week that she always wore on the proper day.

Why that image made him hot, he had no idea.

She was within a block now and he couldn't help but appreciate the view. She was barely five-four. Her pale blond hair and large hazel eyes gave her a cute, fragile, elfin look that in his weaker moments made him want to protect her as much as provoke her. Since he was fairly certain she'd never let anyone protect her—regardless that she looked as delicate as the petals on a yellow rose—provoking her was a much better bet.

And again, she was not his type. She was the exact opposite of Rea, who'd been svelte, sexy and as predatory as a jungle cat. Thoughts of his ex made him shiver. Too bad he'd been so blinded by the svelte, sexy parts that he'd missed the other characteristic until it was too late.

Whoa, what's this, he wondered when he saw Chrissie cross the street. Without a doubt she was on her way up to see him.

Fine. He walked away from the window, picked up the box and set it on his desk. He'd been about to have his secretary call a courier to pick it up and deliver it to Chrissie anyway. This would save him a buck or two. He'd had his fun. Now she could have her precious box. And the musty-smelling saddlebag that was in it.

His secretary, Janice Smith, who had been with him from the beginning seven years ago, buzzed him on the intercom as he settled in behind his desk.

"Yes, Janice."

"Christine Travers is here to see you, Mr. Thorne."

"Send her in."

He rocked back in his chair. Propping his elbows on the arms and steepling his fingers beneath his chin, he prepared to be magnanimous. It wasn't nearly as much fun as being obnoxious, but, hey, if nothing else, it would be a kick to throw her off guard by being nice.

* * *

She should have called, Christine realized when she found herself standing outside Jacob Thorne's office door. Her palms began to sweat. She should have saved herself the stress of a face-to-face meeting.

But that was the coward's way out and she'd never been that. She wasn't starting now. Not for someone like him.

She turned the handle and stepped inside, expecting...well, not really knowing what to expect when she entered his inner sanctum. He did, however, manage to surprise her.

The office was large but not ostentatious. The furniture was top-of-the-line but functional, all stylish black lacquer and shining chrome. There wasn't a dead animal in sight—either on the floor made into a rug or on the wall in the guise of a hat rack or displayed as a trophy. She grudgingly gave him points for that. And for the stunning collection of photographs adorning the walls.

Each dramatically framed photo was of a different oil fire site. And each photo captured all the fury, the danger and the unyielding hunger of the flames shooting into the air like geysers and of the courageous men who risked their lives putting them out.

"Impressive, aren't they?"

She jerked her attention from the photographs to the man lounging idly behind a desk that was far from empty yet neat and uncluttered. He was watching her with a look that made her think of a lion lounging lazily in the sun, overseeing the lioness doing all the work.

Clearly, though, he was a hands-on boss if the stacks of paperwork were any indication. Okay. So he got another point for being involved.

"Very," she agreed belatedly with a nod back to the photos, because what was really impressive was the way he looked behind that desk and she didn't want him to see how he had affected her. Since her cheeks were hot, she figured they were also pink. It was a curse of her fair complexion.

In the meantime she'd never seen him in business mode. She'd seen him at death's door, as pale as the hospital sheets beneath him. She'd seen him all sexy swagger and irritating indolence, as he'd been the other night at the auction. This man-in-charge persona was disconcerting—and unexpectedly appealing.

His shirt was white. The top button was undone and his cuffs were rolled up on his strong forearms. His brown suit jacket and a truly stunning silk tie hung on the coatrack behind him. Style. He had it. In spades.

"That one was taken in Kuwait," he said when she averted her attention to a print that, once she was able to study it without being hyperaware of him, gave her chills just thinking about the fierceness of the blaze.

"I'll go to the ball with you," she said without turning back to him.

Okay. It was out. She hadn't intended to just blurt it out that way but now that she was here, now that she was suddenly aware of him as an entity other than the proverbial Thorne-in-her-side, she wanted to get this over with and get away from him as quickly as possible. And away from this unbelievable resurgence of attraction that not only blindsided her but also shook her composure. The sooner they cut this deal, the sooner she could go on about her business.

When she was met with nothing but silence, she drew a bracing breath and turned toward him.

He was frowning. Not a gloating or even an angry frown, but more as though he was in deep thought or contemplating something heavy.

"I said I'd go to the ball with you," she repeated, and he finally rocked forward in his chair and came to attention behind his desk.

"So you did."

And still he scowled.

Perplexed, she eyed him with wary suspicion. "Wasn't that the condition?"

"Of me turning over the box?"

Her exasperation at the way he was drawing this out came in the form of an impatient breath. "I believe it was."

"Ah. Well, you just said the magic word. Was. That *was* my condition. Two days ago. But *now,* we're dealing with today."

She narrowed her eyes. "There was a time limit?"

"It seems so, yeah."

Sure. *Now* he was smiling.

Because this was still a joke to him. He had never intended for her to go to the dance with him. Just as she'd thought. He'd merely been playing with her, and when she'd called him on it, he'd figured a way to weasel out of the invitation. It shouldn't have hurt so much.

"Why is this stuff so important to you anyway?" he asked, standing. He walked around the desk and settled a hip on its corner.

"Historic value," she said truthfully.

He crossed his arms over his chest and scowled. "Musty saddlebags? Old guns? A lady's purse? What else? Oh, yeah. A faded map."

Her heart jumped over itself. "You looked?"

"You may have heard. It's *my* box. I'm pretty sure that means I'm entitled to look."

This was going nowhere. And she'd had enough of his fun and games. She'd figure out another way to get the box of Jess Golden's things to the Historical Society. Maybe she could get some of the city matriarch types to put a little heat on him or something.

"Sorry to have taken your time," she said and headed for the door.

"Wait. Wait. You haven't heard the new condition."

She stopped, her hand on the door handle, and let out a deep breath. Knowing she was going to regret this, she turned and met his smug smile. "New condition?"

He pushed off the desk. "Tell you what. Let's talk about it over lunch."

"Lunch?"

He reached around her to open the door. "You know. The light meal between breakfast and dinner?"

"But—"

"I'll be back in an hour or so, Janice," he said, herding Christine out of his office and into the reception area with a hand at the small of her back. "Anybody calls, tell 'em I'll get back to them—unless it's Ray. If Ray calls, tell him to phone my cell."

Christine was far too aware of his hand touching her there, ever so lightly at the small of her back. "I'm not going to lunch with you."

"Oh, lighten up, Chrissie, would you? It's noon. I'm hungry. I figure you're hungry, too. It's that simple. It's not like it's a date or anything."

She told herself his last statement didn't sting. And it wouldn't have—at least not so badly—if Janice, stylish and chic in her tailored white blouse and short red skirt, hadn't glanced up and cast Christine a sympathetic look when they passed the desk.

He'd just made it clear to anyone within earshot that Jacob Thorne didn't consider Christine Travers datable.

Which was perfectly fine. She lifted her chin. She didn't want to date him anyway. And she didn't want to go to lunch with him. What she wanted was to get as far away from the reproachable evil twin as she could, considering they lived in the same city.

And that was the truth.

Three

Okay. Jake had surprised himself again. He simply had been going to give Chrissie the box. End of story. So what had happened to the plan?

Why was he sitting across from her in a booth at the Royal Diner happy as a damn clam because little Chrissie looked all pouty and put out?

As usual the diner was packed. It never seemed to matter that the greasy spoon, with its smoke-stained walls, cracked bar stools and chipped countertops, had seen better days. The place stayed popular with the locals for two basic reasons: nobody knew their way around a grill like Manny Hernandez and nobody gave lip like the mainstay waitress, Sheila Foster. A lot of guys came in just to let Sheila rag on them. Himself included.

Montgomery and Gentry belted out a song from the beat-up jukebox as Jake watched Chrissie pick at one of Manny's burger baskets with all the enthusiasm of a *Fear Factor* competitor contemplating eating a box of scorpions.

"You don't like the burger?"

"Do you know how much fat is in one of these things?" she grumbled.

"So why did you order it?"

"I didn't. *You* did. I wanted a salad and you said I was too thin and why didn't I eat something with some substance. So I said fine, I'll have what you're having."

"Oh, yeah." He grinned. "I forgot."

Actually he hadn't forgotten anything. He'd wanted to see her eat something that he figured she would consider sinful. And then he wanted to watch the lady enjoy sinning. Wait until she saw the pecan pie with ice cream that followed his standing lunch order.

He didn't know why but he was suddenly determined to loosen her up and make her enjoy herself in spite of her determination not to. Not, he told himself, because he particularly cared, but because sometime during the course of this day—okay, if he were being honest, it was long before today—she had started to become a personal challenge to him.

People liked him. Pretty much without exception.

Chrissie Travers was the major dissenter. For whatever reason, he wanted to change that.

As a rule, folks liked his teasing. They liked his sense of humor. They liked that he thought life should be lived to the fullest whenever possible because so much in these times was tough to deal with. And they liked that he knew about tough from the trenches. Just as he knew what it was like to face down death and come out on top.

A near-death experience like he'd had five years ago had a tendency to change a man's outlook on life—it had sure as the world prompted him to want to live the rest of it on terms of his own making. Terms that included squeezing out as much pleasure as possible. Unlike the super-duper-serious Christine Travers, who was his polar opposite when it came to pursuing fun.

So he'd pulled a squeeze play on Chrissie, who really wasn't too thin or all that difficult to squeeze. He'd said she was thin to get her riled again and see the color rise in her cheeks because she looked so pretty in pink. In fact, despite her spinster-slash-warden suits, which ranged in color from navy blue to black to—God save her—dirt brown, she looked kinda cute just the way she was. Well, cute except for the sourpuss attitude that was going to give her wrinkles before she turned thirty.

The woman was a puzzle. Flat out. And he did love a puzzle. Which probably explained why he kept trying to fit the pieces together.

"So. Tell me," he said, digging into his own burger, "what do you do for fun?"

She blinked at him as if she didn't understand the question. "Fun?"

He shook his head, swallowed and wiped his mouth with a paper napkin. "I'm sensing a severe shortfall in your basic vocabulary here. *Lunch. Fun.* Do I dare introduce the word *play?*"

The woman had some expressions. Most of them pinched—as if she was sitting on something prickly and was too polite to take care of the problem in public. *What would people think?*

He wondered what it was going to take to make her smile. He'd given it a halfhearted effort for five years now and so far he hadn't hit the magic word, number or combination. Maybe it was time he got serious.

"I thought we were going to talk about your new conditions."

"Fine. Right. We are." He bit into his burger and chewed thoughtfully. "First tell me why—no smoke screen this time—that stuff is so important to you."

She considered him across her uneaten burger and fries. Instead of answering, she asked a question. "You're a Texas Cattleman's Club member, right?"

"Right," he said, popping a fry into his mouth and letting her play this out.

"And Cattleman's Club members are sworn to certain values. Like loyalty and trust and honor and all that, right?"

He nodded and leaned back on the faded gray vinyl booth, wondering where this was going.

"Then if I tell you something in confidence—something that could affect Royal's future—you're sworn to secrecy, correct?"

He matched her pinched-brow scowl. "Absolutely. Of course, to make certain there's no breach in that confidence, we're both going to have to swear it in blood. You got a pocketknife on ya?"

She let out a disgusted little huff. "Do you take anything seriously?"

"Not if I can help it. Now, for Pete's sake, spit it out. If you want me to keep it on the QT, all you have to do is ask."

"Well, I'm asking," she said, so sober it was all he could do not to laugh.

"Okay. Consider it done. Now give."

"You know the Jessamine Golden legend?"

"Some of it," he said. If you grew up in Royal, you'd heard about Jessamine Golden. It was as staple a part of the town's history as the feud between two prominent families, the Windcrofts and the Devlins. "She was an outlaw, right? Killed the mayor and the sheriff. Stole some gold. Let's see…disappeared somewhere around the early 1900s."

"Right. Okay. Well…the saddlebags?" She leaned in close and lowered her voice.

"Yes?" he said, doing the same. Mostly because it got him a little closer to her and he'd been wondering if that really was gold shot through her pretty hazel eyes. Not only gold but silver, he realized. *So that's what gives them that iridescent color.*

And didn't she have the longest, most lush eyelashes he'd ever seen? Soft as sable, thick as a paintbrush. Why hadn't he ever noticed that before?

Or her freckles. Cute little angel kisses lightly dusted the rise of her cheekbones and skimmed the bridge of her pixie nose. He was surprised he'd never noticed them before, either. Of course, he'd never been this close. Kissing close, if he were of a notion to steal one, which he might be if he didn't have a pretty good idea of how she'd react. Those even pearly whites of hers would probably rip into his lip like tiger teeth.

"I'm sure," she said, and he was mesmerized by the mobility of her full lips, "that those saddlebags belonged to Jess Golden."

"Where did you get that?" he asked, frowning suddenly when he noticed a very fine, very faint crescent line of a scar at the bottommost edge of her pointed chin. It was about an inch long, and of course he'd never noticed it before, either. That close factor again.

She pulled back, looking exasperated. "Where did I get what?"

"That scar," he said, reaching across the battered gray Formica tabletop and gently pinching her chin between his thumb and index finger so he could angle her head for a better look. And on second look, it wasn't so fine and it wasn't so faint. "Man. That had to have hurt like blazes."

"We were talking about the saddlebags," she said,

pulling away from his hold and touching her fingers to her chin in a gesture that was both self-conscious and embarrassed.

Okay. The scar was a sore subject. So he let it drop. For now. But after five years of dancing around the edge of her fire, he seriously wanted to know what fueled her flames. He could be patient when the need arose. "What about the saddlebags?"

"I said I'm certain they belonged to Jess Golden."

He sat back. Shrugged. "What makes you think so?"

She went into an excited diatribe about Jess Golden once living in Jonathan Devlin's house, about the purse and the rose petals and the six-shooters and the map coming from Jonathan's attic. And there was that pink blush on her cheeks again. So. Anger and excitement were two of her triggers. He wondered what else got her going and flashed on an image of her face flushed with the heat of great sex.

Whoa.

That was interesting. And the picture was a little too vivid.

"The roses are a dead giveaway," she finished.

"Hmm. Roses, huh? An outlaw who liked roses?"

"I have always figured there was more to Jess Golden than what was written in the local newspapers at the time and recorded in local history books."

He considered her and realized she'd finally revealed a chink in that airtight armor. "Well, well, well, Chrissie. *You've* got a romantic streak."

She blinked several times in rapid succession, clearly flustered. "I am not a romantic."

"You've romanticized an outlaw," he pointed out.

"Romanticized? That's ridiculous." She blushed again, as if the notion that he might think that she— Christine Travers of the straitlaced, all work, no play variety—would have any thought on the subject of romance was too absurd to consider. Or because he was right and she really was a closet romantic.

Huh. *Who'da thunk it?* And on the heels of that discovery, possibilities abounded. How hard would it be to romance this standoffish little blonde? How soft would she be when she let some of the starch out of her spine?

"The point is," she pressed on, "if I'm right and those are Jess Golden's things, the map could lead to the stolen gold."

"Okay. Hold it. If those are her things, what makes you think the gold is still here? Why wouldn't she have taken it with her?"

She gave him a "duh" look and evidently decided he needed remedial training. "You're an outlaw," she began as if she was talking to a five-year-old.

He leaned back, held both hands up, palms out. "Swear to God, I did not steal that gold."

Nothing. Not even a smirk. And he wanted to pry one out of her so badly.

"I didn't mean that you are an outlaw literally," she said, enunciating each word, again as if she were talking to someone who was intellectually challenged. "I meant, you're an outlaw hypothetically. And you're on the run because everyone in Texas believes you killed not only the mayor of the town but the sheriff, as well. You stole the gold and don't have the time or the means to take it with you. It's heavy and cumbersome. So you hide it. And you draw a map. You hide the map somewhere—like in the house where you live, in the attic or something—and then you run, hoping things will settle down after a time and you can go back and get it."

"Okay," he said, marginally intrigued now. "I'm an outlaw—well, not me specifically, because we're still doing hypothetical, right?"

Only a card-carrying optimist could interpret her sneer as camouflage for a grin.

"What makes you think that I—the hypothetical outlaw—didn't come back and dig up the gold later?"

"Because there are absolutely no accounts of Jess Golden ever being spotted in or around Royal again. Ever. And the gold was in the form of numbered bars. If they'd been converted to cash, there would be a record. There's not. I checked."

She was thorough. He'd give her that. And he'd give her something else. She hid it well, but there was a treasure trove of pent-up passion buried beneath the layers that comprised Chrissie Travers. At least she had passion about this issue. He suspected there might be something else that would fire her up and toyed with the idea of being the man to discover exactly what that something was.

The prospect of peeling those layers and discovering,

little by little, the woman hiding behind the steel facade suddenly fascinated him. For years he'd found a certain sophomoric satisfaction in simply pulling her chain, then leaving her stewing in her own juices.

He didn't feel so much like leaving now. Instead he felt as if maybe he owed it to her to help her come out of her cocoon. Yeah, he thought, warming to the idea. And maybe he owed it to himself to see whether a butterfly or a bug wiggled its way out.

"Tell you what," he said, putting his money on the butterfly. "Since you've made such a compelling argument—" he reached for the ketchup bottle and dumped a generous glob on top of her uneaten French fries "—I think you deserve to have the box."

"But?"

He smiled at her insight and helped himself to some of her fries. "But there are still conditions."

He was getting a little addicted to that icy glare. He didn't know anyone who did it so well. He swiped a few more fries. "Condition number one—you eat at least half of your burger and some of the fries."

"This is ridiculous."

"Pretty minor, really."

She leaned back in the booth, her head tilted with both impatience and irritation. "What do you want from me? Why do you take such pleasure in baiting me?"

"Well, to tell you the truth, I didn't have a clear answer to that question myself until a few minutes ago."

"And what happened to clear things up?"

"I think it's the freckles," he said happily and watched her eyes shift from irritation to confusion to flat-out exasperation. "They're cute. And so are you. Now eat your lunch and then we'll lay out the rest of the terms."

"And one of the conditions is a dinner date?" Alison asked later that evening. She sounded just a little too cheery to suit Christine.

Actually Jacob never did get around to talking about terms. He'd said they would discuss them over dinner. Which was not a date.

"A dinner *meeting,*" Christine clarified. "Saturday night."

She still couldn't believe she'd agreed to it. Not only that, she didn't want to believe it. The man was devious and manipulative and…and he thought she was cute. Right. As if she believed that.

"What do you suppose he's really after?" she asked Alison as they sat side by side on Christine's sofa, wearing their sweats, a popcorn bowl between them, their stocking feet propped on the coffee table as the opening credits to the movie Alison had chosen for their traditional "Wednesday night at the movies" rolled by.

"What's he after? Sweetie, I've been trying to tell you. He's after *you,*" Alison said, grabbing a pillow and hugging it to her chest. "This is a tearjerker," she added offhandedly as if she hadn't just made the most ridiculous statement of the year.

"He is *not* after me," Christine insisted and dug into the popcorn.

"So why did he fabricate yet another excuse to see you in the guise of leveling conditions on giving you Jess Golden's things? No man goes to those lengths to tease a woman unless it's because he's interested in her."

There was no convincing Alison otherwise, so Christine let it drop. She watched the movie. And told herself Alison was all wet. Jacob Thorne was not interested in her. It didn't make any sense that he would be. A man like him. A woman like her. Talk about oil and water.

"So. Where are you two going on your second date?"

"It's not a date," Christine insisted. "And where do you get second?"

"Who paid for lunch?"

"Well, he did but—"

"Then it's a second date. Now, where are you going?"

"Claire's," she finally confessed.

"Oh là là! Big-time date."

Christine only grunted. She'd never been to Royal's swanky French restaurant. Claire's wasn't exactly in her everyday budget. Or even in her special-occasion budget, for that matter. And while she wasn't looking forward to spending an evening—that was *not* a date— in Thorne's company, she couldn't help but be excited about getting a little taste of how the upper crust lived.

"What are you going to wear?"

Christine shrugged and feigned interest in the movie.

"I hadn't really thought about it." Okay. That was a lie. It's all she'd thought about. "Probably my black pantsuit."

Alison sat up straight. "Eeewwww. You can't go to Claire's in that boxy old thing."

"What do you mean, old thing? It's only—" She stopped and thought. Hmm. It had been a long time since she'd bought the suit.

"Tomorrow we're going shopping during our lunch hour," Alison said. "And you're going to buy something sexy."

"I am not."

"Are, too."

"I. Am. Not."

"We'll see," Alison said. "Now let's watch the movie. I'm due for a good cry."

The dress was black. And short. And low cut.

The heels were silver. And spiked. And strappy. And they showed off siren-red toenail polish that Alison had insisted was perfect for the total look.

She had a look, all right, Christine thought, hovering just one notch to the left of panicked on Saturday night. A look she'd never in a million years thought she could pull off. Yet as she took it all in—experiencing a mixture of disbelief and shock and a pleasurable womanly confidence—in her full-length bedroom mirror, Christine had to admit Alison was right.

She looked hot.

"Okay. That settles it. I'm changing."

Alison laughed. "Don't even think about it," she said, standing behind her like a drill sergeant.

Right. She'd forgotten about Alison for a minute there. Her friend had insisted she help Christine get ready for her dinner *meeting* and then informed her she was going to stick around until Jacob arrived just to make sure she didn't chicken out and ditch the new duds for the black pantsuit.

"Alison, I look ridiculous."

"You look fabulous."

"I look obvious."

"I really like the hair, too," Alison added, ignoring Christine's discomfort.

Yeah. Christine had to admit Alison was right about that, too. Her hair did look great. Alison had scooped it up to the crown of her head and wrestled it into a spiky little puff that looked chic and hip and—yeah, she admitted, still amazed—sexy.

It was a word that had never fit her.

Conservative—now, there was a word she wore well. A word that was comfortable, unlike the way she felt wearing this dress. She *had* to change clothes. Desperate times called for desperate measures.

"Okay. Thank you, thank you, thank you for everything. You've transformed the pumpkin into a fancy coach, Fairy Godmother. You must be exhausted. Why don't you go on home now?"

"Yeah, right," Alison said. "And give you a chance to change into something less revealing, less sexy and more conservative the minute I walk out the door? Uh-uh. Besides, it's too late. Mr. Wonderful just pulled up."

Well, yikes, Christine thought and tugged up the plunging neckline in a vain attempt to cover a little more skin.

"Go," Alison said and gave her an encouraging squeeze. "Answer the door. And let the begging begin."

Yeah. As if Jacob Thorne would ever beg for her.

On a deep breath she walked out of the bedroom. Her knees were wobbly as she headed down the hall and regarded the front door to her apartment as if Jack the Ripper were about to make an impromptu appearance.

Not Jack. Jacob. Jacob the Thorne. And his knock was solid and confident.

She wished she could say the same about her knees. This was so ridiculous. The way she looked. The way she'd dressed. The outrageous way her heart was hammering. All because the man on the other side of the door had orchestrated a pretend date to have a little more fun at her expense.

The reminder was all she needed to regain her composure. He wanted to make a joke of her? Fine. At least she was turned out in a way that might give him a twinge of regret.

She wiped her sweaty palms on her skirt and immediately regretted that she may have soiled the delicate silk crepe. Regrouping, she pasted on a smile and opened the door.

"Hi," she said and had the disarming experience of watching his arrogant hey-baby grin slowly deflate to be replaced by a look of complete and utter shock.

Four

"Um…hello?" Christine repeated again after several long, uncomfortable seconds had passed.

He hadn't said a word. He just stood there. Looking her up and down. Slowly. Very slowly.

"Hello," he said finally, his voice deep and gruff. Very, very gruff. "Hello, hello, hello," he repeated slowly.

His smile had returned. A pleased, surprised, uniquely charming smile, and if she wasn't careful, she might start to think he actually was happy to see her. And that he actually liked what he saw.

"You have legs," he said, standing back to take another long, blatantly appreciative look. "Nice legs."

"Um. Well."

Sparkling response, Christine. Just sparkling.

"Nice, Chrissie," he said, meeting her eyes again. "You look very, very nice."

"Um. Well."

Is there a really stupid echo in here? And why are my cheeks so hot?

"I'll…I'll, um, just go get my purse."

"It will be my pleasure to wait here and watch you go get it," he said, another grin in his voice that made her glance back over her shoulder—and get caught off guard by the heated look in his eye.

She turned her head back so fast, she made herself dizzy. At least, that's why she thought she was dizzy. It had nothing to do with the way he looked in his rich cobalt-blue suit and expertly knotted silk tie. Or the way he smelled—like some pricey, seductive, masculine cologne that brought to mind mint and musk and the subtle undercurrents of testosterone.

And it definitely had nothing to do with the way he was looking at her. As if he wanted to gobble her up in one big, wolfish bite.

Wolfish? Get real. This wolf usually hunted for foxier game than her. He probably had indigestion or something.

She felt a hot river of self-consciousness trickle through her. Why was she putting herself through this? Maybe he did like what he saw—but what he saw was an illusion. A surprise in something other than drab mode.

She was still exactly what Jacob Thorne thought she

was—a dowdy, inexperienced, pushing-thirty old maid trying to play dress-up. A woman who was so afraid of men because of what her father had done to her and her mother and so afraid of letting herself fall into that same horrible spiral of humiliation and pain that her M.O. was to make herself as plain and unappealing as possible so men wouldn't notice her. And God forbid a man ever showed any interest in her, because she'd pop out her porcupine quills and warn him away with her bristles and barbs.

She felt chilled to the bone suddenly. And hot all over at the same time. Talk about self-discovery. Why did she have to experience this particular discovery now? And why did it have to have tears gathering in her throat?

"Chris?"

She turned her head to see Alison standing in the bedroom doorway holding her purse. The concern in her eyes had Christine blinking back tears again.

"Oh, sweetie. What's wrong?"

"I can't do this," she whispered. "I'm not the kind of woman who can go out to dinner with that kind of man."

"The hell you can't," Alison said, intuitively sensing that Christine was in the midst of a monumental cold-feet moment. "Don't you dare put yourself down that way."

Alison shoved the little black clutch purse into Christine's hand. "Now, you are not going to waste that dress and that hair and that makeup, do you understand me? You. Look. Incredible. Work it. Enjoy it. Feel the power, girl. You own it tonight. And the way you look, you're gonna own him, too."

Alison hugged her hard, then turned her around and literally shoved her into the hall.

"There you are," her date said when she lurched into the living room. "Thought you'd decided to bail on me."

Alison's words bounced around in her head.

Feel the power. You own it....

As incredible as it seemed, when she looked and saw real interest—not just surprised curiosity—in Jacob's eye, she did feel the power. At least, a little power surge. For all of his smooth words and sexy smiles, she'd never seen him quite the way he was tonight.

Off balance. Just a tad uncertain. As though maybe he really did like what he saw—and it had surprised him.

Maybe the balance of power *had* shifted in that moment when she'd opened her door and he'd seen her standing there. Not looking like Prissy Chrissie Travers, as even she had begun to think of herself. But looking like a woman. A vibrant, self-confident woman who recognized her burgeoning power—yes, power—over a man who had always had the upper hand.

Okay. Maybe that was overplaying it. But there was something. If not power, at least a measure of self-confidence she'd never felt before. With luck, it would last through the evening.

"Bail? No," she said as a calm resolve descended over her. "I'm not going to bail."

The stakes were suddenly too high. This was no longer just about acquiring Jess Golden's things. This was about something bigger. Much bigger. And as soon as she figured out exactly what was happening to shake her and yet empower her, she'd know what she wanted to do about it.

Butterfly, Jake thought as they walked into Claire's and he got a whiff of some exotic, flowery perfume. She'd definitely turned into a butterfly. Sleek, satiny and mysterious. And, man, had it been worth the hassle to witness the full effect of the metamorphosis.

Superserious, profoundly professional and supremely prickly Christine Travers with her sensible clothes and plain-Jane package was long gone. In her place was a sophisticated, sexy siren possessed of an underlying vulnerability that sent his heart rate rocketing.

He liked it. He liked it a lot. And he was starting to think that maybe she might be a woman he could like a lot, too. Not that he hadn't always liked her, it was simply that the dynamics of their relationship had changed drastically when he'd invited her to dinner. He was used to prickly Chrissie. Had taken great pains to bring out that side of her.

Now he was faced with sexy Chrissie—a side of her he'd always known existed if she would just let her come out and play. Yet for some reason this new face made him a little nervous—which was nuts because he was never nervous around women.

She'd done something amazing to her hair. Not that he didn't think it looked cute when she wore it down and straight and framing her pixie face in a businesslike do. It was just that with all that fine blond mass swept up on top of her head...well, it had an effect, was all. It accentuated the model-slim line of her neck and exposed a delectable-looking nape. A nape that tempted him mightily to bend down and place a kiss there when she sat at the table for two he'd reserved and he pushed the chair in for her.

He caved in to a spike of better judgment and had to satisfy himself with wondering how badly him kissing her there would rattle her as he settled across the table from her.

"Good evening, Mr. Thorne."

Jake smiled at their waiter, Claude Jacques, as he produced open menus. "Hello, Claude. How's it going?"

"Superb, thank you. Would you and the lady care for something to drink while you decide on dinner?"

"Chrissie?" Jake said over the top of his menu. "Would you like something? The wine selection is excellent."

"I think I'd prefer a club soda, thanks. With a lime wedge, please," she added with a flash of her gray-green eyes at Claude before she went back to studying her menu.

"Make it two," Jake said, deferring to her choice, although he'd have loved to see the color a little wine would have splashed on her cheeks.

Not that she needed color. She was...hell...glowing? Close enough. Her lips shimmered with color—

somewhere between a wine-red and hot-pink. And he had another I-never-noticed-that-before moment. He'd never noticed that her lips were so full, so lush, and they looked so kissably soft.

He missed the freckles, though. She'd camouflaged them with some powder or blush or bronzer or Lord knew what little bit of magic she'd pulled out of her woman's bag of tricks.

Speaking of magic, the dress was the mother of all illusions. It had been driving him crazy since she'd opened her apartment door and magically drained all the blood from his head and shot it directly to his groin. He was a sucker for black, short and plunging necklines. All that pale, creamy skin against and beneath the black silk was a turn-on of epic proportions.

"Did I mention that you look incredible?" he said, watching her studiously avoid eye contact by gluing her gaze to the menu.

Several beats passed before she lowered the menu and met his eyes. "You did, actually. Or words to that effect. Thank you. You, um, you look very nice, as well."

Aren't we formal now? Again he thought it was cute. So was the way her gaze sort of lingered involuntarily on his mouth before sliding to his chest, then gliding slowly back to his mouth again.

"So, do you see anything you like?"

Her gaze snapped to his.

"On the menu," he clarified with a grin.

There was that blush. The one he loved to fire up. The

one that told him that she hadn't been thinking about food when she'd been checking him out but that there might have been hunger involved and that it embarrassed her to be caught whetting her appetite, so to speak.

"I'm not too knowledgeable on French cuisine," she said, sounding self-conscious.

"That's what Claude's for," he said, wanting to set her at ease. "Let's ask him what's good when he brings our drinks."

He watched with interest when she did just that, leading the waiter through a series of questions, both polite and businesslike in manner, until she finally settled on whitefish in wine sauce.

"Make mine beef, make it red and make it big," he said when it was his turn. "And I'll have whatever the lady's having for side dishes."

"You will enjoy." Claude scooped up the menus. "The lady has excellent taste."

And then they were alone. If you didn't count the discreetly hovering army of wait staff—one who placed ice in their water glasses with sterling tongs, another who dropped in a wedge of lemon and yet another who finally got to the task of pouring the water.

Her expressive eyes relayed her amazement over all the fuss about filling a water glass.

"Not exactly the Royal Diner, huh?"

"Not exactly."

"It's a little pretentious," he agreed, "but the food's great."

"It's a beautiful place."

Ritzy is what it was. Valet parking, white linen table-cloths, red roses in crystal vases on every table. Women liked it. Besides the great food, the part he liked was the candlelight—something he'd never really paid much attention to before tonight.

Tonight the lighting seemed the perfect accompaniment to the woman sharing his table. It also played into a little fantasy that had been growing in size and scope since the blonde in black had opened her door and rocked his world.

He'd been anticipating staid, stodgy and subdued. The last thing he'd expected was sexy with a capital SEX. And again he felt that niggling sense of unease that he wanted to discount as nothing more than pleasant surprise. Oh, yeah. Had she ever surprised him.

"Are you having a good time?"

"Is that what this is about? Me having a good time?"

It didn't take much to put her on the defensive. His fault. He'd done little more than give her grief for five years. He wasn't even sure why he'd changed the game plan now. "Well, I would hope so. What did you want it to be about?"

"Jess Golden's things."

"Ah. But I don't want to talk about that yet."

A frown brimming with rebuke crinkled up her forehead.

"Later," he promised. "I want to talk about you first."

Clearly she hadn't been prepared for that.

"Jacob—" she began to say, a clear preamble to another roadblock.

"Jake," he interrupted. "My friends call me Jake. And for once don't argue, okay? Let's enjoy the evening."

He sat back in his chair, toyed with the stem of his water glass and watched her face. It didn't hide her emotions nearly as well as it hid her secrets. She was uncomfortable. It was one thing for him to put her on edge with a little good-natured teasing. It was another for her to feel discomfort because she thought she was out of her element, which is what he suspected was going on right now. And he wanted to remedy that situation ASAP. "How about we start with something easy? Do you like your work?"

"I do. Yes," she said without hesitation—and with a noticeable lack of elaboration.

Okay. So he was going to have to pry every snippet of information out of her. "Why a respiratory therapist? And yes," he insisted at her doubtful look, "I really am interested."

"My freshman year of college," she said at long last, "I was awarded some work-study money. My assignment was at the university hospitals and clinics. Cleaning rooms, if you really want to know. I rotated between several floors and got interested in respiratory therapy when I was working in that unit."

"Work-study? So you worked your way through school?"

"Pretty much, yes."

"What other types of jobs did you have?"

Their bread came about that time, so she busied her hands with it and seemed to let down her guard a little in the process. "Too many to count. Let's see...I tended bar, worked the night shift at the front desk of a couple of motels, cashiered at a convenience store. Whatever it took to make tuition and board."

His admiration for her kicked up a couple more notches. "Sounds tough."

She shook her head, not an ounce of regret registering on her face. "Sometimes, yes, but for the most part I enjoyed it all. Appreciated every job I had. Without them, I wouldn't have gotten my degree."

"Your family wasn't in a position to help?" He broke off a chunk of bread and picked up his butter knife.

What little reserve she'd let down jumped back up with a vengeance. Instead of answering, she asked her own question. "And what did you study in college? I don't recall ever seeing any courses in oil-well fire-fighting on any course catalogs."

All righty, then. Talking about her family was off-limits. Since she'd struggled to make her own way through college, he had to figure one of two reasons was the cause. Either her family was very poor and she felt self-conscious about it or she was estranged from them, and that just made him more curious about what had precipitated the break.

Regardless, it explained—at least in part—why she was such a serious Sara all the time. She knew hardship.

She knew if not poverty, at least slim pickings. He supposed if he'd had to work as hard as she had to get his education, he'd have a tendency to take life a little more seriously too.

He would have liked to press a little harder about her family, but he took his cues from her and let it drop. "Actually I majored in business management with a minor in accounting."

"Oh, well," she said, buttering a piece of bread, "I can see how that would make a natural transition into fighting oil-well fires."

His smile at her little joke was slow. "So she *does* have a sense of humor."

"When motivated, I can be funny," she said, sounding a little defensive.

"Well, then, I'll have to see what I can do to motivate you more often."

Yeah, he thought when she gave him a wary look. *That means exactly what you think it means. We are going to do this again. This is not a one-time deal, so get used to it, sweetie. I plan to see more of you.*

He wasn't sure when that intention had become apparent to him or why he was so certain he wanted to see more of her. For that matter, he didn't understand the edgy sense of calamity that accompanied his thoughts. He shook it off and rationalized the situation instead. Why did some men find it impossible to resist the lure of Mount Everest? Why did some risk their lives jumping out of planes? Why did he make a living with men

who marched into the jaws of oil fires risking everything, including their lives, in the process?

Sometimes the why wasn't nearly as important as the
want itself. And right now he wanted to get to know this
woman better.

"This bread is delicious."

Nice table talk, but the segue wasn't going to work.
"So is the view."

She actually looked behind her to see if she'd missed
seeing something. When she turned around and correctly read the look on his face, she didn't exactly roll
her eyes, but he could tell she wanted to.

"That was a compliment, Christine."

She set her knife on the edge of her plate, propped
her forearms on the table and took his measure. "You
don't have to flatter me, Jacob."

He wagged his knife at her. "Jake. And I'm just calling it like I see it."

Oh, that long-suffering look. Oh, that heavy sigh. She
was just too much. Was she really that naive?

"You don't really think that tonight is just about Jess
Golden's things, do you?"

Now she looked wary again. Maybe not naive. Maybe
it was more a question of distrustful. Again. His fault.

"I want to get to know you, Chrissie."

"For what possible reason?"

From any other woman he'd consider the question
coy. From her it was exactly what it appeared to be: utter
puzzlement.

"I've been giving that some thought." He shrugged. "Maybe because you intrigue me. Maybe because I find you a contradiction. Or maybe because the way you look tonight only increases my curiosity about something that's got me wondering."

She'd grown very still. Even her eyes didn't so much as flicker, although they were wide with the unasked question, *What have you been wondering about?*

"I've been wondering," he said, responding to both the wariness and the anticipation revealed by the accelerated pulse thrumming at the base of her throat, "why you normally go to such lengths to hide the fact that you are a very beautiful woman. And why it embarrasses you to be told that you're beautiful."

"I'm not embarrassed."

Yet she was flushing pink—something he chose not to point out. "What, then?"

"Uncomfortable," she finally said. "I could do without the scrutiny."

He laughed. "Then you shouldn't have worn the dress."

"My thoughts exactly," she grumbled under her breath.

"Okay, look," he said after a moment of her looking as though she wished she was anywhere else but here with anyone else but him, "just lighten up a little. You're taking yourself way too seriously."

"Right. Something you're an expert on."

"Hell, no." He grinned, appreciating her sarcasm. "That's the point. Life's too short to take so dismally serious. You, sweet woman, need a few lessons in loosening up."

"And I suppose you're just the man to teach me."

"There you go. I am definitely the man. And starting tonight, I'm leading the class in the education of Christine Travers, good girl with a yen to go bad."

She smiled. A full-out, bona fide, no-holds-barred smile. Okay. So it was laced with the same sarcasm that sometimes put a bite in her words, but it was a smile. The first one. It felt like a major victory.

"You are so full of it, Thorne," she said, sitting back in her chair when the waiter brought her salad.

"I am, for a fact. Full to bursting with possibilities on how we can loosen you up."

"Not going to happen."

"Because?"

"Because," she said on an exasperated breath, "this is a ridiculous conversation."

He couldn't resist baiting her even more. "Scared?"

Her head snapped up. "Scared? Of what?"

"Of letting go, sweet cheeks. Of living life."

"Just because I'm cautious, just because I'm discriminating, doesn't mean I'm scared. Believe me, I know what scared is…it's something I no longer choose to be. No matter what you think."

Whoa.

I know what scared is…it's something I no longer choose to be.

Her statement shouldn't have come as a surprise, but

it had—to her as well as to him. The expression on her face said she hadn't meant to reveal something so intimate about herself. He hadn't expected the revelation. He'd guessed that there had been some not-so-great events in her life that might have shaped her, contributed to her defensive reserve, but he hadn't wanted to think it was something ugly.

I know what scared is....

Not knowing what she'd endured, only that she had endured it, increased his desire to show her how to have a good time.

"What's the wildest thing you've ever done?" he asked as he dug into his salad. On the other side of the table, she shoved the greens around on her plate. "And don't say it's that you wore your Monday panties on Tuesday 'cause that ain't going to cut it."

He could see that she was a deep breath away from telling him to take his question and put it where the sun don't shine. But reserved, controlled soul that she was, she swallowed back the urge.

"I cut class once," she said.

He grunted in disbelief. "That's it? That's the best you can come up with?"

She shot him a defiant look.

"Oh, Chrissie. Sweetheart. That's pathetic."

"So sue me. I'm a model citizen."

He leaned forward, his fork poised over his salad. "Don't you ever get the urge to be bad? Just do something a little shocking? A little wild?"

Her silence as she finally met his eyes said it all. No. No, she didn't.

"I often work double shifts. I volunteer hours at the Historical Society. I don't have a lot of time left to pursue a sideline of mischief and mayhem. Much like you don't have time out of your fun and games to get involved with something of a little more substance."

"Sticks and stones," he singsonged and pried another reluctant and very small grin out of her.

"You know, there is such a thing as being too frivolous," she pointed out.

"And I would be a prime example?"

"You said it, I didn't."

"So, what if I stepped up to the plate and did something...oh, let's say, civic? You'd consider that a move in the right direction?"

"What direction you move makes no difference to me."

She'd tried to make her words sound snippy but didn't quite accomplish it. She also tried to make him believe it. He didn't.

"I think it does. I think that if I did something—how did you say it? something of substance?—that you might begin to see shades of gray instead of black-and-white and that might prompt you to loosen up a bit."

"It is still beyond me why you care about what I do or think."

"It's a little beyond me, too—or it was until you wore that dress. The fact is, I think we could help each other. I can loosen you up and you can straighten me out."

She patted her mouth with her napkin. "Do you ever quit?"

"No, really, listen. I'm beginning to like this idea." He leaned forward conspiratorially. "How about we make a little deal? I do something you categorize as adult and you do something I categorize as juvenile."

"I'm already doing something juvenile. I'm a party to this conversation."

"You get to pick my project," he pressed on, "and I get to pick yours."

She was about to launch into another protest on the ludicrous content of their conversation—which Jake admitted he'd started and pursued on a lark but now was warming up to—when Gretchen Halifax appeared at their table.

Only his mother's insistence on good manners prompted him to stand and acknowledge her presence.

Five

"**H**ello, Gretchen," Jake said stiffly when the city councilwoman made it clear she expected an audience. "How are you?"

Gretchen Halifax was not on his list of favorite people. The tall, severe-looking woman with the cold gray eyes and pale blond hair was self-righteous, humorless and demanding. He'd gone toe to toe with her a time or two at city council meetings when she'd refused to see reason and failed to compromise.

"I'm wonderful, Jacob." She smiled, all gleaming white teeth and politician sincerity. She'd perfected that sincerity along with her manipulative ways and somehow had managed to build a large circle of influence in the city.

"I'm sorry to interrupt," she added with barely a glance at Chris, "but I saw you sitting over here and knew I simply must stop by and say hello."

Not on my account, Jake thought but made nice anyway. "Gretchen, this is Chris Travers. Chris, Gretchen Halifax."

With a cool smile Gretchen turned to Chris and extended her hand. "My pleasure, Ms. Travers."

"Gretchen is on the city council," Jake added as Chris extended her hand and said a soft, "Hello."

"Should I know you from somewhere?" Gretchen asked after swiftly appraising Chris.

"I do some volunteer work for the Historical Society," Chris said. "We worked together a couple of times on the Edgar Halifax exhibit."

"Oh, of course. I'm so sorry. Forgive me for not recognizing you. I saw the finished display on Edgar at the museum this afternoon. It's marvelous, don't you think?"

"Display?" Jake asked, not because he was particularly interested in Halifax but because he was interested in Chris's part of it.

"Of my great-great-great-uncle Edgar's historical artifacts," Gretchen explained, oozing self-importance. "It's so exciting that he's been given his rightful place in Royal's history as one of the city's outstanding leaders.

"Edgar was the mayor of Royal in the late 1800s and early 1900s," she added when Jake made an I've-got-no-clue-what-you're-talking-about face.

She beamed while telling the story, making it sound as if old Edgar had come over on the Mayflower.

"Unfortunately Edgar was killed by the outlaw, Jessamine Golden, over a stolen shipment of gold. Speaking of Jessamine Golden, Jake, dear, I heard that you purchased something at the auction the other night that may have belonged to her."

"Where did you hear that?" Chris asked, sounding a little shocked. Clearly she'd hoped to keep the contents of the box between the two of them, Jake thought. At least until he handed it over to her.

"Why, I believe it was your secretary, Jake, who said something to mine over lunch yesterday," Gretchen said, dismissing Chris. "I'd love it if you'd show it to me."

"I can't imagine that you'd be interested in a box of musty old junk."

"Interested? In something that belonged to the woman who killed one of my ancestors? Why, of course I'm interested. Actually I was hoping you'd be willing to part with the items."

"Even if I were, Gretchen, I already have another interested party."

"That's easily solved. I'll double any offer you've got on the table."

He shook his head and from the corner of his eye saw Chrissie's shoulders sag in relief. "If you wanted it so badly, you should have been at the auction and bid on it."

"I would have, but I had a meeting I simply couldn't miss. Okay. I'll triple what you paid for it," Gretchen said, pouncing on him in such a demanding voice, other diners turned to see what was going on.

"Sorry," Jake said, puzzled by Gretchen's almost desperate bid for the box. Even more puzzled about why she was so determined to have Jess Golden's things—if they even were indeed the outlaw's things. "It's not about money."

"Then what would I have to do to get you to part with it?"

He imagined that Gretchen perceived her smile as seductive. He perceived it as predatory. And when she leaned toward him, blatantly inviting him to a view of her cleavage and in effect putting the moves on him without any regard for the fact that his date was watching, he'd had enough. "Give it up, Gretchen. This conversation," he cautioned when he sensed she was about to push a little harder, "is history."

He sat, dismissing her. Gretchen's gray eyes heated in anger, then cooled by slow degrees as she visibly got control of herself. She smiled. Calculated. Tight. And patted her perfectly coiffed hair. Clearly she was not happy that both of her offers had been rejected, but she was determined not to let her anger show.

"Speaking of history," she said, attempting to save face by changing the subject, "I plan to make a little myself. I've officially announced that I'm running for mayor of Royal. Isn't it exciting?"

"Very," Jake said, then covered his obvious lack of excitement with a question. "Who are you running against?"

"At the moment? No one. The incumbent, Maynard Willis, isn't going to run again. Isn't that marvelous?"

Jake shrugged. "Depends on your platform."

"Why, tax reform, of course."

"Tax reform?"

"Specifically as it applies to the oil fields. We've been far too lax in that area—with other local businesses, as well. As a result, we've missed considerable revenue for the city."

The woman was too much. "From where I stand, the local businesses—oil companies included—already are digging pretty deep into their pockets. You get too heavy-handed, they may just decide to relocate to a lower tax base."

"Jacob," she said, as if addressing a rowdy child, "you might want to leave politics to the politicians. All you need to be concerned about," she added with a cheeky smile as she slipped him a business card, "is that a vote for Halifax is a vote for progress."

"Progress my ass," Jake muttered under his breath when she finally walked away.

Christine had listened to—and watched—the exchange between Jacob and Gretchen with interest. Not just because it was a welcome respite from the ridiculous conversation that Jacob—Jake—had insisted on pushing past the limit, but because Gretchen had been so interested in Jess Golden's things. Christine supposed there would be some natural curiosity over items belonging to a woman who had allegedly killed one of her ancestors, but Gretchen had gone a little over the top with her insistence that Jake sell them to her.

Speaking of over the top, could Gretchen have been more obvious making a play for Jake?

The penetrating looks, the subtle brush against him when she'd handed him her card. Christine had seen enough women in action to recognize a come-on when she saw one, even if Gretchen's had been veiled by talk of politics.

Even more amazing than Gretchen making a pass at a guy when he was on a date with another woman was that it hadn't even fazed Jake. He hadn't seemed to care that Gretchen, for all her brassy, fake sincerity and sharp features, was still a very attractive and powerful woman.

"I'm sorry about that," Jake said.

Christine set her salad plate aside. And the words were out before she was aware she'd been thinking them. "Sorry that she was flirting with you?"

He grunted. "Ballsy, huh?"

Took the words right out of her mouth.

"In any event, don't let it bother you. Gretchen flirts with everyone." He scowled at the business card, then tossed it on the table. "As a matter of fact, it's one of the things she does best. Too bad she's not as capable as a city leader."

"So, you wouldn't support her bid for mayor?"

"Hell no. If she gets in, there's no telling what kind of chaos she'll create."

"Because she's a woman?"

"Because she's Gretchen. Whatever gave you the idea that I'm gender biased?"

"Oh, I don't know. Could be the ridiculous conversation we were having earlier."

"Darlin', that wasn't about gender bias. That was about gender equity. I want you to experience some of the fun I have." He waggled his brows. "Show you what it's like to take a little walk on the wild side."

He was incorrigible. And, drat it, he had her smiling again with his silly words. And, yeah, part of the reason she was smiling was because he so clearly was not fazed by Gretchen Halifax's cool sexuality.

Until Gretchen had arrived at the table, Christine had actually started to feel a little less...what? Tense? Self-conscious? Less defensive maybe, despite Jake's questions about her history. She'd even enjoyed his silliness. That had come as a big surprise. Much of this evening had been a surprise—starting with his reaction to seeing her when she'd opened the door. The way he'd looked at her made her feel warm all over, aware, aroused even. And that was the biggest surprise of all.

Their entrées arrived and for a little while they ate in silence. Christine contemplated the way Gretchen had tried to put the moves on Jake. Witnessing Gretchen in action—smooth, sophisticated, worldly—had reminded Christine of one unalterable fact.

While she could enjoy tonight for what it was—one single night—the truth was she wasn't only way out of her element but also was way out of her league. Fancy French restaurants were not on her usual flight path. Men like Jake Thorne moved in privileged circles; she moved in stagnant squares.

She felt let down suddenly. Evidently the power surge sparked by her outfit was officially over. But she decided she was going to make the most of the evening since she'd probably never enjoy the pleasure of Claire's again. With a blissful sigh, she enjoyed a bite of her fish. The wine sauce smothering the whitefish was absolutely decadent.

"Now that's a look you ought to have on your face more often."

She hadn't realized she'd closed her eyes while savoring the rich explosion of flavor saturating her taste buds. "This is delicious."

"And a very sensual experience from where I'm sitting."

She blinked at him, saw the hot appreciation in his gaze and felt herself blush. Again. "How's your steak?"

"Exceptional. And rare. Just the way I like it."

And just the way he liked his women, she figured. There was nothing rare about her. And yet she couldn't quite stall a little shiver of awareness as his gaze swept from her face to her neck, then dropped ever so subtly to the swell of her breasts before he smiled into her eyes.

"Have another bite of your fish. I want to watch you indulge some more."

He'd done it again. Managed to make her face burn with a fire that wasn't fueled as much by irritation as it should have been. Awareness...of him as a man...of herself as a woman, played a bigger part. And it was time to get on top of the situation.

"I think I've waited long enough. It's time to talk about your other condition for turning over Jess Golden's things."

"You haven't been paying attention," he said, that maddeningly amused grin tipping up one corner of his mouth. "I already named it. The condition is we strike a deal. I'll agree to do something you deem as adult and you'll agree to do something I deem as juvenile."

He insisted on pushing. Okay fine. She'd push back. But how?

And just like that, it came to her how she could call his bluff.

"Okay. You're on."

He did a double take. Then sat back in his chair and considered her with a pleasantly disbelieving look. "For real?"

She nodded. "For real."

"Well, okay then, Chris-tine," he said, drawing out her name, "what do I have to do?"

"Run for mayor."

That wiped the smile off his face. "What?"

"You're so confident that Gretchen Halifax will make a lousy candidate? Then you need to make sure she doesn't get the position."

"Hell, sweet cheeks, I'm no politician."

"All the better. You already run a business. It's not much of a stretch to run a city."

"This is ridiculous."

"Oh. *Now* it's ridiculous. Now that I've called you on it."

"But it's my game," he whined with the express intent of making her laugh.

And she did. It just sort of bubbled out, surprising her more than it surprised him.

"Lord, that's sweet," he said. "You really ought to do that more often."

"You make me sound like I'm a stuffy old curmudgeon," she grumbled, but she was still grinning.

"There is nothing stuffy about you, darlin'. And nothing old. Everything's new—especially that laugh. Did you know your eyes sort of dance in that beautiful face when you laugh?"

His eyes had turned dark again, fueled by a fire that was far too warm and far too intimate for her comfort. She felt exposed...and as alive with sensation as if he'd physically touched her.

"You're full of charm, Mr. Thorne. And you do so love to use it, don't you?"

"When it gets results like that, yes, ma'am. I truly do." He reached across the table, took her hand in his. "You have the most kissable mouth. I bet you didn't know that, either, did you?"

Yikes. Okay. Time out. He was way too fast on his

feet for her. And the way she was feeling about him was too confusing.

"If you'll excuse me," she said, pulling her hand from his. "I'll be right back."

Then she hightailed it to the ladies' room while her bones were still in solid form. Another few minutes under his seductive gaze and said bones might just fold like licorice. And then where would she be? Believing he didn't say those things to *all* the girls, that's where. That belief would be a mistake of major proportions.

She knew that for a fact. But knowing it didn't take the sting out of the truth that a teeny, tiny part of her wanted to believe he really thought she was special.

Wasn't that just the most asinine thing? She didn't even like him. Well, she *hadn't* liked him. She still didn't *want* to like him. And yet…she was having fun tonight. Kind of. When the mood struck him, he could be very sweet and attentive and… Stop!

Just stop. This was the same man who had tormented her for the past five years. For all she knew, tonight was just a precursor to another kind of torment. The kind that could leave her wounded instead of just ticked off.

"Had a good time tonight, Chrissie," Jake said as he pulled up in front of her apartment.

As he walked her up the sidewalk to the door of her first-floor apartment, his hands were tucked oh-so casually into his trouser pockets. Of course, to accomplish that he'd had to brush his suit jacket aside. So, of course,

Christine's peripheral vision was filled with the way his white dress shirt hugged an abdomen that, if memory served, exemplified the term *six-pack* abs.

"The dinner was excellent," she said, aware of the warmth of the July night, ultra-aware of the height and the rich scent of the man walking beside her.

"Exceeded only by the company."

When she'd returned to the table after her trip to the ladies' room, she'd very quickly steered him away from the topic of dancing eyes and kissable lips. Fortunately he'd taken her cue and backed off all the Mr. Charm talk. They'd discussed the weather, her work at the hospital and the Royal Museum. When she'd pressed, he'd reluctantly told her about his business—if you counted, "It's doing well," as talking about it.

Since he hadn't seemed to want to talk about it any more than she'd wanted to discuss her family, they'd opted for talk about their alma maters. She was an Aggie and he'd been a Longhorn, and since the two schools were huge interstate rivals, verbal competition about which university was better had kept them occupied through the ride back to her apartment.

But now he was in flirt mode again. And she was going to nip that in the bud because no good could come from her falling for his practiced lines. She had it all planned in her head. She would turn to him when they reached her door, shake his hand, thank him for dinner and get while the getting was good.

She no longer cared that they hadn't sealed the deal

over Jess Golden's things. She'd revisit the issue another time when she wasn't so confused. With all his charming talk and heated looks and walk-on-the-wild-side banter, he'd thrown her totally off-kilter.

She wasn't used to feeling so off balance. She didn't know how to handle the sensation. But she did know how to handle him.

Thank you, handshake, good night. A good, solid plan.

"Thank you," she said when they reached her front door and focused on the hand she extended. "Good night."

Long moments passed and he just stood there.

Finally she was forced to look up and meet his gaze.

Damn him, he was smiling.

Her lungs deflated on a slow, weary sigh. "What's so funny now?"

"You, sweet cheeks. You are a laugh a minute." The warmth and affection in his voice and his expression stirred a herd of butterflies into flight in her tummy. "But then, I'm easily entertained. Come here. Let me show you how easy I am."

And then he kissed her. Just like that. No long, lingering meeting of eyes in the moonlight as a prelude. No dodging and weaving or wondering when it was going to happen.

One minute he was a safe three feet away announcing his intentions. The next he gathered her gently into his arms and lowered his head.

Did she fight it? No.

Did she want to fight it? Um. Guess not.

That was the surprise of the century.

She stood there, her head tipped back, watching as that beautiful mouth descended. Actually she more than watched. She actually rose up on her tiptoes to meet him. Then she lifted her hands to his biceps to steady herself, to mold herself closer. And she let him show her exactly how easy he was.

He showed her just fine. He was easy like a down comforter on a cool winter night. Easy like a daydream on a lazy summer afternoon. The caress of his mouth as he opened it over hers was slow and sweet, soft and undemanding.

It was wonderful. It was amazing. She didn't think about raising her arms to his neck and burying her fingers in the hair at his nape. She simply did it, only tactilely aware of the silky softness of his hair, the warmth and strength of the muscle beneath his skin, the heady heat and hardness of him against her as he wrapped her closer, deeper into his big body.

And he was big. So strong yet so gentle as he cradled her against him, changed the angle of his mouth over hers and with a groan that reverberated against her breasts, took the kiss to a whole other level.

His mouth urged hers open. His tongue entered when she gladly acquiesced. Through the ringing in her ears and the trembling of her entire body, she recognized his hunger, melted into the pleasure, rode the wave of mutual need.

She felt dizzy with the knowledge that a man like him truly could be aroused by a woman like her. He definitely was aroused, no hiding that with her belly pressed against his this way. She felt the power of that knowledge surge through her like a current. Imagined the full measure of his passion with a shiver, then felt wrenched from the heat of sensual pleasure to the cool rush of reality when his big hands rose to hers and untangled them from around his neck and he set her physically away.

"Whoa," he said in a voice that was gruff with passion. With one small step he put a mile of distance between them.

She blinked, her lips pulsing and swollen, her entire body buzzing on sensual overload.

"Whoa," he said again. Then he shook his head and after a look that was searching and stunned and wary, he turned on his heel and hightailed it down the walk to his car.

That was it. Not another word.

A little stunned, Christine watched him go. Got the distinct impression that he was running away, when only moments ago he hadn't been able to get close enough fast enough.

She was still standing in the same spot when he peeled away from the curb. Her lips were still tingling from his kiss when she went to bed half an hour later. And her mind—Lord above, her mind was still spinning.

Her experience with sex was limited and for the most part unsatisfying. Her fault, is what she'd always figured.

She didn't do well with touching. Didn't do well with trust. Sexual encounter made for more tension than passion. But Jacob Thorne had just proven there were exceptions to some rules she'd taken for granted as unbreakable.

To her utter surprise, she'd liked being touched by him. She'd loved being kissed by him. Trust hadn't even been an issue. Or maybe it had been the entire issue and she'd instinctively trusted him when he'd drawn her in, wrapped her tight and made love to her mouth with the enthusiasm and the expertise of a lover. One who sensed exactly what she wanted, exactly what she needed, and made it clear with the touch of his hand, the heat of his mouth, that he knew precisely how to deliver.

And he had delivered—until he'd abruptly dragged himself away, looked at her as though he didn't know how she'd ended up in his arms and hadn't been able to leave fast enough.

He had acted as though it had been a colossal mistake to kiss her.

But it hadn't felt like a mistake. It had felt...wow. It had felt incredible.

Now, however, she felt incredibly confused.

And alone. Most of all, alone.

Of all the things in the world she'd ever wanted, ever dreamed or fantasized about, being alone for the rest of her life hadn't been one of them. Never had she been more aware that the choices she'd made and the barriers she'd erected might have guaranteed that she always would be alone.

She was so lost in those dismal conclusions that it didn't even dawn on her until much later that they had never gotten around to discussing the hoops she had to jump through to get him to give her Jess Golden's things.

Six

Later that night, Jake sat at the bar in the Texas Cattleman's Club nursing a beer. Normally he found a certain amount of contentment in the sprawling, exclusive gentlemen's club Henry "Tex" Langley had established nearly one hundred years ago. Everything about the place was male, from the rich, dark paneling, heavy leather furniture and massive fireplace to the huge oil paintings, animal heads and antique guns displayed on the walls.

He needed the no-frills, no-female atmosphere. But tonight instead of enjoying it, he was brooding. He'd left Chrissie Travers over two hours ago. Kissable, crushable, vulnerable, incredible Chrissie Travers.

Lord above, could he get lost in that woman's kisses. And he had been lost—without-a-map-or-a-compass lost—until his brains had finally come in and, with a mad scramble, he'd gotten his bearings. Then he'd run, not walked, away from the glut of emotions that had scuffled with his better judgment.

He kept seeing her and her sweet, soft, swollen lips. Her and her gray-green eyes, wide open and wondering.

Whoa.

Seemed to be the word of the night.

"You look like you're in a mood."

He glanced over his shoulder, surprised to see his twin brother, Connor, ease onto a bar stool beside him. It was like looking into a mirror. Folks still remarked that if it weren't for the hair, they wouldn't be able to tell the twins apart. Connor wore his dark brown hair in a clipped military cut—a holdover from his Army Ranger days. Jake preferred to let his hair grow, sometimes to the point of being shaggy—a holdover from his rebellious youth.

"*I'm* in a mood?" Jake grunted and returned his attention to his beer. "This from Mr. Mood Swing himself."

Immediately Jake regretted the offhand remark. Par for the course, he always seemed to say the wrong thing to Connor lately, and in this case Connor was right. Jake *was* in a mood.

Jake motioned to the bartender. "Give us two more, would ya, Joe? Seems the Thorne boys are of the same mind tonight." He turned toward his brother, prepared to make atonement. "What brings you out this time of night?"

It was getting close to last call. Connor wasn't known for frequenting the bar, so Jake had been surprised when his brother had sat beside him. Jake had been so mired in his own pickle, though, he hadn't given it much thought at first.

"Couldn't sleep," Connor said with a throwaway shrug as he reached for his longneck and took a deep pull.

Tell me about it, Jake thought but didn't say as much. Ever since he'd left Chris Travers standing at her front door, he'd been as revved as a DuPont Chevy on NAS-CAR race day.

"Figured there'd be a poker game goin' on," Connor added while Jake huddled over his beer and tried to forget the things that prickly woman had done to him. Like turn him on, fire him up and wring him out.

"Game broke up about midnight," Jake said. He'd turned down the offer to join in. In his state of mind, he would have lost the business and wouldn't even have cared.

But he wasn't so self-consumed that he didn't notice something was up with Connor. Jake cared about his brother. Connor hadn't been the same since returning from the Middle East. He had followed their father's footsteps in an attempt to win the old man's favor by becoming a U.S. Army Airborne Ranger and then an engineer.

Jake, an adrenaline junkie, had opted for a different type of career adventure. After his four-year hitch with the Army, during which time he took college credit classes that he finished up at University of Texas, he'd gone to work for Red Adair fighting oil-well fires.

He'd became so addicted to the danger, he'd wanted a greater hand in it and left Red to form his own company, Hellfire, International. While his twin had been fighting terrorists in the Middle East, Jake made his own statement for freedom and patriotism by fighting oil fires in the same war-torn countries.

They'd both been there. Now they were back. And some things had never changed. Such as sensing when there was a problem.

"Heard from the old man lately?" Jake asked, wondering if a recent set-to with their father was at the root of Connor's dark mood.

Connor's grunt gave Jake his answer. Yeah, Connor had had another tangle with their father. Even though his folks had moved to Florida, James Thorne still could reach out and touch all kinds of raw nerves.

When Connor had retired from active duty, he'd made the ultimate sacrifice. He'd taken over the family engineering firm when their father retired. Jake owed his twin big-time for that. It had gotten the old man off his back.

Some would call his father's repeated wish for Jake to take over the business the burden of the favored son. Jake called it something else—damn unfortunate.

He knew that their father's blatant favoritism toward Jake had always made Connor feel like second banana. Oh, Connor had never said as much. He didn't have to. Actions spoke louder than any words. Even when they were kids, Jake often had talked his way out of a sound pounding with the old man's belt. Connor, on the rare occasion he bucked the old man, never even tried. He just took the beating. And as a result, Jake had watched Connor turn deeper into himself, bottle up his pain and anger until the dark mood would hit him.

Like tonight.

"Tell you what, brother mine," Jake said, slinging an arm over Connor's shoulder, knowing there were some things embedded so deep, no amount of heart-to-heart sessions would drag them out, "how about we blow this place, dive into a case of brew and the two of us get rip-roaring drunk? I haven't tied one on in a coon's age. You game?"

That finally made Connor smile. "Must be woman trouble."

"Got that right," Jake muttered as he dug into his hip pocket for his wallet, then tossed some bills onto the bar. Big-time woman trouble.

What in the hell was he going to do about Chrissie Travers? Things had gotten out of hand tonight. He'd set out to do a little seducing. Just a little good-natured fun and games.

But then he'd kissed her...and she'd come alive like a flame set to a candle.

And it hadn't seemed so much like fun and games after that. He'd felt the subtle give of her body, the gentle swell of her breasts against his chest. It had been much more than a kiss to her. Not to him, of course. No, he thought and wiped at a bead of sweat that had pooled on his forehead. Not to him.

Now he knew what that niggling sense of catastrophe he'd been experiencing on and off all night was about. He'd screwed up. When he'd crossed the line from teasing to appreciating, from tormenting to kissing... Well, he'd changed the dynamics between Chrissie and him.

When she was a prickly little prude, he'd been as safe as a Boy Scout on a supervised campout. But when she'd transformed into a vibrant, alluring woman before his eyes, he'd ditched his Scout troop in favor of a little sweet talk and seduction. And the safety factor had flown out the proverbial window.

Words such as *serious* and *relationship* and *future* and other scary notions leaped to mind. He simply didn't do those things. Not any more. Jake had gone the marriage route once and he'd gotten used, burned, battered and beaten. Ever since, fun and games had been his stock-in-trade. Just fun. Just games.

Prissy Chrissie, however, kissed as though she planned on changing the rules and the stakes. And well, that just wasn't going to happen. Not to him. Not again.

That's why he'd walked. Before the harm. Before the foul.

So why was he sitting here fighting the urge to walk right back to Chrissie? Get a better, longer, bigger taste of what he'd just walked away from?

He dragged a hand over his face. He had to think. He had to think about this a lot. But not tonight.

"Come on," he said. "My place. Gotta be something on ESPN to take our minds off what ails us."

"This time of night? Nothing but reruns," Connor said, walking beside him out of the club.

"Good enough for me," Jake said.

When the light finally dawned, it lit up Christine's world like a ten-thousand-watt bulb and darn near blinded her. That's why Monday at noon she had a mission on her mind when she maneuvered her flashy, brand-new red convertible—purchased just fifteen minutes ago when she traded in her used tan compact—into a space in front of Hellfire, International.

She was turning over new leaves left and right. No more dull and drab and ultrasafe for Christine Travers. From now on it was flash and fire, razzle and dazzle. She was filled with determination to change a few more things when she fed the meter, drew a deep breath and headed into the building.

She'd thought about her meeting-slash-date with Jake Thorne all weekend. Mostly she'd thought about the way he'd kissed her. She'd gotten all warm and tingly inside. And she liked the feeling of excitement and anticipation. She'd considered his offer to teach her about walking on the wild side. And she liked the prospect of treading a new path. Yeah, she was still getting used to this brave new Chris.

She had Jake to thank for this awakening. The man, she thought with a smile as she pressed the elevator button that would take her to Jake's fourth-floor office, was full of the devil and full of life and teasing and fun.

After five years of scowling over his antics, cursing him for his insensitivity, she'd done a one-eighty. She now was convinced that he'd had the right idea after all. She'd been doing it all wrong.

She wasn't sure of the exact moment when she'd come to that conclusion. It wasn't that the bulb had been off one second, then suddenly burned full blast the next. No, the wattage had steadily increased over the weekend. It had finally powered to full glare about the same time she'd started asking herself what her strait-laced, all-work-no-play mind-set had netted her all these years. And she'd realized she didn't like all the answers.

Well, she was going to ask some new questions. Starting today.

"Hi, Janice."

Jake's secretary looked up from her desk when Christine breezed in the door. "Well, hello. You're look-ing...bubbly," the secretary said with a curious smile.

Christine felt bubbly. And it was about time. "Is Jake in?"

Janice picked up the handset. "Let me see if he's busy."

Christine hadn't even settled into a chair when Janice said, "You can go in. Great outfit, by the way," she added with an approving nod. "I love what you've done with your hair."

Christine's new plan had called for new look. That's why she'd headed out to the mall Sunday afternoon and spent some of her moldy money—Alison's words—on some snappy new sandals, a pair of snug white capri pants and a white spaghetti-strap tank. Over top she wore an off-the-shoulder, light-as-air silk-scarf blouse in a soft pink print that gave the entire outfit a breezy, sexy and fun look. She'd also gotten a makeover. A short, sassy haircut and some makeup secrets made her look vibrant instead of invisible.

The look fit her mood. Right up until the moment she walked into Jake's office. Then all of her hard-won confidence crumpled in the face of what she planned to do.

Can I really do this?

Jake had a smile firmly in place. The smile, however, deflated like a leaky balloon as he looked her up and down.

"Chrissie. This is a…surprise."

More than a surprise. Christine could see that by the way his dark eyebrows were pulled together. He seemed wary about what her presence in his office meant. Was he worried about her reaction, given that he'd kissed her silly Saturday night, then galloped out of Dodge as fast as three hundred and fifty horses could take him? Maybe more than wary. Maybe he was worried sick that she'd read too much into that kiss.

Well, she hadn't. But she did intend to stay the course.

"Sorry to barge in like this. I was wondering if you had a minute to talk."

He leaned back in his chair. Tossed down his pen and gave her another appraising look. "Well, um, sure.

What's on your mind? Wait. Stupid question. You're here about Jess Golden's things."

"Not exactly."

Okay. This was much harder than she'd thought it would be. She took a deep breath, let it out and put it all on the line.

She blurted out what she wanted from him.

Then she waited for the fallout as a stunned and, if she wasn't mistaken, panicked look froze on Jake's handsome face.

"You want me to what?"

Oh, God, Jake thought. This was not what he needed today.

"I want you to make good on your offer. I want lessons on how to walk on the wild side."

No. No. No. He'd had it all worked out. It was a done deal. He'd crossed the wrong line with Chrissie Saturday night—a line he'd decided he wasn't going to cross again, no way, no how, no time. He was going to forget about her innocent, lusty kisses and go back to being her biggest pain in the butt.

That was the safe way.

But now here she was, all girly and gorgeous and pink and sexy as hell with that handkerchief of a top sliding off her left shoulder and leaving it bare. She'd done something to her hair, too. Cut it in a sassy do that gave the illusion she had just gotten out of bed and run her fingers through it—or a lover had.

And her lips. Lord, they looked plump and pouty, painted the prettiest shade that had him licking his own lips over the thought of licking the color off hers.

Double hell. Just when he'd had all his ducks lined up in a neat and tidy row, Miss Quick-Change Artist had come rushing in and sent them scattering in every which direction.

"Um…Jake?"

Her voice was thick with uncertainty, and suddenly he felt guilty. It wasn't her fault that he wanted to turn back the clock to a time when the hot-looking woman standing anxiously in his doorway had been a stodgy, prickly, schoolmarm-of-yore type who had interested him only from the standpoint of how much of a rise he could tease out of her.

Funny how the tables had turned on *that* level. If he wasn't careful, the memory of that amazing kiss they'd shared coupled with the way she looked today might make him rise to the occasion. Literally.

He manufactured a stiff smile when she eased his office door shut behind her.

"Chrissie. I was joking when I said that."

You could dress the girl up in soft, sexy clothes, but you couldn't quite iron the starch out of the girl. Her chin went up and her shoulders stiffened, and suddenly he understood how much this request had cost her. "So you didn't mean it when you said you wanted to volunteer to teach me how to loosen up?"

"Um, well," was the best response he could manage

to say because he couldn't stop looking at her, knowing that this new Chrissie presented a whole lot more complications than the old one. The one who would have poked him to death with her quills instead of melting into his arms like a candy kiss.

"Life's short, Jake. You above all men should know that."

"Well, yeah, but—"

"And you got me thinking Saturday night. Well, not just Saturday night but all weekend. Do you know how old I am?" she asked, abruptly shifting gears.

She didn't wait for him to answer but barged on like a steamroller on a diesel high. It was as if she had to get the words out all at once or she'd lose her nerve.

"Twenty-eight. I'm twenty-eight years old and I still don't know what I want to be when I grow up. I don't truly know what I want out of life and you want to know why?"

"Um—"

"I'll tell you why."

He puffed out a breath between his cheeks and prepared to listen.

"Because I've never given myself an opportunity to think about what I really wanted. How sad is that?"

He opened his mouth but no sound came out because she continued to speak, her tone growing reflective and regretful.

"I've been too busy toeing the line. And what has it gotten me?"

He didn't bother to try to respond. Clearly she'd

come here on a mission to get some things off her chest—her soft, voluptuous chest that at the moment was pressed quite nicely against her silky blouse as she drew in a shaky breath.

"What it's gotten me is respectability. Okay, fine. Respectability is good. And it's gotten me security. Also good. But has it gotten me contentment?"

"I'm thinking the answer might be no?" he said cautiously when she paused and appealed to him as if she really did expect an answer.

"No is exactly right. I do not have contentment. Not for even a second have I led what I consider to be a contented life. Dull, yes. Contented, no. There has to be at least a little excitement for a person to be content, right? Well, where's my excitement? Where are my thrills? Where are my…my magic moments?"

Oh, sweetie, don't cry, he thought when her lower lip started quivering in the face of a self-assessment that was both harsh and humiliating. On top of everything else, he didn't think he could take it if she cried.

He stood and made his way around his desk. Easing a hip on the corner, he crossed his arms over his chest to keep from holding her close and telling her there was still hope.

But then a big, glistening teardrop spilled down her cheek and he was a goner.

He reached for her and patted her back clumsily. "It's not really so bad," he lied kindly.

"It's…awful. P-Prissy Chrissie," she sputtered

against his chest. "That's what they call me behind my back. Did you know that?"

Oh, yeah. He knew. Was probably the worst offender. Her little sniffle twisted the knife of guilt deeply embedded in his gut. He patted with a little more sympathy.

"The worst part is, they're right. Well, they *were* right. I've been nothing but a…a goal-oriented workaholic. All my life I've been so focused on my need for respectability and stability and safety that I've ignored my other needs. A woman's needs," she said and lifted her head to look up into his eyes.

Gulp. Not those big hazel eyes. He was a sucker for her eyes.

"I want to know what it feels like to be appreciated as a woman. To be desired by a man. To have power over a man."

Sweetheart, if you only knew how much power you had right now. She could have brought him to his knees. First with guilt. Then with the desire to kiss her tears away, to bite gently into the quivering softness of her lush lower lip.

He resisted. Only God knew how, because she felt so soft and warm and wonderful cuddled up against him. But he'd made up his mind Saturday night between a six-pack and an ESPN classic football game. He was nipping in the bud this new twist to their relationship that he'd had the misfortune to initiate.

Chris Travers needed a man who would stick around. One who was in for the long haul. Didn't matter how much Jake loved her kisses, didn't matter that he found her a sweet surprise, a sexy temptation, he was not the kind of man she needed.

"I'm a spinster," she said on another teary sigh. "An old maid. And all because I've been too scared to take a chance on life."

"Aw, Chrissie," he said, feeling sad that she was bullying herself this way.

"But that's all going to change," she said, finding her composure again and pushing away from him.

Just look at those freckles, he thought. Dusting the bridge of her nose, riding on her cheeks like little angel kisses. It made him feel soft and sentimental in his chest. And hard in other places.

Until she said, "And you're the man who's going to make it happen."

Seven

Jake's mouth opened as wide as his eyes. "What? *Me?* What am I going to make happen?"

"For five years you've needled me, teased me, made fun of me and in general goaded me into burying my feet deeper into my principles and my head deeper into the sand. Well, Saturday night changed all that. You were nice to me. In fact, you were into me. I liked it."

Damn. "Chris—"

"Oh, don't worry," she said, some of the old starchy Chrissie back in her speech and her bearing. "I know you were just playing. I know what you are. You're a flirt and a good-time guy. And you were just being you on Saturday night because I wasn't being me. At least,

I wasn't being the old me. I was being the new me when I didn't even realize I wanted me to be a different me."

His head was starting to hurt. "Huh?"

She waved a hand. "Doesn't matter. What does matter is that you offered to teach me how to loosen up and have fun and I'm going to hold you to it. Starting right now."

And the next thing he knew, she kissed him. She reached up, placed her hands on either side of his face and pulled his mouth down to hers. There wasn't any finesse to it. It was all about impulse and determination and flat-out moxie.

It should have been funny. But for some reason he thought it was sweet. At least, he did during the moments he wasn't alternating between panic that warned him he could easily go down for the count here and a flat out case of pure, animal lust.

That mouth. She did have a way with her mouth. It wasn't practiced. It wasn't expert. But, oh, was it enthusiastic. And that enthusiasm was infectious. He hadn't planned to kiss her back. But there was the surprise factor. And the heat factor. And the warm, soft woman factor that, combined, sucked him in, egged him on and dragged him under.

He widened his legs, pulled her between them and dived into the kiss like a pearl diver on a treasure hunt. He urged her mouth open, swept inside her sweet, wet heat with his tongue while pressing her into his growing erection with one hand at the small of her back. His other hand pressed between her shoulder blades, encouraging the pressure of her breasts against his chest.

And sweet ambrosia, she tasted good. The soft sounds she made deep in her throat fostered a low growl of his own that had him leaning back on the top of his desk, bringing her with him. He heard something crash to the floor, didn't care what it was because her full weight covered him now—sexy and hot and pressing in all the right places.

If their sudden horizontal tango gave her pause, she didn't let on. In fact, she really got into the kiss then. She'd let go of his face and buried her hands in his hair, all the while squirming and sighing and doing a little pressing of her own.

He loved it. Loved the honest lust. The exuberant response. But most of all he loved the way they fit, the heady friction as she moved above him, dragging him deeper into the heat of the moment and further away from the consequences.

He was ready to take it to the next level. Make love to her right there on the top of his desk, in the middle of Monday, when she lifted her head. Looked down into his eyes through those drowsy hazel eyes of hers and in the most slumberous, seductive voice he'd ever heard, she whispered, "Consider that payment for lesson one. Come through with lesson two and there'll be more where that came from."

Then, as if she hadn't just played the most amazing game of tonsil tag he'd ever been a party to, she pushed herself off him, straightened her top and left him flat on his back.

"When you do come up with lesson number two," she said, turning around with one hand on the door handle, "give me a call." Then she left him. Hot and bothered. Hard and hungry.

When the blood returned to his head several long minutes later, he eased himself to a sitting position. When he could take a breath that didn't smell of her— something fresh and citrusy—he carefully stood.

For the longest time he just stared at the closed door. Finally he raked both hands through his hair, swore, then dropped into his desk chair. He let his head fall back and stared at the ceiling.

What the hell had just happened here?

He felt as if he'd been hit by a tank. At the very least, by a whirlwind in the guise of Chrissie Travers.

Prissy? He'd never again think of her that way.

But he would think of her. She'd made sure of that.

He'd be thinking about just how silky her skin might be. How those soft breasts would feel pressed against his palm, how they'd taste on his tongue. About how much heat the two of them could generate on a big bed instead of a hard desk.

None of that was supposed to happen. He wasn't supposed to kiss her again, to flirt with her again, to charm her again, let alone think about making love to her.

But she's the one who had done the kissing. And the flirting. And the charming.

And the challenging, he realized as a tight knot of grudging respect twisted into anger. The minx had turned the tables on him. She'd leveled a dare. He was the one who had always been in control of their relationship—if you could call what they'd had until Saturday night a relationship. Mostly it had been a good-natured—at least on his part—razzfest. He teased. She bristled. He'd liked it that way.

But then he'd been stupid enough to kiss her. He'd used the weekend to put that kiss into perspective, chalked it up to stupidity. End of story. Until the woman had barged in here, added another chapter to the book and confused the hell out of him with her talk about "old me" and "new me" before attacking him with those sizzling, mind-bending kisses.

Now he was in a daze. And that just plain fried his circuits. He did not get bent out of shape over a woman. It wasn't allowed. It wasn't supposed to happen.

So why had it?

He stood and walked to the window. Maybe he was bored. Since he'd damaged his lungs in that damn fire five years ago, he'd had to be satisfied with the management end of his own business. Sure, it was rewarding. But it was dull. He'd joined the Texas Cattleman's Club hoping for a little excitement, but so far all the thrill he'd gotten was to listen to the exploits of other club members. Hearing those stories about saving countries or princesses only served to remind Jake of his limitations.

Chrissie had been a handy distraction. One that he'd let get out of hand.

Well, there was only one thing to do about it, he decided as the haze began to lift. This couldn't go on. He had to regain the upper hand. And he knew how to do it.

He was going to call her bluff.

Little Chrissie wanted to take a walk on the wild side? Well, then, he would give her the walk of her life. That would put an end to her hit-and-run kisses. Put an end to her messing with his head.

He'd come up with something so wild and so foreign to her straitlaced nature that she'd run like a rabbit and he'd never see her sweet face again. Yeah. He'd fix her little red wagon and reclaim his equilibrium in the process.

He felt marginally better about the situation until he dragged a hand over his face and realized how unsteady he still was.

Why in the hell hadn't he let her win the bid on Jess Golden's things? Then none of this would be happening.

She'd done it.

Between sharp bouts of disbelief that left her tummy tumbling and moments of pride at her own audacity, Christine couldn't stop grinning. She'd marched into Jake Thorne's domain and told him what she thought, told him what she expected from him. Then she'd kissed him.

Well, okay, there had been a little waffling in there, but she'd gotten it together. Oh, had she gotten it together.

Another one of those waves of disbelief swamped her as she signaled for a left turn and headed out of the city. She'd shocked him. Heck, she'd shocked herself. Never in her life had she initiated a kiss. Never in her life had she experienced such a strong sexual reaction. Okay, so her experience was severely limited, but could it get any hotter than that kiss in Jake's office? On his desk?

She wasn't sure where her actions had come from—instinct maybe. Maybe from years of watching movies and reading books and living vicariously through them. Whatever, she'd been a tiger.

She felt good. She felt great! The sun was high and hot, her brand-new convertible's top was down and the wind whipped her hairstyle around her face—something she'd never allowed with her longer hair. It was freeing. And exciting.

"It's the new me!" she shouted into the wind, inched her speed up to a shocking two miles per hour above the speed limit and switched her radio station from the classics to classic rock. She felt like a little kid writing on the walls with crayons or a teenager skipping class.

Actually she was skipping work. Technically she was taking a personal day—something she never did just for the heck of it. It felt naughty. And, wonder of wonders, she liked it.

She couldn't wait to call Alison to tell her what was going on.

And she couldn't wait to hear from Jake to find out what the second lesson would be.

There would be another lesson. She may have discovered some new sides to Jake Thorne during the past few days, but there was one thing about the man she'd always known.

He never backed down from a dare. He wouldn't back down from this one.

"Bring it on," she said aloud. Whatever he fired at her, she was up to it. "The new me is up to it."

The new her wasn't deluding herself into believing that what was going on between her and Jake was a long-term notion. She wasn't foolish enough to think that she was the one who could tame him for a serious relationship when any number of beautiful, sexy women hadn't been able to accomplish the same.

No, she wasn't that foolish. She simply was ready to experience life. For some reason, she trusted Jake to be the man to help her. And when the challenge was over and she'd had her fill, she'd be ready to walk away.

It helped to know what Jake Thorne was—a game player. He couldn't help it. And she wouldn't change him. Even if she wanted to.

The thought of things between them ending—before they'd even really begun—flooded her with an unexpected sadness. She turned up the radio and, at the top of her lungs, sang along with the Boss about being born to run.

Jake left the office early that day and hightailed it to the Cattleman's Club for a little diversion. He breathed a sigh of relief when one of his buddies, Logan Voss, spotted him and motioned him over to join a poker game. A friendly game of five-card stud was exactly what Jake needed to take his mind off Chrissie and the way she'd turned him inside out yet again.

"So, how's it shakin', Jake?" Logan asked as Jake hung his black Stetson on a brass hat rack in the corner of the bar.

"Can't complain. How about you boys?"

He got what he'd expected—mumbled "fines" and head nods. While members of the club often tackled matters of grave importance and danger within these walls, it was also a haven. As a rule, a man didn't come to the Cattleman's Club to talk about his troubles. He came here to get away from them, to simply hang out with men of like minds.

Of all of his friends at the club, he felt a particular kinship to Logan Voss. Voss ran a large cattle ranch just outside of town. Like Jake, the rugged rancher, who was a hands-on owner, was divorced. Unlike Jake who took pains to see that no one saw his pain, Logan's scars occasionally showed in the bleak look in his eyes and the weary set of his shoulders. Or maybe Jake was just sensitive to Logan's situation since he'd gone through an ugly divorce himself.

"You in, Thorne?" Mark Hartman asked. "Or you gonna sit there and admire your cards the rest of the night?"

"Yeah, yeah, I'm in," Jake said and called Hartman's good-natured haranguing.

Jake didn't know Mark Hartman as well as he knew Logan, but he liked what the guy stood for. Jake didn't know the entire story, but the retired soldier had lost his wife in a violent mugging. Mark played his cards—and his feelings—pretty close to the vest, too. The African-American appeared to be independently wealthy but still spent hours at his gym where he gave self-defense classes to women. No one had to wonder what motivated him.

"Read 'em and weep, boys." This came from the fourth man at the table, Gavin O'Neal, as he laid down a diamond flush.

Jake groaned and tossed in his cards. He hated this run of luck. But how loudly could one complain about losing to the sheriff? A decent one at that. O'Neal had been a wild man in his day, but he took the shiny badge that he wore on his chest seriously. The badge also didn't hurt his standing with women. As a rule, Jake loved to give O'Neal grief about his reputation.

Tonight, though, Jake just wasn't in much of a joking mood—mainly because of one particular woman giving him so much grief.

O'Neal dealt Jake another stellar hand. Not. He arranged his cards, rolled his eyes and folded. When Voss won the hand, Jake was down fifty bucks—and he hadn't been in the game a full hour. He was starting to think his luck had deserted him altogether when Voss dealt him a pair of queens. Finally. A bidding hand. He was about to raise Gavin's bet when a commotion by the front door had the entire table on their feet.

"What the hell?"

It was Nita Windcroft. Her violet eyes were shooting sparks and the slim young woman, who had recently taken on one helluva responsibility when she'd assumed management of her father's horse farm, appeared to be in one high and mighty snit.

"Sheriff," she said, marching toward the table. "You've got to do something."

O'Neal met her halfway across the bar and laid a settling hand on her arm. "Good Lord, Nita, settle down before you bust a vein. Not another word until you calm down. Take a deep breath now. That's it. Give me another one. Okay. Now tell me what's wrong." He steered her toward the table where the men had been playing.

Even off duty and out of uniform, Gavin had an air of command that Nita responded to.

"The Devlins are at it again," she said, rage coloring her voice. "And if you don't put a stop to it, so help me, I will. I can't let them destroy my ranch."

"Okay, Nita. Settle down," Gavin repeated with a soothing calm that seemed to make Nita at least stop and take stock of her surroundings.

Besides their table, only a half a dozen other TCC members sat in the bar. After Nita's initial outburst, they all returned to their respective conversations.

"You want to talk to me in private?" Gavin asked.

"I don't care if the whole county hears what those snakes have been up to! You've got to do something."

The Windcrofts and the Devlins had nursed a Hatfield-and-McCoy-style feud for close to a century. Old Jonathan Devlin had liked to keep the situation stirred up, but Jake had thought things would settle down now that Jonathan was gone.

Judging from the look on Nita's face, he'd thought wrong.

If he had his facts straight, the Windcroft-Devlin feud had started when Richard Windcroft lost over half of his land to Nicholas Devlin in a poker game. The Windcrofts always had maintained the game was rigged. A Devlin ended up getting shot and killed over it, and of course, the Windcrofts got the blame. The accusations and squabbles had been going on ever since.

"Why don't you tell me what's going on out at the ranch that's got you so upset, Nita," Gavin suggested.

"In the past few weeks I've been dealing with downed rails, cut fence lines and spooked horses. At first I tried to write it off as wear and tear, but then I found wire cutters by a downed section and some of my new board fences have been broken, as well. I spent three days rounding up stock from the last time those bastards did their dirty work. But the last straw, the very last straw—they poisoned my horse feed."

Nita's cheeks were fiery red. "If my foreman hadn't noticed something off, there's no telling how much stock I would have lost. It's bad enough I'm treating over a dozen head of very sick horses—some of them my customers'—but it will cost me a small fortune to replace that tainted feed. And do you have any idea what this is going to do to my business once word gets out? It could ruin me. Not to mention, I'm worried sick about the horses. Only a Devlin would stoop so low as to try to kill innocent animals."

No wonder Nita was upset, Jake thought. The Windcroft ranch boarded and trained horses. She'd start to lose customers if they felt the safety of their stock was compromised. She was leveling some pretty serious charges, and the Devlins were prominent citizens in Royal. Tom Devlin was even a member of the Cattleman's Club and Jake considered him a friend.

"Those are pretty strong allegations, Nita," Gavin warned, echoing Jake's thoughts. "You have some proof that the Devlins are behind this?"

"Who else would it be? They've finally come up with a way to ruin us. It's what they've always wanted. And they'll shut us down if they aren't stopped!"

"Have you had any direct threats on your life?" Gavin asked.

"My life is my ranch, so you can play it anyway you like.

"Okay, no," she admitted when Gavin gave her a stern look. "I haven't been personally threatened, but that doesn't mean it won't come to that. I'm worried about my stock. I'm worried about my help. Now, what are you going to do about it?"

"Come on," Gavin said. "Let's go down to the station. You can write out a statement and I'll dispatch an officer to your ranch to take stock of all that's happened. Maybe he can find a lead on who's doing this."

"I told you who's doing it. And I want to press charges," Nita insisted.

"Do you have anything—anything but your gut instinct—tying the Devlins to this?"

Nita's silence was Gavin's answer.

"Go ahead," he said. "I'll meet you at the station."

"I know what that means," she said, her tone expressing her anger. "It means you can't do anything. Okay fine. You can't. You have to follow the letter of the law. But what about you?" she asked, turning to Jake, Mark and Logan. "I know it's supposed to be a secret but it's common knowledge that you TCC guys get involved in situations like this when people are in danger."

Whoa, Jake thought. The club's missions were kept under wraps, so it was a little unsettling to hear Nita announce that their covert operations weren't all that covert. But more unsettling was the fact that Nita felt she was in danger at the hands of a fellow club member and wanted them to investigate. Even though from the sound of things there was really nothing definitive to indicate either danger or Tom Devlin's involvement.

"Nita," Jake said, "I feel real bad for what's happening out there, sweetie. Hell, I'm sure we all do. But for all we know, you're just the unfortunate and random victim of some ugly pranks. Anyone could be responsible. Kids. Vagrants. As to the feed, have you had it tested? Is it possible you just got a bad batch from the elevator?"

"No, I haven't had it tested. It just happened today and I've been too busy saving horses to investigate."

"So, when did you get your last batch of feed?" he pressed.

"Yesterday," she said defensively, "but we always order the mix from the same elevator, so it's not likely that they're responsible."

Jake cut a glance at the others. Mark, Logan and Gavin all wore looks that said exactly what Jake was thinking. Most likely she'd just gotten a bad batch of feed, but in her panic over the possibility of losing the horses, she'd decided someone needed to take the rap and the Devlins were the most likely target.

"Check with the elevator," Jake said gently. "If you come up blank there after the feed is tested, then maybe we'll consider looking into it."

"Consider?" Her eyes snapped with fire. "Thanks. Thanks so much for nothing."

She stomped out of the club in as much of a huff as when she'd stomped in.

"That's one upset woman," Logan remarked.

"Can't blame her," Jake said. "She's stubborn and outspoken and I've known her to go to great lengths to get her way, but I've never known her to lie about anything. This is her livelihood that's being threatened. I'm sure she's scared."

"Let's keep our ears open for word from the elevator regarding the feed," Mark suggested.

"What about the fences?" Logan asked.

Jake shrugged. "Who knows? Could be kids. Could be any number of possibilities. What do you guys think of checking with Tom Devlin to see if he has any ideas on what's going on?"

"He's out of town right now. Business trip," Gavin said.

"When he comes back, then," Jake said. "We'll find out what he thinks. Man, when old Jonathan was alive, he loved to stir the fire on the Windcroft-Devlin feud every chance he got. I thought maybe after he died that this stupid feud business would die a quiet death, too."

"I should be so lucky," Gavin said on a weary breath. "See you boys. I'd better get down to the station before Nita raises hell with my officers."

"But I was about to get into you for some serious coin," Jake complained, thinking about his pair of queens.

"You can break my bank another night, buddy. I've got a mad woman waiting and it's not going to do any of us any good if I keep her that way too long."

Didn't it just figure? Jake thought. These days there always seemed to be a woman complicating things for him. Nita was leaning on the club members for help, and his pair of queens hadn't shown up until after he'd dropped a bundle and the game was over. Then there was Chrissie. Lord. She had materialized this afternoon as a different woman, then issued a challenge he couldn't see his way clear to walk away from.

Eight

"**M**y place. Tonight. Midnight. Wear jeans and boots."

Christine's heart knocked her a couple of good ones in her chest when she listened to the message on her answering machine.

That the message was from Jake was without question. She'd recognize his barbed-wire-and-velvet voice anywhere. That he'd answered her challenge so soon—the day after she'd lain her metaphorical cards on the table—was a big surprise.

"So, what are you going to do?"

Christine looked at Alison, who had dropped by after work to check out Chris's sports car.

"I'm going to go. It's what I want."

Alison eyed her with appreciation. "You are serious about this personal alteration, aren't you?"

"Like I said—" Christine made a concentrated attempt not to chew nervously on her lower lip "—I'm tired of playing it safe and dull. I know it sounds funny given our history, but I trust Jake not to hurt me."

"Jake is it? He's not the evil twin or the insensitive jerk anymore? My, my. That must have been some dinner date Saturday night."

"Let's just say the evening opened me up to new possibilities."

"Well, I say, you go, girl. Just…well, be a *little* careful, okay? I don't want to see you get hurt."

"I'll be fine," Christine assured Alison even though she wasn't one hundred percent sure herself. "I know what I'm doing."

Six hours later, however, as Christine pulled into the drive of Jake Thorne's ranch south of Royal, one burning question kept surfacing like a stubborn cork in a choppy sea: *What am I doing?*

She eased her convertible around the circular drive, then stopped in front of a portico that flanked a pair of massive double doors framed in a stucco structure the color of sand.

Money. The place reeked of it with its understated elegance and style. The house was new—one of many in this area where land was sold in five-hundred-acre parcels of rolling hills and the occasional thicket of timber.

Only the wealthy and privileged could afford the property here.

Lot of house for one man, she thought as her gaze roamed over the impressive facade. A light mounted under the portico came on and the front door swung open.

Make that, a lot of man for one woman.

Neither the businessman nor the tease strode out to meet her. A cowboy did. And Jake Thorne as an icon of the American west personified the cowboy mystic in resounding three-dimensional color.

His boots were a rusty-brown color. His Wranglers looked soft and worn and tight. On his head was a black, well-shaped Stetson—black for bad guy, she thought—and his shirt was as white as snow with mother-of-pearl snaps running down his torso and on the breast pockets. The blue bandanna he'd tied around his neck lay in stark contrast against his white shirt and tanned throat. Spurs jingled with every long, purposeful stride.

The only thing missing was a pair of six-shooters strapped on his lean hips. Still, she got the feeling that he was gunning for her.

"Nice wheels," he said by way of greeting as he looked her car over.

"It's new," she said inanely.

One corner of his mouth turned up. Not a smile. Not a sneer. Small clue as to what he was thinking.

"Got your boots on?"

She got out of the car and showed him. And his not-a-smile-not-a-sneer expression turned into a frown. Big clue as to what he was thinking.

"Let met guess—those would be new, too?"

She glanced away from his look of disgust at her pretty red boots. "What's wrong with them?"

"I was thinking *cowboy* boots."

"These *are* cowboy boots."

"If you're strutting down Rodeo Drive in California maybe. Not if you're planning to ride a horse."

She'd suspected he had a midnight ride in mind, even though she'd held out hope for something else. She didn't ride. In fact, she'd never ridden—guess the choice of boots might have given that away. Somehow she figured he already knew that, too, but she wasn't going to give him the satisfaction of admitting it.

"These boots will do just fine," she said.

He grunted and shook his head. "Come on." Then he walked away from the house toward a mammoth, pristine white barn.

"This is Cletus," he said opening a box stall.

Inside was what Christine considered to be a very big—strike that, an exceptionally huge—brown horse.

"Does he bite?" She could have kicked herself, but the question was out before she could stop it. Talk about sounding green.

"Only blondes," Jake said, leveling her a look. "But since you'll be on his back, you should be safe."

Her stomach sank toward her knees as she looked up the broad length of him. But she smiled. "Oh. Well. Good."

Jake studied her face. "You have ridden, right?"

"Sure. Lots of times." Why was she playing this game? What did she think it was going to net her?

A broken neck, probably, but something about his smug attitude just wouldn't allow her to let him see that she was scared senseless.

"You two get to know each other," Jake said. "I'll go get my mount."

"Good. Great. I'll be fine," she said, lying through her teeth. "Nice...horse," she whispered when Jake was out of her line of sight. "Be nice, okay? I brought you something."

Again, because she'd figured a ride might be what Jake had in mind, she'd hedged her bets. She fished into her hip pocket and pulled out a sugar lump. She'd heard that horses like sugar.

She'd heard right. Cletus went for the sugar like a bear after honey. It was icky feeding it to him. He snuffled all over her palm before finally lipping the sweet treat into his mouth. When he was finished, he lowered his head and nudged her hip pocket where she'd tucked the rest of the sugar, evidently smelling it there.

"Okay, okay," she said, laughing in spite of herself, and gave him another hit. "Now we're friends, right?"

In answer, the horse nipped at her pocket.

"Hey," she sputtered, stepping back. "Easy on the jeans."

"They as new as your boots?" Jake asked, startling

her as he walked down the aisle of the barn, a big buck-
skin in tow.

She manufactured a smile. "You're right about the
biting thing."

His blue eyes pinned hers in the dimly lit barn. "Any
guy is liable to bite if a woman has something in her
pants that he wants."

Oh. My. This must be where the walk on the wild side
came in. He was letting her know. *You came out here to
learn, and I'm just the man to teach you.*

"Busted," she said, conceding that he'd caught her
with the sugar but not going anywhere near the sexual
innuendo. "Who knew he'd be such a glutton?"

"Offer me sugar. See what kind of a glutton I become."

He gave her another one of those long, smoldering
looks that held undertones of all kinds of gluttony, along
with shades of warning. She actually thought about
turning tail and running as fast and as far as her new red
boots would take her.

The old Christine would have run. The new one followed him as he led the two horses out of the barn and
into the moonlight.

"Come on. I'll help you up into the saddle," Jake offered. "Cletus is long on leg, and you're just a little
short on one end. Um, you always mount from the left,
Chrissie."

Face flaming red, Christine walked back around to
the horse's left side. "I knew that. I was just checking
out the, um, stirrup."

"Sure you were," he said. "Now grab the saddle horn. It's that tall thing right behind the mane and in front of the seat," he added with another shake of his head.

"Well, if I could reach it, it would help," she sputtered, angry with herself for not being better informed and angry with him for knowing it. "Oh, whoa." The next thing she knew, she was airborne.

Jake's strong hands had gripped her around the waist, lifted her up and deposited her on the saddle like a sack of potatoes.

"Here are your reins," he said when she'd managed to push herself to a sitting position. Problem was, she was gripping the saddle horn for dear life and didn't have any intention of letting go, even if it was to take the reins.

"What's he doing?" she asked, near panic when the big body between her legs seemed to pitch and roll like a ship in a rough sea.

"Shifting his weight from one back leg to the other," Jake said, grinning openly now. "You ready to give up the pretense?"

"Yes," she all but whined. "Am I going to get hurt?"

He chuckled. "Not on Cletus. He's a pussycat. And you nailed his soft spot with the sugar, so he's not going to take a chance of dumping you because you have his sugar stash. Just sit easy, rock with the motion and trust him to take you where we want to go."

Trust. There was that word again. And that was what this was all about.

"Well, then, yee haw," she said and smiled when it made him chuckle.

Jake mounted up and they were on the move. The night was warm. The wind that usually kicked up during the day in this part of Texas had mellowed to a breeze. It played gently with her hair, cooling her skin yet somehow warming the night.

Or maybe it was the fear of falling off the horse that made her so warm. More likely it was the prospect of what the evil twin had in mind. Cletus proved to be a real gentleman as he plodded along beneath the stars. So far Jake had been a gentleman, too. Despite the temperature of the night, despite the blanket of stars shining down, she shivered in anticipation of what he had in mind for lesson number two. In all likelihood, being a gentleman was the furthest thing from his mind.

"Greenhorns," Jake sputtered good-naturedly an hour later when he helped Christine down out of the saddle. "How can you live in Texas and be such a greenhorn?"

"Not all of Texas is yippee-yi-yo-ki-yay land, you know," she grumbled. "I grew up in Houston. We had cars."

Cute. She was too cute. And a little sore, if Jake didn't miss his guess. But she was game, he'd give her that. Once she'd found her seat, she'd taken to the midnight ride like a trooper.

Of course, he never would have paired her with a

horse that would have placed her in any danger. Old Cletus was pushing twenty-five, and if a random thought
of bucking ever did cross the old boy's mind, Jake was
confident it would get lost somewhere between Cletus's head and the execution. So, no, Christine had never
been in any danger.

At least, not from the horse.

Not for the first time he told himself that what he had
planned was not a good idea. But it would work, if it
didn't backfire on him.

"So, is this like a rest stop?" she asked, tugging down
on the thighs of her jeans as if they'd crept up and into
places they didn't belong.

Places he'd noticed. Places he'd been thinking about
way too much as he'd ridden in relative silence beside
her, a silence broken only by his limited advice on the
finer points of riding and his reassurances that no, Cletus had no intentions of bucking.

He'd noticed other things, as well. Like the way the
starlight shined on her silver-gold hair. Like how cute
she looked in those ridiculous boots and how tiny her
waist was with her white tank top tucked into her jeans.

Who knew that Miss Chrissie was the complete package? Who could have possibly known? If he hadn't seen
her dressed to kill Saturday night, if he hadn't felt all
those sexy curves against him when they'd kissed—
twice now—he never would have guessed it. She'd
seemed to make it a mission to disguise that she was
even remotely feminine—even though he'd seen

glimpses of the china doll lurking beneath all that starch.

Hell, it had crossed his mind a time or two that, as prickly as she was toward him, maybe she played for the other team. He'd never seen her with a guy, never heard of her dating. In fact, when he did see her, she was either alone or with a friend. So, yeah, it had crossed his mind that maybe it wasn't just him that turned her off but that women turned her on. Not that there was anything wrong with that. But, man, what a waste, he thought, watching her now as she stretched her arms above her head and worked out some of the kinks.

Now he knew for sure that she definitely liked the opposite sex. No woman could kiss him the way she had and not be totally into it. It shouldn't have made him so happy because tonight, after all, wasn't about seducing her. Tonight was about scaring her back to where she didn't want to come within ten feet of him except to hurl insults.

Yeah. Tonight was about reestablishing distance, because distance was the best thing he could give her.

"Come on," he said, leading his gelding by the reins. "Let's walk over this rise."

"Oh," she said when she saw what was on the other side of the small hill. "It's beautiful."

The little man-made lake was, for a fact, pretty in the moonlight. But Jake had confidence that what he was about to suggest was going to put the prissy back in

Chrissie and that there wasn't enough "pretty" in the world to entice her to do it.

And then life, as he knew it where she was concerned, could get back to normal.

"So, Chrissie," he said oh-so casually, "let's lose the duds. We're going skinny-dipping."

He could have sworn he heard a teeny, tiny "Help" from her as he hung his hat on a low-hanging branch of a nearby tree.

And when he reached for his belt buckle, he knew he heard one.

Her eyes were as big as dinner plates when he turned toward her.

"Skinny-dipping?"

"As you ordered," he said, undoing the buckle and the metal button on his waistband. "Lesson number two."

He almost felt sorry for her—almost—as he slid down his zipper then tugged his shirttails free. "Any walk on the wild side has to include a midnight dip."

"N-n-nude?" she squeaked out as he shucked his shirt and tossed it to the ground.

"Naturally," he said, sitting on the ground to tug off his boots and socks. When he stood again, he was wearing nothing but his jeans and a smile. "You're falling behind, sweet cheeks," he said and dropped the jeans.

Her little gasp was punctuated by a small, lingering "Oh" that escaped like a sigh.

He gave her a good eyeful, liking a little too much the way her nervous gaze flitted from his face to his chest to his face again, then to his groin—which was liking the way she looked at him a little too much, too. Mixed in with the fear and surprise in her expression was a very female appreciation.

"Time's a-wastin'," he said and showed her his back—just a little too late to hide what her hot looks had done to him. He walked to the bank, waded to midthigh before executing a shallow dive. Like it or not, he needed cooling off. The look in her eyes had heated him to the point of boiling.

When he surfaced, she was still standing on shore, looking exactly the way he thought she'd look—ready to bolt. Which was exactly what he wanted her to do. Nip this nonsense in the bud, that's what he planned on. A little more goading ought to do the trick.

"How come you've still got your clothes on?"

"I…um…isn't it cold?"

"Nah." He wiped his wet hair out of his eyes. "Just right."

She glanced toward Cletus and he thought, *Go for it. You know you want to.*

"Tell you what," he said, standing chest-deep in the water. "I'll count to three, then you make your choice. Either ditch the duds and join me, honey, or hightail it on back to the house and we'll forget this ever happened. Cletus knows his way back to the barn."

"One," he said and watched her bite her lower lip between her teeth.

"Two." *Go ahead, darlin'. Get out of here.*

"Three."

She closed her eyes and took a deep breath and he thought, *Bye-bye*. Until she reached for the hem of her top.

"Oh, hell," he muttered when the shirt came off. And then all he could think was, *Oh, hel-lo*.

Skinny-dipping. It always sounded so...playful. But what it was was intimate, Christine thought as she sat on the bank in her bra and jeans and tugged off her boots. It meant getting naked. In this case, it meant getting naked with a man.

Not just a man. A beautiful, well-conditioned, amazing specimen of a man who didn't think twice about stripping to the skin and flaunting himself in front of her.

Well, she wasn't a flaunter. Heck, sometimes she still undressed in the dark. And it may be well after midnight, but with the cloudless sky and the full moon and complement of stars shining down, it was far from dark out here. As a matter of fact, she felt as though she had a spotlight shining directly on her body.

Don't think about it, she told herself. *Just do it. It's what you want. It's what you need to do if you're ever going to break the pattern.*

Mouth pinched in determination, she finished pulling off her boots and socks, then stood and, with her back to the pond, unzipped and stepped out of her jeans. At the last minute, she reached into a pocket of her jeans and took out one of the packets of protection that Alison—dear, sweet, conscientious Alison—had pressed into her hand earlier today with a smile and a "Just in case."

With a deep breath Christine turned to face Jake and slowly walked toward the water.

"Nope," he said in that gruff, velvet drawl. "All of it or it doesn't count."

So much for hoping he'd overlook the underwear.

"Turn around," she said.

"Not on your life." His voice was sexy and low.

Another deep breath and she reached behind to unhook her bra. She couldn't look at him, but she knew he was watching. It was so quiet, she could hear the soft ebb and flow of his arms as he glided them slowly back and forth through the water. So quiet, she could hear her heartbeat and the soft snuffle of the horses where they grazed on the grass nearby.

She let her bra drop to the ground by her jeans, but she held her forearm over her breasts. She couldn't help it. One-handed, she tugged down her panties, stepped out of them, then tried to look casual as she covered the important parts below her waist with her other hand.

If he laughed, if he so much as snickered, she was going to drown herself.

He didn't laugh. He didn't snicker. He didn't make a sound.

In fact, even the sound of his arms skimming the water had stopped.

She took another deep breath and looked up. Met his eyes. And almost lost her breath.

He was just standing there. Not even smiling. His eyes were hooded with shadows, but even so, she knew his gaze was locked on her. Only when he swallowed and she saw the muscles work in his throat did she realize that he was as riveted by the moment as she was. She felt a power surge sweep through her again.

Feel the power, girl. Use it.

Buoyed by the memory of Alison's words, she stood straighter. And slowly lowered her hands.

This time it was *his* breath that caught. This time it was Jake doing the appreciating, as she'd appreciated the fluid muscle, the lean lines, the impressive part of his anatomy that distinguished him as a man.

She knew that he liked what he saw. When he took a step toward her as though it was involuntary, she knew that he loved what he saw. For the first time in her life she felt like celebrating the fact that she was a woman— a woman who intuitively sensed that this moment with this man was going to change her life.

Nine

"**H**oly mother of God," Jake whispered, so low that even he barely heard it.

She was so freaking beautiful. A moon witch. A night nymph. Pale skin frosted to shimmering silver in the moonlight. Pert, perfect breasts. An hourglass waist. Hips that were slim yet round and a soft little triangle of pale blond curls at the apex of her femininity.

Time out. Time out. Time out. The words kept racing through his mind as she walked toward him.

This wasn't supposed to happen. She was supposed to run. In the opposite direction. She wasn't supposed to be walking toward him, the water licking at her thighs, with that look in her eyes that was part uncertainty, part triumph and held all the trust in the world that he would know what happened next.

Well, hell. He didn't know. He hadn't planned on this part. He'd only mapped the evening out to the place where she lit out for parts unknown and this supposed walk on the wild side that he'd known in his heart she really wasn't up for was over.

Well, guess what? She was up for it.

Unfortunately so was he. He was a man. And like most men, he led with his libido.

"Stop," he finally managed in a gruff whisper. Not because he didn't want her to come any closer. Not because the water was just lapping at the underside of her breasts now and it was so intriguing to watch. He needed her to stop because he needed to make sure she understood what was on the line while he still had the wherewithal to muster up a shred of chivalry.

"Chrissie," he said, his chest feeling full, his hands aching to get a hold of her. "You don't have to do this."

She watched him for the longest time, searching his face before finally smiling. "Yes. Yes, I do."

So much for knighthood.

He was only so strong.

And he wanted.

He wanted her.

He wanted her bad.

He reached for her—hadn't realized just how much he'd been wanting to reach for her—and pulled her toward him.

Her back was warm and lean and wonderfully wet beneath his hands. Her breasts were buoyant and beautiful where they pressed against him, her nipples puckered tight, their velvety tips submerged in the little pool of water trapped between their bodies.

Her arms rose slowly to his shoulders as he backed them into deeper water. Her legs separated and wrapped around his waist, smooth as velvet, sleek as silk.

"Sweet, sweet heaven," he groaned and leaned his forehead to hers. "You sure you haven't done this before?"

She smiled, a little bit shy, a little bit pleased. "I'm sure."

He met her gaze then, loving the look of her by moonlight as that smile turned sly.

"I'm sure of something else, too."

"Oh, yeah?"

"Yeah. I'm sure that I've been missing out on a lot all these years."

Again he groaned.

"And I'm sure I want you to be the one to show me what I've been missing."

And damn if she didn't produce a condom.

Well, that did it. This hadn't started out to be a seduction. At least, he hadn't planned on seducing her. Just the opposite. He'd meant to scare her away.

Now he couldn't get close enough. Couldn't get suited up fast enough. Right versus wrong, reasonable versus rash. In the end it was no contest. And who was seducing whom got lost somewhere in the moment.

He lowered his mouth to hers, submerged himself in a kiss that was all wet heat and honest, uninhibited passion. He'd known it would be. The first time he'd kissed her, she'd given him exactly the same response. The second time she'd given him even more. She didn't have it in her to hold back, didn't have it in her to pretend. She was all reaction to his action, give to his take. And the more she offered, the more he wanted until he skimmed his hands down her back across her waist and filled his palms with the satiny softness of her sweet sexy bottom.

She made a throaty sound and squirmed against him. And he couldn't hold back anymore. He reached between them, made a quick pass of his fingers over her open, vulnerable flesh and guided himself home.

With his tongue buried in her mouth and her fingers knotted in his hair, he tilted his hips and drove himself deep. She gasped into his mouth, then settled herself with a throaty groan and started moving against him.

Bracing his feet wide on the bottom of the lake bed, he gripped her hips in his hands and helped her find a rhythm. Seemed he didn't have to worry about that because she knew exactly, instinctively what she wanted.

She wanted him hard. She wanted him fast. And she wanted him now.

"Easy. Easy," he whispered between deep, drugging kisses while his heart damn near beat out of his chest. "You're going to drown us."

"Don't care." Her lips raced over his face as she moved frantically against him. "Don't…care…"

Well, he did. At least, the part of him that wasn't going to be satisfied with having her and dying in the process cared a lot. With her mouth still mated with his and her hips still pumping against him, he stumbled toward the bank, half wild with the effort of holding back, half crazed with the way she was moving against him.

Finally, *finally,* he found dry ground. It was enough. He went down on his knees and, still buried deep inside her, let her do whatever she wanted with him. He was putty. He was clay. He was anything she wanted him to be as long as she didn't stop moving like that and kissing him like that and making those throaty little sounds that drove him beyond the limit.

"J-Jake." Breathless, she whispered his name. Restless, she rode him until he thought he'd go blind.

Just when he thought he couldn't take anymore, she shuddered and cried out and, with a long, sighing breath, melted into a puddle against his chest.

Gripping her hips in his hands, he went the same way she did, burying himself, riding with the contraction of her inner muscles, dying just a little from the sheer, pure pleasure.

He'd made a bed of sorts for them out of the towels he'd stuffed in his saddlebags—just in case. Christine lay naked as the day she was born, curled into his side, feeling boneless and brazen and about as wonderful as she supposed a woman could possibly feel.

Her head rested on Jake's shoulder, and his hand slid in a slow, steady glide up and down the length of her back.

It felt incredible to lie with him this way. Like Adam and Eve in the Garden of Eden. The smooth musculature of his shoulder pillowing her head, his heart rate slow and steady beneath the palm of her hand.

The night smelled of summer grass and a little of the leather saddlebags. And it smelled of him. Musky and clean and sexual.

"You okay?" he murmured, sounding just as drowsy and satisfied as she felt.

"More than okay." And though she was still drifting on the currents of her orgasm—my goodness, she'd actually had an orgasm—she couldn't wait to feel that amazing climb to the summit and the dizzying ride from the top all over again.

"Thank you," she whispered and, emboldened by the intimacy of their tangled limbs, pressed a kiss to his neck.

"Oh, no," he said, a smile in his voice. "Thank *you*."

She giggled. Giggled. Her.

"You don't understand," she said, pushing herself up on an elbow and looking into his eyes. His beautiful, beautiful eyes. "That's never happened to me before."

The lazy smile left his mouth. He stared at her. Long. Hard. "You were a virgin?" he asked, sounding so appalled that she laughed.

"Relax. I wasn't a virgin. I mean—" She hesitated, feeling self-conscious suddenly.

"What?" he said, touching a hand to her hair. "You mean you never came before?"

She nodded. Lifted a shoulder. "Pretty sad, huh?"

"Man," he said after a long moment, "those other guys must have been jerks."

"Guy," she said, again feeling self-conscious and horribly pedestrian and inexperienced. "There was only one. And...well, he said I wasn't very good at it."

"Major jerk," he said, hugging her again. "More like he wasn't any good at it, or I wouldn't be your first time."

It was a nice thing to say. And she realized he was probably right. She felt overwhelmed with this wonderful new feeling of power.

"Lots of firsts for me tonight," she said, rising above him. Twisting at the hip, she reached for her jeans, dug around for another condom, then grabbed his hat from the tree branch and put it on her head. "Never rode a horse before, either," she added and watched as his eyes went all stormy and dark when she placed a foot on either side of his hips and slowly sank to her knees. "Never rode a cowboy."

"Sweet thunder," he whispered on a groaning sigh as she dressed him then sank on top of him.

Okay, so he'd made a miscalculation, Jake thought the next morning as he drove to town. He'd thought Chrissie would run. He'd never dreamed... Well, he'd never dreamed they would do what they'd done.

He was an ass. A weak-willed, ruled-by-his-dick opportunist. He ought to be drawn and quartered.

So why was he grinning?

Well, hell. What man who'd experienced some of the best sex of his life less than—he checked his watch and rolled his eyes—four hours ago wouldn't be grinning?

Damn, did that woman turn him on. Those freckles were going to be the death of him. She had them on her shoulders, too. And on the very tops of her pretty breasts.

Still waters do, for a fact, run deep. Chrissie of the china-doll eyes and silky-smooth skin was a tiger disguised as a kitten. And soft. She'd felt so soft in his arms afterward, vulnerable and spent.

His mind flashed on an image of her wearing nothing but his hat and a smile, moving above him, and he damn near drove off the side of the road.

It was kind of a blur how they'd gotten back to the house. They'd ridden double on his mount. He did remember that—and all the friendly touching and kissing that had gone on between them, while Cletus had happily plodded behind them.

He flipped his turn signal when he hit a main intersection in town, then stopped at a light two blocks down. Waiting for the light to change, he drummed his fingers on the steering wheel and stared into space. She hadn't clung when it was time to leave, he'd give her that. When they'd reached the house, she'd kissed him goodbye and with a coy smile said, "If you think I need any more lessons, just let me know."

He wiped a hand over his jaw, contemplating all kinds of lessons he'd like to give her. Problem was, he wasn't sure who had been teaching whom last night.

A car honked behind him and he realized his light had changed. Gunning it, he drove toward the office, damning his slow reaction. Running on one, maybe two, hours of sleep, he could hardly see straight, let alone think straight.

He was mentally exhausted and clearly not in control of his faculties. It was more than enough excuse. When he finally reached his office, he shut his door behind him and reached for the phone.

He got her answering machine. "Lesson number three. Tonight. Seven o'clock. My place. Wear the black dress."

She wore the dress. And the silver heels. And, as he was soon to find out, that was about it.

"Hi," she said when he met her at his front door.

"Hi," he said and that was the extent of the talking for the next hour or so.

"I think you're teaching me to be a nymphomaniac," Christine said when she caught her breath.

She lay on her tummy in the middle of Jake's big bed, her dress in a tangled heap on the floor, her heels still on her feet. Beside her Jake lay on his side, his hand resting gently at the small of her back, his thumb stroking lazily along her spine.

"And so far it's going quite well," he said.

She smiled into the pillow, hugged it to her breasts and turned her head to look at him. He was smiling, too.

"You're amazing, Chrissie."

"Thanks. You're pretty amazing yourself. A girl couldn't ask for a better teacher."

His smile suddenly faded. He rolled to his back, crossed his hands beneath his head and stared at the ceiling.

"Chrissie—"

"No," she said, interrupting him softly. She had a pretty good idea what was going on here. Mr. Independent was starting to worry that she was pinning more on their "lessons" than he wanted her to. "It's okay," she said and reminded herself that it really was. "You don't have to worry. I'm not going to get the wrong idea about what's happening between us."

He turned his head and looked at her. Beautiful, beautiful face, she thought. So rugged and male and still unconvinced she meant what she said.

"Look. It's all fun and games. I know that. And it's fine. I don't expect more from you. I don't want more from you."

"How can that be?" he asked, his eyebrows pinched together. "Every woman I know wants commitment. Why not you?"

It was her turn to sober. She thought of all the pain commitment had brought her mother. Not that she figured Jake for a closet abuser—he was too gentle, too kind to ever be that. It was just that she never wanted to allow herself to count on anyone but herself. Life was less disappointing that way.

"I know the difference between fantasy and reality, Jake. Commitment doesn't necessarily mean happiness. And now that I'm better educated on life, thanks to you," she added with a smile, "I'm happy to go on and experience a little more. I don't need a serious relationship to do that."

He frowned again and she wasn't sure why. She'd thought reassuring him that she didn't have any long-term expectations would be a huge relief.

"Now," she said, feeling a need to lighten up things between them, "if you have any more lessons that you—devoted instructor that you are—feel compelled to put to the test, I'm burning to be enlightened."

Slowly, very slowly, his face lost that solemn look and he smiled. Sexy. This man was oh-so sexy.

"Have I got a lesson for you."

He moved over her. The look in his eyes was so tender and searching when he lowered his head and kissed her. His lips were gentle, persuasive, as he settled them over hers, moved them over hers, softly caressing, expertly nipping, seducing her into very willing submission as he taught her more fine points of a kiss.

She could kiss him forever, she thought as he changed the angle and simply sank into her. Strong yet gentle. Tender yet forceful. He devoured her mouth, feeding her hunger, rekindling her need. She stretched beneath him on a blissful sigh when he left her mouth to give special attention to her jaw. The slight abrasion of his closely shaven beard whispered across her skin, making her shiver, making her yearn.

She arched to his mouth when he trailed a string of kisses—employing teeth and tongue and those amazing lips—along the length of her throat. She urged him toward her breast as he made his way slowly downward, his lips at her shoulder, his tongue flicking across her collarbone until she was begging, "Please, please." He finally took her nipple into his mouth.

Oh, did he know how to love her. He cupped his hand around her breast, plumping her for his pleasure, lifting her to his mouth so he could suckle and tease with the flick of his tongue, the whisper of his breath. She loved it. Loved how he knew what she needed.

When he moved lower, pushed himself to all fours above her and trailed a path down the center of her body with his tongue, she understood that she was about to experience another intimate lesson in loving.

The first touch of his mouth to her most vulnerable flesh was electric. She sucked in a harsh breath, let it out on a long, low moan and groped helplessly for a hold on the sheets on either side of her hips when he made the first lush pass with his tongue. And when he tunneled his hands beneath her bottom and lifted her hips to his open mouth, every pulse point in her body met there, between her thighs, where he made the most incredible love to her.

She closed her eyes, felt tears leak down her temples as sensations she couldn't begin to name assaulted her.

Pulsing, surging pleasure so intense, it radiated to her fingertips, to her toes, flooded inward again, propelling her to an orgasm so huge and so powerful, she bucked into his mouth, cried out in wonder and awe and disbelief. It seemed to go on forever and yet not long enough, and even as she started the slide down, his mouth caressed her, whispered praise, settled her.

When she finally came back to herself, he was moving up her body, his dark eyes intent on her face, his lips wet and swollen. She'd never seen anything so moving in her life. She reached for him. Whispered his name. Whispered her gratitude, then gasped on another storm of pleasure as he entered her, stroked her deeply and, on a mind-numbing explosion of sensation, took her to the limit yet again.

The next couple of weeks passed in a blur of fun and sensation for Christine. In between her busy schedule at the hospital and the time she committed at the Historical Society, she still managed to meet Jake often. They never seemed to get around to talking about Jess Golden's things, and frankly that was fine with her. She didn't want to end their...fling. My God. She was having a fling.

It made her smile just thinking about it. And about how often they made love. Jake was an inventive, sensitive and giving lover.

But there was one thing she always had to remember—he didn't love her.

As she drove across town on her lunch break one day, heading for Hellfire, International because Jake had called this morning and asked her to meet him at noon, she reminded herself of that fact. He did not love her.

It was something she found herself doing more and more often because, well, it would be easy to misconstrue the way he looked at her sometimes, the way he would reach out for no reason at all and touch a hand to her hair or to her arm, the way he made love to her. As if she was the one thing, the only thing, that mattered in the world.

Yeah, it would be easy to mistake all of those gestures for love. And that was a mistake she just wouldn't let herself make. Just the way she wouldn't let herself mistake her feelings for him as love.

"Hi," she said, poking her head inside his office after Janice had said she could go on in.

"Hi," he said, his face solemn as he took in her white hospital uniform. "Shut the door. Lock it."

"Is there something wrong?" she asked, feeling a little surge of alarm at the dark look on his face.

"Nothing's wrong. Unless you count the fact that I'm just itching to make love to you in that uniform."

She grinned when he walked up to her and put his arms around her. "You'd look a little silly in my uniform, but hey, if it trips your trigger, go for it, cowboy."

"Smart mouth," he said, then covered her mouth with his in a hard, demanding kiss.

The next thing she knew, he'd reached under her

skirt, stripped off her panties and deposited her on his desk. The shock of it, the heat of it, the urgency in him stole all reason. It thrilled her that he wanted her so badly. She couldn't get his pants undone fast enough. Couldn't get him suited up and inside of her soon enough.

It was all over in minutes. And it was incredible.

Panting, spent, she stroked his head where it lay on her breast, too satisfied to care that the desk was hard and unyielding beneath her back.

"Wow. That was quite a lesson," she ventured with a smile.

"Not a lesson. A pop quiz," he murmured and bussed her nipple with his nose.

She laughed. "So, how did I do, teach?"

"Well, I was going to make it a pass-fail, but since you obviously studied so hard, you get an A-plus."

Ten

"**Y**eah. I miss it," Jake confessed a week or so later as he sat with Chrissie in a booth at the Royal Diner one evening after burgers. They'd talked about a lot of things during the past couple of weeks, but this was the first time firefighting had come up.

Had someone else asked, he might have hedged the way he usually did. Brushed it off. Made some lame statement such as, "Are you kidding? Miss walking into a wall of fire as hot as hell? Do I look stupid?"

"Miss it a lot," he confessed because this was Chrissie. He caught her sympathetic look and firmed his lips because he just couldn't smile about it with her.

She was easy to talk to. Easy on the eye. Easy to make love to. He liked her. A lot.

But he didn't love her. And that, he told himself several times a day, was why things worked so well between them. All the silliness about "lessons" aside, things worked for them because they both knew the score. Love was not on the table. And it never would be.

"Tell me about it. What is it you miss?" she urged gently as she cradled a cup of decaf coffee between her hands. The same hands that could stroke him to arousal, ease him into sleep, amaze him with their gentleness.

He stared into space for a bit. The diner was quiet this time of night. Besides the two of them, there were only a few other hangers-on sitting in booths on the far side of the room.

Finally he shrugged. "I don't know specifically. I've always been an adrenaline junkie. Love the rush. Live on the thrills. And I hate it that my men are out there putting their lives on the line and I'm twiddling my thumbs on the sideline."

"Running the machine—the *business* machine—isn't exactly twiddling your thumbs. You give them everything they need to ensure they can do the job. You keep them safe in many ways."

"And I'd still rather be there beside them. Watching their backs. You don't know how often I've found myself heading for a fire—"

"You almost died," she interrupted. "You cannot risk

another incident with smoke inhalation. The additional stress to your lungs could kill you."

He nodded. "I know. Doesn't make it any easier."

She covered his hands with one of hers. Stroked her thumb over his skin, then squeezed.

"Is Connor as…oh, what's the word I'm searching for?"

"Pigheaded?" he suggested, needing to lighten things up a bit.

She smiled. "That'll work. Is Connor as pigheaded as you?"

He shook his head. "Connor is driven."

"He seems very serious. At least, the few times I've seen him, he strikes me as that way."

"When you grow up in the shadow of someone who was always perceived as the golden boy and the popular twin, it has a tendency to make you try a little harder."

"Had to be hard," she said. "For you, too."

Very insightful, this woman. Just one more thing he appreciated about her. "Yeah. I was who I was. Am who I am. Life's been easy for me. People like me. It wasn't that way for Connor. The old man leaned on him a lot—and it made for tension between us.

"The odd thing is," he added after a while, "Connor always was the smart one, yet our father put him down. Hard man, my dad. Never in all the years we were growing up do I remember him showing either of us any affection. Favoritism, yes, sadly. But not affection. It never bothered me, but Connor—well, he needed more. He tended to bottle things up inside, you know? Let them fester."

"And you?"

"Hell, I acted out by pushing things to the limit."

Okay. He'd talked more about himself in this one session with her than he ever had in the years he'd been married to Rea.

"What about you?"

"Me?" she asked, pulling her hands back, looking surprised.

"Yeah. What makes you tick?"

"Oh, well," she stammered, and he could actually see her withdrawing emotionally as well as physically. "Just your basic, run-of-the-mill childhood. Nothing remarkable there."

Chrissie was not a good liar. It shouldn't have bothered him that she'd lied. Aside from the fact that he'd just spilled his guts to her, it ticked him off that she couldn't trust him with the truth.

That's what people who loved each other did. They trusted.

Whoa.

His heart ratcheted to about one-twenty. Where had *that* come from? He didn't love Chrissie. He *liked* her. Had great affection for her. Admired her. Lusted after her.

But he did not love her.

He'd been there, done that. Wasn't going to do it again. Ever. He knew himself too well. He knew that he couldn't survive another hole like the one Rea had blown in his heart when she'd left him. He didn't want to ever again put himself in the position where he was that vulnerable to a hit.

And because Chrissie sometimes made him question a stand that had held him in good stead for several years, he figured now was a good time to get his head on straight again.

"What do you say I take you home?" he said, standing and digging into his hip pocket for his wallet. "I've got an early day tomorrow. I'm sure you do, too."

"Sure," she said, looking surprised by his abruptness but also as if she wanted to get away from this conversation as much as he did. "It's been a long day."

She didn't have reason to feel guilty about closing up on Jake just now, Christine told herself as she stood beside Jake at the cash register and Sheila Foster rang up the ticket for their meal. Still, Christine felt guilty for shutting him down.

She'd come a long way in the trust department. However not far enough to trust him with the truth of her childhood, even though he'd been honest with her about his feelings.

Intellectually she knew that she had no reason to be ashamed. The shame was her father's and, in some part, her mother's for not standing up to him and for not getting herself and Christine out of that horrible situation.

But still, the shame was as sharp as a slap from the

back of her father's hand, as acute as the verbal abuse he'd heaped on her with dump trucks then ground in with steamrollers. *You're not cute enough. Not smart enough. Are too much of a mouse. Always in the way.*

Someday maybe she'd get past it. But right now, well, it wasn't going to happen.

The little bell above the diner's door tinkled, and she shifted her attention there to see who had entered. It was Gretchen Halifax and some smarmy guy Christine knew she should recognize but couldn't quite place.

He was in his late thirties, maybe early forties. His hair was a dull brown, the same as his eyes. Small eyes. Snake eyes, she thought for some reason. Maybe it was the suit. It was a shiny gray material and made her think of snakeskin, covering a well-fed, bulky body. She wondered if he thought he looked the part of a smooth, savvy guy. Certainly the way he looked at her—big smile, come-on eyes—said that he thought he was quite the ladies' man.

She thought he was quite the loser but he hadn't figured it out yet.

Then again, he was with Gretchen, so what did Christine know.

"Well, well," Gretchen said when she spotted Jake at the counter. "If it isn't the backstabber."

Christine frowned. *Backstabber? What is she talking about?*

"Now, Gretchen," Jake said, sounding as patronizing as he could possibly be, "nobody is stabbing you in the back."

"Oh? Then what do you call running against me for mayor?"

Christine blinked from Gretchen to Jake. *What?* "Running for mayor?" Christine echoed, dumbfounded. "You're running for mayor? Seriously?"

"You know I'm a serious kind of guy," Jake said, glancing at her before returning his attention to Gretchen. "Not afraid of a little competition, are you, Councilwoman?"

"I'm not afraid of you. But then, I don't see you as competition."

"If that's the case," Jake said, smiling his best candy-eating smile, "it shouldn't bother you that I entered the race. See you around, Gretchen." Then he added, "Devlin," nodding to the man at Gretchen's side. With his hand at Christine's back, he guided her outside.

Durmorr. Malcolm Durmorr. That's who the man was, Christine realized from the muddle of her confused thoughts as she walked down the street.

"When did this happen?" she asked when they reached her car, still a little dizzy with shock and surprise. And with something else. Disappointment. Jake had done something major in his life and he hadn't even mentioned it to her. Hadn't seen fit to tell her. Which meant he hadn't thought she mattered enough to tell her.

"Just this morning."

She felt her stomach sink a little lower. Okay. So he hadn't told her. He wasn't obligated to tell her everything he did. In fact, he wasn't obligated to tell her anything.

It was just that, well, she'd thought— She'd thought she mattered more to him. And it shouldn't come as either a surprise or a disappointment that she didn't.

"Why?" she asked, feeling the need to fill the uncomfortable silence.

"Why run for mayor? You're the one who said it. I need to do something adult. Something civic minded. So I'm doing it.

"I don't like that woman's platform," he added as he opened her car door for her. "She wants major tax increases—for the local oil business as well as other businesses. She wants to cash in on increased tax revenues, and I am totally against that. Her platform not only affects my business but those of many of my friends and the people who keep Royal prosperous. She'd have a negative effect on the town—we'd lose business right and left—if she gets elected.

"Besides," he added, "I don't like her or her methods. And I don't like the people she runs with. Malcolm Durmorr—unlike the rest of the Devlin family—is a lowlife, a deadbeat opportunist. The fact that Gretchen keeps company with him just reinforces my decision to run against her."

"Well," Christine said, fighting that sinking sensation of exclusion that she had no right to feel, "good luck. And good night. Thanks for dinner."

She got in her car and drove off. Without another word. It was a little hard to talk through tears. And damn it, she was crying.

It made no sense. It made no sense at all that he hadn't told her about his decision. He had to have been thinking about it for quite a while if he actually filed the papers today.

His silence might not make sense unless he was trying to make a point, she realized, wiping her eye. And the point was she was not a staple in his life.

Now the really bad news. She hadn't realized until this very moment how badly she wanted to be.

She was in love with him. Damn her naive, foolish hide. Against all her own warnings not to, despite what she'd known about him going into this, she'd made a fatal mistake.

She'd fallen in love with Jake Thorne.

He'd hurt her.

As Jake lay awake alone in bed that night, he knew that he'd hurt Chrissie by not telling her about his decision to run for mayor. And the worst part? He was pretty certain he'd done it on purpose.

He'd kept thinking he'd tell her that he was seriously considering running, but in the end he hadn't. He hadn't told her because he'd known that if she found out from someone other than him, it would put their relationship in proper perspective. There was no future for them. Something they both knew.

So how come he'd felt as if he'd kicked a kitten when she'd looked at him with surprise, then hurt, then a dawning understanding? She'd known exactly the message he was trying to send. He'd wanted to make sure that she remembered—hell, he'd wanted to make sure that *he* remembered—what their arrangement was about. No promises. No future. Only fun for now. For as long as it lasted.

His cell rang, blasting him out of the doldrums. He was still picturing Chrissie's face when he flicked on the bedside light, saw that it was nearly five in the morning and answered his phone.

It was his site manager, Ray. There was an oil fire near Odessa. A bad one. They needed a crew. And they needed them fast.

He split the calling list of available men with Ray, then assembled his half of the crew. They'd all be there, on-site, within an hour—two max.

When he hung up the phone, he ran through a mental checklist. He hadn't missed any beats.

Everything was under control. Except his heart. It was waging a helluva war in his chest.

Each hard pump said, "Go, go, go."

But he knew he wasn't needed on-site. Knew he had no business at any oil-well fire. He wouldn't be able to stand back and simply supervise. He knew he'd get one whiff of the oil smoke, feel the burn of the blaze against his face and dive into the thick of things.

He dragged a hand through his hair, steeled himself against the need. Braced himself for the fight.

But not hard enough.

"The hell with it," he swore and vaulted out of bed.

He needed… He needed…something. Something to remind him he was still alive. Something to prove he was vital.

He needed Chrissie.

And because he needed her so badly and because he didn't dare give in to that need, he dressed in battle gear and headed for the fire.

Christine had the TV on in her kitchen as she always did in the morning while she got ready for work. She was rinsing out her coffee cup in the sink and about to shut off the set to head out the door when the reporter's voice stopped her.

"It's a bad one, all right, Mike." The reporter was doing a live remote from the site of an oil-well fire south of Odessa. "Hellfire, International—the Royal, Texas-based firefighting company—arrived in force about six o'clock this morning."

"Hellfire," she whispered aloud. Jake's company.

"At least two of the firefighters are being treated for minor injuries by EMTs," the reporter continued to say, "and it's not looking as though they're going to be capping this bad boy for a while yet. Let's roll some tape we shot earlier of an interview with Hellfire's head man, Jake Thorne."

Christine couldn't believe it. There was Jake. At the site. He was covered in smoke smudge and sweat, suited up in full firefighting gear, rattling off techniques and solutions and probabilities, then hurriedly excusing himself as he donned gloves and helmet and headed toward the plume of fire that boiled out of the ground like a geyser on a straight line from hell.

For a moment she couldn't breathe. Refused to believe that Jake was actually there. Not just there, on the site, but actively involved in fighting the fire.

"The fool," she sputtered aloud. "The damn fool."

It wasn't just a question of *if* he suffered more smoke or fire inhalation it *maybe* could kill him. There were no ifs or maybes about it. He was risking everything. *Everything.*

"And for what?" she asked aloud as she grabbed her purse and headed out the door at a run. "An adrenaline rush?"

Heart racing, she did something she'd never done in her entire career at the hospital. She called in sick from her cell phone. Then she floored the convertible all the way to Odessa.

She'd recognized the area from the news report, so she knew exactly where to find the fire. Still, the hour-long trip felt like forever. When she finally arrived, she was met with more frustration because she couldn't get to Jake. The police and local fire departments, as well as the drilling operation's security, were out in force to keep the area secure and free of curiosity seekers.

After parking several blocks away, she quickly locked her car and, at a trot, headed toward the source of heat. The heat factor grew outrageous the closer she went to the fire. So did the security.

"I'm EMT support," she lied, flashing the name tag on her uniform.

She figured it was the Respiratory Therapist title under her name that did the trick.

"Go on in. We've got triage and treatment set up over there." The guard pointed in the general direction of a pair of ambulances where several medical personnel were treating firefighters in need of oxygen, rehydration and first aid.

All of them appeared to be fine and getting the treatment they needed. None of them was the man she was looking for.

Working hard to control the tremor in her voice, she approached one of the firefighters where he sat resting on the tailgate of a pickup. "Where's Jake?"

He poured cold water over his head, then wiped soot from his face with a red handkerchief. "Down there somewhere," he said, nodding toward the fire.

Her heart sank just before a roar went up from the gathered crowd.

"She's capped!" someone shouted just as Christine turned and saw that the fire was out.

"Thank God," she whispered under her breath, then felt her heart take another dive.

"Man down!" The shout came from the center of the activity.

She didn't think. She headed toward the site at a dead run.

Frantic, she searched the weary faces of every man

who turned to look at her as she ran past. Ahead, a knot of firefighters hovered over the prone figure.

She pushed her way through them, grabbing one man's shoulder and shoving him aside. "Let me through," she snapped, then almost broke down and wept when the firefighter she'd tried to move out of her way turned around and looked at her.

It was Jake.

"Chrissie," he said, confusion and surprise clouding his face. "What the hell are you doing here?"

"Looking for you!" she said, not knowing whether to kiss him or hit him or bawl all over him. "I thought you were hurt. I—I thought you were…dead."

"Oh, sweet cheeks. Sweetie. It's okay. I'm right as rain. Old Ben here didn't fare as well, though. He might have a broken ankle."

The EMTs arrived right behind Christine and immediately went to work on Ben.

"Chrissie?"

Shock. She supposed she was suffering from a little shock. First from the scare. Now from relief.

"Chrissie," he said more gently. He turned her to face him, cupping her elbows in his big hands. "I'm okay."

His gaze locked on hers, his brilliant blue eyes searching from his smoke-smudged face.

Latent fear made her breath ragged. Frustration made her voice tight. "Why did you do this? Why when you know the risk?"

He had the sense to look guilty before he lifted a

shoulder, defiant, defensive. "They needed me," he said, but without the conviction to ring true. He knew what it could have cost him. So did she.

"What if I said I needed you?" She hadn't intended to confess. Hadn't wanted him to know. But now that it was out, there was no turning back. "What if I said I love you? And I was scared to death that I'd lost you? What if I said that?"

He looked as though she'd punched him and knocked every last breath from his lungs. He blinked, looked away, then back into her eyes. Finally he shook his head. He opened his mouth, but nothing came out.

"Yeah," she said, feeling very weary suddenly. And so lost. Lost in love with a crazy, foolish man who hadn't had a clue how she felt or what the thought of losing him had done to her. A man who clearly felt uncomfortable with her revelations. "That's what I thought you'd say."

She pulled out of his hold and started walking away.

"Hey… Hey, Chrissie," he said, catching up with her. "Let me walk you back to your car."

She laughed. No humor. Just sad acceptance. "Don't bother. Just…don't bother," she said, knowing that he was as uncomfortable with her being here as she was with the fact that she loved him.

She loved a man who didn't care enough about himself to ever care about her.

She'd hoped. Deep down inside she'd foolishly hoped that she meant more to him than a good time and good sex. Okay, that made him sound shallow and cruel. He was neither.

He was, however, exactly what she had always known him to be—a man who had no intention of committing to a woman. Especially not her. He couldn't have made it more clear. First by leaving her out of the loop on joining the mayoral race. And now with his total disregard for his own life.

No man who loved a woman would unnecessarily put himself in danger the way he'd just done.

Christine went to work. She came home. She cried. That went on for two days. And then she'd had enough. She'd survived worse than Jake Thorne's nondeclaration of love. And she would survive this, too.

But what she would not do was talk to him. She couldn't. She was too raw yet. And too needy for the sound of his voice. No, she would not talk to him. Cold turkey was hard, but it was the only way to get over him.

So she didn't return his calls or answer the messages he left on her machine. She did not want to hear him say things such as "It's me, not you." Or "I never meant for you to get hurt." Or "I thought we both knew there was nothing serious going on."

Well, nothing serious was going on. At least, not from where he stood. And from where she stood? Well, she'd eventually find firmer ground. She'd get over it. She'd get over him.

She'd get over a damn fool of a man who didn't have

enough sense to know that he could not take chances with his life for the sake of an adrenaline rush. A damn stupid man who did not know that she was the best thing that had ever happened to him.

Eleven

Jake waited five days. Five long, frustrating days.

Then he drove to Chrissie's apartment.

Stupid.

Par for his course lately. He'd pulled a stupid stunt when he'd suited up to fight the oil fire at Odessa. Okay. Water under the bridge. He hadn't intended to compound a gross error in judgment by going to see Chrissie.

So much for what he hadn't intended to do.

Man. Why couldn't he just stick to the plan? Even before Odessa he'd decided to cut off his relationship with her. He'd been worried that maybe she might be getting too attached to him. And he'd been right.

He could still see her face when she'd found him. Relief, anger. Pain.

Pain that he'd caused. See, this was exactly what he'd wanted to avoid. The possibility that she'd cry. The probability that she'd cling.

He flipped his left-turn signal and headed down Western Avenue, then stopped at a red light.

"Well, none of that has happened, has it, ace?" he muttered aloud. She hadn't cried. She wasn't clinging. Hell, the woman wouldn't even return his calls.

So why wasn't he happy about that? It was a clean break. Exactly what he'd wanted.

He scowled straight ahead. Five days had gone by since she'd charged onto the oil-fire site like an avenging angel, asked him what he'd say if she told him she loved him, then made herself as scarce as peace in the Middle East.

Love. She didn't love him. In the heat of the moment she'd just…hell, he didn't know. She'd been overly emotional, that's all. Clearly she didn't even want to see him anymore.

So why wasn't he as pleased as spiked punch about that, either?

For Pete's sake, he should be relieved.

The light changed and he punched it.

He should be feeling mighty fine that he didn't have to lie, make excuses or watch her cry. Or wonder if maybe she wasn't crying. Wonder if maybe she'd already moved on—asked someone else to give her "lessons."

There'd be no shortage of guys lining up to take his place, that's for sure. Since she'd quit hiding her beautiful assets, he'd seen the way other men looked at her.

His jaw started aching at about the same time he realized he was clenching it so hard, he could have crushed his molars into powder.

So, he didn't like the thought of some other guy looking out for her. Watching over her. Teaching her. That didn't mean anything except that he didn't want to see her get hurt.

That's what tonight was about. He pulled to a stop in front of her apartment. He told himself he was going to make sure she was all right. Just check on her. Make sure she knew what she was getting into with some of these other creeps.

But then she answered her door. Opened it a crack and frowned at him.

And he knew why he wasn't happy about anything.

He'd missed her.

He'd missed that sassy blond hair. Those crazy hazel eyes. Those whimsical freckles that drove him crazy with lust. He'd missed her spirit and he'd missed her spunk and he'd missed the way she looked at him.

But most of all he'd missed the best opportunity to tell her that he needed her in his life.

Since he'd figured that out just this moment—he'd never claimed to be the sharpest tack in the drawer—he cut himself a little slack.

And then he set out to make things right.

"We have to talk," he said.

"I, um, I don't mean to be rude, Jake," she said, clinging to the door, keeping it open only a crack so he couldn't walk inside, "but now really isn't a good time."

He froze as the light slowly dawned. She had a man in there.

"Yeah, well, I'm real sorry about that, but I'm afraid this can't wait."

He shouldered his way around her and stomped into her apartment. He stopped short just inside the door, ready to give whatever lowlife had moved in on his territory a real good reason to move on.

What the hell?

The place was a mess. There were newspapers spread on every inch of the floor. Plastic sheets were draped all over the furniture. And not a man in sight.

"You're painting," he said, feeling a huge smile spread across his face.

"I'm *about* to paint," she said, sounding a little testy.

That's my girl, he thought and started rolling up his sleeves. "I love to paint. What's this?"

She gave him a long-suffering sigh. "A paint roller."

"Oh, yeah. I knew that. So, where do you want me to start?"

"How about by heading back out the door?"

He smiled, picked up a paint can and started shaking it.

"This is ridiculous. I haven't got time for your games.

I need to get to the paint store before it closes and get some masking tape."

"You just run along and get what you need, sweet cheeks. I'll start without you."

She stared at him for the longest time. Then she swallowed and her eyes got a little misty. "I really don't think—"

"Go to the store," he said gently. "Before it closes."

After another long, searching look, she gave up and snagged her car keys. "If—if you ever cared anything about me," she said in a faltering tone that he'd never heard before, "please be gone when I get back."

Then she left, shutting the door softly behind her.

It was just like him, Christine thought when she pulled up in front of her apartment and saw that Jake's car was still parked in front. Just like him to do what he darn well pleased, regardless that she'd asked him to leave.

She cut the engine, let out a deep breath and told herself to just deal with it. Jake was Jake. He wasn't mean. He wasn't stupid. He knew she was hurting over him. And being who he was—Mr. Good Time, Everybody Likes Me—he simply couldn't handle thinking she hated him.

So his plan, evidently, was to make nice and put them back on friendly terms so he could live happily—and singly—ever after.

Fine, she thought, slamming her car door. He clearly wasn't going away tonight, so she'd have to play his game to get rid of him. She could survive it. As she so often reminded herself, she'd survived worse.

Head down, she trudged up the walk, then let herself inside.

And stopped cold when she walked into the room.

Eyes wide with disbelief, she turned a slow circle trying to take it all in. Good to his word, Jake had started the painting without her—only it wasn't the kind of painting she'd had in mind.

On the wall directly in front of her he'd painted in big sloppy letters *What would you say if I said I love you?*

She pressed her fingers to her mouth, walked farther into the room and felt her eyes fill with tears when she read the rest of his handiwork. Above the front window he'd painted a stick figure of a man with a huge, sad frown. He'd painted his name above it and the words: *I'm such a jerk.*

On the wall where the entertainment center usually sat was *Can you forgive me?*

Everywhere she looked, he'd painted a message. He'd painted a big, splashy heart with an arrow through it. Inside the heart were his initials and hers.

But the kicker, the one that finally had the tears overflowing, were the two words she never, ever figured she'd have from him: *Marry me.*

He walked through the kitchen doorway about that time, looking rugged and gorgeous and, God bless him, as uncertain as a skydiver on his virgin jump.

"Told you I could paint," he said, his gaze searching hers.

"You are such a fool," she said and launched herself into his arms.

He hugged her hard against him, lowering his head to hers. "A fool for you," he murmured, then picked her up, carried her to the wall that was foremost on both of their minds.

"Yes," she said, lifting her head long enough to kiss him. "Yes, yes, yes, I'll marry you."

"I think I could get to love this bed," Jake murmured into Chrissie's ear as they lay side by side, snuggled together like sardines in a can on her double bed, tiny in comparison to his king.

"You hate this bed," she said on a soft chuckle and wrapped her bare leg around his hip.

"But I love you and I love being close to you. This bed makes sure that happens."

She pulled back far enough to look into his eyes. "Say it again."

"I love you."

They'd made love. Then they'd talked. He'd told her about Rea, how she'd used him to get what she wanted, how she'd soured him on love and marriage. Christine had told him about her childhood and she'd fallen a little deeper in love when his eyes had misted with tears for her. He'd tenderly kissed the scar on her chin that her father had given her when she was six years old. That one tender kiss did more to ease the pain of abuse than years of trying to put it behind her.

And Jake had made promises. "I'll be good. I won't give you reason to worry about me. My firefighting days are over. Hell, they'd been over. The only reason I went to Odessa was because of you. You had me running scared, sweet cheeks. So scared, I did the one thing I figured would push you away for good. I figured you'd never forgive me for doing something so stupid."

Of course, she forgave him. They snuggled even deeper into the bed.

"You know," he said, reflecting on the events that had led them together, "if it weren't for Jess Golden's things, we never would have found the new you and me."

"That's right. We sort of forgot about that during the past few weeks, didn't we? You made me forget my name half the time," she confessed.

"I did that to you?" He sounded pleased and just a little too cocky.

She pinched him. "You know darn well what you did to me."

"Yeah. I do. Want to know something else? I never forgot about the lady outlaw's things. I think maybe subconsciously I was holding them as my ace in the hole."

"How so?"

He nuzzled her neck and kissed her there. "Well, why wouldn't I have turned them over if I really wanted out of this hot little thing we had going on? I mean, duh. Could it be any more obvious that I knew deep down that as long as I had them, I had some hold on you?"

"I don't care what the reason was. You will always have a hold on me," she confessed as he slipped lower and took her breast into his mouth. "Always."

Twelve

Logan Voss stared at Jake as though he'd said he'd grown a tail. "You're what?"

"Getting married," Jake said, grinning around a cigar similar to the ones he'd passed around to his buddies. Logan was late joining the poker game, so he was also late hearing the news Jake had shared first with Connor and then the other men at the table. "You gonna ante up or what?"

Jake and Connor, along with Logan Voss and Mark Hartman, were winding down from a meeting finalizing plans for the anniversary ball, which would take place at the Cattleman's Club on Saturday night.

Still looking stunned, Logan tossed his chip into the pot in the middle of the table. "It's almost too much to take. First you get respectable and run for mayor and now this. I've gotta think about this last piece of news for a while."

"Don't we all," Connor agreed. "I'll see your bet and up it twenty."

"I fold," Mark said and tossed his hand toward Connor, who had just dealt.

"Well, I think I can see that," Logan said. "Let's see what you got."

"Three ladies," Jake said, laying down his three queens.

"Guess luck's with you tonight, bud," Mark said as Jake raked in the pot.

"And don't I just know it. Thank you, boys," he said with a smile.

"Hey, Gavin," Jake said when the sheriff walked in. "You're just the man I wanted to see. Damnedest thing happened. Chrissie and I took that box of stuff I bought at the auction to the museum yesterday."

"What things?" Mark asked.

Jake explained about the saddlebags with the purse and six-guns and the map that Chrissie was so certain belonged to Jessamine Golden. "Looks like she was right, too," he added. "According to the historian at the museum, they're authentic. Those folks are as excited as kids on Christmas morning over what they called 'an exceptional and significant find' of Royal's history.

"Anyway," he continued, "you know that display set up to honor old Edgar Halifax?"

"The one your competitor, Gretchen, is so excited about?" Connor asked.

"Yeah. But it seems someone isn't as happy about the

display as Gretchen because they vandalized the hell out of it. Sprayed paint mostly. Wrote, 'It's all lies!' across the glass case."

"Already heard about that," Gavin put in. "I was just going off shift when we got the call. I sent one of the boys out to check it out."

"What's up with that?" Logan asked.

Gavin shrugged. "Total mystery at this point. Got another mystery on my hands that's taking priority at the moment. That's why I stopped in. I need your help with something."

"What's up?" Jake asked. "Or does this fall into the category of you'd tell us but then you'd have to kill us?"

"Actually," Gavin said, "I do have to ask for your pledge of confidentiality on this one."

Jake glanced at Connor, sensing something big was about to be revealed.

"We got the autopsy results back on Jonathan Devlin today."

"Autopsy?"

Gavin nodded. "Standard practice when there's even a hint of a question as to cause of death."

"Didn't know there was a question," Mark said.

"Yeah, well, like I said, there was enough of one. Long story short, the report got put on the back burner due to backlogs at the lab. Anyway, I just got it back today."

"Something tells me you're going to tell us he didn't die of natural causes," Connor speculated soberly.

Gavin cast a dark glance around the table. "Seems we've got a murder on our hands."

A stunned silence fell while the four of them absorbed Gavin's news and waited for him to continue.

"I had his house cordoned off this afternoon. For all the good it will probably do. It's going to be hard as hell to pick up anything from a crime scene that old."

"Crime scene? I thought the old man died in the hospital," Logan said.

Again Gavin nodded. "Look, I can't disclose any more information yet. Not until the state boys do their work. As it is, I'm sticking my neck out breaking this news to you, but I figure it's only a matter of time before the media gets a hold of it."

Gavin was right, Jake thought. Jonathan Devlin was a prominent figure in Royal business and society. Word that he was murdered would make fodder for the media for months.

"I just want you boys to keep your eyes and your ears open for me. If you see anything suspicious going on—"

"Like that business at the museum and the Halifax exhibit," Jake interjected.

"Or what's happening out at Nita Windcroft's," Mark put in soberly.

Gavin shrugged. "Hell, I wouldn't discount anything at this point. It's been almost a month since Jonathan died, so we've got a cold trail and a big, high-profile murder. I'm shorthanded and will be for a while with Wilson out on extended disability and Smith transferring to Dallas. To make matters worse, we've got a budget issue and a hiring freeze, so I'm dying here."

"You know you can count on us," Jake said. "And you

can bet that Tom Devlin will want to lend a hand, too, when he gets back to Royal."

"Okay then," Gavin said, looking and sounding weary. "I've gotta go. Let's plan on getting together on a regular basis and I'll fill you in on what I can when I can."

To a man, they watched the sheriff leave. And to a man, they knew they'd do everything in their power to help him.

Royal's one hundred and twenty-fifth anniversary ball was special for more than one reason. Besides the milestone event itself, for one of the few times in history, the private Texas Cattleman's Club was open to the public. That in itself was enough to bring out the residents of Royal to the gala ball in droves.

The posh club was renowned throughout Texas for its lavishly appointed bar, private rooms and extravagant ballroom. Those who attended that night and had never been inside the club were not disappointed in what they found.

Polished walnut paneling graced the foyer, rare Oriental rugs covered the floors. Gleaming brass fixtures and chandeliers dripping with cut-crystal teardrops adorned the ballroom. Presiding over it all was the one thing all club member held sacred—a plain wooden plaque over the door heralding the club's motto: Leadership, Justice and Peace.

It was a night for celebration. A night for sumptuous evening gowns and tailored black tuxedos. And it was a night that Jake hadn't even known he'd been looking forward to when he'd conned pretty Chrissie Travers into attending the ball with him.

She looked amazing. Her gown was red and strapless, and he couldn't get enough of looking at the contrast of all that vibrant crimson satin against her ivory skin.

"You are the sexiest campaign manager I've ever slept with," he said, grinning down at her as they waltzed around the room. He loved it that she'd thrown herself into the campaign, insisting that she handle his PR. Turned out she was a natural, too. He spotted any number of Thorne for Mayor—a Leader for Tomorrow pins on tuxedo lapels.

Personally he liked the pin she wore on the waist of her dress—Thorne for Husband.

"And you are the sexiest and the smartest and the best candidate for mayor I've ever agreed to marry. And unlike the other candidate, I haven't seen you cast a single glaring sneer the entire night."

He laughed and, as luck would have it, caught a glimpse of Gretchen Halifax as she danced by with Malcolm Durmorr. And sure enough, the look she knifed his way could have cut glass.

Gretchen didn't bother him. Jonathan Devlin's murder bothered him, as it bothered all of the guys Gavin had confided in—Mark, Connor and Logan. They had jumped on the bandwagon, too, and were actively campaigning for him for mayor—everyone but Gavin, since his own elected position of Sheriff kept him from campaigning openly. Still, Jake knew he had Gavin's support.

"Who's that with Logan Voss?" Chrissie asked when they waltzed by the bar area. "Oh, wait, isn't that the TV reporter who's covering the celebration?"

"Melissa Mason," Jake said, following Chrissie's gaze and seeing the reporter with Logan.

"They seem pretty familiar," she observed. "She's gorgeous, isn't she? I've seen her newscasts, envied her. She's even prettier in person."

"She's pretty enough," Jake said and waited for Chrissie to meet his eyes, "if you like that type. Me? I go for a hot blonde with wild hazel eyes and the sweetest body to ever skinny-dip in the lake on my south forty."

"I'd better be the only blonde who ever skinny-dips in that lake, Mister."

"The one and only," he promised, loving her more than he had ever imagined was possible to love a woman. "Always and forever my one and only."

He lowered his head to hers and kissed her, right in the middle of the dance floor, not caring that half the county was watching, and smiling as he did.

* * * * *

LESS-THAN-INNOCENT INVITATION

BY
SHIRLEY ROGERS

Shirley Rogers lives in Virginia with her husband and an adorable Maltese named Blanca. She has two grown-up children, a son and a daughter. As a child, she was known for having a vivid imagination. It wasn't until she started reading romances that she realised her true destiny was writing them! Besides reading, she enjoys travelling, seeing movies and spending time with her family.

Prologue

From the diary of Jessamine Golden
August 10, 1910

Dear Diary,
Something happened today that I will always cherish in my heart. Something wonderful. Sheriff Brad Webster kissed me.

Me. A woman who walks on the opposite side of everything he stands for.

Though we have chosen different directions in life—his honorable and noble, mine a path that creates a barrier between us—this magnificent, proud man kissed me.

It was a glorious ending to a perfect day. Brad took me on a picnic down by the lake, and we spent a whole afternoon together on a blanket in the shade of a willow tree. As we talked, he took my hand in his, and I grew warm all over.

As the sun set low in the sky and our day together began to slip away, Brad leaned close to me and stroked my lips with his thumb. Every single inch of my body responded to his touch. My skin tingled and my face flushed hot, so hot that I knew he could tell how much he affected me. He smiled at me then and, for a moment, I thought he was going to laugh at me.

But, he kissed me instead. Oh, my, he kissed me. And his kiss was so tender, yet full of promise. His arms held me with gentle strength, and I wanted it to never end. In that instant, I forgot that our lives are worlds apart. I forgot everything except being with Brad.

Oh, diary, it felt as if the entire universe had shifted, and for that moment in time, that one captivating moment, I wanted only to be with him for the rest of my life.

But that can never be, can it?

I wish with all my heart that our circumstances were different, that the path I must follow wasn't against the code of honor Brad holds. But just as the darkness of night has fallen, the time to change my course in life has passed. Tonight I will fall asleep and dream of another time when Brad and I could be together. A time that embraces forever.

One

Logan Voss checked his watch for the third time in the space of fifteen minutes. Damn! The 125th Anniversary celebration of Royal, Texas, had started only an hour ago, but he felt as if he'd been there for hours. From the excitement in the air, it appeared to be a huge success.

Scanning the festively decorated ballroom of the Texas Cattleman's Club, he took a sip of the whiskey he'd been nursing for the past half hour. The August event was in full swing. Conversation and laughter flowed just beneath the song being belted out by a local country band. Logan knew just about everyone here. Many of the men were members of their elite club, some of them the same men who had talked him into attending this party.

He spotted Jake Thorne and Christine Travers dancing and smiled. Seeing as Jake had sworn he wasn't ready for anything serious with a woman, and most especially with Christine, Logan couldn't have helped but give his friend a hard time when he'd greeted him earlier in the evening. Now Jake had taken the proverbial fall, and he and Christine were planning to be married

Better him than me, Logan thought, loosening the tie around his neck. He'd been down that road before, had ended up buying his freedom from a marriage that never should have taken place.

Despite their divorce and financial settlement, Logan held no hard feelings for his ex-wife. It had been mostly his fault that their relationship hadn't worked out. Though he'd failed to realize it at the time, he'd married her for all the wrong reasons—his breakup with Melissa Mason being at the top of the list.

Melissa.

Hell, he hadn't thought about Melissa in what…at least a month. That was probably a record for him. Even after more than ten years apart, she usually crossed his mind every week or so. It was said that you never really forget your first love. Logan had to agree. Melissa's beautiful smile and sexy green eyes still haunted him.

He sighed and shoved away from the wall. What was wrong with him? The last person he needed to think about tonight was Melissa.

"Hey, Logan. What are you doing over here by yourself?"

"Mark." Logan greeted Mark Hartman, another single member of their elite club. After the death of his brother and sister-in-law, Mark had been named the guardian of his nine-month-old niece. How he managed taking care of a baby, operating his ranch and running a self-defense studio puzzled Logan, especially since Mark seemed to have trouble holding onto a nanny. "Actually, I was just thinking about leaving," Logan admitted.

"You're kidding, right?" Mark took a sip from his glass, then gestured with the same hand toward the crowd. "With all these pretty ladies to dance with?"

"I notice you're not out there." From their conversations, Logan had learned Mark was also hesitant about becoming involved with a woman. Years ago while he was overseas on a mission, the ex-marine's wife had been abducted and killed. Though he rarely spoke of her death, from the sadness that lingered in his friend's eyes, Logan suspected Mark had never gotten over it.

"Point taken." Mark drained the last of his drink. "Some celebration, though. There's even a reporter with a crew here from a Houston television station."

"Yeah?" Logan wasn't really interested in the coverage of the city's anniversary. Working his ranch didn't leave much time to watch television. Even if he met the reporter, he doubted he'd recognize the guy.

Mark nodded his head, indicating a group of people across the room. "A woman. Pretty, too. I heard she used to live here."

The small hairs on Logan's neck prickled. He shifted his attention to the crowd. He didn't see anyone who he suspected could be the reporter. But… He scanned the group again, slower this time, and his gaze landed on a woman, her back turned to him.

Layers of auburn curls cascaded past her shoulders. She wore a sparkly white cocktail dress made to enhance her slender figure. As if she sensed him watching her, she looked in his direction.

Logan's breath whooshed out as if he'd received a hard punch to his midsection.

Melissa.

"Damn," he muttered.

"You know her?" Mark asked, not missing the change in Logan's demeanor.

"I used to." Logan tracked her movements as she lifted her hand and brushed a strand of hair from her eyes. Every muscle in his body tightened.

How could she have an effect on him after all this time? It had been more than ten years since he'd set eyes on her. But watching her now, it felt as if it had only been yesterday when he'd fallen in love with her and asked her to marry him.

Pain sliced through him. Logan remembered only too well how she'd come to his ranch the day after she'd accepted his proposal and told him she'd changed her mind and was leaving town. Melissa had spoken of leaving Royal when they'd begun dating. But after seeing each other nearly every day, he'd believed her when she'd said she loved him. Apparently she hadn't meant it.

The music throbbed around him as he thought about the last month he'd spent with her. Everything in his life had fallen into place. He'd always loved the Wild Spur, the ranch he'd been raised on. He'd loved it as much as his younger brother, Bart, who had been spoiled by their father, hated it. He'd moved into Royal as soon as he graduated and Logan rarely ran into him.

When their father had died of a heart attack, the

brothers had made plans for Logan to buy out Bart's portion. The plan suited both of them. They'd never been close and Bart had wanted no part of the Wild Spur. But neither of them had known about the stipulation their father had put in his will.

The first son to marry would get the Wild Spur.

At first angry at their father, Logan and Bart had discussed how to get around the will. Then they realized they didn't have to worry. Logan was already in love with Melissa. When they married, everything would be his and he still could buy out Bart's part of the inheritance.

So he'd proposed to Melissa and she'd accepted.

Except a day later she'd changed her mind.

Without looking back, she'd dismissed him from her life. He hadn't been able to tell her she was ripping him apart inside.

Vulnerability wasn't an emotion Logan was familiar with. Losing his mother at the age of eleven, he'd been raised by a demanding father who hadn't encouraged sharing feelings. Logan had learned to hold what he thought and wanted to express inside.

He watched now as Melissa laughed at something the man beside her said and his chest began to ache. Afraid that she'd met someone else, he hadn't gone after Melissa, hadn't given her a chance to hurt him further. He'd always believed himself a smart man. He knew he should let bygones be bygones. The last thing he needed to do was to stir up unwanted memories. But damn it, he wanted answers. He wanted to know why she'd left, why she hadn't talked to him.

Would he accomplish that if he confronted her?

Would he see a fraction of the pain that he'd felt for years in Melissa's face? Would that make him feel any better? Would it heal his heart and let him move past the torment he'd endured?

And how would he react if it didn't? What if she looked at him as though she barely remembered him? God, if she did, he didn't know how he'd handle it. Could he walk away from her and salvage his dignity?

What if she gazed at him and he saw regret in her lovely green eyes? It wasn't as if they could pick up where they left off before, right?

And he wouldn't want to, anyway. He wouldn't trust his heart to her again. No, sir. Not again. But he damn sure wanted some answers from her. And if she didn't want to talk, he'd figure out some way to convince her.

He threw back the remainder of his drink, then set the glass down with a thud on a nearby table. Whether hearing the truth from Melissa would heal his pain or not, he deserved to know what had happened and he wasn't letting her leave town until he knew.

"See you later," he muttered to Mark. Logan's boots echoed with a steady beat on the hardwood floor as he started across the room.

With something close to fear squeezing her chest, Melissa watched Logan Voss storm across the ballroom, aimed in her direction. No, not fear, she quickly corrected herself. Anxiety? Oh, yeah. Anticipation? Most definitely. Awareness? Yes, even awareness, she admitted to herself, unable to deny the quick stir of her heart.

From the moment she'd been given the assignment

to cover the anniversary celebration of her hometown of Royal, Texas, she'd known the odds were high that she'd run into Logan.

But considering the promotion she'd been promised if she did the story, the risk had been worth it. Of course, that was *before* she'd arrived.

And before she'd seen Logan.

She should have known that she'd run into him tonight. All day while filming in Royal, she'd been feeling edgy, almost sensing impending doom about to strike her. Now that doom was heading straight for her in the form of one very determined and grim-faced rancher.

Melissa quickly searched the room for the nearest exit. After the rumors she'd heard about the secret missions of the wealthy members of the Texas Cattleman's Club, she'd wanted to satisfy her curiosity by talking with a few of the members.

Too bad she had to cut her visit short.

Hoping to escape before Logan reached her, she broke off her conversation with her videographer and sound person, Rick Johnson. However, before she could take a step, Logan blocked her path. Her gaze traveled up his broad chest, over his set jaw and finally connected with his gorgeous gray-green eyes.

She acknowledged what any warm-blooded female had to admit—the years had been awfully good to Logan. He was what, thirty-four now, three years older than herself. The only wrinkles she could make out on his sexy face were tiny lines crinkled around his eyes. Laugh lines, weren't they called?

Only Logan didn't look as though he had laughing on his mind.

Steeling herself, Melissa offered Logan a polite smile, one she'd perfected as a reporter. She'd be damned if she'd let him know just how hard her heart was beating.

"Logan, hi. It's been a long time." It was an effort to keep her voice light and appear at ease when it took all of her strength just to stand there in front of him.

"Over ten years," Logan replied, then cursed under his breath for making it sound as if he'd been counting. At least she knew who he was. One hurdle crossed.

Melissa tilted her head as if trying to recall the time, when in reality it was etched permanently in her mind. "Yes, I guess you're right. How have you been?" she asked, her tone more nostalgic than she'd intended. It wasn't every day she made polite conversation with the only man she'd ever loved, the same man who had ruthlessly used her for his own greed.

Logan propped his hand on his hip as his gaze dropped lazily over her. "Well, sweetheart, I've been just dandy. How about you?"

Melissa's breath dammed in her lungs. Though barely discernable, she caught the underlying sarcasm in his voice. What did *he* have to feel put off about? He was the one who had hurt *her* all those years ago.

But she refused to be baited by him. Dredging up unpleasant memories was not on her list of things to do while in town. "I've been fine. I'm in Royal covering the anniversary celebration," she explained, feeling it was safer to keep their conversation on a neutral subject.

He remained silent, forcing Melissa to pick up the

conversation again. "I'm a reporter for WKHU, a television station in Houston."

Logan's jaw tautened. "So you got what you wanted." *A life away from Royal.*

Away from me.

He mentally shut himself off from the hurt of their breakup. Crossing his arms, he stared at her. He'd heard rumors that Melissa was a journalist somewhere, but the rare times her name came up in a conversation, he excused himself because he didn't want to know where she was.

Or who she was with.

Houston. All these years she'd been here in the state of Texas. Hell, what did it matter? She'd made her choice a long time ago.

Melissa stiffened her carriage. "A life as a reporter? Yes." Her answer held little truth. She'd wanted him. Forever. Until she'd learned the selfish truth of why he'd asked her to marry him.

Logan raised a skeptical eyebrow. She frowned, a bit put off by his cynicism. "Don't look so shocked. I've been doing this a long time, and I've worked hard, taking assignments other reporters have turned down."

Including coming back to this town.

After years of proving herself by covering every type of story imaginable, she'd begun to believe if she was ever going to get a desk assignment, she might have to move to another station in a larger market. Although she liked and respected the station's news director, Jason Bellamy, he had yet to give her a chance.

Until last week. She had Jason's word that if she covered this one last story, she'd be promoted to a weekend news position becoming available in a month. Her dreams lay before her. She only had to complete this last assignment.

"Actually, I'm impressed," Logan admitted. And he was. His love hadn't been enough to make Melissa happy, but apparently she'd found what she'd been searching for in her work. Had her satisfaction also come in the form of another man? He glanced at her left hand and noticed it was free of any wedding rings.

"Thank you." From the hard edge in his voice, Melissa doubted his sincerity. Their parting had been traumatic for her. How had he handled it? She wanted to know, but she wasn't going to ask.

Silence fell between them. With her emotions in turmoil, she had to get out of there. She sent Rick a desperate look, but he was engaged in a conversation with Daniel, her story producer, who had come to Royal as part of their crew.

The upbeat country tune changed to a slow, heady song about lost love. The melancholy words of the tune mimicked her past relationship with Logan. One of her favorites, she'd often played it when she'd wondered if she'd done the right thing breaking up with him.

"Dance?"

Logan's request jerked her from her thoughts. "What?"

"Would you like to dance?" He wasn't about to let her get away. Taking a step toward her, he closed the distance between them, her panicked look giving him a sense of satisfaction. Apparently she wasn't as immune to him as she wanted him to believe.

"With you?" Surprised he'd asked, she struggled to maintain her composure, knowing she stood little chance of holding herself together if he touched her.

He gave her a wry grin, the idea of holding her in his arms more appealing than he wanted to admit. "Well, sweetheart, since I'm the one who's asking…"

"I, um, I'm not sure that's such a good idea." Melissa shivered at the thought of being held again by Logan. Until now, she'd compartmentalized her feelings for him. Dancing with him would be tantamount to opening the lid on her personal Pandora's box.

Trying to stall, she glanced around, only to notice that several of her crew were watching them with more than a passing interest. So were some of Royal's finest citizens, people she'd known when she'd lived there. She quietly groaned. The last thing she wanted to do was to cause a scene right there in the middle of the ballroom.

"It's just a dance, Melissa," Logan coolly stated. At the indecision in her eyes a sudden rush of desperation shot through him. He *wanted* her to say yes—but for all the wrong reasons.

Yeah, sure, he wanted answers from her, but he found himself wanting to hold her once again. The knot in his stomach twisted a little tighter. At sixteen she'd been cute, at twenty, pretty. Now, at thirty-one, she was flat-out beautiful. Her long chestnut hair fell in curls around her face, setting off her fascinating green eyes. His gaze drifted lower, over her bare shoulders and slim, athletic figure. Her dress hid very little of her perfect skin. No wonder the television industry had her in front of the camera.

Shaking his head, Logan forced himself to stop thinking about how beautiful she was and centered his attention on what he really wanted from her. Answers about why she'd left. If she'd lied about loving him. And now, after seeing her again, he needed to prove to himself that these new feelings of awareness were based on nostalgia and nothing more, that the desire he'd felt for her all those years ago was long gone.

"Are you here with someone?" Melissa asked. She looked at his hand, searching for a wedding ring but finding none. She told herself it didn't mean anything. Because work on a ranch could sometimes be dangerous, even if he *was* married, he probably didn't wear a ring.

He grinned at her. "No."

"All right," Melissa answered, more than a little surprised at his response. And curious. Did that mean there was no one special in his life? Or that he was alone just for this evening?

She held out her hand and Logan closed his around it. They walked to the dance floor, and a shiver of anticipation whispered through her as he pulled her into his arms. Her lungs constricted with a needy ache. She was a fool to do this, to be this close to him, to let him anywhere near her heart. Even as she acknowledged she was playing with fire, her hand traitorously trailed across his shoulder to rest close to his neck.

Closing her eyes she breathed in his scent, and the enticing, woodsy smell took her back to another time, another place, when he'd held her in his arms in more intimate ways as his big hands caressed her skin until she'd trembled with anticipation.

Oh, this is not a good idea, her mind chanted over and over again. She leaned away, placing some much-needed distance between them. Opening her eyes, she searched his face to see if she'd had any effect on him. His emotionless mask, however, gave her no clue to his thoughts. She quickly looked away. "It's a nice party," she commented, struggling to ground herself.

Logan nodded. "The town's planned a lot of events to commemorate its anniversary."

She gave him a practiced, on-camera smile. "And the Texas Cattleman's Club is doing its part."

"We aim to please."

Which meant he was now a member of the Texas Cattleman's Club. She found that interesting, but under the circumstances, she wasn't about to stroke his ego by pursuing that topic. "A lot of work has gone into putting this ball together."

"It isn't every day the town has something this exciting to celebrate." Logan felt the softness of Melissa's hand in his and was suddenly very glad that he hadn't left the ball. Not that he intended to have more than a dance with her.

His mind drifted to the last time he'd made love to her, how she'd... No he wasn't going to punish himself with the memories. What they had shared together was a long time ago.

Done.

Over.

He'd asked her to dance to confront her, not to reminisce about how it felt to hold her, to touch her skin, to run his hands over her body.

His goal was to get her to tell him why she'd broken up with him.

Nothing more.

Maybe once he knew the truth he could truly forget her.

God knows he'd tried.

"When my story producer heard about the legend surrounding Jessamine Golden, he insisted on coming with me and my videographer to learn about it firsthand."

"Yeah, history has it she was quite an outlaw," he answered. "A lot of people believe the gold she stole is still hidden around here somewhere." His struggle to keep Melissa at a distance was proving more difficult than he'd imagined. Her perfume filled his senses. Her scent hadn't changed. He'd never quite forgotten her smell— like sunshine and lavender.

Excitement lit her eyes. "If it's true and the gold was found, it would be quite a story." Tempted to stay in Royal and dig up some additional material on Jessamine Golden and the treasure she'd supposedly stolen and hidden, Melissa hesitated. If she did, she'd chance running into Logan again—a risk she wasn't ready to take. This one encounter with him was definitely enough.

Truthfully, her heart had never quite healed. She'd thought she'd successfully dealt with her feelings for Logan, but now in his arms, she realized she hadn't. Though not in love with him anymore, her emotions for him still went deep. It was best to finish this dance and say goodbye.

"So, is this what you've doing all these years?" Logan asked, changing the subject to one that would help him keep his focus. "Chasing leads and reporting the news?"

"Pretty much." She lifted a shoulder in a soft shrug as they slowly moved to the music, conscious of how Logan used that moment to pull her closer. Rather than make an issue of feeling his hard, lean body pressed to hers, she pretended that she didn't notice. Or notice how easy it would be to lean the few inches separating them and kiss him. She focused on his chin instead of looking into his eyes. "Of course, I haven't always been given assignments like attending glamorous events. I've covered a lot of stories over the years, paid my dues, as they say."

"Was it worth it?" Logan asked, his voice low, yet determined. He'd planned on waiting until the right moment to ask her, but the words spilled out of his mouth. He told himself it had nothing to do with the way she felt.

Melissa's eyes grew wary. "I enjoy what I do."

"That's not what I asked." A hard edge crept into his voice, an underlying current of tension he hadn't been able to conceal.

"I thought you wanted to dance for old time's sake." Melissa stopped moving and tried to disengage from him. She came up short when he wouldn't let her go.

"I did," he told her, aware he wasn't being totally truthful. Grimacing, he admitted, "But I also want to know what made you break our engagement. You owe me that."

"No, Logan, I don't." When she pulled away this time, he let her go. It startled her as much as when he hadn't.

"The hell you don't."

"This is ridiculous! Why would you want to dredge up old memories anyway, Logan? What happened between us was a lifetime ago. It's water under the bridge. Over." Her lungs lacked air. Calming herself, she managed to take in a short breath.

His jaw hardened. "I guess maybe to you it is."

Melissa eyes widened. Did his comment mean that to him it wasn't? His rigid stance revealed nothing more than that she'd provoked his anger. Well, she was pretty angry now herself. How dare he imply that their breakup was her fault? "I'm not responsible for what happened between us, Logan Voss. You are and you know it."

Logan stared at her in disbelief. "Me?"

"Yes, you!"

"You're the one who left, Melissa." His tone was sharp as he tried to speak over the music. He glanced around the room, irritated as people started to turn toward them. Damn, this was getting out of hand, and he wasn't about to give anyone a show. Frustrated, he grabbed her wrist.

"What are you doing?"

"I don't know about you, but I'm not too crazy about providing tonight's entertainment. Let's take this outside."

Two

"Let me go!" Melissa's voice rose a notch. At that moment, the music ended and she realized he had a point. Many of the guests had stopped dancing and were watching them with something between amusement, surprise and blatant curiosity. Heat burned her face. Back in Royal only one day and already Logan was turning her life upside down

Logan dropped her hand. "We can go out the quiet way or not. The decision's yours."

Forcing herself to smile, she nodded. "Fine." He started walking toward the door. She kept up with his long strides, her heels clicking on the polished hardwood floor.

As soon as they entered the impressive foyer, Logan came to an abrupt halt beneath the glow of a rustic antler chandelier. Preventing herself from running into him, Melissa steadied herself with her palm on his sculptured back.

She sucked in a breath. As his muscles shifted beneath her hand, memories of making love with him dulled her senses. Giving her head a shake, she stepped back.

"Are you crazy?" she demanded, glaring at him. "People were beginning to stare at us back there."

Logan glanced toward the door, then back at her. "They wouldn't have even noticed us if you'd just answered my question."

Melissa tossed her head back. "I have no intention of getting into a discussion about…about…" She stopped speaking and took a calming breath. Why hadn't she heeded her inner warnings about returning to her hometown and the possibility of seeing Logan again? If her promotion hadn't been riding on this assignment, she would never have come back. Never have taken the risk of seeing him.

Ever.

"Look, this is ridiculous."

"Is it?" He leaned toward her. "Ridiculous is the way you suddenly left, Melissa." His hands went to his hips. "More than once I've tried to figure out why. What went wrong between us?" Cursing under his breath, he held her gaze. He didn't admit that thinking about what had happened that last day, thinking about her and what they'd shared, could still drive him crazy.

"I didn't just take off," she reminded him, her tone scorching. "I came to see you."

He made a sound of disgust. "Yeah, to toss my ring

in my face and tell me you were leaving. Why?" he demanded. "Was it because you fell in love with someone else?" Though he braced himself for her answer, he didn't want to believe she'd been seeing another man. It would kill him.

"No!" Her face drained of color. "Is that what you thought?"

"Hell, I didn't know what to think. I believed you loved me. Then all of a sudden, you were telling me you didn't want to be married." His voice softened. "Do you even remember what we had together?"

Melissa licked her lips. "Of course I do." As soon as she said the words, she wished them back.

Logan closed the distance between them. Unable to stop himself from touching her, he cupped his hand around her neck. Despite the anger that had simmered inside of him for so long, he wanted to pull her against him. "Do you, Melissa?" Something drove him to find out if she'd thought about him since she'd been gone, if she'd ever regretted leaving.

Swallowing hard, Melissa's eyes locked with his. Oh, how she'd loved this man. "Yes," she whispered.

Logan lowered his head, his lips lingering just above hers. "Then you remember just how good we were together."

Her gaze drifted lower to his mouth. "Oh, Logan."

At that moment the door to the ballroom whisked open. Logan straightened and stepped away from her as a man entered the foyer and walked hurriedly toward them.

What the hell was he doing? He had no business even thinking about kissing Melissa Mason. He'd let his heart get tangled up with her before and their relationship had ended badly. Hadn't he learned his lesson?

Apparently not. After only a few minutes in her company, his mind had drifted to the memories of touching her.

Kissing her.

He wanted to know if she tasted as sweet as he remembered.

No, it was more than curiosity. Dancing with her had stirred up all kinds of emotions inside him, made him aware of her in ways that time had blurred.

"Melissa, there you are!"

"Daniel!" Expelling a breath, Melissa turned away from Logan as her producer approached, relieved he'd chosen that moment to find her.

After all the years apart from Logan, she never would have dreamed she'd give in so easily to him again, but God knows, if left alone a minute longer, she would have kissed him. Now that she knew she wasn't immune to him, she'd keep her distance until she could get out of town.

She gestured toward him. "This is an old friend of mine, Logan Voss. Logan, Daniel Graves. He's the story producer for the feature on Royal's anniversary."

"Mr. Voss."

Logan held out his hand. "Call me Logan," he told the man as he tried to absorb Melissa's description of him as an "old friend." It stung more than it should have.

Daniel clasped his hand with a firm grip. "It's a pleasure to meet you."

"I hope you're enjoying yourself at the ball," Logan said as he studied the man. Twice his own age, Daniel

Graves was thin and wiry with a nervous energy that made him look as if he was fidgeting even while he stood still.

"I am." He turned toward Melissa, his eyes wide with excitement. "And I've just heard the most exciting news. I was talking to one of the guests and heard that some of Jessamine Golden's personal belongings have turned up at an auction!"

"Yes, I know. I heard about it when I arrived in town yesterday and I have notes on it," Melissa told him. "Apparently they auctioned off a saddle bag and a few other things. I was going to discuss the information with you on our trip back to Houston."

"So you already know about the map?" Daniel asked.

Melissa frowned. "I know there was a map of some kind, but I fail to see what you're so excited about."

"Inside the saddlebag was a treasure map."

She rolled her eyes. "Daniel, please don't tell me you're falling for that tale," she scoffed.

The producer ignored her remark and turned to Logan. "You don't seem to be surprised."

Shaking his head, he replied, "The legend of Jessamine Golden burying a cache of gold bars somewhere around here has been circulating for years. The map and the rest of her items are on display at the Historical Society Museum." The common thought among his friends at the Cattleman's Club was that if Jessamine had indeed heisted the gold, the map was proof she'd intended to come back for it. Something must have prevented her from returning.

"I hope to see them while I'm here," Daniel stated.

Logan settled back into a comfortable stance. "One of my friends, Jake Thorne, donated them to the museum after he bought them at the auction."

"The same Jake Thorne who's running for mayor?" Melissa asked.

"Yeah. Jake outbid Christine, who is now his fiancée."

"Really?" She frowned. "Why would he do that? Was he trying to increase the amount of money for charity or something?"

Logan shrugged. "I don't know. They weren't dating at the time. Christine wanted the items for the museum. Jake eventually made it up to her by donating them."

At the excitement building in Daniel's eyes, Logan remarked, "You know, it's only speculation that the map may lead to a treasure."

"That's true. And we all know how rumors are always built out of proportion," Melissa said. She didn't want her producer getting ideas about staying in Royal any longer than they originally had planned. But from his excited expression he already seemed intrigued, which meant nothing but trouble for her. She was ready to leave Royal tonight, to put Logan and memories of their love affair behind her. Now, thanks to a hokey map, her plans were in jeopardy.

Daniel's excited expression faltered a fraction. "There's a chance that the map is real."

"Daniel—"

"You don't *know* it isn't and you won't if you don't look into the story. Also, one of the guests said he'd heard someone had vandalized an exhibit at the museum and it was close to where Jessamine's things are on display."

Melissa frowned. "Which exhibit?"

"The one on Edgar Halifax." Daniel looked at Logan. "Who was he?"

"Edgar was Royal's first mayor and is credited with establishing the town," Logan informed him. "He was shot and killed and the person responsible was never caught. For the anniversary celebration and because Gretchen Halifax, his descendant and also a mayoral candidate, pushed for it, an exhibit in his honor is on display at the museum."

"Do they have any idea why it was vandalized?" Melissa asked.

"Not from what I've heard." Daniel shifted his attention to his reporter.

She raised an eyebrow. "Sounds like someone has an ax to grind, but I fail to see any connection to Jessamine Golden's legend."

"That's where you come in," her producer told her. "We're going to stay in town for a few days. You can spend some time working on the connection, if there is one. It'll make a great addition to your story."

Melissa all but groaned, even though she had to admit that something suspicious was going on. Still, in her opinion it didn't warrant them staying in Royal. "I think we have enough footage and information for the story we're planning."

"Maybe for what we originally planned, but I've already talked to Jason. We're covering Royal's anniversary celebration, but we're also planning a series on historical mysteries. Let's investigate Jessamine Golden more thoroughly. And I want you to report on the vandalism when you put the story together. Do some digging. There's no telling what you could turn up."

"Jason?" Logan asked, noticing the panicked look on Melissa's face.

Melissa explained, "Jason Bellamy is the news director at our station." She turned toward her producer, her eyes wide. "This could take a while. Daniel, I don't think—"

"People love a mystery, and this one is rich with historic significance. You might even find a way to connect it to the town's celebration."

Logan watched the two of them with interest. By Melissa's replies and body language, it was clear she wasn't crazy about staying in town. Why? Because of him? He discounted that theory. She'd walked away from him before without batting an eye.

Well, he wanted her to stay until he found out what he wanted to know from her.

"Do you have hotel reservations?" he asked, hoping they didn't. If they hadn't made reservations, they were going to need a place to stay.

Melissa gave him a frustrated look. "No, we don't. We checked out today because we *weren't staying*," she reminded her producer, pinning him with a hard stare. Remaining in Royal wasn't an option. Nearly kissing Logan tonight was enough to tell her that her feelings for him went deeper than their years apart could erase.

"Then you have a problem," Logan stated, already thinking about setting them up at his ranch. "You won't be able to get a hotel room."

"Nowhere in town?" her story producer asked. "Are you sure?"

Relief rushed through Melissa and she released a pent-up breath. "Well, that's that, then." She almost did a happy dance. Now they could leave. And if Daniel wanted a more in-depth piece on Royal, he could come back—with another reporter.

"Yes. Everything has been booked for weeks because of the celebration." Logan checked the time. "At this hour, you'd have to drive for miles before you'd find an available room, if you're lucky." As Daniel's face fell, Logan put his plan into action. "Tell you what. I'll be glad to help you out."

Daniel leaned toward Logan. "How?"

"I own a ranch just outside of town. I can put you and your crew up while you're here."

"What?" Melissa squeaked.

"That would be great." Daniel missed his reporter's look of alarm. "Thank you!"

"Wait a minute—"

"My pleasure." Ignoring Melissa's protest, Logan shook Daniel's hand, sealing the deal. "How many are in your crew?"

"Three. The two of us and Rick Johnson, our videographer and sound person."

"I have plenty of room. I'll give my housekeeper a call and let her know to expect you later tonight."

"Logan, wait!" Melissa grabbed his arm as he started to turn away. "We can't possibly impose on you."

He smiled at her. "It's the least I can do."

Not fooled by his innocent expression, she dropped

her hand. "So you're doing this for the town, is that it?" She knew better than to trust him. He had an ulterior motive, but at the moment she was at a loss as to what it could be.

Logan looked down at his arm where she'd touched him. He could swear he'd felt the heat of her through the fabric of his suit. His gaze swung up to her face. "What other reason could I have?"

"I don't know. Why don't you tell me?"

"None, I assure you, sweetheart. Now if you'll excuse me, I have a call to make."

She glanced at the bracelet watch on her arm. "It's late," she blurted, stopping him again, this time with only her words. "You can't expect your housekeeper to make up rooms for us at this hour."

Logan grinned at them both. "Wait until you meet Norah. Believe me, she won't mind a bit. She'll make you feel right at home."

Melissa's heart sank. *This can't be happening!* She did not want to stay in Royal.

And she surely did not want to stay at Logan's ranch.

That would be just too darn close to the man for comfort. The farther away from Logan she was, the better. She started to protest again, but Logan turned away and began dialing his cell phone.

Melissa frowned at Daniel. Though she wanted to argue about his decision to stay at Logan's ranch, how could she? Daniel would want to know her reasons. As it stood, her colleagues knew nothing about her past with Logan.

And she wanted to keep it that way.

"Staying on a ranch. This will be exciting," Daniel said, breaking into her thoughts.

"Yeah, exciting." Her voice revealed she was anything but. It was just her luck to have a boss who was a history buff.

Logan punched a button on his phone, then tucked it inside his jacket. He turned toward them. "Everything is all set. Norah will have your rooms ready for you by the time you arrive."

Daniel clapped him on the back. "We can't thank you enough, Logan."

Logan was glad things had turned in his favor. "The pleasure's mine." He looked at Melissa. "All mine, I assure you."

Daniel's face lit up like a Boy Scout earning his first merit badge. "If you'll give us directions to your ranch, we'll leave the celebration in a short while. The last thing we want is to be an inconvenience."

"That's not necessary. Stay as late as you like. I wouldn't want you to miss a minute of it." He gave Melissa a long look. Putting her on the defensive, he said, "Besides, Melissa can find the Wild Spur. She already knows the way, don't you sweetheart? I'll meet you when you arrive." Touching the brim of his hat, he walked away.

Her mouth dropping open, Melissa stared after him as he exited through the doublewide front doors. From her producer's silence, she knew Logan's comment had left him speechless, too. Facing him, she explained, "I knew Logan in high school." She hoped that would be enough information to satisfy his curiosity.

It didn't work. Daniel's raised eyebrows caused her stomach to wrench.

"I got the feeling there was more between the two of you than being school chums," he commented. "So there's another side to my wonderful workaholic reporter?"

Melissa's lips tightened into a straight line. "I am not a workaholic."

"No? Dear, you haven't been on a date in months."

"I've been busy working for a promotion, which Jason has promised me after this assignment," she reminded him.

"I know, and you'll get it. But that doesn't mean that you can't slow down occasionally, have a little fun."

"I do things for enjoyment. I went out with the gang last week."

Daniel shook his head. "Going out for drinks with a group of friends from work isn't the same as dating and you know it. You only travel in a pack." As if jolted by his own words, he looked at the door Logan had just left through, then back at Melissa.

"Don't go reading anything into that wicked mind of yours. I knew Logan a long time ago. That's all."

"Oh, really?" Daniel raised his dark, bushy eyebrows. "C'mon, Melissa. I'm surprised I'm not singed from the vibes between the two of you."

"What you were feeling is your imagination getting away from you."

"You can deny it all you want, but there's something going on between you and Logan Voss."

"Daniel, you're crazy! I haven't seen the man in years. How could there be anything between us?" Logically, it made sense and she hoped Daniel bought it. Because before he'd walked into the foyer and interrupted them, Logan had been about to kiss her. And she would have let him.

Worse, she would have kissed him back.

Oh, Lord, what had she been thinking? When she'd learned the reason Logan had wanted to marry her, her heart had broken in two. She'd prayed that Logan would come after her and tell her she'd been wrong to believe what she'd heard. But he hadn't. It had been years before she'd been able to think of dating again.

Now, back in Royal for a few hours, she'd been tempted by that same destructive path.

Exasperated, Melissa glared at Daniel. "Let's go into the party. There are a few more people I want to talk to."

"All right." Daniel followed her. "I'll find you, say, in about an hour." He opened the door for her. After she entered, he walked in behind her. "Let me know if you're ready to leave earlier."

Melissa nodded as she made her escape, Daniel's words echoing through her mind.

Let me know if you're ready to leave earlier.

Ha! As if that was even a possibility. The last place on earth she'd thought she'd end up tonight was at Logan's ranch.

There had to be some way to get out of going there. Perhaps Logan had been wrong. It was possible that the hotels weren't solidly booked. How could he even know that for sure, anyway?

She looked around for Rick. Since she'd ridden to Royal with him, she didn't have a car, but maybe she could borrow his truck and check a few of the hotels on her own. There had to be some other place she could stay.

Because going to Logan's wasn't an option.

Three

"There it is." Melissa pointed out a road off the highway to Rick as they passed a small country food market that had long closed for the day.

He put on his blinker and made a sharp right turn onto the narrow paved road. In the distance caught beneath the moon's glow, she could just make out a house beyond several fenced pastures.

"So this guy you know has a real ranch?" Rick asked.

"Yeah, it's the real thing." Melissa turned her head away from the window and gave Rick a faint smile. Five years younger than her, he was what women referred to as beautiful—not a common word used to describe a man, but it fitted Rick completely. His black hair was pulled into a ponytail, which accentuated his high cheekbones and gorgeous blue eyes. Surprisingly, he didn't seem to realize how perfectly God had made him. He was a nice person, too, and they shared a great working relationship.

"How do you know him?" he asked, shooting her a glance.

A flash of her past whipped through her mind. "We met at a party when I was twenty." Actually, because she and Logan had gone to the same high school, she'd known who he was. He'd been three years ahead of her and hadn't even known her name. Back then, all the girls had had crushes on Logan Voss.

Except she'd never grown out of hers. A couple of years after graduation they met and began dating and she'd fallen madly in love with him. Ruggedly male and hard-working, he was also as gentle as he was intense, as loving as he was stubborn.

"An old boyfriend?" Rick wiggled his eyebrows suggestively.

"Something like that." An old boyfriend. A former lover. The man she'd planned to marry.

The man who had broken her heart.

Rick slowed the truck to navigate a sharp curve. "So you grew up here?"

"My father was in the service and was transferred to Reese Air Force Base near Lubbock when I was twelve. We passed through Royal on our way there. He liked it here, so he commuted to work. Once I graduated high school I didn't want to move with my parents when they retired to Florida. So I stayed in Royal."

To be near Logan. But she didn't say that.

She'd never forgotten the moment she'd seen him sitting alone at that party. For years she'd admired him from afar, so, gathering her courage, she'd sat beside him and struck up a conversation. They'd spend the remainder of the evening together, then Logan had taken her home.

The instant chemistry between them had led to a heated kiss. A few dates later, with their passion still burning hot, she'd given him her virginity.

Over the next few months, their relationship had grown more intense. And emotional. As a teenager, Melissa had sworn she wouldn't turn out like her mother, a talented dancer who had given up her chance at stardom to become the wife of a career military man and follow him from base to base as he moved up the ranks.

Not her. She had wanted to do so much more.

Until she'd fallen in love with Logan.

For the first time in her life, it all made sense. Love, happiness, being with the man you couldn't live without. Having his children. Growing old with him.

She'd wanted all those things with Logan so much that she'd tossed away her dreams of leaving Royal and becoming a reporter.

Logan had asked her to marry him.

Melissa sighed just thinking about how happy she'd been at that very moment. "Yes," she'd whispered. And Logan had kissed her tenderly. Then he held her in his arms and said, "I'll have everything I've ever wanted, Melissa. I'll have you and the Wild Spur."

It hadn't occurred to her that it might be an unusual thing to say at all. He'd always loved the ranch. But the next day she'd learned from a casual friend the cold truth of why Logan had asked her to marry him—a far cry from his whispered words of love.

The truck traveled over the cattle guard, jarring Melissa out of her thoughts. Her stomach felt like lead as they drove under the Wild Spur entrance and up the long drive to the main house. She stared out the window, mesmerized by how the landscape had changed. Three cottages dotted a circular drive she couldn't recall. Next to them, the trees had flourished, blocking their view of the main house.

Several outbuildings lay to her right, each very large and well-kept. Beyond them in the distance stood an impressive row of stables and several large corrals. Progress and improvements had changed the small ranch she'd known into a major, thriving business.

The truck rounded a small curve and at the sight of Logan's home, she caught her breath. It barely resembled the small, functional ranch house she'd remembered.

Pulling into a driveway of cocoa-colored stone, Rick stopped his truck in front of a grand courtyard enclosed with an equally impressive stone wall. A majestic fountain stood like a monument in the center of it, welcoming them.

She opened her door, climbed out of the truck and her stomach knotted tighter as she took in the massive house. Although she recognized a part of the original building, the majority of it had clearly been constructed since she'd left town.

It was, in a word…stunning.

The Spanish-style house boasted a low-pitched terracotta roof, rounded windows and stucco walls painted a pale shade of peach. An array of native foliage gave the iron-gated entryway and courtyard lushness, as did the beautiful flagstone patio and walkway.

It seemed Logan's management of the ranch had paid off nicely. He'd always been devoted to this place, she thought with a sense of resignation—enough to marry her to acquire it. Obviously he'd succeeded in getting the ranch, despite the fact that she'd refused to be used as a ticket to secure his heritage.

Had he and his brother Bart struck another deal of some kind, or had one of them married to lock down their legacy? What had happened to Bart? she wondered.

The brothers had had little in common. Unlike Logan, Bart, a few years younger, had hated living in the country, raising cattle and handling horses. Though Melissa hadn't thought he'd been a bad seed, he'd found his way into his share of trouble. Aware Logan's father had favored Bart, Melissa once had asked Logan why.

He'd told her that their mother had died of cancer when he was eleven and Bart was six. At first, Bart had withdrawn, then later he became difficult to handle. His father had tried to compensate for his distress by giving into his demands. Logan hadn't expressed bitterness or jealousy; he'd simply accepted his father's obvious favoritism without complaining. Or showing emotion.

What had happened between the two brothers since she'd left? Had Bart followed through with his plans to leave Royal for good when he got his share of his inheritance?

Following Rick to the back of his truck, she retrieved

her bag, which held little more than her makeup and one change of clothing. Having tailed them from the celebration, Daniel parked his car behind Rick's truck in the wide driveway. Melissa waited as he got out and joined them.

When she'd agreed to this assignment, it had been with Daniel's assurance that they'd only be in Royal for an overnight stay. No longer.

And surely not as long as it would take to do a series of feature stories on Royal.

Disgruntled at the turn of events, she debated letting someone else approach Logan's door, then decided if she acted as though something was bothering her, it would make her coworkers more curious about her relationship with him. And after the way she and Logan had disappeared from the ball, the last thing she wanted to do was to give either Daniel or Rick anything additional to talk about.

As she started toward the house, the door opened and Logan walked out. He was followed by a short, stout woman with rosy cheeks and a smile big enough to win over Snow White's dwarf, Grumpy.

"I see you made it," Logan commented, centering his gaze on Melissa as he greeted the group. "This is Norah Campbell. Officially, she's the housekeeper, but she's really the boss. She keeps the place running smoothly."

Norah gave Logan a fond look, then smiled widely at them. "Welcome to the Wild Spur. We're pleased to have you stay with us. We want you to feel right at home, so if there's anything you need, please let me know."

Melissa extended her hand and shook Norah's. "Hi,

I'm Melissa Mason. This is Daniel Graves and Rick Johnson. We appreciate having a place to stay at the last minute and hope we haven't put you to too much work."

"Not at all. It's nice to meet you. I have your accommodations ready." She nodded to Logan. "Why don't you take the men to their quarters, and I'll show Miss Mason to her room."

"Melissa, please."

"And I'm Norah. Let's go inside. I'm sure you're tired."

As she started to follow Norah inside the house, Melissa heard the groan of a car door opening. Turning back, she saw Rick and Logan get in Rick's truck and Daniel climb in his car. Her heart began to pound as they started their automobiles, then backed out of the driveway. Turning to Norah, she asked, "Where are they going?"

"Logan's taking them to one of the guest cottages. You passed them on the way in. Come, let me show you to your room."

Melissa watched the vehicles drive away, then pull in several hundred yards from the main house.

Why would Logan locate the men in one of the cottages, separating them from her? Did he want her in the main house to corner her? She knew he wanted to talk about why she'd left years ago, but she had no plans to let him have his way. No good could come from revisiting that emotional nightmare.

"Logan thought they'd be more at ease in one of the cottages," Norah added as they went inside. "We talked about having you stay in one as well."

"Why didn't you?" Melissa asked as she took in the breathtaking foyer. Polished wood floors reflected light from a delicate chandelier hanging overhead and an antique grandfather clock stood watch in the corner.

"He thought you'd be more comfortable here in the house."

Melissa didn't believe that for a minute. Logan had always been as tenacious as a pit bull when it came to getting his way. Apparently that was one thing about him that hadn't changed.

As she followed the housekeeper, Melissa found the rest of Logan's house as extraordinary as the foyer. All on one level, it was spread out, easily more than five thousand square feet. When they neared the living room, Norah stopped and Melissa stared in awe at its richness. Wide framed windows, a large flagstone fireplace and soft leather furniture gave it a comfortable, yet luxurious feel.

"This is beautiful. Everything looks so different."

"So you've been here before?" Norah asked.

Melissa realized her blunder and forced a smile. "It was a long time ago. How long have you worked for Logan?"

Norah led them down another hallway. "I moved here about eight years ago. My husband passed away and my sister lives nearby and wanted me close to her. I was happy to get a job here. Logan was in need of help and I needed something to do."

"So you enjoy working for him?" Melissa asked.

The housekeeper smiled. "Oh, I do. I wouldn't want to work anywhere else."

"He's fortunate to have you," Melissa commented.

Norah shook her head. "I'm the lucky one. I never had children so I think of Logan as my son."

Curious to learn a little more about him, Melissa asked, "Is he difficult to work for?"

"Oh, quite the opposite."

"Really?" She couldn't stop herself from pumping the housekeeper for more information.

"He's awfully quiet sometimes and doesn't go out much. I worry that he's never going to find the right woman and settle down."

Melissa followed Norah into a bedroom and put her bag on the floor. Did Norah's comment mean that Logan had never brought a woman here? She couldn't help being curious about his past. She walked over to the bed and ran her finger along one of the fluffy pillows.

"How lovely." The cherry furniture was simple, yet elegant, the queen-size bed covered in a beautiful comforter of burgundy, teal and gold that matched the long drapes at the windows. Iron wall sconces with candles burned a delicate scent of vanilla throughout the room. She looked at the older woman. "Did you decorate it?"

Norah shook her head. "Heavens, no."

"The room definitely has a woman's touch," she commented.

"Logan hired a decorator to redo the entire house. He didn't want anything here to remind him of his ex-wife."

Melissa's gaze snapped to Norah's. "*His ex-wife?* Logan was married?" she asked, breathless.

"Only for about a year from what I've heard. He

doesn't mention her very often, well, truthfully, pretty much never."

"When was he married?"

"I believe he got divorced about ten years ago."

Logan had married someone else.

Pain sliced through her. That meant he'd met and married someone shortly after she'd left Royal. Or worse, was he seeing someone else when he was dating her?

Oh, God.

Balling her hands into fists, Melissa fought back waves of heartache. He hadn't loved her after all. He'd wanted this ranch desperately enough to ask *her* to marry him. When she'd left, he hadn't wasted time finding another woman to take her place.

She'd always thought that she'd been right about Logan's motives for proposing, but over the years doubts had plagued her. Having her beliefs confirmed shouldn't have hurt her, but it did.

The bastard!

Who was the woman he'd married? Where had he met her? And more importantly, when?

"I hope you'll be comfortable here. The bathroom is through there. It's completely furnished with toiletries, but if you need anything at all, please press this button." She pointed to an elaborate intercom system on the wall.

"Thank you." Numb, Melissa watched Norah leave. All Melissa wanted was this night to be over. And to sleep. Tomorrow would be a long, difficult day. She'd need her wits about her when she saw Logan again.

If he continued to pressure her, she had a few questions for him—ones she was sure he wouldn't want to answer.

She wasn't too sure she wanted to hear what he had to say, either.

Setting her bag on the bed, she searched through it for the clothes she'd worn during the day—a pair of black slacks and a blue silk blouse. She'd need to wear those tomorrow. Perhaps the first order of business in the morning would be shopping for some clothes and shoes.

Spotting her nightgown, she pulled it out and tossed it across a pillow. Restless, she paced across the room and glanced out the window. Her room was situated at the front of the house and she could clearly see the nearby cottages. Why had he chosen to install her in his home?

To embarrass her? To make her feel uncomfortable? Well, he'd accomplished both.

Feeling edgy, Melissa walked over to the bed. At this rate she wasn't going to get an ounce of sleep. She needed a book or a newspaper, something to take her mind off seeing Logan again, sleeping in his house. Then she remembered seeing some magazines in his living room when she'd passed it earlier. Hoping she could find the way, she went in search of it.

A few minutes after leaving her room, she'd gotten turned around and wasn't even sure where the living room was, but she passed by what looked to be Logan's study and noticed a few magazines on a table. Stepping inside, she picked one up and thumbed through it. She was turning to leave when she was startled by Logan's voice.

"I didn't expect to see you again until morning."

Melissa dropped the magazine to the floor. "I'm sorry. I didn't realize you were in here." He must have been sitting in his chair with his back to her. Darn!

Logan watched her pick up the magazine and straighten. "Somehow I figured out on my own that you hadn't come looking for me."

"I couldn't sleep, no thanks to you."

Logan stood. "You're annoyed."

Fire flashed through her eyes. Annoyed? No, she was angry that he'd professed to love her, only to marry another woman shortly after she'd left. "I don't like being manipulated."

"All I did was offer you and your coworkers a place to stay." Despite Melissa's terse tone, Logan couldn't take his eyes off her. Even mad at him, she was beautiful. He'd dreamed of seeing her again, but he'd never allowed himself to believe she might one day be in his house. To have her here brought a wealth of emotions to the surface. Frustration. Hurt. Anger.

And desire.

She clutched the magazine to her. "Don't, Logan."

"Don't what, sweetheart?" he asked, shoving his hands in his pockets.

"Make light of what you've done."

"Meaning?"

"Using our situation of being without a hotel room to install me in your house. Or should we start where you approached me at the ball? Take your pick," she told him, still angry with him.

Logan walked over to her. "I thought I was doing you a favor."

She held up her hand. "It won't work. You're not going to make me feel guilty about leaving."

He stepped closer until only inches separated them. "You're the one who brought it up this time, Melissa. Maybe you do feel guilty. Care to talk about it?"

"No." At his nearness, Melissa swallowed hard. He was too near. Too dangerous. Too tempting. She stepped back. "I think I better leave."

"Really?" he murmured, his voice hoarse. Logan closed the distance between them and slipped his hand behind her neck, his fingers inching into her hair. He wondered how, after she'd left him, he could feel anything more than pain. But he couldn't deny that he wanted to kiss her.

Melissa pressed her hands against his chest. "Yes." She lifted her face to his, stared into his eyes, refused to back down.

"Did you ever think about me, about what we had together?"

Sensations of awareness coiled through her as he watched her, his gaze intense. "No."

"You're lying." Logan ran his thumb over her bottom lip, wanting more than ever to taste her. But he'd be foolish to get involved with her again. She'd proven to him once that she couldn't be trusted with his heart. "When the time is right, you'll admit it. I can promise you that." With every ounce of willpower he had, he let her go and went to the door.

"Logan." Melissa waited for him to look at her. When he did, her knees went weak even as her confidence returned. "Don't push me," she said boldly. "You might not like what you hear."

Without answering, he walked out, leaving her wondering what would have happened if he'd kissed her. Would kissing him have proven that she was over him? Or, God forbid, would it have reawakened feelings for him she'd buried deep inside?

She began to pace. How was she going to stay in his house and be able to keep her emotions under lock and key? Every time he came near her, every time he touched her, she wanted to know what it would be like to taste him again. The longer she stayed, the more difficult it would be to keep him at arm's length.

And that's what she wanted, no *needed,* to do.

As Melissa returned to her room and put on her nightgown, she decided that tomorrow she'd focus on gathering information for her story. Once she covered all aspects of it, she'd leave Royal, and Logan, behind.

This time forever.

In his bedroom, Logan stripped off his clothes and took a cold shower. It did little to take his mind off the woman sleeping across the hall. Having Melissa walk back into his life had disrupted his otherwise placid life.

He was the one who had orchestrated getting her here to his home so if he lost a night's sleep obsessing about her, he had only himself to blame. What *had* he been thinking? Their past relationship and subsequent breakup should have warned him to stay away from her.

When she'd broken up with him and left town, he'd been hurt and disappointed and disheartened. She'd never given him the chance to talk to her. Why? He'd been foolish enough to believe she loved him. But a better opportunity clearly had come her way and she'd grabbed it without even thinking about him.

He'd been in a well of pain, given to feeling sorry for himself until eventually, feeding on the need to survive without her, he'd pulled himself together enough to think about the ranch.

Then he'd met Cara through his brother, Bart. Attractive and provocative, she'd stroked his ego. Before he knew what hit him, he was knee-deep involved with her. When she began talking about getting married, Logan hadn't taken her seriously because they hadn't been dating very long. But then, he'd thought, he hadn't known Melissa long, either, and he'd wanted to marry her.

But Cara had kept talking about marriage and he warmed to the idea. He cared for her, and they'd enjoyed being with each other.

Though he could honestly say he'd tried, his relationship with Cara hadn't worked out. She hadn't been any happier on the ranch than Bart had been. While Logan and Cara had gotten along well when dating, they'd argued often during their marriage. Finally, Logan hadn't been able to take it any longer. When he'd asked her for a divorce, she hadn't fought him. It was only after she'd left that he'd faced the truth—he hadn't loved her.

Not like Melissa.

Half aroused from thinking about her sleeping across the hall, he threw his damp towel on the bathroom vanity, went into his bedroom and climbed into bed. As he lay down, he interlaced his hands under his head and stared at the ceiling.

Was he a fool to have brought Melissa here? He'd thought he'd been smart by keeping her in town to confront her.

And to give himself peace of mind.

So far, at every turn, instead of putting his past with Melissa to rest, she'd stirred up feelings of frustration, anger and awareness.

And lust.

The sex between them had always run hot, the reason he'd become so deeply involved with her. The first time he made love to her, he'd known that what he felt for her was different than for any other woman he'd been with. She'd gotten under his skin.

Now things were different. When she'd left him before, she'd severed any emotional attachment he'd had for her.

Lust he could handle.

His goal in getting Melissa to stay in Royal wasn't about getting her in bed.

As long as he remembered that, his heart was safe.

Four

The next morning, Logan walked in the back door after meeting with his foreman about a new roof for one of the barns. The aroma of bacon and eggs filled the air as he headed to the dining room for breakfast.

He hadn't seen Melissa yet this morning, and after their encounter in his study last night, he half expected her to avoid him.

As he stepped into the kitchen, Norah approached him, the phone pressed to her apron.

"Gavin is on the telephone. He said it was important and he couldn't reach you on your cell."

Logan checked his belt where he usually clipped his cell and realized he'd left it in his room. "Thanks, Norah," he said, accepting the phone, "I'll take it in the study."

Recently elected to the position of sheriff, Gavin O'Neal was well-respected throughout the community. As a member of the TCC, his experience in law enforcement was invaluable. With their property lines next to each other, Gavin and Logan were neighbors as well as friends.

So why was he calling so early?

Dropping into his chair behind his desk, Logan picked up the telephone. "Hey, Gavin."

Gavin's voice drawled across the line, "Morning, Logan."

"What's up?"

"Can you meet at the club this morning?"

At the seriousness of his friend's tone, Logan sat straighter in his chair. "What's going on?"

"I want to discuss the autopsy findings on Jonathan Devlin. As you know, I'm down a few deputies and I may be needing your help with the investigation."

The recent murder of Jonathan Devlin, the town's main historian, had everyone concerned. After falling into a coma, he'd been hospitalized. In the days prior to his death, he'd begun showing signs of improvement and the doctors cautiously had believed he would recover.

Instead, he'd died of a sudden heart attack.

An ornery man, Jonathan hadn't been especially liked by the community. The circumstances of his death were peculiar, so an autopsy had been performed.

"I've already talked to Jake, Thomas and Connor," Gavin said. "I'll call Mark as soon as I hang up with you."

Logan glanced at his planner. "What time do you want us there?"

"Ten-thirty."

"I'll be there." Logan disconnected the line.

Grimacing, he stood and left the study. What had Gavin found? From his hard tone, it couldn't be good.

Logan arrived in the dining room to find Daniel and Rick across from each other at the table already eating.

Rick looked up. "Hi, Logan. We were going to wait for you, but Norah insisted that we start eating while the food was hot."

"I'm glad you did. I had a call I needed to take." He sat at the end of the table nearest them. "Where's Melissa?" Logan hadn't meant to ask, but the words had just spilled out of his mouth. Annoyed with himself, he buttered a piece of toast, then added some eggs and bacon to his plate.

"Haven't seen her yet," Rick said.

Logan raised an eyebrow. When he'd dated her, she usually had been out of bed before him. "Not a morning person?"

"Are you kidding?" Daniel took a sip of his coffee, made a grunt of approval, then took another sip. "She's usually the first one into work every day."

Chewing his food, Logan found that interesting. It could only mean one thing. Melissa *was* in her room avoiding him. Well, if she thought she'd wait him out, she was in for a surprise.

He wasn't going anywhere until he saw her.

The scent of bacon and eggs hit Melissa as she left her room the next morning. The thought of eggs made her stomach roil. She'd settle for a cup of coffee and a piece of toast. She'd hardly slept at all, and she wasn't in the greatest of moods. It had nothing to do with her conversation with Logan last night. Nothing to do with being tempted to kiss him.

Nothing to do with sleeping only a few rooms away from him.

Today she would borrow Daniel's car to run some errands. Before she did any additional investigation on her story, she needed to buy some clothes.

Her steps faltered as she entered the dining room and saw Logan. He was sitting at a large walnut table, a cup of coffee in his hand. Daniel and Rick also were seated at the table.

"Good morning, everyone. I was hoping to find a cup of coffee."

Logan looked up at her approach. "Have a seat. I'll pour you some."

She saw the coffee urn on the table and reached for it. "Thanks, Logan, but please don't get up. I can do it," she said without looking at him.

"Morning, Melissa," Daniel said.

Rick finished a bite of his food, then swallowed. "Hey, Melissa."

With her cup full, she pulled out a chair and sat down, thankful that Rick and Daniel were seated next to Logan and she didn't have to sit near him. She added sugar and cream to her coffee, then looked up at Daniel. "I'd like to borrow your car for a while this morning. I have some errands to run. I also need to head over to the museum and check out the Halifax exhibit, get the details on what happened with the vandalism."

Daniel shook his head. "Sorry, Melissa, but my plans have changed. As much as I was looking forward to staying here for a few days, I have to head back to Houston."

Melissa's hand froze in the middle of reaching for a piece of toast. "What? Why?"

"Jason called this morning. There's a story breaking in Houston about busting a drug ring."

"Then we're leaving," she concluded.

"I am," he clarified. "I'm leaving you and Rick here to work on the Jessamine Golden story and how it might tie in with the Halifax exhibit."

"Are you sure you want to go there, Daniel?" she asked, trying one last time to dissuade him. "There's probably nothing to it. So far, no one even knows what it means. And the map is hardly worth mentioning."

Daniel picked up his cup, then paused before taking a sip. "Stay on it. The appearance of the map is interesting enough to follow. And I want more about the historical mystery." He nodded. "Contact me when you've finished your first segment on the ball and the Halifax exhibit."

Frustrated, she set down her coffee. "I'll work on it. I hope the mystery surrounding Jessamine Golden doesn't disappoint you."

"It's going to go over big. I just know it. A lot of wealthy, influential people live here. Who knows who could be involved?" He sat back in his chair and looked at Logan with gratitude. "Well, I've gotta run. I can't thank you enough for your hospitality, Logan." He stood and extended his hand. "Don't get up. I'll see myself out."

"You're welcome anytime." As Daniel left, Logan

glanced at Melissa, who didn't look at all pleased that her producer was leaving her in Royal. From the cold shoulder she'd been giving him, he had a feeling she was eager to avoid him. More determined than ever to pin her down, he said, "I can give you a lift into town, Melissa." Being alone with her in the car would be the perfect opportunity to question her. She couldn't avoid answering him there.

"I appreciate it, Logan, but Rick will still be here. I'll ride in with him."

Rick stuffed the last of his bacon into his mouth, chewed it, then swallowed. "Logan said I could hang around the ranch this morning and take a look at his operation."

She stared at him with disbelief. "What?"

He shrugged his shoulders. "C'mon, Melissa. You're not going to be shooting this morning, are you?"

"Well, no, but—"

"Then you don't really need me. The ranch foreman's already agreed to let me tag along with him for a while."

"I have a meeting at the Cattleman's Club so I'm going into town anyway," Logan cut in. "You might as well ride with me."

Melissa finished the last of her coffee. This wasn't working at all the way she'd planned. The last thing she wanted was to spend more time in Logan's company. Why? she asked herself. Because she didn't trust Logan? Or because she didn't trust her own feelings for him? "Thanks anyway, but I can take Rick's truck."

"If you take my truck, then later want me to meet you, I won't have any way to get there," Rick told her.

"All right," she said, accepting her fate. "But keep your cell phone with you in case I need you." Fine. She'd ride into town with Logan. Maybe after she poked around a little at the museum, she'd learn that the vandalism of the exhibit was merely a prank. If so, she'd write a conclusion to her story and leave Royal by tomorrow.

And say goodbye to Logan. Again.

Logan's pickup rocked as he hit a pothole on the back road before turning onto the main highway and heading toward Royal. "Do you plan to remain silent the entire ride?" He glanced at Melissa. "Or do you plan to talk to me?"

Melissa looked up from her reporter's notebook. "I'm not ignoring you. I'm thinking about the story I'm working on." She went back to flipping through the pages. If she were inclined to talk, she'd demand to know who he'd married. Which she could never do because it would seem as if she were interested in him. Which she wasn't. Really.

Still, it grated on her nerves to know he'd married within months of her leaving. His actions only solidified her reason for breaking up with him. He'd needed a wife to secure his inheritance. It hadn't mattered who the woman was.

Old hurt coiled through her as she recalled the day she'd found out why he'd proposed. She'd run into a friend from school, Cara Young, who had been dating Logan's brother, Bart. Cara had revealed that the terms of their father's will dictated that the first of his sons to marry would inherit the ranch.

Because he didn't want the ranch, Bart had refused to marry Cara to get it. He'd told her that he and Logan had made a deal. Logan would marry Melissa, thereby securing the ranch, then he'd buy out Bart's portion. Cara had been furious.

Crushed and betrayed, Melissa hadn't wanted to believe Cara. But she'd thought about Logan's words right after he'd proposed.

I'll have everything I've ever wanted, Melissa. I'll have you and the Wild Spur.

The truth had been right there for her to hear. She had been too in love with Logan to see it. So she'd done the only thing she could to save her self-respect. She'd given Logan his ring back and left town, using her desire to be a reporter as the reason she'd changed her mind about marrying him.

Did he really want to dredge all that up?

Glancing at him, Melissa noticed his taut jaw, his white knuckles as he gripped the steering wheel. This certainly wasn't going to be a pleasant experience if they couldn't be civil with each other. She'd probably be with him for only a few days at the most. How hard could it be?

"I appreciate your giving me a lift into town."

"Where do you want to go first?" Logan asked, deciding not to press her now. They'd be in town in a few minutes. When he talked to her, he wanted time on his side.

"Shopping."

Her response evoked a grin from him and lightened his mood as he thought about the times they'd gone shopping together. "You always did like clothes." And she'd looked damn good in whatever she wore. Even better when she was naked. He stole a look at her, letting his gaze drift over her breasts. Though she was still thin, her body had gentle curves and swells that were hard to ignore. He dragged his eyes back to the road.

"I can't very well wear these same clothes every day that I'm here," she said, feeling the need to defend herself because he probably hadn't forgotten how much she loved shopping. He used to go with her often.

"I was just teasing you."

"Oh, gee, I missed that."

"You can walk around naked for all I care."

Her eyes widened. "Logan!"

Thinking about her naked sent all kinds of erotic images through his mind. Ever since she'd arrived, Logan had been fighting the desire to kiss her. Though he'd started this, he needed to clear his thoughts. Otherwise he would be very uncomfortable for the remainder of the ride into town—and the rest of the day. "All right. Do you want to go to the museum after you shop?"

She watched him warily. "Yes. I think that's the best place to start investigating the vandalism of the Halifax exhibit."

"I don't know how long my meeting will be. I'll drop you downtown, then come back and pick you up."

"Thanks." She turned to a fresh page in her notebook and jotted down her phone number, then she ripped out the page and handed it to him. "This is my cell number. Call me when you're on your way and I'll let you know where I am."

He stuffed it into his front shirt pocket. "I shouldn't be too long."

She turned a little in her seat to face him. "As a long-time resident, why do you think anyone would vandalize the Halifax exhibit?"

He shrugged. "Beats me. Maybe someone's just trying to tarnish Gretchen Halifax's name. Could be someone doesn't want her to win against Jake for mayor," he speculated.

Her brows dipped in thought. "Do you think she *will* win?"

"It's hard to say. Jake is a strong candidate. He's a local businessman and he's well liked in the community."

By his tone, Melissa read into what he hadn't said. "And Gretchen Halifax isn't?"

"I didn't say that, but, truthfully, I don't know her that well. She comes across as very ambitious. I guess that's not always a bad thing."

Intrigued, Melissa jotted some notes on her pad. "Does she have any secrets?"

"None that I know of." He had a gut feeling there was more to her, but with nothing solid to go on, he didn't speculate further.

"Does Jake Thorne?"

At her focused, intelligent questions, Logan let his gaze drifted over her feminine features. She was a beautiful woman, but he'd always known there was more to Melissa than her appearance.

He looked back at the road as he turned onto the street leading to the center of town. "No. He's running against Gretchen because he feels her platform on tax reform may have a negative effect on local businesses in Royal."

"What about you? Do you think Jake is a better candidate for mayor, or as a businessman, is he protecting his own interests?" Melissa knew he was one of Logan's close friends. Did his loyalty to Jake make him blind to his flaws?

Logan's mouth tightened. "Jake is as upstanding as you get."

Melissa had to stop herself from grinning. Obviously she was right. Jake was Logan's friend, and Logan was loyal to a fault.

Except with you.

Melissa tamped down on her feelings of resentment and tried to keep her focus on her story. "I wasn't suggesting that he wasn't," she replied, softening her tone. "I'm just trying to find out what's going on."

"Right." Just like he was trying to find out why she'd left. And eventually he would. He just hoped he wouldn't be sorry when he did. He tabled his thoughts as he pulled up to a curb in the upscale shopping district. "My meeting shouldn't take more than an hour or two."

She reached for her door handle. "I'll be ready when you are."

"You don't have to rush."

"Thanks." Melissa got out of the truck, then gave him a wave. Maybe she didn't have to rush shopping, but she did have to rush to get this story done so she could return to her life in Houston.

So far today she'd avoided any further personal discussions with Logan. She didn't expect her luck would hold out, though, not with the looks she'd been getting from him. Or the innuendos.

Still, the question of his marriage burned in her mind. Maybe talking with him would be worth the pain if she forced him to admit the truth. Maybe she'd leave Royal this time with her mind clear of Logan Voss.

And her heart.

Logan pulled to a stop in the parking lot of the Texas Cattleman's Club just as Connor Thorne, Jake's brother, got out of his car. Unlike Jake, who was outgoing and easy to know, Connor was on the quiet side. Though his hair was cut short the way he'd worn it when he'd served as an army Ranger, he'd resigned his commission to return home and run the family's engineering business. Connor didn't talk about his reasons, but Logan suspected something had happened to cause him to give up his chosen career.

"Hey, Connor," Logan called as he got out of his truck and met him in front of the club. They exchanged pleasantries, then Logan said, "It looks like Jake, Mark and Tom Morgan have already arrived." He gestured toward their vehicles.

Connor nodded. "Yeah. Now we're only waiting for Gavin."

Together they entered the club and went to a private room in the rear. Moments later, Gavin walked in and everyone but the sheriff seated themselves around the large conference table.

"I'm glad you all could make it," Gavin stated. He took off his hat and dropped it on the table. He looked at every man in the room, his gaze pausing briefly on each. "Since I'm down a few deputies I could use your help."

"Anything we can do," Logan said. The rest of the men voiced their agreement.

"As you know, Jonathan Devlin was murdered." All of the men nodded. "Until I made headway into the investigation, I've kept the results of the autopsy confidential, even from the family, because I don't know who was involved."

"And now?" Logan asked.

"The investigation is snowballing."

Jake was the one who asked the question on all of their minds. "So how was Jonathan Devlin killed?"

Gavin released a sigh. "Lethal injection."

"What was in it?" Tom asked, leaning forward.

Logan understood Tom's interest. Recently, Tom had learned that Jonathan was his great-grandfather. Adopted at birth, it wasn't until after his mother died that Tom had returned to Royal in search of his family.

Meeting Jonathan must have been an eye-opener. The man had had a reputation of being difficult and he'd ruled his family with an iron fist. There was no telling who had murdered him.

"Potassium chloride," Gavin told them. "Which is why it looked as though he died of cardiac arrest."

"Did they find any needle marks on him?" Connor asked.

The sheriff tapped his fingers on the table. "No. We believe it was given to him through his intravenous drip."

"Then the killer got to him in the hospital." Logan voiced what they were all thinking.

"That's a fair assumption, but so far there's no proof. My main focus at this time is hospital staff members, anyone who has worked there in the past year and family members who could have had a grudge against him."

"Do you have any leads?" Tom asked.

Gavin sighed. "More than my men and I can handle. I don't like the idea of a killer running loose in our town. We're following up the leads as quickly as we can."

Jake rested his elbows on the conference table. "How about suspects?"

Gavin pulled out a chair, turned it around and straddled it. "No one solid. I went out to Jonathan's house, but found nothing significant to his murder."

"Anything else?" Logan asked.

"Not yet. We're still analyzing evidence and hoping something will turn up to lead us to the killer."

"What about one of the Windcrofts?" Jake asked. "They've been fighting with the Devlins for more than a hundred years over whether Nicholas Devlin cheated Richard Windcroft out of half of his land in a poker game."

"But their feud has never led to murder," Connor reasoned out loud.

"Except when Nicholas was shot," Tom offered. "My family still talks about it. They believe a Windcroft was responsible."

"But why would a Windcroft want Jonathan dead?" Gavin asked. "What would they gain?" He shook his head. "I don't know. It just doesn't add up."

Mark crossed his arms over his chest. "Okay, let's take this in another direction. What about the appearance of the map? Jonathan lived in the same house as Jessamine Golden did. If someone really believes she engineered a gold heist, they might have been after something in the house."

Connor nodded. "Like the map."

"But the map only turned up when Opal Devlin began cleaning out Jonathan's things," Logan pointed out.

Tom rubbed his knuckles against his chin. "Maybe someone already knew about the map's existence."

"Say someone *was* after it," Mark speculated. "Without knowing if the map is authentic, who would want it bad enough to kill Jonathan?"

Connor sat forward. "How about Malcolm Durmorr?" he suggested. "He's related to the Devlins, but he's never been welcomed into the family fold and he's been on the wrong side of the law more than once."

"Could be him, but hell, with the map made public and on display at the museum, it could be anyone who believes it might lead to a treasure of gold bars. There's something else." Logan dreaded this part because he knew his friends were going to get on his case about a reporter staying at his ranch. "Melissa Mason, the reporter from WKHU in Houston, is staying at my ranch and is doing a story on Royal's celebration and history. She's planning to mention the map in her feature. When it airs, every kook within a thousand-mile radius will be after it."

"Another reason I need your help," Gavin stated. "As I've said, the Devlin murder case is keeping me busy. Aaron Hill at the Heritage Society Museum would like some assistance safeguarding the map. I suggested the TCC handle the duty since my department is short on manpower. Can I count on you to keep the map secure and do some discreet investigating on Jonathan's murder? Use your own contacts and report back to me if you find anything that could be connected to it."

Logan nodded. "You got it."

Tom gave Logan a contemplative look. "Melissa Mason is quite a looker. How are you standing it having her under your roof?"

Jake chuckled. "Yeah, Logan. Hell, I want to know how you managed to get her out to your ranch."

"If I'd known she needed a place to sleep, I would have offered her a bed," Connor stated, then quipped, *"Mine."*

All of the men laughed—except Logan. He didn't find Connor's comment amusing. The thought of Connor sleeping with Melissa irked him. "She's not available."

At his gruff tone, Mark's eyebrows shot up. "Oh, is that the way the wind blows?"

"Don't go reading anything into it. She's planning to return to Houston as soon as she finishes her report here." Logan stood, cutting off any further discussion about Melissa. "When Gavin has more news, we'll meet back here and discuss any action we need to take. In the meantime, let's keep a watch out for anything unusual."

Five

Having called Melissa to let her know he was on his way, Logan pulled up to the curb in front of the same department store where he'd left her. Though he'd told her not to rush, she'd assured him she'd finished shopping and was ready.

As he opened his truck door and got out, he spotted her walking toward him, her arms loaded with packages of all shapes and sizes, several full shopping bags hanging from her hands. Walking around the vehicle, he relieved her of most of the packages.

"Have fun?" he asked. It looked as if she'd bought out the store. Logan opened the tailgate and deposited her items inside.

"Actually, yes." Her eyes sparkled with excitement. With her busy schedule, she rarely had time to shop.

More often than not, she would run into a store for a specific item. The couple of hours that Logan had been gone had passed rather quickly, but she was surprised at what she'd managed to buy.

She'd also used the time to put her feelings for Logan into perspective—or rather, to face her attraction to him. It was there every moment he was near her, that breathless feeling of anticipation.

When she'd been young and naive, she'd loved him with all of her heart so it only made sense that she still had feelings for him buried inside. Denying her obvious attraction toward him would only make her stay here harder. From her earlier response to his touch, Logan knew it, too.

What she'd do about them remained to be seen.

Daniel had accused her of being a workaholic. He was right. It was the way she protected herself. Work had provided a perfect excuse not to become involved with the men she'd dated.

Why should she? She'd never felt that rush, that endless excitement that should accompany intimacy.

Because those men hadn't been Logan.

And because Logan had hurt her, she'd been afraid to open her heart to anyone else.

Seeing Logan again stirred up yearnings for him that had lain dormant. Even though she'd promised herself she could handle her attraction to him, with him close enough to touch, her entire body tensed as if bracing itself.

How did he have the power to do that to her after all these years? Disconcerted, she handed the rest of her packages to him and he put them in the truck along with the others.

Closing the tailgate, Logan turned to her. "Ready to go to the museum?"

"Yes, I'm anxious to get a look at the Halifax exhibit." And to get away from him. The man had an effect on her that should be outlawed.

"Melissa—" Logan started, then heard someone call his name and straightened. He saw Gretchen Halifax coming across the street toward them, her stride purposeful. Though not especially pleased to see her, he was grateful she'd interrupted his errant thought of acting on his attraction to Melissa.

"Hello, Logan," Gretchen said, stopping in front of them. "It's good to see you." She shifted toward Melissa with an engaging smile.

"This is Councilwoman Gretchen Halifax," Logan said by way of an introduction. "Gretchen, Melissa Mason. She's a reporter from Houston. She's doing a series of reports on Royal's anniversary."

"It's nice to meet you," Melissa said, shaking Gretchen's hand. Impeccably dressed from head to toe, Gretchen projected a professional image that few could find fault with. Melissa had noticed the councilwoman last night at the celebration gala. She'd intended to strike up a conversation with Gretchen, until Logan had cornered her and thrown her whole night into chaos.

"I'd heard there was a reporter in town. It's a pleasure to meet you. Our town appreciates your interest. Your stories are bound to draw more visitors to boost our economy."

"Thank you."

"Logan, the ball last night was delightful. Miss Mason, I do hope you were there and enjoyed it."

Melissa had a feeling Gretchen knew specifically that she'd attended and was fishing for details of her and Logan's encounter. Few people could have missed the exchange between them on the dance floor and their quick departure from the room. "Yes, I was there with some of my coworkers. We had a wonderful time."

"I'm glad to hear that. We want you to feel right at home here. How long are you going to be in town?"

Smiling politely, Melissa replied, "For a few days."

Irritation touched Gretchen's face, then she quickly recovered and pasted on her smile. "I'd be happy to do an interview with you if you'd like. I'm running for mayor."

"Yes, I know. I'll keep that in mind," Melissa replied, not at all interested in promoting Gretchen Halifax's political ambitions. Obviously Gretchen was trying to cash in on some free publicity. It was rare for Melissa not to like someone on introduction. Gretchen held herself in a regal way, strived to appear cordial, but Melissa's investigative reporting had honed her skill at reading people. The woman's eyes revealed her to be clever and ambitious.

"Great. I'll look forward to hearing from you." Gretchen turned to Logan. "I wanted to talk to you about the map found with Jessamine Golden's saddlebag."

Logan shifted his stance, curious as to why she was interested. "What about it?"

"Do you think it's wise to have the map displayed at the Historical Society Museum indefinitely?"

"It belongs to them, and it's under lock and key," he reminded her.

"Yes, but with what happened to my ancestor's exhibit, it might not be safe there." To Melissa she added, "Edgar Halifax was my great-great uncle, the first mayor of Royal."

Melissa forced a patient smile. "Yes, I know."

"I think it'll be fine," Logan assured Gretchen, but he couldn't help wondering what she was up to. Her concern about the map intrigued him.

Melissa touched Logan's arm. "I was planning to ask if I could use the map for my story, display it where the camera can get a clear shot of it."

With a sniff of disapproval, Gretchen tilted her chin up and gave Melissa a patronizing look. "That's not a good idea, Miss Mason. The map may be valuable. Left out in the open, someone could steal it."

Logan stiffened at Melissa's side. "The director of the museum has asked the members of the Cattleman's Club to safeguard it."

The councilwoman's lips thinned to a line. "I'll be happy to secure it in my safe."

"I'll talk to the members of the club and we'll get back to you, Gretchen, but I don't think that'll be necessary." Logan's tone was firm.

"I'm just trying to help," Gretchen declared, her tone turning slightly brusque.

"And we appreciate it." He gave her a nod. "I'll be in touch."

With a tight smile, Gretchen said goodbye and strode away, her heels tapping sharply on the sidewalk.

Melissa released a slow sigh, then realized she was still holding Logan's arm. He looked at her at that moment, and she pulled away. "Sorry," she mumbled.

He shook his head. "That woman is something else."

"She has quite an overwhelming presence, doesn't she?" Melissa remarked. "Why do you think she was so interested in holding onto the map?"

"No idea," Logan answered. "She could be concerned about preserving the town's history as part of her platform."

"Probably."

He opened the passenger door of his truck and waited for her to get in, then went around and climbed behind the wheel. After merging into traffic, he headed out of town toward the museum.

"How did your meeting go?" she asked, curious to know what he and his friends had talked about at the club. She'd asked around about the Texas Cattleman's Club. Some people had suggested it was a social club where the men could go for conversation and relaxation. But when she'd lived in Royal she'd heard rumors that the club was some sort of secret organization of men who performed dangerous missions, solved crimes and ran rescue operations.

It was a silly notion, of course. It wasn't as though they were superheroes. But she did wonder about Logan's involvement.

"The meeting went fine," Logan replied, not revealing what he'd discussed with his friends. Melissa would find out soon enough about Jonathan's murder. For now, he'd keep it under his hat, use it as leverage to keep her involved in reporting from Royal if she made noises about leaving.

"Really?"

Her inquisitive expression sent a warning to him. "Yes."

"Hmmm."

Not sure he really wanted to know, but curious as to the direction her mind was going, Logan asked, "What's that 'hmm' for?"

"Who else was there?" she asked, ignoring his question.

Logan shrugged. "A few of my friends."

"Such as…" Melissa waited for him to fill her in.

"Jake Thorne and his brother, Connor."

"Jake, who's running for mayor against Gretchen, right?"

"Yes."

"And what does Connor do?"

"He runs his family's engineering firm."

"Ah. And who else was there?"

Studying her, he said, "You sure are full of questions." He began thinking he was treading on dangerous ground. It wouldn't do for Melissa to know too much about the club or its operations. As far as the public was concerned it was an ordinary club.

"Just curious." She smiled.

"Right." The force of her smile hit him all the way to his heart. He'd always loved her shapely mouth, her tempting, kissable lips. After all these years, he still remembered her taste. Hot, sweet—and capable of driving a man to his knees, begging for more.

"I *am* a reporter," she reminded him.

Logan hadn't forgot that. She'd be leaving within a week or so, as soon as she'd finished her story. "From what I've heard you're good one." Her smile grew wider, reminiscent of the younger woman he'd loved.

"Don't try to sidetrack me with a compliment." His comment was interesting. Had he been checking up on her? Or had he seen one of her reports?

He chuckled. "All right. Mark Hartman, who is another rancher and runs a self-defense studio in town, Tom Morgan, who's related to the Devlins and owns a demolition business, and the sheriff."

She raised her eyebrows.

He glanced at her, his expression guarded. "What's that look for?"

"Well, you're a busy rancher, right?"

"Yeah, so what?"

"Yet you sneak off in the middle of the day for some kind of meeting at the Cattleman's Club."

He laughed. "I wasn't sneaking. It's broad daylight."

"You know what I mean. What's going on? Why are you meeting with the sheriff?"

He hesitated, taking a moment to decide how to answer her without raising her suspicions. "Gavin's asked us to help out the sheriff's office for a while. With budget cuts and a hiring freeze, he's down a couple of deputies." That much was the truth.

She considered that. "So why you guys?"

To appease his desire to touch her and to throw her off balance, he reached over and toyed with a silky strand of her hair. "Most of our members have a military background."

At Logan's touch, Melissa struggled not to lose track of their conversation. Though his explanation sounded reasonable, his hesitation before he replied made her suspect he wasn't being totally upfront. She started to ask him another question, but they approached the museum. The parking lot was almost half-full.

As Logan parked, she smiled. "The museum looks the same." It made her feel good to know that some things never changed. As a teenager she'd loved visiting the museum. The large, two-story, stately brick building, once the home of prominent landowners, was adorned with four ornate white columns and an array of beautiful flowers and shrubs.

They walked up the wide steps and through the arched doorway. Inside, two circular stairways with decorative wrought-iron railings led to the second floor. Original wood floors creaked under their footsteps as they climbed the stairs. Antique cases displayed artifacts of Royal's history, and visitors roamed from room to room.

"It's busier than it used to be," Melissa commented.

"The museum has become a landmark in Royal. It's one of the most popular places for tourists to visit."

"That's wonderful." She looked around, then turned back toward him. "Do you know where the Halifax exhibit is?"

"This way. Both the Halifax Exhibit and Jessamine Golden's items are on display in the gallery up here." At the top of the stairs, Logan guided her to a large room framed by two arched entrances.

She stood in the middle of the room and turned a complete circle. "This will be the perfect place to do a video." Pointing to the black, iron, Western-style chandelier hanging from the ceiling, she nodded. "And there's plenty of light from the chandelier. I'll have Rick check it out, but I believe this will work nicely. All I'll need is a podium to set the map on."

Her excitement over her job drew his attention. She loved what she did. It showed in her eyes, in her voice when she spoke. She'd already said she was up for a promotion. Melissa was going places, had her career planned out, it seemed.

"This way," he said, his mind sizzling like hot pavement. He showed her the Halifax Exhibit first. "Looks like the vandalism has been removed."

"This exhibit will be barely worth mentioning if I don't have any evidence of the damage."

"Aaron Hill, the museum director, may have some pictures and Gavin may have some crime shots, as well."

"Great. I'd like to see if the sheriff will release copies of the photos to me to include in my report."

They moved to Jessamine Golden's display. "Look at the roses tooled on her saddlebag, Logan," she said quietly. A sense of sadness overcame her that she couldn't explain.

Logan reacted to the trace of wistfulness in her tone. "From what I've heard, the rose was her trademark."

"It must have been. It's on the handles of her guns, too." She drew a quick breath, her heart not quite steady. "And there are rose petals from her purse." Dried petals in muted colors of purple and pink lay scattered about the small, antique purse. "A woman who could shoot and was considered an outlaw, yet she kept rose petals."

Meeting Logan's eyes, her gaze softened at the sentimentality. "The roses must have been from someone she loved." Running her fingers across the glass protecting the items, she ached for the outlaw, a woman who also possessed a soft heart.

Logan reached over and touched her shoulder. "You think so?"

Reeling from his touch, Melissa felt heat rush to her cheeks. "I can't explain it. I just feel it inside." She struggled to maintain her distance from Logan. Clearing her throat, she focused on the display to get her bearings. "Do you think the map is authentic?"

"Authentic is one thing, but accurate is another." Not wanting to, but knowing he should, Logan removed his hand from her shoulder. "The markings are unusual and difficult to understand. It may be useless."

"Unless someone figures it out and uses it to find the treasure."

He shrugged. "Anything's possible."

Studying it, Melissa sighed. "Look at all the hearts on it."

Logan leaned over the display case, which brought him within inches of her. Her gentle lilac fragrance drifted to him, shifting his already active libido into high gear. He steeled himself to ignore his body's urges. If he touched her now, he might do something reckless, such as kiss her the way he'd been wanting to since he'd seen her at the ball. "Yeah," he replied, aware his voice wasn't as steady as he'd like. "But it's anyone's guess as to what the hearts mean."

"It's an interesting design, as if Jessamine made sure

she was the only one who could decipher it." Melissa turned toward him. "Look, Logan, I know I have no right to ask a favor, but with your association with the Cattleman's Club, apparently you have some influence. I really want to use the map in my story."

"When do you think you'll be ready to shoot it?"

"In the next day or so. Do you think you can arrange it?"

Logan shoved his hands in his pockets. "Depends."

"On what?"

"What do I get in return?"

Wary, her eyes narrowed. "What do you want?"

His jaw set, he stared her straight in the eyes. "The truth, Melissa. Why did you leave me?"

Gritting her teeth, she sighed heavily. "That's not fair. You're putting this on a personal level."

Logan shrugged as if he didn't care what she thought. "No one ever said life was fair. You want the map. That's my offer. Take it or leave it."

It took Melissa several seconds to calm down before she could speak. When she did, she surprised herself. "All right." She'd tell him what he wanted to know. But what would happen when she did? Was it possible that she'd been wrong to believe Cara? No, she told herself. Logan himself had confirmed what Cara had told her.

Melissa couldn't have been wrong.

"I'll see what I can do," Logan said, pleased with himself.

"Thanks. I'm going to find the museum director, set up a time to meet with him and ask for permission to film here. I'll be right back."

Logan watched her walk away, mesmerized by the sway of her hips. He sighed. Whether it would bring relief or anguish, finally he'd get what he wanted from her.

They decided to double back to town and stop at the Royal Diner for lunch. Logan had to twist Melissa's arm because she'd wanted to head straight to the ranch and start working on her story. So he'd used hunger as a diversion to keep her with him a while longer.

Foolish, he knew. He was kidding himself. The more time he spent with her, the more he wanted to be with her. Though she'd broken his heart, it was as if the years she'd been gone had melted away. The attraction between them still sizzled. Had all of the work he'd done to get her out of his system been for nothing? He needed peace of mind, not complications.

And Melissa had *complication* written all over every inch of her luscious body.

As they were approaching the door of the diner, Logan was surprised to see Lucas Devlin, a local rancher, leaving.

"Hello, Lucas." Logan shook his hand. He'd deemed Lucas, Jonathan's grandson, as the peacekeeper of the Devlin clan. When trouble started brewing between the Devlins and the Windcrofts, Lucas was the one always willing to listen to both sides of the argument. With good sense and a cool head, he attempted to calm down his family.

"Hi, Logan. How are you?"

"Doing fine. How about you?"

Lucas nodded. "Can't complain."

Logan touched Melissa's arm, then slid his hand behind her back, drawing her forward. "This is Melissa Mason. She's a reporter from Houston. They're doing a story on Royal. Melissa, Lucas Devlin."

Melissa smiled. "Hello. It's nice to meet you."

"The pleasure's mine, Miss Mason." A muscle worked in Lucas's jaw. He turned to Logan. "I hate to keep you if you're busy, but I'd like a few minutes of your time."

"Sure," Logan replied. "What can I do for you?"

"I'm concerned about my grandfather's autopsy findings."

At the sparkle of interest in Melissa's eyes, Logan suggested she have a seat and he'd join her in a few minutes.

Melissa nodded. "Yes, of course."

After Melissa left them, he turned to Lucas. "So word of the autopsy has already reached your family," Logan stated. Gavin's investigation at the hospital must have started rumors flying. It didn't take long for news to travel in the town of Royal.

Lucas nodded. "Now that the autopsy is in, we know he was murdered, but we haven't been told how it happened. Since he was in the hospital, I assume it took place there, but I don't know for sure. I wanted to know if you've heard anything else."

Gavin had made it clear that he wasn't ready to release the autopsy findings to anyone, including the family, until he investigated the circumstances further. Unable to tell Lucas what he'd learned, Logan replied evasively, "There's nothing I can tell you that the sheriff hasn't. He's actively investigating the murder."

Lucas put his hand on his hip. "My family's upset and rightly so."

"Gavin will get to the bottom of things."

"I hope so. He was out to my place asking questions, but said he didn't have anything concrete as yet."

"These things take a while. Be patient and give it some time."

Lucas nodded reluctantly. "All right. Well, I'll let you be on your way." He settled his hat on his head and walked away.

Logan joined Melissa at their table. One glance at her and he could read the questions in her eyes.

Melissa tilted her head with determination. "Okay, what was that all about?"

Six

"Lucas?"

"Yes." Melissa studied Logan with interest. "I get the feeling you know something. Want to fill me in?"

"Let me ask you a question. Do you have enough information for your story?"

"Not yet. I have to work on the Jessamine Golden angle, then compile my notes. Rick and I will come back into town over the next couple of days and go to the library to research the history of the town and the legend of Jessamine, then go to the museum. I still have to interview Aaron Hill."

"And then what?"

She shrugged. "Daniel wants more on Jessamine and the map. Do you know something that's connected to the investigation that you're not telling me?" she asked pointedly, picking up on his elusiveness.

As a reporter, she suspected Logan knew more than he was admitting. As a woman, she hoped he wasn't. If she finished the story in a few days without another lead, she could leave by the end of the week.

For her, it was easier not living in the past. She'd put her love for Logan under lock and key in her heart. It frightened her to think of opening that box. Because leaving Logan while loving him had been the hardest thing she'd ever done.

"I see." Logan thought about that. Although Daniel had assigned her to work on the mystery aspects of the map and the vandalism of the Halifax exhibit, Logan was sure she would try to leave Royal as soon as she could.

Too bad. He was just as determined to see that she stayed. "I may have something that will keep you here a while longer."

Melissa looked at him, her expression serious. "Okay, you've got my attention." All of her journalistic instincts kicked into high gear. Something was definitely going on with the Devlin murder case and Logan was in on it, which probably was related to his secret meeting at the Cattleman's Club this morning. Which was another subject she'd like to investigate. What exactly was that club all about?

"Off the record?"

"All right. Off the record."

"You know about how Jessamine apparently stole that gold, then disappeared, right?"

"Yes, we've talked about that."

He leaned toward her, propped his elbows on the table and folded his arms. "Well, there have been more recent developments than what I told you." Logan relayed the facts Gavin had given him. "Valid or not, someone seems to believe the map leads to the gold, someone who seems willing to kill for it." These new details definitely added to the mystery of Jessamine Golden.

"Why do you think Jonathan didn't use the map himself to look for the treasure?" Melissa asked.

"We don't know that he wasn't doing that. Maybe that's what got him killed," he suggested.

"That's possible. This definitely adds a twist to the story. If there's a killer on the loose, I want to continue investigating."

Logan should have been happy that he'd manipulated Melissa into staying in Royal, but the way she'd said *investigating* made him uneasy. He gave her a stern look. "I don't want you out asking questions that could get you hurt or, worse, killed."

Finding his statement humorous, she bit her lip to keep from laughing. "That's ridiculous, Logan. I'm an investigative reporter. This is what I do for a living."

A muscle worked in his jaw. "I'm not doubting your experience, but until we know what's going on here, you're not going to stick your neck out. Whoever's behind the murder has proven they'll stop at nothing to get what they want."

Her green eyes narrowed. "You can't stop me."

"I don't intend to. I know you have to do your job. But wherever you go, I go," he told her, his tone resolute.

Melissa frowned. "I don't need you watching over me."

His gaze drifted over her. The problem was he liked watching over her. Too much. "Are you ready to order?"

he asked, changing the subject. When she nodded, he signaled the waitress. As Melissa set the menu aside, the fabric of her silk blouse stretched tightly over her breasts, defining them, teasing his imagination.

Yeah, he wanted her, plain and simple. But this time if anything happened between them, she'd be a sweet diversion while she was in town.

He wasn't looking for anything except a good time.

Later, as they drove back to his ranch, Logan stole a glance at Melissa while she talked about her work. He was struck once again by her beauty and the way her eyes darkened with passion telling him about the stories she'd done. She was sharp, intuitive and persistent.

And sexy as hell.

How would it feel to have all that sexual power focused on him?

By settling her in at his ranch, all he'd done was manage to torture himself. He didn't want to be attracted to her, but from the way his heart squeezed whenever he thought of her, he couldn't deny that he felt something akin to what they had shared years ago.

And that was the crux of his problem.

He didn't love her.

No, his feelings had nothing to do with love. Hell, he'd loved her before and it had only brought him heartache. And that was when she'd been young and pretty. Now she was beautiful and intelligent and fascinating, everything a man could want in a woman.

Everything *he'd* wanted.

But she wasn't the same woman now. And he wasn't

the same man. For years they'd lived two completely separate lives. Yes, he still found her attractive, but it didn't mean he wanted to do anything about it.

Logan simply wasn't interested in getting hurt again. He wasn't searching for a long-term relationship. If he wanted sex, he knew women willing to go to bed with him without strings attached.

He tightened his hand on the steering wheel. Who was he kidding? He wanted Melissa all right—wanted to touch her, wanted a chance to feel her beneath him, to feel himself inside her.

"Logan?"

Realizing she'd asked him something, he shook his head to clear his thoughts. "Yeah?"

"Where were you?" Melissa asked.

What could he say? That he'd been fantasizing about kissing her? That he'd been dreaming of stripping her naked and loving her until dawn? Wouldn't that make her day?

"Thinking about Jonathan Devlin and who would have wanted him dead."

"I'd like to talk to Gavin about the investigation."

"So would a lot of other reporters."

"Still, I'm going to call him when I'm in town tomorrow."

Logan shrugged. "It's worth a try," he agreed.

At the ranch, Melissa spent the afternoon compiling her notes and verifying her facts. While the stories about the anniversary of Royal and the vandalism of the Halifax exhibit were interesting, she decided she would use those stories to draw attention to the town's history and the legend of Jessamine Golden.

Having the map displayed while she did her report remained her goal. Maybe she'd been foolish to give in to Logan's ultimatum, but she knew she'd have to face him at some point and discuss their past. He wasn't going to let up until she did. At least now she'd get something she needed while satisfying his need to hash out what had happened between them.

Actually, Melissa was ready to get it over with. Thinking about whether or not she'd made a mistake years ago was exhausting. What if Cara Young had been wrong? What if Logan hadn't tried to use her?

No, he had. Logan's marriage shortly after she'd left was all the proof she needed.

Trying to get her mind off of Logan, she called Daniel to discuss the story. Melissa told him about Jonathan Devlin's murder and the possibility that it was tied to Jessamine Golden's map. She wasn't at all surprised when Daniel instructed her to keep digging to find a clear connection.

After hanging up with Daniel, she went to Rick's cottage. They spent an hour or so discussing their itinerary for the next day and talking about the map at the museum.

Heading back to the house, Melissa wondered if Logan had made the necessary arrangements for them to film the map. But she wasn't able to ask him because it wasn't until dinnertime that she saw him again.

When Melissa walked into the dining room, Logan looked up. "Hi, I'm sorry I kept you," she said.

"You didn't," he assured her. "Where's Rick?"

She chuckled. "He said he was going to a bar to check out the hot cowgirls. His description, not mine," she clarified. Logan was sitting at the end of the table so she took the seat to his right.

Melissa took one look at the starchy foods gracing the table along with the roast beef and green beans—macaroni and cheese and homemade biscuits—and nearly sighed. She loved this kind of meal, but usually kept herself on a more moderate diet. She took a helping of each and decided to enjoy the meal. Buttering a biscuit, she took a bite of it.

"This food is delicious. You know, I usually jog a few days a week at home to combat my indulgences. I should have bought some running shoes while I was in town. Maybe I will tomorrow."

"Speaking of tomorrow, what are your plans?"

She sipped her sweetened iced tea. "Rick and I are going to the museum. If all goes well, we may shoot a segment." She was dying to know about the map. Unable to wait for him to bring it up, she put her fork down and looked at him. "Did you find out if I can use the map in my story?"

"Yeah, it won't be a problem. Mark Hartman will keep an eye on it while you're using it."

She frowned. "Won't you be there to do that?" He'd said he was going everywhere she went. Apparently he hadn't meant it. She should have been pleased by the change in his plans, but couldn't deny feeling a bit disappointed.

Logan finished the last of his meal. "I'll be there."

Looking confused, she asked, "Then why won't you be guarding the map?"

He gave her a direct look. "Because I'll be watching you."

Melissa tilted her head as she thought about his answer. "Me? What on earth for?"

"Because if someone's after the map and you're using it, that makes you a target."

"I don't live in Royal. Why would anyone hurt me?"

He shrugged. "They might not want to hurt you, but if you get in their way, you could be in danger. The map will be out in the open near you so that's reason enough."

"I think you're worrying about nothing."

"Then it shouldn't bother you if I'm there to guard you."

"All right," she conceded. "But you're just wasting your time."

Logan seriously doubted that. Watching her could become his favorite pastime. Definitely a bedroom activity. "Now that you have approval to use the map, it's time you held up your end of the bargain."

Melissa finished the last bite of her meal and wiped her fingers clean with her napkin. "All right. But is there somewhere more comfortable we can talk?"

Logan stood. "We can go into my study."

Getting out of her seat, she preceded him into the hallway. She'd made a deal with him and he'd held up his end of the bargain. Now it was time for her to do the same. Well, that was fine by her. She couldn't wait to hear Logan admit the truth. After they talked, he would regret that he had forced the issue.

Stepping into his study, she looked around. When she'd been in here last night, she hadn't paid attention to the decor. Bookcases lined the wall behind a large wood desk where a computer sat. The brown sofa looked soft and inviting, as did the man-size chair in front of the desk. The faint scent of leather gave the room a masculine appeal.

"Make yourself comfortable," Logan said from behind her as he shut the door.

How was she supposed to do that? Except for the one on the day when she'd broken up with Logan, this was going to be the most difficult conversation she'd ever had.

Choosing one end of the sofa, she sat, then watched Logan move across the room to occupy the other end of it. He leaned toward her, his elbows resting on his knees, his hands clasped together.

Under his direct stare, doubts about her sanity in agreeing to talk with him arose. "I don't know exactly what you want to hear."

"Don't play coy, Melissa. You're too good at what you do to pull that off." She'd done good job of dodging his questions until now.

Her defenses went up. "You were good, too, Logan. Good at fooling me, making me believe you cared about me."

He frowned. "I loved you, Melissa. I thought you loved me until you broke up with me and said you were leaving to become a reporter."

Shaking her head, she said, "That's not why I left and you know it." Melissa had to give it to Logan. He still was trying to pretend that he was innocent of hurting her. Why? What good would it do him? He was the one who wanted to get to the truth.

"What are you talking about?"

She gave a bitter laugh. "You were using me and you know it."

"Using you?" He straightened. Suddenly he had a bad feeling about where this was going.

"I knew about your father's will."

Logan didn't move. How could she have known about his father's will? "What about it?" he asked carefully, panic thrumming through his pulse.

"You wanted to get this all out in the open," she stated harshly. "Tell me about how you asked me to marry you so you could hold on to all of this." She swept the room with her hand.

He felt the blood drain from his face. "I asked you to marry me because I was in love with you."

"Right. And the fact that if you married before your brother the ranch would be yours never played into it?"

He wanted to deny her accusation. Would she believe him if he did? Trying to figure out the best way to explain, he shifted topics to buy some time. "How did you know about the will?"

"So it was true." She didn't want to break down in front of him, didn't want him to know that what he'd done still mattered to her. But it did.

Logan couldn't lie to her. "That I'd get the ranch if I married before Bart did? Yes. But what did that have to do with us?"

Melissa dragged in a breath. Until now, she'd held out the tiniest hope she'd been wrong. Her chest ached at his betrayal. "Everything, Logan. I ran into a friend who had been dating Bart. Right before they stopped seeing each other, he'd told her everything, that you even bragged about beating him to the altar."

"That's not true, Melissa. Bart and I thought it worked out great, you and I getting married. I never bragged about anything to him."

"Really?" she said with sarcasm. "Tell me it's not true that you ask me to marry you to keep the ranch."

"I'll admit that learning about the stipulation changed my thinking, but only about the timetable of our relationship. I wouldn't have asked you to marry me if I hadn't loved you."

"Oh, Logan, I'm not that young, naive girl anymore."

"It's the truth," he persisted, hurt that she doubted him now as well as then. "You left me because you thought I'd marry you to keep the ranch?"

"You said as much to me the night you proposed," she reminded him.

Confused, he shook his head. "What did I say?"

"You said, 'I'll have everything I ever wanted, you and the Wild Spur.' I didn't know what you meant until I heard about the will."

Logan reached out to touch her, then stopped himself when he realized she didn't seem receptive to his gesture. "I don't even remember saying that, Melissa. I just know that I loved you. I did. It was hell when you left me."

Had she misinterpreted the meaning of his words? Melissa wanted to believe him, but her distrust was hard to overcome.

"You loved me so much that you married another woman?" she challenged.

Logan's breath exploded in his lungs. "You know about Cara?" Hell, this was getting worse.

Her eyes speared his. "Cara?" For a moment she couldn't speak as she processed his words, then her heart sank with their meaning. "Cara Young?" When he nodded, she hunched forward and placed her hands over her face, dragging in deep breaths, wishing she was anywhere but there. Why had he been so adamant about dredging up the past when the result was that she'd be hurt even more?

"Melissa?"

Suddenly he felt like scum. Logan had never felt more helpless than at that moment. He wanted to hold her, comfort her, but he held himself back.

Melissa lifted her face and looked at him, her cheeks flushed. "You married Cara Young?"

"Yes, but—"

"Damn you." Her eyes glittered with tears as she stood. "Were you seeing her while we were dating?"

"No!" Logan said. "I swear I wasn't. I didn't even meet her until after you left."

"How could you not have known her? She was dating your brother."

Logan's expression changed to confusion. "She never dated Bart. He knew her, sure. He was the one who introduced us. After a few months of seeing each other, she kept saying that she loved me, that she wanted to get married." He shrugged. "So...we did."

"Let me get this straight, Logan. You loved me. But

after I left, you met Cara, and after a few months when she kept saying how much she loved you, you married her?"

"It sounds bad, I know. I was miserable after you left. On the rebound from you, I married her. It was a stupid thing to do. Our marriage lasted less than a year. I'm sure that she never dated Bart. They were just friends."

Melissa shook her head, confused. Something wasn't right here. "Logan, she dated Bart."

"That's not possible."

"Apparently it was." She released a slow breath. "It was Cara Young who told me about your father's will."

Seven

Logan's eyes glittered with anger. "What?"

"Cara dated Bart. They'd been seeing each other for a while before they broke up."

"That can't be true," he said, his words hot with denial. He had no idea where she'd heard such a thing, but she was mistaken.

"The day I ran into her, Bart had already told her about the will and had broken up with her," Melissa said, her throat dry. "Cara had been so angry at your brother. She said she'd wanted to marry Bart so he'd get the ranch. Then they could sell it and live off the money. But Bart had said he wasn't interested in getting married and he was leaving town as soon as he got his money."

"It's true that Bart wanted only the money, not the ranch." Logan cursed beneath his breath. Everything was beginning to make sense. "If what you're saying is true, she must have told you about the will to get back at Bart. If we broke up, he wouldn't have gotten anything."

Melissa swallowed hard. "I'm telling you the truth, Logan. Cara was really upset that day. She wanted to marry Bart."

"Did she? From the way she came on to me, it seems like she wanted the money even more," he answered soberly. He felt like a fool. Cara had used him.

"Maybe she did. But that doesn't explain why your own brother would have set you up by introducing her to you."

"Yes, it does," he said, aching at the cold actions of his brother. "That's how much he wanted to leave Royal. The only way for him to get the money was to get married, or to make sure I did."

Rising, he paced the room. "When you and I were engaged, he must have figured it wouldn't be long before he got his cash. Knowing he'd be leaving and with Cara pressuring him to propose, he must have ended things with her." Logan should have seen through Cara, but during that time, he'd been blinded by the pain of Melissa leaving.

Melissa looked at Logan. "And when I broke up with you, it messed up Bart's plans."

"Yeah." He gave a bitter laugh. "He wanted his money bad enough to conspire with his ex-girlfriend to get it." Bart always had been selfish, and after he'd left Royal, they rarely had seen each other. As brothers they'd never been close, had never been friends. Now, they never would be.

She stood and walked over to him. "How could he have done that?"

"After my mother died, my father doted on Bart, gave him anything he wanted. Bart was used to having his way. I guess he figured that applied to the money as well."

She touched his arm. "They why didn't your father just leave the ranch to Bart? Why put the stipulation in the will about one of you getting married?"

"Honestly, I'm not sure," Logan answered, baffled. "My father was a difficult man to understand. He didn't talk much, kept a lot inside. I think he knew how much I wanted the ranch, but he loved Bart more. Maybe my father thought it would make Brad grow up and settle down."

"Oh, Logan, I'm so sorry," Melissa said on a soft whisper. Despite what had happened between them, how much it had stung when she'd found out Logan had married another woman, she felt deep sorrow for him. It must have been hard being raised in the shadow of his brother.

"I'm the one who's sorry. Bart ruined what we had together." God, he couldn't believe it. All these years he'd blamed Melissa. Bart had stolen their past together. Anger boiled inside him. If he ever saw his brother again, there wouldn't be enough left of him to think about.

"And Cara Young." She turned toward him. "Leaving you broke my heart. I loved you so much then."

"So you didn't leave for a career?" he asked, his eyes questioning.

She bit her lip, then a moment later said, "No. I just said that to save face. I didn't want you to know how much you'd hurt me."

"I hope you can believe now that I loved you, too."

She shrugged. "I want to." It wasn't easy to give him her trust. Or to let the past go. But the attraction between them...oh, that was something else altogether.

Logan draped his arm around her and pulled her close to him. Giving in to the need to be held by him, she rested her head against his chest with a sigh.

"But you're not sure?" He understood. No matter what she said, it still hurt him that she'd left him.

Looking up at him, she said, "It's hard to believe that you married Cara."

He swallowed past the knot in his throat. "I made a terrible mistake."

"I don't think what happened between us is something we can easily get past. But I want you know one thing." Her heart pounded wildly inside her. "I'm still attracted to you," she said candidly. "Does that count for anything?"

He sighed and the tension left his body. "Oh, yeah, sweetheart. I'm attracted to you, too."

"Let's enjoy what time we have now, Logan." She wasn't staying. They led different lives in different cities. More importantly, she refused to lead her heart into such danger again. But she wanted this moment with him, wanted a chance to rediscover what they'd had together, to learn about the man he'd become.

Though she hadn't said the words, Logan knew what she meant. "I like the way you think," he whispered huskily, then covered her mouth with his.

Melissa sank into his kiss. The feelings she'd kept locked inside were threatening to break loose. Could she stop them? Did she have a choice? Despite the promise she'd made to herself before she came back, she wanted to be with Logan again. Could she indulge in an affair with him and leave with her heart intact?

If she couldn't, was she ready to face the consequences of sleeping with him, then walking away again?

He groaned as she kissed him back and pressed his erection against her. "You always did have that power over me," he whispered. He cupped her breast with his hand, massaged it gently.

Melissa's knees went weak. She licked her lips, tasting him, wanting more than ever to feel his powerful body inside hers.

Logan ran his tongue along her lips, then past her teeth to explore her mouth. Heat exploded through him. Sweet. Tender. Exotic. She sucked on his tongue and he moved his hips in response.

"Should we be doing this here?" she asked quietly when he shifted his attention to her throat. Even as she'd asked the question, her mouth sought his in a heady, explosive kiss that left them both breathing hard.

Logan continued to touch his lips to hers with a nibbling, seductive motion that teased and tempted. "Want to go to my room?"

"Yes," she answered in a desperate sigh. Gliding her hands around his neck, she dragged his mouth down to hers. He nipped her lips with his teeth.

"I've never forgotten your taste," he told her huskily. "Never." He'd tried. Hell, all these years he'd been haunted by it. But Melissa was in his soul. There was a connection between them that separation hadn't erased. "After all this time, I want you in my bed."

All night. And he suspected making love to her all night long wouldn't be enough to atone for years of wanting her.

She took his hand in hers and he led the way through the house to the room across the hall from her own. Once inside, she glanced around. His bedroom was large and masculine, decorated in burgundy and brown with an inviting king-size bed. "This is nice," she said. With a sexy smile, she added, "I really like the bed."

Logan's eyes flashed with desire. "Then come share it with me." He drew her to it, sat and pulled her toward him. She stood before him, her hands on his shoulders as he began unfastening the buttons of her blouse. It fell in a heap to the floor.

Melissa leaned down and kissed him as his hands covered her breasts, moaning softly as he caressed them through her bra. She unfastened his shirt and pushed it off him, then explored his hard-muscled shoulders, his corded neck.

It had been a long time since she'd been with him, but suddenly it felt as though it was only yesterday. There was no pretense, no awkwardness, no hesitancy to give herself to him. Her body was attuned to his and he was an expert at igniting her passion. Continuing to kiss her, he found the catch of her bra. With little effort he released it and she freed her arms. His tongue continued doing wonderful things to her mouth as his hands again found her breasts, his fingers pleasuring her.

"Logan." She held her breath as his mouth moved lower, pressing hot kisses to her throat, her shoulder. Lower and lower until his hot mouth closed over her tight, rigid nipple. A fever began simmering deep inside her as she moaned. Her hands held his neck, pressing him to her.

"You are so beautiful," Logan murmured, then he divided his attention between her nipples, kissing one then the other, laving them with his tongue.

His words, whispered in passion, fueled her desire. "I want you," she told him. Her body was no longer hers. It belonged to him and only he knew how to soothe the delicious ache building inside her.

Lifting his head, he leveled his gaze on her. "I've wanted you ever since I saw you at the ball," he confessed. He lay back on the bed, taking her with him, then he rolled her to her back and stretched out beside her. He unfastened her slacks and skimmed his hand along her warm, velvet skin. His fingers grazed the tuft of hair between her legs. Cupping her, he slipped them between the yielding folds.

Hot. Soft. Wet.

For him.

"You're driving me wild," she whispered. "Come inside me." The words were boldly spoken, a challenge that let him know she was ready for him.

"Woman, you really know how to turn me on."

Her gaze drifted over him, pausing on the bulge in his jeans. Her eyes met his again. "Show me."

Logan left the bed. He hooked his fingers in the waistband of her pants and drew them down over her thighs, removing them along with her heels. As he shed his jeans, he made love to her mouth. She rewarded him with a groan of satisfaction and longing. Her hips rocked back and forth as he caressed between her legs, stroking her slowly, making her ready for him.

It took every ounce of strength for Logan to stop touching her, but he moved his hand up her body to her breast, then whispered, "I'll be right back."

Melissa dragged her eyes open. "Where are you going?"

"I need to protect you."

"Right."

He opened the drawer to the nightstand beside his bed, then returned with a foil packet in his hand. His gaze locked with hers, he stood before her, naked. All of him. All six-foot-three of rugged, muscled man.

All hers.

At least for the moment.

She banished that thought from her mind as he sheathed himself. Melissa's throat went dry, her desire for him intensifying as he moved over her and spread her legs apart, positioning himself.

Wanting to enjoy every single moment of loving Melissa, Logan took it slow, joining their bodies, then withdrawing. Inch by aching inch he filled her, her body stretching to accommodate him. She opened her legs wider, and as he pushed himself fully inside her, he kissed her again and again, building their ecstasy, bringing her to the brink of the ultimate pleasure. Her hips began writhing against his own, and still he made love to her in slow, rhythmic strokes.

"Oh, Logan." Melissa whispered his name, half plea, half demand. He seemed to know intuitively what she wanted, moving faster, plunging deeper into her over and over. Her arms went around him, holding him to her, wanting the rush of heat to last forever.

But it didn't and her release came swiftly. She closed her eyes and gave herself to him completely. Shifting against him, she chased the gratification he promised with each movement of his body inside hers. And then she was falling over the edge of bliss as sensations exploded through her.

She tightened her arms as he pushed even deeper, seeking his own release. When it came, he groaned and his hands gripped her, claiming her as his.

After a few moments, when she could breathe again, Melissa ran her hand along Logan's back. His body was hard, lean, his skin so hot. It felt wonderfully delicious to have the freedom to touch him so intimately.

Logan shifted his weight from Melissa, then held her as he tried to catch his breath. She sighed and moved closer to him, ran her hand along his belly. His muscles clenched at her touch. He'd gone into this with his eyes wide open. He had told himself that he could handle his attraction to her, that he could handle what was happening between them, and come out unscathed.

Now he wasn't so sure—one taste of her and he wanted more.

He forced himself to face facts. Melissa had walked away from him before and she was going to again, this time for another reason. The difference now was that he knew it.

His pulse began to slow and he couldn't stop himself from asking, "Why didn't you talk to me, Melissa?" He had to know in order to put what had happened totally behind him.

She raised her eyelids and looked at him, regretting that she hadn't given him the benefit of the doubt. "I thought I knew the truth after what Cara had said. It pretty much confirmed what you'd said the night you proposed. I was hurt. I was so young, Logan, and you were so…" she smiled "…so male. You knew exactly what you wanted. It was a little overwhelming for me. I should have talked to you. I know that now." She gave a soft shrug. Realizing she'd played a part in their breakup staggered her.

Cara. His gut twisted. How could he wonder why Melissa had listened to Cara's lies? Like a fool, he'd trusted Cara, too. And his brother. "Hell, sweetheart, we both believed her."

She ran her hand along his shoulder, then touched his face. "I thought if you loved me, you'd come after me."

"I did love you." Logan raised himself above her.

She stared into his eyes. "Why didn't you try to find me?"

He swallowed hard. "At first I thought you wanted a career as a reporter and I didn't want to stand in your way."

"At first?"

"I've never been good at this kind of thing, Melissa," he confessed.

She frowned. "What kind of thing?"

"Talking. Sharing what I'm thinking. My mother was gone early in my life and my father wasn't very sociable. Bart and I never got along. I never had anyone to talk to. After some time had passed, it was easier for me to let you go than to deal with why you left."

Melissa reached up and kissed his cheek. "You're getting better at it," she said. "Logan, why didn't you tell me about the will?" she asked, needing to know.

"God, sweetheart, I don't know. I guess somewhere inside I was afraid you'd think exactly what you did, that I was using you."

Which showed he hadn't trusted her feelings for him, Melissa thought. No more than she'd trusted what he felt for her. "I guess we were both young and vulnerable." Now, though together temporarily, they'd both changed.

Except her love for him hadn't faded at all. It was still there, threatening to consume her.

Logan traced her thigh with his finger, running up her rib cage to her nipple. He began toying with it and she sighed sweetly. Aroused, he moved over her, straddling her thighs. Her auburn hair spread out on his pillow and he couldn't get enough of looking at her.

Melissa felt his hardness pressing against her as his mouth took hers on a passionate journey.

Sweet.

Sensitive.

Hot.

Demanding.

Her eyes closed as she arched against him and eagerly responded to his lovemaking. He shifted and his hands found hers. Holding them on both sides of her head, he pushed inside her when she opened her legs for him.

Logan groaned as he ground his hips against hers. "Open your eyes, Melissa. I want to see you come apart for me."

She did and met his burning gaze. His eyes held hers

in a spell as he pushed even more intimately into her. The sensual journey began again, slowly at first, then building in intensity until she could no longer think. Her mind splintered in a thousand pieces as he ground his teeth together and called out her name, taking them both over the cliff of ecstasy.

Within that precious moment, Melissa knew Logan had broken through the barriers she'd erected around her heart.

Melissa stirred and lazily opened her eyes. Morning sunshine peeked through the curtains. She lay in bed with Logan, her body pressed against his. It had been a long time since she'd spent the night with a man, but with Logan it felt so natural.

Their night together had been incredible. Logan had been tender, yet demanding, evoking a response from her that only he was capable of. Melissa had never forgotten how Logan's touch could build her desire for him until she couldn't do anything except feel how perfectly they responded to each other.

It had always been like that between them. And, oh, it was almost devastating to know it still was.

Until now she'd never faced the truth. Moving away from him hadn't purged her love for Logan from her heart. She'd only successfully kept it locked away where she wouldn't have to analyze her feelings.

So where did that leave her?

For the past several years, she'd focused on her career. She'd worked her butt off to move up the ladder of success. Now, this promotion was at her fingertips.

It was what she wanted, right?

She sighed wearily. For the first time, she wasn't sure. Being with Logan was incredible. There had been no feeling that she'd been making a mistake. Here, in his arms, was where she wanted to be.

"What's wrong?" Logan asked, his voice hoarse from sleep. He'd heard Melissa's sigh and alarms went off inside him. Was she regretting sleeping with him?

Melissa turned in his arms until she was facing him. "Nothing."

She smiled, but he saw sadness lingering in her eyes. He suspected she was holding something back, but, not willing to break their fragile bond, he didn't push her. "Are you all right?"

"Oh, yeah." She stretched, then trailed her hand down his chest to his flat stomach. "How about you?"

Logan's hips moved as blood surged through his body. His erection was immediate and intense. His gaze met hers. "Take your hand lower and you'll find out."

She did, and he groaned with pleasure as she stroked him. Leaning closer, she kissed him deeply as her hand continued to explore him. He was hard and smooth, and oh, so hot.

After a moment, Logan clamped his hand around her wrist. "If you don't stop, you're not going to be able to join the party."

"Well, we can't have that, can we?" She made quick work of the condom, then shifted over him, straddling him, taking him inside her.

Logan pushed deeply into her until he was completely surrounded by her feminine heat. "No, sweetheart, we can't." Straining, he held back his release as she began moving her hips. His hands cupped her breasts, massaged her nipples, then skimmed to her back and pulled her to him.

"You feel so good inside me," she murmured, her breathing growing rapid as gratification swiftly changed to an ache so desperate that she thought she'd die if he stopped moving. Her body convulsed as her climax began. "Now, Logan," she cried, and let him take over the rhythm.

Logan's hips rocked faster, until she tightened all around him and cried out his name. His own climax came and, unable to hold back, he joined her in the sweet release, his pleasure deep and intense, overwhelming him. And he knew Melissa had not only eased his desire for her.

She'd eased the ache in his heart.

Eight

Breathing heavily, Melissa lay sprawled across Logan. "I hope you have a drawer full of those." She raised herself up and gave him a teasing look.

Logan grinned at her. "Don't worry. If we run out and you get pregnant, I'll make an honest woman of you."

Although he was joking, his words touched a place in her heart. If she hadn't been so naive ten years ago, she'd already be his wife and maybe they'd have had children. But that could never happen now. "Right. And you'd move to Houston?" She shook her head. "I don't think so."

He propped his arm on the bed and watched her gather her clothes. A tense silence fell between them. Melissa stopped in the process of looking for her bra and faced him. "C'mon, Logan, let's not fool ourselves.

What's happened between us is wonderful, but it can't last. We both know it."

Logan sobered. She'd said the words he'd been thinking ever since they'd kissed last night. He'd told himself that he could live for the moment, that he could be happy being with Melissa—making love to her—even if it couldn't last between them. Hearing her confirm his own thoughts disturbed him more than he'd expected. "Yeah, I know." But he didn't have to like it.

She licked her lips. "I don't want any secrets between us, Logan." She sat on the edge of the bed, leaned over and kissed him, sighing when his tongue met hers. She ended their kiss and looked at him, unsure what to think of the apprehension in his eyes.

"Can you stay for a while after your story is done?"

She shook her head. "I'm up for a promotion as soon as I return."

He raised his eyebrows. "What kind of promotion?"

"There's an opening for a weekend news anchor. If everything falls into place, this should be my last assignment as a reporter."

A dull pain stabbed him in the chest at the thought of her leaving. As much as he wanted her to stay, he didn't have the right to ask her to. She'd worked hard to get where she was. It would be selfish to ask her to give it up. "I see."

At his quick compliance, sadness filled her. What had she wanted? That he'd beg her to stay? If she were honest, a part of her had. Which was a foolish thought. Her life was in Houston. "It's what I do, Logan."

"I know." She was being forthright with him, and he

had to accept it or risk ruining what time they had left together.

Melissa brushed her fingertips across his forehead. "I've got to get dressed. If I don't find Rick, he's liable to go off on some cowboy roundup or something. I think he's forgotten that he's working."

Logan drew her to him for a kiss, then let her go. She stood and looked down at him. "Do you have a robe or something? I don't want to get caught sneaking across the hall-naked."

"Hold on."

Logan went into the bathroom and returned with a blue terry robe. Its thick softness enfolded her as he helped her into it. Breathing deeply, she noticed his scent clung to it. She halfway decided to take it when she left. "Thanks."

"You're welcome." He hugged her. "When are you going into town?"

"Within the hour. I'm going to ask Sheriff O'Neal if he'll release the pictures of the Halifax Exhibit vandalism. Then Rick and I will scope out the museum and determine if I've chosen the best place to tape. We'll visit the library, too. They probably have a genealogy section, which will have a lot of facts."

"I'll come with you."

Melissa recognized his no-nonsense tone, remembered his intent to shadow her. But that had been before they'd slept together and she'd believed his motives were to talk about their past. "Logan, you don't have to babysit me."

Logan pulled on his jeans. Although she wasn't concerned about danger, he wanted to be with her. With Jonathan Devlin's murder under investigation, Logan didn't feel comfortable with Melissa asking questions around town on her own. He didn't care if it was her job or not. He wanted her safe while she was here, while he could take the liberty to watch over her. "I want a chance to see you work."

Surprised, she grinned. "We won't film today. We'll just go over some of the details," she told him, pleased he was interested in her work. "I'll meet you at breakfast in about an hour. I hope Rick will be there. If you see him first, tell him we're going into town."

Leaning up on her toes, she kissed his mouth. What started out as a simple kiss grew into an intimate mating of their tongues. With reluctance, she pulled away. "You're trying to sidetrack me."

Logan skimmed his hand down until he cupped her breast. "Is it working?"

"Yes, which is why I'm leaving now. Another minute and I'm going to have my way with you."

He groaned. "You're killing me."

When he reached for her again, she batted his hands away and walked to the door. "Work, then play."

"Is that a promise?"

Melissa looked back and gave him a wink. "No, honey, that's a threat." She darted out before he could answer.

Several days later, Melissa and Rick began preparations for filming from the Historical Society Museum. She'd spent the past few days researching Jessamine

Golden and had gleaned a wealth of material at the local library with the help of the informative staff. Gavin O'Neal had granted her a few minutes of his time, as well as photos of the Halifax Exhibit vandalism. In the meantime Jonathan Devlin's autopsy results had reached the Devlin family and Logan had told her they were anxious for his killer to be caught.

She and Rick had nosed around town on their own. It seemed there was a lot of interest in Jessamine's map. Word had gotten out that Melissa would be filming today and a crowd had gathered to watch, more visitors than usual for the middle of the morning.

Aaron Hill, the director of the museum, had met with her yesterday, and he'd shared his knowledge of the intriguing Jessamine Golden legend. It was going to make quite an interesting story.

A nervous energy filled the room as Rick positioned the camera at the correct angle for shooting the segment. If there was indeed gold hidden somewhere in Royal, Melissa felt the map held the key. She looked around at the many people gathered to watch—Aaron, the museum employees and visitors—and couldn't help but wonder if one of them was Jonathan's murderer.

Logan stood at one of the entrances to the gallery, mesmerized by Melissa's movements as she talked with her videographer. Due to a special function being held at the museum, they hadn't been able to do the shoot the previous day, but the director had given them permission for today.

Dressed in a red blouse and a black suit with a skirt

that came to her knees, Melissa looked both beautiful and professional—the essence of a career news reporter focused on her responsibilities as she prepared for filming. Logan had been here for a couple of hours, keeping an eye on things as Melissa and Rick worked. Now Rick was doing the last sound check as Melissa went over her notes again.

It almost hurt to watch her. This was what she lived for.

Hearing his name called, he turned to see Mark Hartman walking toward him. "Hey, Mark."

"Logan." Mark scanned the area. "What do you want me to do?"

"Melissa is about ready to film. With so many extra visitors here today, Aaron asked that we be more vigilant when the map is out of the display case. Stand at that entrance and keep your eyes on the map at all times. It's going to be on that podium." He pointed to the stand in the center of the room. "My focus is going to be on Melissa as well as the map."

Understanding flashed in Mark's eyes. "You're involved with her."

Logan gave his friend a dark look. "We knew each other a long time ago." He didn't confirm or deny Mark's comment.

"The way you disappeared from the ball together, I figured that." Mark adjusted his hat, then his gaze traveled to Melissa and back.

Color climbed into Logan's face. "I hadn't expected to see her there," he answered. "We had a few things to discuss in private." The rest of his friends had yet to mention it, but he suspected the time was coming when they would.

"You were in love with her once?"

Swallowing hard, Logan nodded. "Yeah."

"And now?"

Logan shrugged. "Now we lead separate lives. Hers is in Houston."

"And she's going back?" Mark asked, his tone subdued.

"Yes. When she's finished with her work here."

He frowned. "Do you think she's in danger?"

"I don't know, but with Jonathan's murder, we can't rule out that someone may be desperate enough to kill to get the map." Logan looked around. The visitors were gathering to watch. Surrounded by glass walls, the gallery was accessible from two doorways. Logan was standing at one. "I'm not taking any chances with Melissa's life. I'll be watching from this angle." He pointed across the room to the door opposite him. "With you over there, we'll have a good view of everything."

"Right."

Melissa walked up to them, and Logan broke off the conversation to put his arm around her possessively. "Melissa, this is a friend of mine, Mark Hartman."

Melissa smiled at Logan's handsome friend. Nearly as tall as Logan, his cropped black hair and teakwood brown skin set off his hazel eyes. "It's nice to meet you, Mr. Hartman."

"My pleasure, Miss Mason," Mark returned, his slow Texas drawl seeming to caress his words. "Please, call me Mark."

"All right, if you'll call me Melissa. I appreciate your helping us out today, Mark. I hope this won't take long. One take, maybe two, and we should have it."

Rick signaled to her.

"I think we're about ready."

"Take your time. If you'll excuse me, I'm going to take up residence at the back of the room." Mark sauntered away.

Meeting Melissa's eyes, Logan pulled her closer. "I'd kiss you, but I don't want to wreck your makeup."

She laughed, then lifted her face. "Don't let that stop you. My lipstick is right here in my pocket." She patted her hip.

Logan gave in to his need to taste her, albeit briefly. His mouth touched hers, lingered momentarily, then he set her away from him. "You'd better go before I get carried away."

Her gaze glittered with awareness. "See you in a few minutes."

Logan watched her walk to the middle of the room. She picked up the microphone and waited for her cue. After a few moments, Rick gave her a prompt, then she began speaking. Pride filled him. Melissa was articulate and savvy, her voice eloquent and expressive. It was easy to understand why she'd been offered the anchor position.

A pang struck his heart as Logan thought of her returning to Houston. But he steeled himself to accept that she wasn't his to have.

Not all those years ago.

Not today.

Logan heard a loud *crack* and his body tensed as he scanned the room, unsure of what had caused the sound.

Another crack reverberated, this time louder and more threatening.

Logan's gaze shot to the iron chandelier above Melissa. It was shaking precariously. At the juncture of its base, plaster crumbled as the chandelier began to rip away from the ceiling.

"Logan!" Mark shouted from across the room at that same instant.

Logan bolted for Melissa as people began screaming. In one fluid motion, he tackled her, protecting her from the fall with his body as they hit the floor. Holding her tight, he rolled away from where she'd been standing a second before.

Iron landed with a thud as glass shattered, spilling across the floor like fragmented diamonds. Logan felt a sting as a piece of flying glass hit his forehead.

As the chandelier settled, screams from the fleeing observers filled the sudden stillness. He steadied himself, looking around to see if he could spot any further danger. Still covering Melissa, he saw Mark racing toward them and waved him off. "Secure the museum!" he shouted, then he lifted himself off Melissa.

"Are you all right?" Not waiting for her to answer, he ran his hands over her, checking for himself. She'd almost been killed. Fury rushed through him as he wrapped his arms around her.

Melissa sat up and touched her head. "I'm a little bruised, but I think so." Her heart pounded as she realized what had happened.

At risk to his own life, Logan had saved hers! A few more seconds and the chandelier would have crushed her. Her knees shook as he helped her stand. Then she saw the cut on his forehead. "You're bleeding! Oh, my

God." A streak of red oozed from his wound and began to trickle into his dark eyebrow.

"I'm all right," Logan insisted, though he felt the warm dampness on his skin. Reaching up, he brushed at it with his fingers, then wiped his hand on his jeans.

"No, you're not." She pressed her hand against his head to try to stop the flow.

He put his hand over hers. "I'm fine. It's just a scratch," he assured her.

Worried, she lifted her hand so she could look at it. "It needs tending."

His heart warmed at her concerned expression. "I'll let you take care of it personally once we sort this out."

Melissa sighed as she pulled her hand away. Though his wound continued to ooze, it didn't appear to be a deep cut. "All right," she answered, not happy about waiting. They shook the remaining shards of glass from their clothing. Looking around the room, she searched for her videographer. "Rick!"

"Yeah?" Rick shouted over the din.

"Are you okay?"

He nodded as he rubbed his shoulder.

"See if you can get some of this," she said. "We can use the footage with our story."

Rick lifted the camera to his shoulder and began scanning the room.

"You don't miss a beat," Logan commented.

"It's my job," she answered simply. "What on earth happened?" She stared aghast at the clutter around them. The broken chandelier lay crookedly on top of the podium, which was turned over and partially broken. Glass and shards of wood littered the black marble floor, which had cracked from the impact.

"You were nearly killed, that's what."

The implication of how close she'd come to dying hit her again as Aaron Hill rushed up to them. "Miss Mason, are you all right?"

"I think so."

"I'm so sorry. I don't know how this happened," he exclaimed, his face red. "What can I do for you?"

"Please, see to your employees and visitors," Melissa suggested.

"And don't let anyone leave," Logan ordered.

"Of course."

They watched him hurry away and disappear into the crowd of people outside the room. "I can't believe this." Melissa looked around. "How could the chandelier fall?"

"I don't know." At this point, Logan suspected it wasn't an accident, so he wasn't letting Melissa out of his sight until he knew her life wasn't in danger.

Her gaze took in the hole in the ceiling, swept the room, then landed on the toppled podium.

The map!

A sick feeling came over her as she pulled away from Logan. Her pulse began to accelerate again and a knot formed in her throat. "Oh, no."

Please don't let it be gone!

One glance at her and Logan knew something was wrong. "What is it?"

"I don't see the map." Carefully navigating her way,

Melissa went to the podium, broken glass crunching beneath her steps. Logan was hot on her heels.

Together they searched the area. The map wasn't anywhere to be seen.

"Damn." Logan let out a harsh breath. Someone *had* been after the map. Melissa's use of it had provided the perfect opportunity. Her life had meant nothing to whoever wanted it.

Dread filled Melissa's stomach. It had been at her request that the map had been unsecured. "I'm so sorry, Logan."

"It's not your fault." Rage tore through him as he looked at the chandelier again, and he thought about what it could have done to her.

"Yes, it is. The map was out because of my story. You warned me about the possibility of danger, but I didn't take you seriously."

"If someone killed Jonathan Devlin because they were after the map, they could have gotten their hands on it by breaking into the museum. Filming your story only gave them another option."

She caught her breath at the anger on his face. "I've put you in a bad position. I don't know what to say."

He stared at her. "You think I'm angry at you?" She bit her lip and nodded. "God, no. But whoever did this is going to be sorry when I get my hands on them." He stroked her hair from her face.

Mark walked up, tucking his cell phone in his pocket. "I've called Gavin. He's on the way."

"The map is missing," Logan informed his friend.

"What?" Mark took in the damage to the podium.

"Damn." His jaw muscle twitched as a look of guilt filled his face. "I took my eyes off it after everything broke loose. Like you, I was heading for Melissa." He swore a few choice words under his breath, then looked at Melissa. "Sorry."

"That's okay, Mark. I'm the one who's responsible. This wouldn't have happened if I hadn't asked for the map to be displayed," she told him.

"Let's focus on getting it back," Logan suggested.

"The camera!" Melissa said suddenly. "Maybe we caught the thief on film." She glanced around for Rick. Spotting him across the room, she walked over to him, Logan and Mark right behind her.

Rick stopped filming and looked at them. "Yeah?"

"We need your help." She introduced Mark to her co-worker, then explained that during the commotion, Jessamine Golden's map had been stolen. "We're hoping you caught the thief on film. When did you stop shooting?"

He shook his head. "I didn't. The camera's been running the whole time. I heard someone shout, then I heard a loud *crack*. The next thing I knew someone knocked into me. I almost dropped the camera."

"I'm sorry about that," Logan apologized, knowing he was the one who'd crashed into Rick. "I only had seconds to get to Melissa."

"It's okay," Rick said, rolling his shoulder as if to check for pain.

"Can you run the film back and play it for us?" Melissa asked.

"Sure." Rick pushed the buttons on the camera, reset the film, then put it on play mode and turned the small screen toward them. The replay showed Melissa speaking, then began to blur. "This is when Logan pushed me," he told them.

Logan muttered an oath when the screen showed distorted footage for the next minute, then it returned to normal. Rick rewound it and played it again for them.

"Stop it there." Logan pointed to a blurred image moving into range in the direction of the podium. "That's our thief."

"It's not much help," Mark commented. "You can't even tell if it's a man or a woman."

"Maybe you could if I put it on a video and you played it on a bigger screen," Rick suggested.

Logan's gaze cut to him. "Good idea. Can you do that for us?"

"Sure, but I'll need access to some equipment."

"Would they have the equipment you need at a television station here in Royal?" Mark asked. He and Logan shared a look.

Rick shrugged his shoulders. "Probably. I think we have an affiliate station here in Royal, WRYL. It'll take a few phone calls, but I can probably use their equipment once I get permission."

"Don't worry about it. We'll arrange it," Logan told him.

Rick raised his eyebrows. "You can do that?"

Mark reached for his cell phone. "Consider it done," he said, then he left them.

"All right," Rick said. "Let me know when I can go there. Until we leave, I'm going to shoot some more footage," he told Melissa.

Melissa waited until Rick had walked away. "Let me get this straight. One phone call and we have access to a room full of technical equipment at a local television station?"

Logan studied her curious expression. "We have contacts."

"Sheesh." She blew out a breath. "Who else do you have contact with? The President?" she asked flippantly.

Grinning, Logan admitted, "We've chatted a time or two."

Nine

Three hours later, Melissa and Logan were still at the museum. The area where the accident had occurred had been cordoned off with yellow crime scene tape. Sheriff O'Neal had arrived on the scene quickly and Logan had left Melissa to talk with him. A short while later he'd returned and informed her the sheriff wanted her to wait until he'd cleared the museum of everyone else.

Logan and Mark had assisted the sheriff by talking with witnesses and taking notes until everyone had been interviewed. Melissa watched them work, impressed by their efficient handling of the crisis. She was seated on a folding chair that a museum employee had gotten for her when Logan and Sheriff O'Neal finally approached her. She stood and held out her hand in greeting. A handsome man, the sheriff's muscular body moved with authority and confidence.

"Melissa, I'm sorry to make you wait so long."

"I understand." She smiled, but inside her heart was beating harder and faster than normal. "Believe me, as a reporter I'm used it."

Gavin flicked a glance around them. "Only a tornado could have caused more damage. You have my word we'll do a thorough investigation. I'd like to hear what happened from you. Though we're lucky to have your video, it may not have been focused on something that will help us solve the case."

She shrugged. "I'll tell you what I can." She recounted how she'd been taping her story when the ceiling fixture fell.

"Did you hear anything suspicious?"

"I heard a loud noise, like something breaking or ripping. I'm not sure which. After that, I heard it again, louder." She looked up. The chandelier had left a jagged hole in the ceiling when it pulled free.

"Pretty much everyone else's story," Logan commented. "Including mine."

"Then what happened?" the sheriff asked.

She smiled at him. "Then I was hit by a two-hundred-pound man."

Gavin smothered a grin when his gaze met Logan's. "What happened next?"

"I was on the floor, Logan on top of me. I didn't realize the fixture had fallen until I got up and looked around. Logan rescued me just in time. Do you have any idea of how this could have happened?"

"From what we can tell right now, the bolts holding the chandelier came loose and it fell."

Though Gavin's expression remained composed, Melissa detected the underlying thread of anger in his tone. "So someone could have tampered with it?"

He shrugged. "It's one of the possibilities."

She gave him a direct look. "Which means it wasn't an accident?"

He nodded.

Melissa thought about that. "So whoever was responsible, were they targeting me or were they after the map?"

"At this point I'm not sure."

"Am I in danger?"

Shooting a look at Logan, Gavin raised his eyebrows. "Why do I feel like I'm the one being interviewed?"

Logan smiled wryly. "She's a reporter, remember?"

Melissa's instincts told her they were holding back information. "Something else is going on here. That the chandelier fell is strange enough, but then the map disappeared. This *accident* is tied into Jonathan Devlin's murder, isn't it?"

Folding his notebook, Gavin tucked it in his pocket. "That case is still under investigation. As to whether they're related, it's too soon to reach that conclusion. We're not ready to reveal any of our findings on Jonathan Devlin's murder to the press."

She gave his comment consideration, then said, "I can appreciate that, Sheriff, but I'm obligated to report to my station what I've learned."

He met her gaze. "Fair enough. How about if you

sit on this for a while and when it breaks, you get the exclusive?"

"All right," she agreed, knowing in the end she'd get an even bigger story—one that would further boost her career. A nice finish to her reporting days before her leap to a desk assignment. "I'll keep it quiet for now."

Gavin nodded. "Until we know more, be careful. Whoever did this could be trying to stop you from bringing attention to the map and alerting others that it could lead to a treasure. Even if it doesn't, the perpetrator may think it does and not want anyone to get in his way of finding it."

They said goodbye and after the hectic day, Melissa was more than ready to leave. By the time she and Logan arrived at the ranch, exhaustion had hit her. Her nerves were shot and her muscles were sore and stiff. It had been easy to function right after the accident while her adrenaline was pumping, but once the excitement was over, her energy had disappeared. She leaned against Logan as they walked to the house together.

Norah met them at the door. "What happened? Someone called and said there was an accident at the museum." She surveyed the two of them and noticed Melissa disheveled appearance and the cut on Logan's head.

"A chandelier fell near where Melissa was filming."

"My goodness! Are you all right?" she asked Melissa.

"Yes, I'm just tired."

"I'm taking her to my room to rest," Logan told his housekeeper, not at all hesitant about letting her know that he and Melissa would be sharing his room.

"I'll be all right," Melissa assured them. "Logan has a cut that needs attention. Do you have a first aid kit or something?"

"There's one in his bathroom." She winked at Melissa. "Don't worry about Logan. He's hard-headed."

"Thanks," he replied dryly.

"You take care of her, Logan. I'll bring you both a pot of tea and something to eat."

Logan took Melissa's hand and led her to his room. Shutting the door behind them, he dragged her against him, desperate to hold her, to taste her, to know she was truly safe.

Melissa pressed her body against Logan's, a shiver running through her as his mouth crashed down on hers. She hung onto him, her hands clutching at his shirt, her heart beating so hard she was sure he could feel it.

He lifted his head. "You risked your life to save me," she whispered into his mouth as he continued to kiss her.

"Thank God I got to you, sweetheart." Despite his gentle tone, anger still simmered inside him. Someone had tried to harm her. Someone evil. Whoever dared to hurt her would answer to him.

She leaned back and touched her hand to his forehead where the blood had dried around his gash. "I need a quick shower and we need to take care of this."

"Shower with me," Logan suggested huskily.

Smiling, she licked her lips. "Mm, I like the sound of that."

Their quick shower turned into a lengthy one as they took turns washing each other, kissing and touching, teasing each other until Melissa could barely stand, her body burning with desire.

After towel-drying her hair, she located the first aid kit under the vanity and set it on the counter. "Sit down," she ordered Logan as she took out the hydrogen peroxide.

Logan's gaze dropped to her perfect breasts, her beaded nipples. "That can wait." He reached for her and she slapped his hand away.

"Sit."

He groaned. "You're awfully bossy for someone who owes me for saving her life."

She rolled her eyes. "Your cut needs tending."

"It's not that bad," he protested. "It's not even bleeding." Seeing she wasn't going to budge on the issue, he begrudgingly sat on the lid of the toilet.

Melissa smiled mischievously, then straddled his lap and sat on his thighs, her body pressed intimately against his engorged manhood. She kissed him. "You be good and let me take care of this and I'll pay you back." Pouring some of the liquid on a gauze pad, she dabbed it on his cut.

Encircling her with his arms, he asked, "Yeah? How do you plan to do that?"

Shifting closer, Melissa grazed his chest with her breasts. "Oh, I'll think of something."

He rolled his hips as his erection grew so hard that he hurt. Their intimate position was killing him. He wanted to be inside her, wanted to keep her beneath him all night long. "Hurry up. I can't take this much longer."

Melissa smiled. "Just a minute."

Logan gritted his teeth. "I'm only human, you little flirt."

She laughed low in her throat as she dabbed his cut one last time. "I think you'll live."

"I'm not so sure." His hands cupped her head, dragged her mouth to his. His tongue delved past her teeth, exploring, tasting, demanding a response.

Twining her arms around his neck, Melissa kissed him back hungrily. His hands gripped her butt as he stood and carried her out of the bathroom. He stopped at the bed and Melissa slithered down his body until her feet found the floor.

A soft knock sounded at the door and she pulled away. "You'd better get that."

He found a tray on the floor outside. He brought it inside, set it on the dresser, then turned toward Melissa. "Are you hungry?" he asked.

"Not for food," she whispered as her gaze traveled boldly over his body.

Logan stared at her, half crazy with wanting her. She was beautiful and sexy and he had to stop himself from going over to her, tossing her on the bed and burying himself deep inside her.

Because he loved her.

He loved her fascinating green eyes, her determination, her strength in the face of danger. He loved looking at her, knowing that he alone could strip her clothing from her and touch her intimately.

Logan's throat went dry as she lay on the bed, then beckoned him with her sexy smile.

"Make love to me, Logan."

He joined her, his mouth taking hers with fierce need. He wanted to make her his in every way—with his mouth, his hands, his body. He wanted her to feel as desperate at the thought of leaving him as he did. He wanted to brand her his in every way possible so when she did leave she would know that no other man would make her feel what he could.

She arched against him as his hands explored her body, moaned as his mouth left hers and trailed kisses down her throat and shoulder to her breast. Sucking gently, he drew her nipple into his mouth, nibbled it with his teeth, savored her taste, her smell, her essence.

He looked at her as she writhed beneath him, watched her eyes glaze with passion as she bit her lower lip. And still he moved lower, kissing her belly, her thighs, between her legs.

Melissa's hips thrashed as Logan's tongue stroked her. Something had changed between them, something emotional and intimate and earth-shattering. The intensity of his lovemaking, of her response to him, took her breath away. Her heart swelled with love as he moved over her.

She welcomed him inside her, tightened her arms around him as he slowly entered her. Opening her legs, she arched upward, wanting more of him than he was giving her. But Logan took his time, filling her ever so slowly. Hot and hard, building on the fire he'd created within her, he teased them both as he withdrew then entered her again. When she thought she could no longer stand it, he answered her unspoken plea and stroked her body with his over and over until they crested the peak of desire together.

Feeling as though she'd never be normal again,

Melissa ran her hands over Logan's back, loving the feel of him on top of her, still inside her. Her heart shifted. She'd known becoming involved with Logan was dangerous, but she'd also known that she couldn't have stopped what was happening between them. And as much as it hurt to think about leaving one day soon, she couldn't regret loving him.

Had she ever stopped loving him?

Tears filled her eyes and she tried her best to stop them. Despite her valiant effort, they spilled down her temples and fell into her hair.

Logan lifted his head and looked at her, his expression one of concern. "What's wrong?"

"Nothing," she told him, hoping he'd believe her. She wasn't surprised when he didn't let the subject drop.

"Are you all right?" he asked, his tone serious and caring. "Did I hurt you?"

She shook her head. "No, I'm fine. Really. It's just…"

I love you.

Clamping her lips together, Melissa stopped herself from blurting out the words.

Logan studied her face, his heart pounding. "What, sweetheart?"

She couldn't tell him. Confessing that she was in love with him would only complicate everything between them. He didn't love her. And once she wrapped up the story, she'd leave. "I guess what happened earlier is finally hitting me."

"It's over now." He kissed her tenderly, then moved to her side and drew her into his arms. He didn't want to let her go. Ever. But he knew in his heart he would have to. He'd asked her to stay once before and she hadn't.

Their circumstances were different now, but the end result would be the same. She lived in Houston. There was a big promotion waiting for her. He knew she had a future in broadcasting and that one day he'd turn on his television to see her anchoring for a major network. He wouldn't be able to live with himself if he stood in her way.

All those years ago he'd been selfish, expecting her to stay in Royal because they were in love. He knew he no longer had the freedom, or the right, to ask that of her. She cared for him, he knew. He could tell by the way she touched him, kissed him.

But that wasn't love—at least not for her.

No, he couldn't ask her to give up everything she'd worked for to stay here. He toyed with the idea of going with her to live in Houston, but knew that would never work.

What would he do in a big city? How long would it be before his missing the hard work of ranching came between them? He was a rancher. Like so many ancestors before him, the dirt of the Wild Spur was in his blood. He'd feel useless anywhere else.

Hell, if he offered to move, would she reject him as she had years ago? No, going with her wasn't an option.

Melissa sighed. "I know. I'm just feeling emotional, I guess."

"That's natural after something traumatic happens."

She turned in his arms, raised herself up on her elbow and propped her head on her hand. "I suppose." Tracing his chin with her finger, she said, "I'm glad you were there, Logan."

"I am, too, sweetheart."

"Do you think Rick will be able to get access to some equipment tomorrow?"

"Yeah, it's probably already set up. I'll call Mark in the morning."

"I'd like to ask another favor, then."

Logan kissed her, then cupped her breast. "Anything you want."

"Mm, that sounds promising," she answered. "But that's not the kind of favor I was thinking of."

He dropped his hand to her hip. "All right, what?"

"I was wondering if your contact at the station would let Rick and me do some work on our story there. Since we're not on a schedule, we could go in any time they'd have the equipment available."

He faked a frown, then laughed. "Just my luck. I have a naked woman in bed with me and she's thinking about work."

Melissa playfully smacked him. "I can always go back to Houston." Afraid of losing what little time she had with him, she hadn't wanted to leave until she was due to return to her job. But she and Rick had a lot of footage so far and she wanted to get some preliminary editing done.

The thought of her leaving, even for a day, made his gut twist. Sitting up, he said, "I don't think it'll be a problem."

"Great!"

"What do I get in return?"

She traced a path down his belly and caressed him.

"I'll think of something," she whispered, then crawled on top of him.

Logan groaned as she scooted down his body, kissing his belly, her tongue wet and hot as she moved lower.

He wondered if she needed any more favors.

"Joe Fisher is the manager of WRYL, your affiliate here," Logan stated at breakfast with Rick and Melissa the next morning. He'd talked to Mark while Melissa was dressing and had learned that arrangements had been made for Rick and Melissa to use the station's facilities. "He's agreed to see you at nine this morning and to set up slots for you to use their equipment while you're putting your story together."

"You're quite the miracle worker," Melissa commented, then gave Logan a sweet, yet seductive smile as she bit into her buttered toast. He'd worked miracles with her in his bed several times during the night.

Rick cleared his throat, breaking the obvious spell between his coworker and his host. "That's great." Swallowing the last of his coffee, he sat back in his chair.

Giving Melissa an impressed look, Logan told her, "Joe recognized your name when Mark mentioned you."

Surprise lit her eyes. "Really?"

"Yeah, he said something about seeing some of your work. Mark said he seemed really interested in meeting you."

"It's nice of him to help us out."

"As soon as you're done, I'll call the sheriff." And the members of the TCC. They were planning to meet to view the video, hoping to recognize the figure.

"I want to go with you to meet with him," Melissa said. "I have some more questions I want to ask him."

Logan had started to speak when his cell phone rang. "Excuse me." He left the room. After a few minutes, he returned and sat. "That was my foreman. There's a fence down and about a hundred head of cattle free." He released a heavy sigh. "I'm going to have to stay here and help round them up." His expression became serious as he looked at Rick. "I want you to stick with Melissa every minute while you're gone."

Rick nodded. "I will. Don't worry about her."

Melissa pushed her plate away. "Okay, you two, I'm sitting right here." She pinned Logan with a stare. "I don't need a keeper."

"I just want you safe. The best way to be sure of that is to have Rick watch out for you."

"I'm not in any danger," she protested.

His lips twisted. "We don't know that for sure."

"But you suspect that the person who caused the accident was after the map. It doesn't make sense that they would harm me."

"You and Rick might have caught the thief on tape," Logan pointed out. "The thief might be responsible for killing Jonathan Devlin and may kill to get the tape. Until we know what's going on, you stay with Rick."

"Do you trust Joe Fisher?" Rick asked.

Logan had known Joe for years. "Yes," he answered without hesitation.

"Then Melissa will be with either Joe or me the entire time we're gone."

"Thanks. And give me a call as soon as you have the tape finished."

Melissa pouted, but that Logan showed his concern for her sent a warm feeling all through her body. "All right," she told him. "You win this time." It was easy to give in to Rick and Logan because, at the moment, she didn't have any plans otherwise. "But I do want to go with you when you talk to the sheriff. And don't even try to talk me out of it."

Ten

"**W**hat's going on with you and Logan?" Rick asked, breaking the silence between them as they drove toward WRYL.

"What do you mean?" Melissa asked coyly.

He smiled at her and his eyes twinkled. "Sugar, you're not fooling me with that innocent act. You and the cowboy have been joined at the hip since we arrived."

Blushing, she gave him a sidelong glance. "We're old friends. We're just getting reacquainted."

"Reacquainted in bed?"

"Rick!"

At the honk of a horn, he turned his attention to the road. "Look, the sparks have been flying between you two since the night of the anniversary ball."

"Oh, *pleeeze*." She rolled her eyes.

"The man wanted you that night. It was written all over his face when he walked up to you."

She shook her head and chuckled. "No, actually, I think he wanted to throttle me."

"Not hardly, babe." The song playing on the radio filled the cab for several moments, then Rick looked at her again. "He's been very accommodating since we've arrived."

"Yes, he has," she answered softly. Melissa thought about Rick's comment. Logan *had* been helpful. He'd gone out of his way to be open and friendly. For years she'd mentally forced him into a tiny box that he no longer seemed to fit, and no matter how hard she tried, he wasn't going back into it.

She still didn't want to believe that she was in love with Logan again, but it was silly to deny it. Sighing as Rick turned right off the highway onto the main road that led to the center of Royal, she stared out the window.

Where was her relationship with Logan headed? He hadn't made any promises and she hadn't asked for them. To believe they could have a happily-ever-after ending between them was foolish. In a few days she was going back to her job in Houston. Back to where she belonged.

But after being here with Logan, living in Houston seemed a lifetime ago. She'd once thrived on the excitement of a big city, relished her work as a reporter, looked forward to achieving even more success with her job.

Now she knew they were only replacements for what was lacking in her life.

Love.

Fulfillment.

Logan.

Maybe her heart would survive the trauma of living without him.

She remained silent as Rick parked in the lot at the television station. One thing she couldn't seem to stop thinking about: she'd never been happier.

Getting out of the truck, Melissa waited for Rick to retrieve his camera from behind his seat.

She *was* happy with Logan. She loved him deeply, cherished each moment with him. But that didn't mean they had a future together, did it?

She'd said as much to Logan when she'd pointed out they led separate lives. He hadn't corrected her, hadn't tried to make more of their relationship than the physical love they shared. That, more than anything, told her how he felt.

Yes, she loved him, but he didn't feel the same.

So where did that leave her?

Joe Fisher was waiting for Melissa and Rick when they entered the lobby. About fifteen years older than her, Joe was balding and had the kindest blue eyes of anyone she'd ever met. "Hi. I'm Melissa Mason. This is my videographer, Rick."

"You don't need an introduction," Joe said with a cordial smile. "I know exactly who you are. It's so nice to meet you. And you, Rick. Please come this way.

"Do you have time for a quick tour of the station?" he asked.

"We'd love one," Melissa answered for them. She could hardly say no, and besides, she'd been impressed by the décor. It was both professional and attractive.

The station was smaller than theirs in Houston, but the technology was state of the art. Melissa complimented him.

"We're quite proud of it."

Joe led them through the engineering department and showed them the editing facilities. "Make yourself at home. If you have any questions, there's an assistant production coordinator in the next room."

An hour later they were done copying the accident video. They left with two tapes: one for them and one for Logan. As they drove to the ranch, Melissa called Logan to let him know they were returning. He was standing in the driveway when they pulled up. Rick dropped her off, then backed his truck up and drove to his cottage.

Melissa held out one of the tapes as she approached Logan, but instead of taking it he pulled her to him and kissed her. For an insane moment, she allowed herself to fantasize what it would be like to be greeted with his kisses for the rest of her life, to live on his ranch, to have his love for eternity.

Aware that wasn't going to happen, she banished the longing from her heart and kissed him back, telling herself she should be grateful for having the time with him now.

"Mmm, that was nice. Care to take this inside?" Melissa whispered when Logan lifted his mouth from hers.

Logan could think of nothing he'd like more. The thought of making love to Melissa consumed him. Day and night.

What's happened between us is wonderful, but it can't last. We both know it.

Melissa's words haunted him. She'd made it clear she wasn't expecting more than an affair. His gut twisted. For her, their affair was just about the sex.

He didn't have her heart.

"There's nothing I'd like more, but I have a meeting at the club in thirty minutes." He moved his hips against hers, the bulge in his jeans pressing against her belly.

"Really?"

Taking the tape, he said, "We're going to view this to see if anyone recognizes the blurred image of the person taking the map."

"I want to go with you." Melissa held Logan's gaze. "I know Gavin will be there. I want to talk with him to see if he's learned anything more about what happened at the museum."

"I'll ask him for you. I know he has another meeting to go to after this one. Maybe he can talk with you later today.

"I hope so."

"I don't want you waiting in the truck and you won't be allowed inside," he told her. "The club is for members only."

She snorted. "No women allowed? What kind of things go on inside there, anyway?" she asked.

He grinned engagingly. "Curious, huh?"

"As you said to Gavin, I'm a reporter. Maybe I'll do a story on it."

Logan knew she was teasing by her playful expression but couldn't stop the discouragement from coming out. "I don't think that would be a good idea, sweetheart."

"What? You don't want the world to know that you're heroes who thwart crime and save damsels in distress?"

"Heroes?" He laughed easily. "You have quite an imagination."

Melissa studied his expression and found it just a little too practiced. "My imagination is fine. As a matter of fact, I'm imagining myself naked, crawling on top of you and—"

"Stop it, you're killing me," he said with a groan. Torn between duty and desire, he glanced at his watch. He cursed when he realized he had just enough time to get to his meeting. He kissed her pouty lips. "I really do have to go, Melissa."

"All right," she said with frustration that was a little bit fake and a whole lot real. "Your loss."

"I'll make it up to you when I get back," he promised.

"I'm going to hold you to that."

He grinned as she moved out of his arms. "I was hoping you would."

Mark Hartman was the last member to arrive. Though he walked in only minutes after Logan, who had just taken a seat a the conference table, he still got a good ribbing from his friends for being five minutes late.

"Nice of you to join us," Connor quipped, rocking back on two legs of his chair.

"Yeah, it's not like we don't have other things to do," Jake added with a laugh.

Mark frowned. "All right, knock it off. I've lost another nanny and I haven't had any luck finding a replacement." He plopped into his chair and slumped down, looking both frustrated and worn out.

"Someone will turn up," Logan offered.

Concern etched his features. "Yeah, but in the meantime my niece is having to adjust to temporary sitters. The self-defense studio is thriving and I need someone I can count on, someone who doesn't mind taking care of her on the spur of the moment."

Tom gave him a reassuring look. "It's not like you planned to raise a child. Losing your brother and sister-in-law unexpectedly was hard enough. Not everyone would have stepped up to raise their niece."

"Yeah," Jake chimed in. "We all know how much you love her. You're doing the right thing. Give it some time. It'll work out."

Standing, Logan walked to the corner of the room and fed the tape Melissa had given him into the video recorder connected to large television. "Let's get down to business. You've all heard about the incident at the museum by now?"

"So the map hasn't turned up yet?" Mark asked, still feeling responsible since he'd was supposed to have been guarding it.

"No," Gavin said. "Melissa was nearly killed and we believe it was because of the map."

Connor brought his chair down on all four legs. "So you don't think Melissa was the target?"

"No. But someone wanted the map desperately enough to kill for it. Jonathan Devlin's murder proved that. This latest incident confirms how bold the killer is.

If Logan hadn't gotten to her when he did, Melissa could have died."

Just hearing Gavin state the killer's intent caused Logan's blood to boil. "Which means that if she wasn't the original target, she might be one now. Whoever did this might think they were caught on tape stealing the map. Or, that possibly they were seen by her."

Jake swore. "Is Melissa all right?"

Logan nodded. "She's a little bruised, but she says she's fine." Pride filled him. "She's taking the ordeal like a trooper and continuing to cover the story." He didn't like it, but he respected her dedication to her job. "I'm going to make damn sure nothing happens to her again."

A brief moment of silence followed Logan's declaration, then Mark asked, "Do you know how the chandelier broke loose?"

"Someone definitely tampered with the wiring and the bolts. It was rigged to drop. We haven't determined how anyone could have gotten access to the attic to do so, but we're still investigating," Gavin explained.

Logan hit the play button. The museum room appeared on the screen, the map on the podium in the center. "This is the tape from the accident. We were lucky to capture some of it. Unfortunately, where the killer comes in is blurred because the cameraman got bumped during the melee. But it's obvious that someone comes near the podium after the chandelier fell. That individual has to be the person who stole the map."

The men studied the television in silence. After showing it once, Logan hit the rewind button and they viewed it a second time. "The person isn't very tall."

Connor nodded in agreement. "I think it's a woman. The figure seems too small to be a man."

"Logan, play it again and stop it when the image moves into view," Jake said. As the tape started playing, he walked over to the television. "Stop."

Logan stopped the tape.

Jake pointed to the slender, blurred image. "It's a woman, for sure. Look at the head." He circled a small section with his finger. "She has a black cap on, but her hair is in a ponytail. See here?"

"You're right." Gavin's eyes never left the screen. "The color of her hair is either light brown or blond. But I can't make out who she is. Does anyone recognize her?"

Mark shook his head. "She doesn't look familiar to me."

"Me, either," Logan added. "Wait." He placed his finger against the screen. "There are letters on the cap. See? There's an *S* and a *C*."

Connor frowned, then said, "That's odd. Why would it have letters that far apart? Look here, her ponytail is between the two letters. There's probably more beneath it."

"I think you're right, Connor," Gavin agreed. "At least we now have something to go on. We agree it's a woman?" he asked. They all nodded. "And the letters on her black cap are an *S* and a *C*?" He rubbed his hand over his jaw. "Unfortunately her description fits about a third of the women of Royal."

Satisfied they'd gotten a solid lead, Logan turned off the television, then removed the tape from the recorder. "What's happening out at the Windcroft horse farm?" he asked Gavin, referring to the trouble Nita Windcroft had been complaining about. "Anything turn up about the poisoned horse feed?"

Gavin took a deep breath. "Nita's confirmed that the feed didn't come from her regular supplier. In addition to the cut fences she's already reported, she called me this morning with another complaint. She said the air had been let out of the tires in several of her horse trailers. She's convinced that a Devlin is behind the mischief going out there."

Mark sat forward. "What do you think?"

"That she may be right, but with no actual proof, my hands are tied. We need to consider sending someone out to her horse farm to keep an eye on things."

"If we do," Logan interjected, "it may look like we're taking sides."

"Right. The Devlins might believe we're already suspecting them," Jake said.

"Which could put fire under the feud if they're innocent," Connor reasoned.

"It may be wise to hold off sending anyone anywhere until we have more to go on," Mark suggested. "Nita should understand that."

"She mentioned that she'd heard that Jonathan Devlin was murdered, which only raised her suspicions that the Devlins have something to do with her problems."

"One of us could talk to Lucas," Tom suggested. "That might be enough to calm her down."

"Good idea," Gavin agreed. "But since you're just getting acquainted with your family, let's keep you out of it."

"I could go to see Lucas and his family and ask a few

questions," Logan offered. "I won't suggest the Devlins are behind anything, but it would interesting to gauge their reactions to all of this."

Gavin nodded. "That's a good idea. We'll meet after you've talked to Lucas. In the meantime, everyone keep an eye out for a woman matching our suspect's description. So far she's our best lead in solving this mystery. And Logan, stay close to Melissa. We don't know yet if she's in danger."

Logan nodded, but he'd already made that decision. Someone was going to be with her whenever she was away from the ranch. Whether she liked it or not.

Two days later Melissa sat back in her chair at WRYL's editing facilities and smiled at Rick. "We're done with this part of our story."

"The editing went faster than I anticipated," Rick said.

"Yes. I need to talk to the sheriff to see if he has anything more on the Devlin murder." If something concrete didn't turn up soon, she'd have to start digging more into Jessamine's past. Melissa had already delved into the story about the gold heist Jessamine had engineered. In the process, Melissa had read something about Jessamine possibly being involved with a man— the town sheriff. Supposedly they'd had a love affair, but Melissa hadn't been able to discover if it was true or what had happened between them.

But if Jessamine had suffered a broken romance, Melissa knew how she felt. Her own heart ached at the thought of leaving Logan.

You knew it was only an affair, her mind taunted.

She'd told herself that she could enjoy being with him temporarily, that she could deal with a brief affair.

She'd been wrong.

Sighing, she stood. "I'm going to find Joe and thank him for giving us access to their equipment. I'll let him know we're finished."

She found Joe in his office. When he saw her at his door, he waved her inside. "Rick and I want to thank you again for the use of your facilities."

Joe nodded. "You're more than welcome. Come back if you need to."

She and Rick had finished editing all the footage they had so far. But Gavin had promised to keep her updated on his investigation, so it was possible she'd need access to the studio again.

She and Joe spent a few minutes chatting. He asked her about her career, and Melissa told him a little about her work. He seemed quite interested and even mentioned a documentary she'd done on battered women which had won an industry award. She was surprised he even knew about it.

Joe stood. "I enjoyed talking with you."

"It's been a pleasure." Melissa smiled and shook Joe's hand as she started to leave.

"Look, I can't let this opportunity go by without mentioning that I'd be interested in talking with you about working at WRYL." He took out his card and handed it to her.

"I don't know, I—"

"Oh, I know there's less prestige working in Royal and the pay wouldn't match what you make in Houston because we're a smaller market, but we'd do our best to make it up in perks."

"Thank you. I appreciate your interest."

"Feel free to call me anytime," he said, coming around his desk. He walked with her back to the editing facility. Rick appeared to be waiting for her, his camera and a couple of tapes in his hands. He handed them to her as she approached and she tucked them into her bag.

As they left, Melissa thought about the differences between her station in Houston and this smaller one in Royal. The pace was definitely slower here. She'd had the chance to catch a couple of their newscasts and found their presentation was topnotch, their field reporters professional. The quality of her work certainly wouldn't be jeopardized in the smaller market.

In Houston she lived and breathed her job, rushing to assignments, racing to meet deadlines. All of that effort built her profile so that, one day, she could see herself working for a major news network. That's what her focus in life up to now had been. And, she was on the verge of a major promotion.

Could she even consider staying in Royal? Could she slow down her professional pace and start filling in all those pieces—home, family…love—that had been missing in her life? Could she make a commitment to Logan?

For a moment her heart soared with the possibility of marrying him. She would be greeted by his kisses the way she'd dreamed the other day. She would love him, and he would… Her thoughts paused there. She didn't know if Logan loved her or not. He desired her, yes. But did he love her? Was she really considering changing her career path without the certainty of a future with him?

Because one thing *was* certain, for her career, it would be a move in the wrong direction.

Eleven

"He's beautiful." Melissa laughed as the young calf trotted after his mother in one of the Wild Spur's pastures. Needing to check his stock, Logan had invited her for a tour of his ranch.

Another week had passed. Daniel had called to ask how things were coming along. Melissa had done more research on the town of Royal than she'd ever dreamed she would. She and Rick had spent hours looking at newspapers on microfiche. Sheriff O'Neal had given her another interview, which Rick had filmed.

Today they were both taking a day off. Sharing Logan's love for his ranch, she was glad for the opportunity to ride along with him.

Leaning against the split rail fence, Logan propped his foot on the bottom rail. "He's from prime stock. His father's a descendent in a line of champions. In the future, I'll use that little bull to breed."

Logan's future—one that didn't include her.

Hearing him say the word stopped her heart. She looked around at the never-ending expanse of land, felt the warmth of the sun shining down on her, heating her skin. Yet inside she suddenly was chilled.

When she'd decided to take this assignment and return to Royal, she'd dreaded the thought of seeing him again. She'd never conceived that they would have anything other than animosity between them, let alone enter into an affair.

Amazingly, they'd managed to work through the pain of their past. Though they'd discovered that they had been manipulated by his brother and Cara, their fragile intimacy didn't change the stark truth of reality.

Logan had said he loved her years ago. She'd wanted to believe it. But he'd married another woman shortly after she'd left. If he'd fallen in love with Cara so soon after she'd moved to Houston, could he have truly loved her? Needing to hear his explanation, she rested her arm on the fence. "Logan, I know we talked about this before, but I need to hear some things again…get them straight in my mind." She took a deep breath, struggling to find the courage to speak further. Then she finally faced him. "Did you love Cara?" She braced herself for his answer.

Ever since that night they'd confronted their past, Logan had dreaded this moment. He didn't want to hurt her, but how could he explain why he'd fallen so easily for Cara? "When I married her I thought I did," he answered, his voice carrying an edge of anger at Bart's and

Cara's deception. "And that didn't happen until six months after you'd left."

"Six months." Disappointment and anger flashed through Melissa. Not long to grieve for a broken engagement with a woman he'd professed to love, a woman he'd planned to spend the rest of his life with. "Why didn't you call me?"

"Pride, I guess. And anger." Bitterness mixed with regret in his tone. "I was so damn angry with you." Hurt flickered through her eyes, and he hated being the one who caused it.

"That doesn't say a lot for your love for me, Logan," she responded bluntly.

Heat flushed Logan's cheeks. "Your rejection stung, hitting me where I was most vulnerable." A few moments passed before he forced himself to continue. "After my mother died, I didn't have anyone in my life who really cared about me. Until you."

"And I left you." She couldn't ignore that she'd played a part in their bitter breakup. Young and naive, she hadn't trusted her own instincts, her own love for Logan.

He shrugged as if it didn't matter, but it had. "Cara came into my life at my lowest point. To be honest, she pursued me, made me feel special. She began talking about marriage and I thought, why the hell not?"

"It wasn't long before I realized I'd married Cara on the rebound from loving you. I missed you and I thought I'd never feel whole again. They were all the wrong reasons for marriage. I felt awful and, as the weeks passed, I faced the fact that it wasn't going to work between us. We got divorced within a year. She didn't even fight it—

just took her settlement and walked." He gave a hard laugh. "Now, aware of her and Bart's association, I know why."

"Somehow that makes me feel a little better." Though she accepted that he'd fallen for another woman and had married quickly, it still hurt. But she needed to move past her resentment to heal her spirit. She knew now that she had to give him her trust.

He expelled a harsh breath. "It makes me feel like an idiot."

"You weren't an idiot. You were fooled by Cara." She laid her hand on his arm. "We both were."

"And I was lonely," he told her. "I wanted you and couldn't have you."

Sadness stole over her expression as she withdrew her hand. "I wish we could go back."

"We can't, though, sweetheart." He wrapped his arms around her and tucked her head against his shoulder. She tilted her face and his gaze drifted over her, taking in the shadows in her eyes, the pain. "It took me years to get over you."

Melissa sighed as he held her. But he had gotten over her. He'd moved on with his life. She leaned up on her toes and kissed him. "At least we both know the truth, Logan. Though it can't make up for the past, we've had this time together."

"You're amazing. Only you could find something good in the tragedy of our past." Amazing was how she felt in his arms. Logan tightened his embrace.

Stepping back, she favored him with a smile. "I bet you say that to all the girls."

He chuckled. "There haven't been many. My attempts at dating haven't gone very well," he admitted. "No one could take your place."

She blushed. "That a sweet thing to say."

Unable to stop himself, he asked, "What about you? Has there been someone special in your life?"

Shaking her head, she met his gaze. "When I first started working I didn't have time in my life for a relationship. Later, I dated someone I cared about, but he resented my work and…" Unable to tell him the whole truth, she let her words drop off.

Because I loved you. I always will.

Melissa turned away, not wanting him to read her thoughts.

Logan glanced at his watch. "We'd better get back to the house. I have a meeting with Lucas at the Devlins' ranch."

She entwined her hand with his and they walked to the truck Logan used on the ranch. Old and a little beat-up, its red paint was covered in several layers of dust, but the ride out to the pasture had been smooth. "What are you going to see him about?"

"Nita Windcroft insists the Devlins are behind some trouble she's having out at her horse farm. Recently she found flat tires on several of her horse trailers. She's also had downed fences and their line shack broken into."

"So you're going to see Lucas to ask him if his family is causing the problems?"

He started driving toward the house. "Not in those words. The last thing anyone wants is to encourage trouble between the Devlins and the Windcrofts. I'm going more to see if I can shed any light on it."

"Great. I'll go with you."

Logan gave her a sidelong glance, observed the determination written on her face. "You're staying at the ranch, sweetheart."

Melissa glared at him. "Why?"

Pulling into the yard, he stopped the truck short, his mind made up. There was no way in hell he was taking her with him. After the accident with the chandelier, he wasn't placing her in any further danger. "Because."

"That's not an answer, Logan."

Because I love you.

But he couldn't admit that. She'd already told him one relationship had failed because of jealousy over her work. He wasn't going to make her feel guilty for making that choice.

"Because of the accident that almost took your life," he finally said. "Besides, if you go along, Lucas may not be as open to discussing what's been going on at the Windcrofts'." Logan reached across her and opened her door. "I respect what you do, Melissa, but I want you safe. I'm going to the Devlin ranch alone. With all that's been happening, I don't know what I'm going to be walking into." He nodded. "I'll be back in an hour and tell you what I learned."

"Can you at least ask Lucas if I can talk to him?"

"That I'll do. Stay here until I get back. There are a lot of hands around here who would notice anything suspicious in my absence." It was an order. He could tell she didn't like it, but if it kept her safe, that was what mattered.

Melissa didn't think anyone was after her, but she could tell she'd never convince Logan of that. Giving in, she said, "All right. I'll see you in a little while." Without waiting for a response, she shut the door, then headed for the house.

As Logan pulled out of the yard, he caught a glimpse of her in his rearview mirror as she disappeared inside. He hadn't meant to be curt, but hell, he was worried for her safety. Couldn't she see that?

If something happened to her while she was here, he'd never get over it. Maybe he couldn't protect her in Houston, but here in Royal he could. Whether she liked it or not.

Houston.

Logan knew that the more information she gathered, the closer the time came when she'd be leaving. Having her talk to Lucas at a later date would buy him a few more days with her.

But she didn't have to know that, did she?

Trying to put thoughts of Melissa out of his mind, Logan crossed the cattle guard and drove up the dirt road toward Lucas's house. The large brick-and-frame structure only hinted at the wealth of the family living inside. Stopping the truck, he cut the engine, got out and went to the door.

He hoped the Windcrofts and Devlins could find a peaceable solution. But if the past was anything to go by, he had his doubts.

As Melissa worked on her story in her room, her cell phone rang. She glanced at her watch before answering, surprised to find thirty minutes had passed. She frowned when her producer's name flashed on her caller ID.

"Hi, Daniel, what's up?"

"How's the story out there coming along?"

"There have been some new developments."

"Great. You can fill me in when you get back. I've got some news for you," he said, his voice excited. "Your promotion has come through. We're ready to put you on the air."

"What?" Melissa's pulse quickened.

"I want you to wrap up your work there and get back here by tomorrow."

His words caught her by surprise. Instead of the elation she'd expected at reaching her goal, panic swept through her. "Wait a minute. What are you talking about?"

"We're putting you on the air this weekend. You and Rick need to leave for Houston right away to be back here no later than tomorrow afternoon," he ordered.

"Tomorrow?" Stunned, she stared at her notes. "But I'm still looking into Jessamine Golden's legend. As a matter of fact, there's been a murder in town and there's a possible connection to Jessamine's map."

"Don't worry about that."

"I've put a lot into this story, Daniel," she said desperately. "It's only fair that I finish covering it."

"The story's all yours. You can keep updated on the investigation through phone calls from here. If need be, we can send someone else there to do your leg work."

A beep sounded from her phone, and she groaned

when she realized the battery was low. "Look, Daniel, my phone's going to die. Let me call you back."

"Don't bother. Explain to Rick what's up and you two get back here stat. And congratulations!"

"Daniel—" Melissa stared at her phone in disbelief when it lost the connection. Her promotion had come through. By the weekend she'd be on the air as a news anchor. She'd have everything she wanted, everything she'd worked for.

But if that was true, why did she feel so miserable?

She set her phone in its cradle to charge, then sat back against the headboard of the bed. As she always known it would, the time had come for her to leave. Now, every single minute she could be with Logan counted. She wanted him here with her, wanted to spend her last evening with him in bed.

Touching him.

Kissing him.

Making love with him.

Except he wasn't here.

But she knew where he was. She'd go to the Devlin ranch. Logan had taken the ranch truck, but the keys to his pickup were on the foyer table. All she needed were the directions. Melissa hurried out of her bedroom to find Norah.

A few minutes later, Melissa drove away from the ranch. On the way to the Devlin's, she kept an eye out for Logan, hoping she'd see him and be able to flag him down. He'd been far enough ahead of her to have possibly finished his business and be heading home.

Seeing the name of the road Norah had given her,

Melissa turned off the main highway. She bumped along, then spotted a chimney standing alone on a hill signaling the entrance to the Devlin ranch.

As she turned right at a post with an iron D-V brand on it, she heard a sharp crack and something exploded through the passenger window of the truck. Screaming, she slammed on the brakes and jerked the wheel to the right. The truck lurched to the side of the road, nearly running into a ditch. Ducking, she pressed her face against the seat.

Someone was shooting at her!

The metallic taste of fear coated her throat. "Ohmygodohmygodohmygod!" Her heart slammed against her rib cage.

Were they still out there? Would they approach the truck to make sure she was dead? Logan had told her to stay home. Why hadn't she listened to him?

Oh, God, she was going to die here. And if she didn't, Logan was going to kill her when he saw her. Her hand shook as she frantically searched through her purse. Where was her damn cell phone! She groaned, remembering she'd left it at the ranch, charging.

Think, Melissa, think!

Looking around the inside of the cab she saw Logan's CB radio.

Thank God!

She turned it on and the radio squawked to life. Grabbing the handset, she pressed the side button and shouted, "I don't know if anyone's out there, but I need help! Someone's shooting at me." Releasing the button, she fought for calm as she listened to see if anyone had heard her. Though there hadn't been any more shots, she wasn't about to stick her head up and risk becoming a target.

Her ears still humming from the sound of the bullet piercing the glass, she looked up. The window on the passenger side had a spider-web effect, with a hole the size of a bottle cap in the glass.

When the radio remained silent, she tried again. "Help! This is Melissa Mason. I'm in Logan Voss's truck at the entrance to Lucas Devlin's ranch. Someone shot at the passenger window. I need help!"

"Melissa?"

"Yes!" *Oh, God.* "Hello, can you hear me?" She wasn't sure who was speaking, but she knew she'd heard his voice before. "Who is this?"

"Melissa, this is Mark Hartman. I'm with Jake Thorne."

"Thank God." They were Logan's friends. She could trust them. "Don't lose me," she begged.

"I'm not going to lose you, Melissa," Mark stated, his voice composed and encouraging. "But I need you to calm down and tell me where you are again. This time slowly."

Her nerves shattered, Melissa bit her lip as she tried to collect herself. "Mark, I'm in Logan's truck at the entrance to Lucas Devlin's ranch. Someone shot at me," she said, her voice trembling.

"Are you hurt?" Mark asked.

"N-no. I'm just scared."

"Okay. Now listen to me, Melissa. Jake and I aren't far from you. We'll be there in a few minutes. Stay down until we get to you. Understand?"

"Y-yes. I will. Hurry, please!" Clutching the microphone in her hand, she prayed they'd get to her quickly.

As Logan walked out of Lucas's home, he ran into Tom Morgan who lived in a guest house on the property. "Your uncle insisted your family has nothing to do with the trouble out at the Windcroft farm," Logan told Tom.

"That's pretty much what I expected him to say. Thanks for coming out, though."

"I hope things will quiet down." He started for his pickup. "I need to be heading back. Melissa's waiting for me." At least she'd stayed at home. With her determination to get a story, he'd half expected her to show up at the Devlin's ranch. With a sigh, Logan opened his door.

"N-no. I'm just scared," a voice cried out on his radio.

"Okay. Now listen to me, Melissa. Jake and I aren't far from you. We'll be there in a few minutes. Stay down until we get to you. Understand?"

Logan froze. Melissa? That couldn't be possible. She was back at the house waiting for him.

"Y-yes. I will. Hurry, please!"

"God, that's Melissa!" Logan shouted. Jumping into the truck, he snatched up the microphone. "Melissa, this is Logan. Where are you?"

"Logan!" Melissa screamed, her voice raw with fear. "I'm at the entrance to the Devlin ranch. I'm in your truck. Someone shot at me. The passenger window's shattered."

He muttered an oath. "Are you all right?" he demanded, his chest feeling as if it might explode.

"Yes, I'm just scared. I wasn't hurt."

Logan turned the key and the engine roared to life. "I'll be right there, sweetheart. Stay put and stay down!"

"Please hurry," she whispered, her teeth chattering as icy fear traveled down her spine.

"I'm going with you," Tom said, dashing around to the other side of Logan's pickup. He'd barely made it inside before Logan floored it. Rocks and dirt flew in their wake as the vehicle bolted down the dirt road.

"Logan, this is Mark," his friend said over the CB. "Jake and I are about five minutes away."

"Thanks, guys. I'm closer, maybe two minutes from her. I'll meet you. Keep an eye out for anyone suspicious on your way." He turned his attention to Melissa. "Sweetheart, can you hear me?"

"Yes, Logan. I can hear you."

"I'm almost there." The vehicle rounded a curve practically on two wheels. Logan spotted his pickup parked at an angle off the dirt road. "I can see you now. Have you heard any more shots?"

"No."

"I'll be there in seconds," he promised. He'd never heard her sound so terrified.

As he came out of the turn, he stomped on the accelerator. The tires kicked up clouds of dust as it shot down the road toward her. When they got close enough, Logan slammed on the brakes and jerked the pickup to a stop. Jumping out, he raced toward her, Tom hot on his heels. He yanked open the door, then reached inside and gathered Melissa into his arms.

"Melissa, sweetheart, are you okay?" Logan's body sheltered hers as he held her tight against him.

Relieved to be in Logan's arms, Melissa clung to him. "Yes," she said breathlessly, her body trembling.

Another vehicle pulled up. Mark and Jake hopped out and ran toward them.

"Is she all right?" Jake asked.

"I think so," Logan called back.

"Stay low while we check around," Mark told them.

Logan held Melissa and calmed her as Jake, Mark and Tom, armed with rifles, investigated the surrounding area.

Melissa stayed by Logan's side as she repeated her story, explaining the shot had come as she was turning onto the dirt road.

Searching Melissa's face, Logan kissed her. "God, I was scared to death when I heard you on the radio. Are you sure you're not hurt?"

Burrowing closer to him, she whispered, "No, but I'm glad you were nearby."

"What were you doing out here? I thought I told you to wait at the house for me?" He silently berated himself for leaving her behind. If he hadn't, this wouldn't have happened.

She met his gaze and the intensity of it shocked her. "I know you did. I just wanted to tell you that Daniel called. He wants me to—"

His muscles tensed. *Her job.* "You risked your life for a story."

She searched his tight expression. "No, Logan, it's not like that. I've faced difficult situations in the past, but I—"

"So this is nothing new," he cut in, annoyance creeping into his tone. "You put yourself in danger all the time." He knew her job was demanding, but the awareness she'd almost been killed twice—both in relation to him—made him shake with alarm.

Melissa stared at him in silence, thinking it was best if she left as soon as possible. Logan would never have to know that she'd been coming for him.

He didn't love her. His disparaging tone told her that. Her last-minute attempt to be with him was only putting off the inevitable. Logan wasn't going to ask her to stay.

Taking a breath, she said, "Some stories are more risky than others." Melissa didn't know where the strength to say the words came from. "I've been in some pretty tough circumstances before, but I've never been shot at."

His eyes narrowed. "Doesn't that bother you?"

"Yes, it does," she admitted. "I try not to think about it. It's a risk every reporter takes."

He set her away from him. "But the risk doesn't stop you from investigating?"

She shook her head, her words coming harder than she'd planned. "I do what I'm assigned. I don't always get to pick and choose. I've worked for a long time to earn a promotion. This story is my ticket."

"Your work is that important to you, isn't it?" he asked.

She looked him straight in the eyes, knowing that without Logan, her work was all she had. "Yes, it is. As a matter of fact, Daniel wants me back in Houston tomorrow. My promotion came through. I'm going to be a news anchor beginning this weekend."

"I see." His lips compressing, Logan felt as though

he was being ripped open. She'd been waiting for this call. It was time for her to leave Royal.

And him.

Someone cleared his throat and they both turned to see Mark, Jake and Tom standing behind them. Logan felt his face flame with heat as he took in the speculative looks on their faces. "Did you find anything?" he asked, hoping to stave off comments about what they'd heard.

"No. It appears the shot came from across the road in those woods," Jake said, pointing in that direction.

"Whoever it was is long gone," Mark added.

"Why would they have shot at me?" Melissa asked. "I don't know anything."

Tom shoved his hands in his pockets. "I'm not sure they were shooting at you. Since it was Logan's vehicle, whoever did this might have thought he was driving," he suggested. "They might have done this to scare Logan off."

She frowned. "Why?"

"We're trying to settle things between the Devlins and the Windcrofts. It looks like someone is doing their best to make sure that doesn't happen. The reason is still a mystery." Jake looked at Logan. "What did Lucas have to say?"

"He claims his family isn't responsible for anything happening at the Windcrofts' and he'd like nothing better than to see the feud between the two families settled for good."

"Did he know anything about the map?" Mark asked.

"Only that it had been stolen. He doesn't believe a Devlin had anything to do with it."

Melissa looked away from Logan. "So you still don't know who took the map?" she asked Mark.

"No, but we're showing the picture around. We'll find the woman who took it."

Though interested in learning the details, Melissa found her mind couldn't focus. All she wanted to do was return home with Logan and curl up in the safety of his arms. Instead, she had to face reality and pack.

She extended her hand, her fingers still trembling. "Thank you so much for coming to my aid. I really appreciate it."

Mark briefly shook her hand. "No problem, Melissa. We're glad you're okay." He shot a look at Logan. "You have this under control, buddy?" he asked.

Logan glowered at them. "Yeah. Tom—"

"I'll drive this truck to my place, Logan," Tom said, reading his thoughts. "You can get it tomorrow. I'll also call Gavin and report what happened."

"Thanks." Hustling Melissa to his ranch truck, Logan helped her inside, then climbed behind the wheel, started the engine and stepped on the accelerator, flying past Mark and Jake who were just getting into Mark's vehicle.

Twelve

Frustrated that he hadn't protected Melissa, that she'd almost been shot, Logan kept his mouth shut on the way to the Wild Spur. Though he'd never let himself truly believe they could have a life together, the idea had taken shape in the back of his mind.

He'd been dreaming. But loving her, his heart had hoped. How could he ask her to give up what she loved, what she'd worked so hard to achieve? He understood what drove her to pursue her career. His entire life had been devoted to the ranch. Without it, he'd feel empty.

The trouble was, without Melissa, the ranch didn't go far in filling the hole in his heart. He glanced at her. She sat beside him with her hands clasped in her lap, her face pale. He wanted to be angry with her, wanted to shake her and tell her no job was worth her life.

You don't have that right.

No, he didn't.

They were lovers. Nothing more.

Since her return to Royal, she'd made it perfectly clear her life, job and future were in Houston.

You love her.

Yeah, he did. But he wasn't part of her equation, was he? He wrestled with telling her how much she meant to him, telling her that he couldn't live without her.

Asking her to stay.

Begging her to marry him. To live with him here. To have his children. He could easily imagine her with their child in her arms. A little girl with her mother's beautiful green eyes.

God, how could she even think of leaving? They'd lost many years of being together, loving each other, sharing ups and downs—endless nights of making love.

Over the past few weeks, they'd recaptured part of their past, but it hadn't changed the present course of their lives. He toyed briefly with the idea of combining their worlds, but in his heart he knew that would never work. She didn't belong here on the Wild Spur any more than he belonged in Houston. And he couldn't operate his ranch long-distance. He had no right to hold on to his dreams and ask her to let go of hers.

"When do you have to leave?" he forced himself to ask, breaking the tense silence between them.

Melissa looked at Logan and shuddered. His hands were nearly white as he gripped the steering wheel, and he hadn't even looked at her when he'd spoken. She turned her head and stared out the window. He was so handsome, so strong, so confident and in control.

She wished she felt the same way.

But she didn't. When Logan had walked up to her at the anniversary ball, her entire existence had changed. She'd never stood a chance.

Leaving him years ago had broken her heart. Over time, she'd picked up the pieces and vowed never again to allow herself to be hurt. But the pain she'd endured then was nothing compared to the pain ravaging her soul at this moment.

"In about an hour." It cost her dearly to say the words. Though Daniel had said to be in Houston by tomorrow, Logan didn't know that. With everything between them, there was no way she could postpone her departure until the morning. She needed a clean break. It was the only chance she had of leaving Royal in one piece. "I'll pack my things as soon as we get back."

"I see." Logan could barely squeeze the words past the knot in his throat. What they'd shared the past few weeks came down to one final hour together. He didn't want to spend the time at odds with her. Pulling into his driveway, he parked his truck and turned off the key. "Is there anything you need help with?" he asked in an effort to diffuse the strain between them.

Melissa shook her head. "No, I don't have that much to do." Opening her door, she got out. They walked inside together. As they stepped into the house, she turned and said, "Logan, I'm really sorry about your truck. I'll pay for the damages."

A frown creased his brow. "You think I'm upset about

the damn truck?" he growled. He embraced her. "Ah, sweetheart, come here. Melissa, I'm not angry at you."

She looked up at him, her eyes searching his. "You're not?"

"I'm just having a hard time accepting that your job puts you in danger." A harder time believing that it didn't bother her.

Melissa caught her breath, realizing she'd pulled off her ruse quite well. He'd believed her when she'd said it was her job sometimes to walk on the edge of danger. "Oh."

His arms tightened around her. "And I guess I always knew the time would come when you'd leave." His chest rumbled with quiet laughter. "Being with you for the past couple of weeks was worth the worry you put me through."

Pulling away, Melissa looked up at him, her fingers playing with the button on his shirt. "Thanks, I think." She smiled, then pressed her lips together to maintain her composure. "It's been wonderful, Logan. I'll never forget you."

His gaze met hers. "I want you to know I respect what you do, and I'm proud of you." She was an amazing reporter. He couldn't resent that she loved her work.

"You'll never know how much that means to me." Unsteady, she stepped out of his arms before she broke down and made a fool of herself. "I'd better start packing,"

He nodded and she walked away, step by fragile step. Her vision blurred. By sheer will, she reached her room and shut the door. Leaning against the solid, cold wood, she cried.

This time when she left, it would be permanent.

She'd never hold Logan again. As she dried her eyes, she told herself how fortunate she'd been to have the chance to be with him once more. It had been wonderful—more thrilling than she could ever have dreamed.

Numb, she called Rick, discussed Daniel's call and his request that they return to Houston, then told him she'd be ready in an hour. She stored her phone in her purse, and gathered her clothes. What didn't fit in the one bag she'd brought with her, she stuffed in the shopping bags she'd kept. Finished, she glanced around the room to be sure she wasn't leaving anything behind.

But she was.

Logan.

Every single fiber of her revolted at the thought of never seeing him again.

And then she could no longer hold it inside. Tears flowed hot and fast as she sobbed with soul-deep agony. She buried her face into the bed covers to muffle the sounds of her pain and cried until there was nothing left inside her.

Until she lay exhausted and emotionally spent.

A tap on her door had her sitting up and wiping her eyes.

"You ready?"

"One minute," she replied to Rick, surprised at how calm she sounded when her life was falling apart. At least it wasn't Logan. She doubted she could have handled him now.

With what little life was left in her, she went into the bathroom, washed her face, then repaired her makeup.

Anyone looking at her would attribute her paleness to the shooting, not her heart breaking.

Now, all she had left to do was to face Logan and say goodbye.

Resolving to leave with her dignity intact, without dropping to her knees and pleading for his love, Melissa picked up her things and left the room. As she came out the front door, Logan was talking to Rick in the courtyard. Melissa focused her attention on her videographer. "I'm ready," she said, joining them.

"I'll take your bags." Rick left to put her belongings in his truck.

Pain stabbed Melissa as she turned to Logan. "Well, I guess this is goodbye." Despite her attempt to keep her emotions under control, tears welled in her eyes.

Logan's gaze swept her as regret and sadness stole through him. A hundred men couldn't have stopped him from touching her. He stepped close, stroked her cheek with his knuckles, then cupped her neck with his hand and drew her to him. "I guess," he answered on a rough sigh. Aligning their bodies, he embraced her, then lifted her mouth to his. From somewhere deep inside him he managed a brief smile. "It's okay, sweetheart. As you said, we both knew this wasn't going to last."

Melissa choked back a sob. "I know."

"Be careful out there."

"I will." With her whispered promise between them, she raised up on her toes intent on giving him a brief kiss. But the second her lips touched his, her control shattered. She gave herself to him, body, heart and mind.

Their kiss shifted, deepened until all that remained was sensation.

Hot.

Demanding.

Touching her to her very soul.

Logan devoured Melissa's essence. He wanted to make sure she remembered what they had shared, to show her with this kiss that he loved her. Words he had no right to say. He made love to her mouth, pouring himself into the only way he could to show how much she meant to him.

And then he found the strength to let her go.

He stepped away. "Take care of yourself, sweetheart," he whispered on a harsh breath.

Aching to stay, Melissa nodded. She walked away, unable to look back. She got into Rick's truck and shut the door. As he started the engine, she caught a glimpse of Logan in the side mirror. He stood still in the courtyard, his hands on his hips, his head facing the ground.

A man alone.

A man she loved desperately.

Rick touched her shoulder and a sob escaped her lips. Melissa held her hand up to stave off any conversation. He gave her a gentle squeeze, then put the truck in gear. They traveled down the long drive, each second taking her farther away from the happiest she'd been in her life.

Memories of leaving long ago haunted her. She fisted her hands and fought off another wave of emotion as she looked out over the rolling hills and the cattle grazing in the distance.

Was she doing the right thing? Years ago she'd been a naive girl. Because she'd believed a vindictive woman, she'd doubted Logan's love. Truthfully, she'd never given him a chance.

Melissa thought about Jessamine Golden, the map and the rose petals from her purse. A woman whom legend told lived outside the law…a woman with secrets and a soft heart. A strong woman who had the courage to stand up for herself.

In every other facet of her life, Melissa faced challenges with strength and perseverance. Why not now? To leave without telling Logan she loved him would be reliving her past mistake all over again.

Logan hadn't said he loved her, but then, she hadn't confessed her love for him, either. So afraid of getting hurt by him again, she'd waited and hoped and dreamed. She hadn't given him any reason to admit his feelings for her.

She frowned. Why would he?

Ever since she'd arrived, she'd put up a front by talking about her job. Keeping a shield between them by mentioning her promotion. Though she loved her work, becoming an anchor would mean nothing without Logan in her life.

Sitting up, she wiped the dampness from her cheeks. She refused to leave without ever knowing what could have been. If there was the slightest chance that Logan loved her, it was a risk she was willing to take.

The truck cleared the cattle guard. Melissa grabbed Rick's arm. "Stop the truck!"

"What?"

They drove under the Wild Spur sign. "I said stop the truck!"

Rick slammed on the brakes and the truck skidded to a stop. A plume of dust churned past them, sweeping across the road that led to the highway a short distance away. His head whipped in her direction. "Melissa, are you all right?"

"Yes," she cried, struggling to get her breathing under control. "I've never been more all right in my life."

Rick shoved the truck into park, his expression wrought with concern. "What is it? What's wrong?"

She grabbed the handle and pushed open the door. "I can't leave." Climbing out of the truck, she looked at Rick. "Go to Houston without me. I'm going back to Logan."

Rick's eyes widened, then he grinned. "Are you sure?"

"Yes." And she was. She'd never been more sure of anything in her life.

Pride filled Rick's face. "Well, get in and I'll take you up to the house."

She shook her head and stepped back. "No, I'll walk. I need the time to gather my thoughts. Just put my stuff on the side of the road," she told him, then shut the door and started walking.

"Good luck, honey," he called as he unloaded her bags.

Melissa looked back, waved, then smiled. "I'll call you later." The engine revved behind her then faded as he drove away.

"I love you, Logan," she whispered as she continued up the driveway.

She felt a sense of homecoming. Fear of being hurt

had stopped her from admitting her feelings for the past few weeks, but she wasn't afraid anymore. Melissa had never dreamed that she would see Logan again, or that they would have a second chance. She thought she'd made peace with that. Now she knew that she hadn't really been living.

Yes, she loved working, but there was more to life than chasing stories and reporting the news. There was loving deeply—as she loved Logan. There were friends, not just coworkers. There were birthday and anniversary celebrations and holiday dinners—the kind that left you with a feeling of warmth and togetherness.

As she walked, she thought of a million things she wanted to say to Logan—all of the things she'd kept locked inside for years.

Once, a long time ago, he had asked her to marry him. That day was still vivid in her mind, one of the happiest moments in her life. She wanted to put the past behind them, give them new and special memories to share.

As she neared the house, her pulse quickened as her gaze swept first the corral, then the driveway, then finally the courtyard.

Her heart ached when she saw Logan. He hadn't moved from the spot where he'd been standing when she left.

Oh, Logan, I do love you.

Her eyes began filling with a fresh wave of tears. He must have heard her footsteps, or the whispers of her heart, because he slowly raised his head and their eyes met. Shock flashed across his handsome face. Her footsteps faltered momentarily, then she recovered and continued walking until she was only a few feet away. All the time he watched her, his eyes intense and questioning.

"What happened? Was there an accident?" Logan searched Melissa's expression as she stopped in front of him. Her eyes were red and swollen.

Melissa's auburn hair swayed as she shook her head. "No."

"What are you doing here? Did you and Rick have a fight?" What had taken place between her and Rick that she'd had to walk back to the ranch? She didn't look as if she'd been hurt, but there was a trace of wariness in her eyes.

"No, Rick is…in his truck. I came back because I needed to ask you something," she said softly.

At the raw emotion in her voice, he tensed. Did she have any idea of what she was doing to him? It had been hell letting her go. Though he'd known it was the right thing to do for her, the pain of watching her leave had crushed him. "Do you need a ride or something?" He steeled himself against doing something foolish, such as reaching out for her. If he did, this time he wouldn't be able to let her go.

A small smiled formed on her lips, warming her eyes. "No. At least I don't think so."

Confused, Logan's brows dipped. "What then?"

She stepped closer to him, and took a deep breath as she stared into his eyes. "Logan, a long time ago you asked me to marry you. At the time, I loved you so much. But I made a terrible mistake when I didn't trust you. I'm not going to make that mistake again." She released the breath on an unsteady sigh.

"Being with you these past weeks has been wonderful. No, more than wonderful. It's been amazing. Logan…I'm so in love with you that I hurt here." She placed her hand over her heart. When he started to speak, she touched her finger to his lips. "Let me finish," she said, letting her hand fall.

"Logan, will you marry me?"

Logan's breath got trapped in his lungs. "What?"

Melissa smiled. "That's not the answer I was expecting. A simple yes was what I was hoping for, unless—"

"Yes," he growled, then hauled her against him. His mouth crashed down on hers in a long, drugging kiss. Fire consumed him as their mouths mated in a heat-induced frenzy. Keeping her in his embrace, he lifted his lips and gazed into her eyes. "God, I've missed you."

She chuckled. "I've only been gone fifteen minutes."

"It's been fifteen minutes of pure hell," he confessed, holding her in his arms. "I love you, Melissa. You'd better be damned sure you love me because I'm never going to let you go. You're part of me."

"That's a relief because, for a moment, you had me worried." She wrapped her arms around his neck.

"*I* had *you* worried? When I saw you, my heart was in my throat." He stroked her hair. "I can't believe you're here. I love you so much, sweetheart. I wanted you to stay, prayed that you would."

She touched his face. "Really?"

"More than you'll ever know. I don't think I ever stopped loving you," he said. "When I saw you at the anniversary ball, I couldn't believe it. I knew then that I couldn't let you leave without touching you."

"You were so angry. When you offered us a place to stay, I didn't know what to think," she admitted.

"It was the only way I could keep you here."

"I was upset with you at the time, but that was because I didn't want you to know that I still loved you." At the time she hadn't admitted as much to herself. "I'm glad you were so persistent. I'm sorry that we lost so many years, but we have forever to make up for it." She kissed him.

"You're right." His eyes darkened.

"What matters now is we're together."

"Forever." His fingers wrapped around her neck. "It hurt so much to let you go." He had survived her leaving him years ago, but this time he'd known he would never recover.

"Why did you?" Melissa asked, gazing into his eyes. Though convinced he loved her, she needed to hear his reason.

"Watching you these past few weeks, I realized how talented you are. I know how much your career means to you. I didn't want to take that away from you."

"Logan—"

He kissed away her words, preventing her from finishing. "No, listen," he insisted, his lips hovering above hers. "We both know we can't go back all those years. You've worked hard to build your career. I told you how proud I am of you and everything you've accomplished. I meant it. Together we'll find a way to make this work."

Melissa didn't think it was possible to admire Logan more than she did at that moment. "I enjoy what I do, but it doesn't define who I am. I'm not taking the promotion."

He shook his head. "The promotion in Houston is what you've worked for. I can't let you give that up."

"I don't want to live in Houston, Logan. I want to live here on the Wild Spur, with you."

"Melissa—"

"I think Joe Fisher may have an opening at WRYL. He gave me his card and asked me to call him if I was interested in working here."

His face burst into a smile. "Really? You'd want to work here?"

Her eyes softened as she nodded. "I want to be an anchor and I can be that wherever you are. I know how much you love this ranch. I'd never ask you to give it up. I want a chance for us to enjoy each other, to discover all the wonderful things in life that we were never able to. Until now." She pressed her hand to his chest, felt the beat of his heart. "I want to take pleasure in the freedom of touching you. I want to make love whenever we feel like it. And if you're willing, I want to have your children and raise them right here."

"You want to have children?" The thought of her carrying his child made his knees weak.

"Yes, please," she whispered, loving him. "I love you, Logan. I always will."

Logan swept her up in his arms and started for the house. He'd never dreamed that when he'd seen Melissa at the Royal anniversary celebration, he'd be lucky enough to win her love again. With their past behind them, he intended to spend the rest of his life making her happy.

She laughed. "Logan, what are you doing?"

"If we're going to start on those children, then we'd better get married soon."

Melissa squealed as he carried her inside to his room. "Really?" she asked, her eyes lighting with joy.

"Sweetheart, I love you. And I've waited more than ten years to make you my wife. I'm not waiting a day longer than necessary to start a family."

Starting right now, he thought, as he began unbuttoning her blouse. "Now, what was that you said about making love whenever we feel like it?"

* * * * *

STRICTLY
CONFIDENTIAL
ATTRACTION

BY
BRENDA JACKSON

Brenda Jackson is a "die heart" romantic who married her childhood sweetheart and still proudly wears the "going steady" ring he gave her when she was fifteen. Because she's always believed in the power of love, Brenda's stories always have happy endings. In her real-life love story, Brenda and her husband of thirty-three years live in Jacksonville, Florida and have two sons.

A *USA TODAY* bestselling author of over thirty romance titles, Brenda divides her time between family, writing and working in management at a major insurance company. You may write to Brenda at PO Box 28267, Jacksonville, FL 3226, USA, by e-mail at WriterBJackson@aol.com or visit her website at www.brendajackson.net.

Don't miss Brenda Jackson's exciting new novel,
***One Night with the Wealthy Rancher,* available in**
August 2010 from Mills & Boon® Desire™.

ACKNOWLEDGEMENTS

To my husband and best friend, Gerald Jackson, Sr.

To the members of the Brenda Jackson Book Club.
This one is for you.

And thanks to my Heavenly Father
who gave me the gift to write.

Prologue

From the diary of Jessamine Golden
September 12, 1910

Dear Diary,

Brad and I had another picnic on the lake today and there, beneath the branches of the willow tree, he told me that he loved me. His words stole my breath and everything around us got silent with such a profound statement from him. Then he gave me a heart-shaped pendant that was etched with two intertwining roses. Engraved on the back were our initials and he said his gift would always be a symbol of the love we share.

His words and gift brought tears to my eyes and when I told him how much I loved him, he pulled me into his arms and held me like he never wanted to let me go. And he kissed me in that special way of his that makes me want to be with him always and give up my quest for vengeance.

But I can't.

The circumstances as they are, I know what we are sharing can't last forever, although I want it to, more than anything. But I have to be honest with myself and with him. Brad is a man of duty, honor bound to do the right thing, and I have made a vow of revenge which goes against everything the man that I love stands for.

Oh, diary, my life is filled with so much turmoil. The woman in me longs for Brad's kisses, his touch and the way he makes me feel. That part of me wants to take what he offered me today— a love greater than any I have ever known that will last for all eternity.

However, I can't forget what I must do before my father can truly rest in peace.

I had vowed not to give my heart to any man before I settled a score, but it is too late. I feel the loving heat of the pendant as it rests between my breasts while I pen this entry. Brad Webster has my heart and I am deeply torn between love and duty.

One

"**I** need you, Alli."

Alison Lind's breath caught and she looked up from the papers in her hand and met the intense hazel eyes of Mark Hartman, convinced she had misheard his words.

Her heart flipped automatically whenever he did more than give her a casual glance. His teakwood-brown complexion held features that were rugged, sexy, mesmerizing. Broad-shouldered with a muscular build, he stood tall at a height of six foot one, and whenever he spoke in his deep, husky voice, her pulse raced.

She had secretly loved her handsome boss ever since he had returned to Royal, Texas, two years ago to open his self-defense studio and she had been hired as his secretary. Recently, he had changed her job title to administrative assistant, and the only time he'd ever indicated that he needed her was when he summoned her to his office to confirm an appointment or to discuss some other urgent business matter.

Inhaling in a deep breath, she held his gaze and asked in a hesitant voice, "You need me?"

"Yes," he said, coming around to sit on the edge of his desk. "Desperately."

How I wish, she thought staring at him, trying to keep the heat of desire from showing in her face; and trying even harder not to notice the way his jeans stretched tight across firm, muscular thighs. There was no doubt in her mind a miscommunication was taking place and he hadn't meant the words the way she hoped. In all honesty, there was no reason her insides should be feeling all giddy and she wished she could stop that warmth from intensifying between her legs. Too bad the attraction was one-sided. The majority of the time, Mark acted as if he didn't know she was alive. To him, she was his ever-efficient administrative assistant and nothing more.

Alli took another deep breath and asked, "You need me for what purpose?"

"Erika."

She raised an eyebrow. "You need me for Erika? I don't understand." Erika was Mark's eleven-month-old niece. He had become her legal guardian three months ago when his only brother and sister-in-law were killed in a car accident. Thoughts of the little girl sent a soft feeling through Alli. Erika was such a darling little girl and captured the hearts of all those who came in contact with her.

Alli watched as Mark blew out a breath before answering her. "I'm at the end of my rope and I don't know what to do or where to turn. As you know I've been having babysitting issues ever since Mrs. Tucker left to take care of her elderly parents in Florida. It may be months before she returns, if ever. So far I haven't been able to hire a dependable, not to mention competent, sitter. Yesterday was the last straw when I dropped by the ranch unexpectedly to find Erika's caregiver too absorbed in her soap opera to notice that Erika had crawled away and was outside on the patio, just a few feet from the pool. I told the woman a hundred times to always keep the door to the patio closed but she had forgotten. Yesterday wasn't the first time it's slipped her memory."

Alli shuddered. She didn't want to think about what might have happened had Erika tumbled into the pool, but looking at Mark, it was evident that he had thought about it. "You let the woman go." It was a statement and not a question. She couldn't imagine anyone being that careless where a child was concerned.

"Yes, immediately."

Alli nodded. "Who's keeping Erika today?"

"Christine. She's been kind enough to be Erika's backup sitter. Lately I've been using her more than I had intended. Now that she and Jake are engaged I'm sure she has more to do with her time than watch Erika for me."

Alli had to agree. Christine Travers was one of her closest friends in Royal and had become engaged to Jacob Thorne a couple of months ago. Christine had mentioned that she had taken care of Erika a few times and that she had enjoyed doing so. Alli knew all about Christine's busy schedule, especially since Jake was running for mayor and Christine was his campaign manager.

Alli met Mark's gaze. "You still haven't told me what specifically you need me for." For a moment he stayed silent as he studied her and Alli felt the increase of her pulse as the seconds ticked by.

"I know it's a lot to ask, but you're the only person I know I can truly depend on. I've watched you with Erika before when I've brought her into the studio. Not only that, I've seen you with other kids when the mothers come by for their classes and assume we have babysitting service. You're a natural, Alli. Kids take to you and you are the most responsible person I know."

Alli shrugged. His words weren't exactly the accolades she wanted to hear from the man she loved, but something was better than nothing. Besides, he was right. Her ability to care for children came naturally. She had grown up in a household with her mother and her baby sister Kara, who was seven years younger. Her father had abandoned his wife and daughters when Alison was twelve and never looked back. To make ends meet, Alli's mother had worked two jobs, leaving Alison to take care of Kara the majority of the time. When her mother had died right before Alli's seventeenth birthday, Alli had become Kara's sole caretaker. She couldn't help but smile knowing that Kara was doing wonderfully now in her second year of college at Texas Southern University in Houston.

"I'm asking you to be Erika's nanny."

Mark's words cut into Alison's thoughts and she blinked and looked at him, hoping she had heard wrong. "Excuse me?"

Mark met her gaze. Held it. "I need you to be Erika's nanny, which means you'll have to move in with me at the ranch and—"

"Whoa, wait a minute," Alli said, coming to her feet.

"There's no way I can do that. Have you forgotten that I work every day? I'm your assistant. I'm needed here and—"

Mark held up a hand, cutting her off. "Erika and I need you at the ranch with us even more, Alli. You're the only person I can depend on. The only person I can trust to take care of her. Knowing what could have happened yesterday took a good twenty years off my life. If anything had happened to her…"

Alli swallowed the lump in her throat. She was seeing a side of Mark she had never seen before, a vulnerable side. It was clearly evident that Erika had wiggled her way into her uncle's heart. When his brother and sister-in-law had been killed so unexpectedly, Mark hadn't been prepared to become a parent at twenty-eight, yet he was doing so and was trying to take care of Erika as best he could. But still there were obstacles in the way of what Mark was asking her to do and she decided to point them out to him.

"I'm majoring in computer engineering and attending college two nights a week—Tuesdays and Thursdays."

"I'll make sure I'm at home those nights so that won't be a problem."

Fat chance, Alison thought. He was asking her to move in with him at the ranch, which was a major problem. She was in love with him for Pete's sake. How could she handle being in such close proximity to him? Working with him at the self-defense studio was bad enough; but she wasn't sure she would survive sharing living quarters with him. Although she knew from the one time she had dropped off papers for him to sign that the Hartman Ranch was a huge place, the idea that they would be living under the same roof was unsettling.

"What about my work here?" she decided to ask.

"I'll go through an employment agency and find a temporary replacement. I'm willing to pay you double what you are making here."

Alison's eyes widened. "Double?"

"You heard me right. As Erika's nanny I'll pay you double. I need you just that much and as far as I'm concerned what you'll be doing is invaluable. You can't put a price on peace of mind."

Alison sat back down. *Double?* She breathed in deeply. As his administrative assistant she was getting paid what she thought was a very good salary, but she could certainly use the extra money for Kara's tuition. Kara had gotten a scholarship but that hadn't been enough to cover all the expenses. Alison had gone into her savings the last two semesters and if an emergency was to come up any time soon, she definitely would be in a tight spot. What Mark was offering would put more than a boost in her savings.

"And there will be a bonus."

Alison glanced up and met Mark's gaze. Once again his words had grabbed her attention. "A bonus?"

"Yes. One thousand dollars up-front just for agreeing to what I'm offering."

Stunned, Alison went speechless for a moment. *One thousand dollars?* That was money she could use to put down on another car. She was still driving the one she had bought right out of high school seven years ago, and lately it had been giving her problems. Just last week she had broken down while coming from class. Luckily, someone had stopped to help her, although the man had given her the creeps most of the time he'd been doing so.

She breathed in deeply. Mark was making his proposal hard to resist. And that in itself was the key word. *Resist.* For two years she had had to resist him, refusing to give into temptation and sharing her feelings. Instead she had fought her attraction and fully intended to continue to do so. She knew the last thing she needed was to place herself in a position where her heart could be broken if she assumed too much. But still, what he said was true. He and Erika needed her and there was no way she could not help him out. And she couldn't overlook the fact that he was helping her out financially as well.

"This will be a temporary arrangement, right?" Alison asked, feeling the need to have that point clarified.

"Yes. I'm hoping Mrs. Tucker is coming back to Royal in another month or so."

"And if she doesn't?"

"Then I'll run another ad in the paper and pray the results are better. There has to be someone in Royal who's responsible enough to keep Erika every day."

Alison nodded. "Will it really be necessary for me to move in with you and Erika at the ranch? I can stay at my place and drive to your—"

"No, I prefer for you to be there at the ranch with us. I may have business to take care of at night."

Alison nodded again. She was fully aware that he was a member of the Texas Cattleman's Club. Membership in the state's most exclusive club was restricted to wealthy ranchers, prestigious businessmen and oil tycoons. She'd heard that the members would often get together a few nights a week to play cards, share drinks and discuss business. But most of the good people of Royal knew that wasn't all they did. There were those who claimed through the generations, the club members had accepted the responsibility for the town's security and over the years had put their lives on the line for justice and peace. The only thing Alli did know for certain was that the club did great things for the community in the way of fund-raisers like the annual Cattleman's Ball, where the proceeds went to various charities.

Christine had talked Alison into attending Royal's Anniversary Ball that had occurred several weeks ago, and she had to admit that she had enjoyed herself…at least until Mark had arrived. Once he had walked into the room, she had found herself constantly watching him, as every other unattached woman had done. And as usual, he hadn't noticed her.

"So will you do it?"

Anytime and anyplace with you, she wanted to say. She hated her wanton thoughts, but when it came to Mark Hartman, they just wouldn't go away. She sighed deeply and did what she always did whenever her thoughts toppled onto the side of fantasy instead of reality, which was to scold herself inwardly and get back on track. Mark didn't have a single clue about how she felt about him and she intended to keep it that way.

"Alli? Will you help me out?"

She met his gaze and almost drowned in the plea she saw in his eyes. He did need her, or at least, thought he did. And although it wasn't in the way she wanted, it would have to do.

She stood and smiled. "Yes, Mark, I will help you out with Erika."

* * *

Half an hour later, Mark released a deep breath when Alli walked out of the room, closing the door behind herself. Both elated and frustrated, he moved away from his desk to walk over to the window. The plans had been finalized. He had contacted a reputable temp agency who would be sending someone in the morning. Alli was to train the person and by tomorrow evening she would be ready to move in with him and Erika, which was both a curse as well as a blessing.

From the first moment that Jake had told Mark about Alli and how efficient she would be as his secretary, he had been eager to interview her for the position. When he had seen her, he had gone almost speechless and had immediately known things wouldn't work out because of the sudden attraction he felt toward her. But he had needed a good secretary and everyone in town claimed she would be the best. Although she was a private person, most people knew her from working as a secretary for the Royal school system.

He had hired her on the spot, presenting her with a higher salary than she had been receiving. That was one move he hadn't regretted making. She had been the efficient, if shy, Alison Lind during the early months and had been instrumental in helping to get his studio off the ground. She had done the marketing, promotion, advertising, accounting…just about everything, freeing him to do what he did best, which was teaching the art of self-defense, primarily to women.

To him it was important that all women knew how to protect themselves. He doubted he would ever forgive himself for not being around when his wife had been attacked and killed while leaving the shopping mall late one night. As part of the marine's special forces, he had been away on a mission in the Middle East at the time. He knew he could not bring Patrice back, but maybe what he was doing would help other women who found themselves in a similar situation.

His thoughts shifted back to Alli. During the two years that they had worked together, he had tried like hell not to notice her, not to be attracted to her, not to want her. And for a while he thought he had gotten his pretended nonchalance down to an art form. But then all it would take was for him to walk out of his office and catch her unaware of being watched, as she filed away some document on a high shelf. He'd notice what a gorgeous pair of legs she had, or admire her small waist, pert and firm breasts and curvy thighs, and his nonchalance would be history.

And now she had agreed to move in with him.

His blood heated at the thought, but he quickly cooled it down. Whether Alli worked for him here at Hartman's Self-Defense Studio or at his home as Erika's nanny, their relationship would remain a business one. A serious relationship with any woman was the last thing he wanted or deserved. He had not been there to protect Patrice and, as a result, a part of him felt he couldn't be trusted to keep women safe. No woman needed a man who wasn't trustworthy, so living the rest of his life alone was something he accepted.

Well, he wasn't actually alone, he thought as a smile touched his lips. A few months ago he had been living the life of a carefree bachelor and hadn't been prepared for eight-month-old Erika Danielle Hartman. The first question that had come to his mind was what in the hell was he supposed to do with a kid? But soon the answers had come. He was to do just what his brother Matthew and his wife Candice had known Mark would do. He would provide not only a home for their daughter, but also he would make sure she received every good thing life had to offer, which was something he definitely could afford to do since, during his grandparents' time, oil had been discovered on their property, making the Hartmans instant millionaires.

He glanced at his watch when he heard the sound of the phone. He was expecting a call from Jake. His friend certainly had his plate full with the mayoral campaign while being an active member of the Texas Cattleman's Club, especially now when there were a number of strange things happening in Royal.

Mark reached his desk and quickly picked up the phone. Alli had already left for the day. "Yes?"

"Mark, this is Jake. There will be a meeting at the club tomorrow night at eight. Think you can make it?"

"Yes, I'll be there."

"What about Erika? Do you need Chrissie to watch her for you?"

"No, Alli has agreed to be Erika's nanny until Mrs. Tucker returns or until I can find someone dependable."

"Alli?"

"Yes."

"She's going to be both your assistant and Erika's nanny?"

Mark smiled, knowing Jake was confused. "No. I'm getting someone from a temp agency to handle the assistant duties for a while. Alli will be Erika's full-time nanny."

"Well, hell, Mark, how did you talk her into something like that?"

Mark sat in his desk chair as he thought about Jake's question. "I simply told her that Erika and I needed her." After a short pause he then said, "I also told her I would double what she was making here and I even threw in a bonus of a thousand dollars."

"Whew, you sound like a desperate man."

"When it comes to Erika's well-being, I am."

"Are you sure that you're only thinking about Erika. I can clearly recall your reaction to seeing Alli that night at the Anniversary Ball."

Mark leaned back in his chair. It was at times like this that he wished Jake had a short memory. He couldn't help but remember how speechless he had gotten when he had seen Alli the night Jake was referring to. She had looked nothing like his efficient, shy assistant. She had taken out the knot that she usually wore in her hair and the thick, silky strands had flowed around her shoulders. And that dress…wow! Seeing her in that dress would be forged in his mind as a delectable memory. On any other woman it would have been a simple black dress, but on Alison Lind there hadn't been anything simple about it. He had found himself drinking an entire glass of wine before realizing he had done so while staring at her.

"Okay, so I found her attractive that night. What of it?" he finally asked.

Jake chuckled and then said, "Nothing of it. I'll see you at the meeting tomorrow night. I understand that we have a lot to discuss. Logan heard from Nita Windcroft again today."

Mark rubbed a hand down his face. "She still thinks the Devlins are behind the mischief going on at her place?"

"Yes, and of course the Devlins are still claiming they know nothing about anything."

Mark shook his head. Having grown up in Royal, he knew that Windcrofts and Devlins had been feuding for years. He couldn't help but wonder if perhaps Nita was blowing things out of proportion, given her temper and her obvious dislike of the Devlins. "And what about Jonathan's death? Any new leads?"

It had been discovered a few months ago that instead of dying of a heart attack, Jonathan Devlin had been murdered with a lethal injection of potassium chloride. Sheriff Gavin O'Neal, who was also a member of the Texas Cattleman's Club, was leading the investigation into Jonathan's mysterious death.

"If there are any, Gavin will bring us up to speed. See you tomorrow."

After returning the telephone to its cradle, Mark stood and walked back to the window and stared out. Getting out of the marines after Patrice's death, he had decided to return to Royal to escape the memories. Within a short period of time he had become a member of the Texas Cattleman's Club, a front for members who worked together covertly on secret missions to save innocent lives.

Investigating Jonathan Devlin's death, as well as the incidents Nita Windcroft claimed were happening at her horse ranch, were keeping them busy. Then on top of everything else, there were still the mysteries surrounding the vandalism of the Edgar Halifax display and the map that had been stolen from the Royal Museum.

The latter bothered him more than anything because he had been assigned to keep an eye on the map while it was on the podium. However, he, like everyone else, had gotten distracted when a chandelier fell, nearly killing Melissa Mason, a television reporter, who'd been filming a scene that included the map. During that quick moment of chaos when fellow Cattleman Logan Voss had rushed across the room to save the woman he loved, thwarting an accident that could have been fatal, the map had vanished off the podium. Mark and his fellow club members were determined to get it back. The thief had been caught on film, but it turned out to be just a blurred image of a woman.

And speaking of images… The faces of two females filled his mind. The first was a beautiful little girl who was under his protection and the other was a stunningly attractive woman who could get under his skin if he wasn't careful.

Two

As Alli passed the huge wooden marker of the Hartman Ranch, she couldn't help but ask herself for the umpteenth time whether or not she was doing the right thing. That question was temporarily forgotten when Mark's home loomed into view. It was massive as well as beautiful and she easily could place her modest house inside of it three or four times over.

She recalled the only other time she had been to this ranch and how in awe she had been. She remembered hearing around town how his grandparents had struck oil on the property and, as a result, the Hartmans lives had changed forever.

She also remembered her mother complaining about Mark's father when he would contact her whenever he needed ironing done, which was something Alli's mother had done on occasion to earn extra money. Mildred Lind had often said that Nathaniel Hartman was a cold, heartless and bitter man who hadn't shown anyone—not even his two sons—any love or affection.

When Mark had returned to Royal and contacted her about becoming his secretary, she had been hesitant about working for him, thinking that if he was anything like his father, she would not want him as an employer. Eventually she had decided not to prejudge him. She had worked for him only a couple of weeks before discovering that, although he was a private person, he treated her with kindness and was fair. But it was evident there were demons eating at him.

More than once, especially around the holidays, she had caught an expression of pain and grief in his face and a part of her had regretted all the sadness he had endured in his life. Most of the people in town had heard about the tragedy that had happened to his wife, prompting him to return to Royal. She'd also heard that Mark blamed himself for her death and establishing the studio to teach women self-defense was a way to relieve some of that guilt.

And speaking of guilt, she couldn't help but remember the phone call she'd gotten from her sister that morning. Kara had been all excited about a guy she had met the night before at the library. Alli had listened to her sister go on and on about what a hottie he was and that he had asked her to a party this weekend. Upon hearing that, red flags had gone up in Alli's head, especially after remembering Kara had mentioned earlier in the week how much studying she had to do for a big exam she had next week. Alli had ended up giving Kara some sisterly advice, which included a reminder of how important getting a good education was. Evidently that had been the last thing Kara had wanted to hear and, needless to say, had ended the call quickly. Alli was left wondering if perhaps she had reacted prematurely and laid the lecture on too thick. Kara had concentrated fully on her studies during her first year at Texas Southern and Alli just didn't want her to lose focus now. And Alli especially didn't want this "hottie" to interfere with Kara's studies.

Alli took a deep breath as she brought her car to a stop in front of the huge ranch house with the sprawling front porch, and couldn't help but smile when the door opened and Mark stepped out with Erika in his arms.

Mark had heard the sound of a car approaching and when he had glanced out of the window and saw it was Alli, he had breathed a deep sigh of relief. He had seen her briefly that morning, long enough to introduce her replacement before returning to the ranch to relieve Christine of Erika.

As soon as he stepped onto the porch and watched Alli get out of her car, he was besieged again with thoughts that having her here wasn't a good idea. But it was the only option he had. "Glad you made it," he said, coming to a stop near the steps. She smiled up at him and, although he didn't want it to, his insides felt warm all over.

It didn't help matters when he got a whiff of her perfume. He had long ago accepted that it was the most seductive scent he'd ever come in contact with. She was wearing her hair down around her shoulders, the way he liked. The sunlight slanting on her head made the strands appear more chestnut than dark brown in color.

"I'm glad I made it, too," she said coming to meet him and automatically taking Erika out of his arms to hold her against her shoulder. His niece remembered Alli from the times he had brought her to the studio and went willingly, but then she did the same thing to everyone. It often bothered him how friendly Erika was and knew when she got older he would have to make sure he taught her not to be so open to strangers.

"You need help with your things?" Mark asked, seeing the boxes in the back seat of her car.

He studied the older vehicle and hoped she would use the bonus she would be getting to purchase another one. Recently he had overheard Christine telling Jake how the car had broken down on an isolated road leading into town one night and that Malcolm Durmorr had stopped to offer help.

Malcolm, known around town as a shiftless lowlife who was always on the brink of some kind of disaster, was said to be a distant cousin of the Devlins, although it seemed they weren't eager to claim him. There were a number of things about him that Mark didn't like, especially the get-rich-quick schemes Malcolm had pulled on a couple of innocent, unsuspecting people in Royal.

Mark recalled how Malcolm had come into the Royal Diner one afternoon and had sat eating his dinner while gazing at one particular waitress by the name of Valerie Raines as though he would have preferred having her on his plate instead of the pork chop. The lust in the man's eyes had been disgusting and the thought that Malcolm had been the one to help Alli hadn't set too well with Mark.

Mark suddenly lost his train of thought when Erika,

fascinated with the gold chain around Alli's neck, reached inside Alli's blouse to pull out the topaz pendant attached to it, providing Mark with a generous view of Alli's cleavage as well as the top of a black lace bra. Upon realizing what the baby had done, Alli quickly switched Erica to her other shoulder and snatched the blouse back up in place. When Alli met his gaze, an embarrassing tint flushed her cheeks.

Mark thought it best to pretend he hadn't seen a thing instead of standing there wishing he could get an instant replay. He cleared his throat. "If you give me your keys, I'll bring your stuff inside so you can get settled in," he said as warning bells clanged in his ears.

He had to fight his attraction to Alli no matter what, but already things were getting off to a heated start. With her dressed in a blouse and a pair of slacks wasn't helping. He had decided after the first time he had seen Alli in pants that she'd had the most well-defined, enticingly shaped butt of any woman he'd ever seen. In fact, he didn't know of anyone who even qualified as a close second.

She always dressed professionally while in the office. The only time he hadn't seen her dressed that way was when she had signed up to take his class. He remembered how, like the other ladies, she had shown up wearing shorts. In addition to teaching her the art of self-defense, he had taught himself the art of self-control.

His thoughts returned to the present when she handed him her car key. "I didn't bring over much since I'll have time to do more packing this weekend," she said shifting her gaze from him to Erika. "Has she eaten dinner yet?"

Mark laughed. "Yes. If she was hungry, you would know it. That's the only time she's in a bad mood."

Alli gave herself a mental shake. Mark's laugh threw her, since she had never heard him laugh before. This was the first time she had ever seen this side of him. He was being so pleasant and human. Not that he walked around being a tyrant, but he'd never been in her presence and not acted with reserve and reticence.

He must have seen the strange look on her face because he eyed her for a moment as his expression went from curious to concern. Then he asked, "Is something wrong?"

She shrugged. "No, nothing's wrong." Cautiously, she added, "I just don't ever recall the two of us ever holding a conversation for more than five minutes that didn't have anything to do with business."

Mark leaned against the wooden column and thought for a moment. Neither had he. Even yesterday while they had discussed the arrangements of her becoming Erika's nanny, it had been business. "Well, you're doing me a huge favor by being here. Away from work I'm more relaxed and at ease so get prepared to see another side of me. Believe it or not, I can be a friendly guy."

"It's not that I thought you weren't friendly," Alli rushed to say, hoping she hadn't offended him. "But you—"

He held up his hand. "Hey, there's no need to explain," Mark said chuckling, thinking he liked how Alli looked when she was flustered, which was something he rarely had seen. "Come on in, let me show you around. I'll get the things out of your car later."

She gave him her usual shy smile and said, "All right."

Erika began murmuring words Alli couldn't quite make out as she followed Mark into the house. This was her first time inside. The last time she had been here he had stepped out onto the porch to sign the papers she had delivered.

She glanced around as Mark took her from room to room. She couldn't help noticing how each one was richly furnished with leathered pieces of a rustic, western design. Erika's bedroom was another matter. It was wallpapered with Snow White and her seven dwarfs, and a beautiful white convertible crib sat in the middle of the room. The room's decor was colorful, bright, fit for a little princess, and the bedding accessories matched a miniature chair and ottoman that sat near a window in the room. A huge stuffed bear had been placed in the chair. Alli couldn't help smiling. "It's beautiful in here, Mark."

He turned to her. "Thanks. I hired a professional decorator for this room. I was a bachelor with no experience with kids when I got Erika and had to learn everything and fast."

He automatically took Erika out of Alli's arms when his niece reached for him. He nodded toward all the furniture in the room "The first thing I found out was that a child's room should grow with the child and not the child having to grow with the room. I spend a lot of time in here with Erika since this is also her play room," he said, tipping his head toward the huge toy chest that sat in one corner. "That's the reason for the recliner-rocker over there. When I first got her I would sit in that chair and rock her to sleep. Now I just sit back and watch her play."

Alli nodded as she studied the chair, seeing the image of Mark kicked back, relaxed, while keeping a protective eye on Ericka. Another vision suddenly came to mind: one of her sitting in that chair with him, in his lap, while the two of them watched Erika together. She could actually see herself as she cuddled close to him, her body curled to his with her head resting on his shoulder, while the warmth of his breath fanned her face.

She blinked and swallowed deeply, not believing she had allowed such thoughts to enter her mind.

"Alli, are you okay?"

She snapped her head around and met Mark's curious eyes. "Yes, I'm fine."

It seemed that he focused his gaze on her for the longest time before saying, "Okay, then let me show you the room that you'll be using."

Before they walked out the room they passed a framed picture sitting on the dresser. Alli stopped and picked it up. It was a photograph of an attractive couple who were smiling and holding an infant.

"That's Matt and Candice when Erika was only a few months old," Mark said softly.

Alli stiffened slightly. She hadn't been aware that he was standing so close. He was leaning down to peer at the picture and she could feel the moist warmth of his breath against her neck. His closeness was causing a sensation she had never felt before to slowly inch its way up her spine. There was also the heat she felt pooling her belly.

She forced herself to stay focused on the picture, fearful that if she turned her head even the slightest inch, her lips would connect to his. "They were a beautiful family and look happy together," she finally said, forcing the words out while keenly aware the heat had moved from her stomach, traveling lower down her body.

"Yes, they were happy together and they loved each other very much. I always envied what they had."

Noting that Mark had taken a step back, Alli turned slightly and met his gaze. He'd sounded so heartrending. She couldn't help looking deep into his eyes, and then she saw it clearly—pain. He was still hurting. But for whom? His brother and sister-in-law? His wife? For all three?

Her gaze shifted to the rest of his features. They were prominent. Handsome. He had beautiful brown skin, thick eyebrows, a nose that was the perfect shape and size for his face. And then there were his lips...

She couldn't help but study his lips. They had a seductive shape to them and had such a smooth texture. They looked soft, which seemed odd for such a rough man. A part of her yearned to figure out the contrast for herself. It wouldn't take much for her to ease her mouth to his, take her tongue and go from corner to corner and lick the—

"Da-da! Down da-da!"

Erika's words snapped Alli around. She had no idea just how long she had been standing there mesmerized by Mark's mouth. What had he thought of her staring at him like that? Heat flooded her cheeks and, instead of meeting his gaze, she placed the picture frame on the dresser.

"No, I can't put you down, sweetheart," she heard Mark say to the baby. "We still have to show Alli around."

Feeling more in control, Alli turned but kept her gaze focused on Erika and smiled when the little girl reached for her. She scooped her out of Mark's arms and planted a kiss on Erika's cheek, liking the sound of her giggle. "She calls you dad."

"Yes, but I prefer that she didn't do that."

The agitation in his voice made Alli's head jerk up, not being able to avoid eye contact with him any longer. She saw the deep frown that marred his handsome features. "Why?" she asked.

"Because I'm not her daddy."

Alli lifted an eyebrow in confusion. "I know you're not her daddy, Mark, but calling you that is as natural and familiar to her as eating and sleeping. You represent a permanent fixture in her life. She might or might not remember her parents and—"

"I want her to remember them, Alli. That's the reason I have this picture in here. When she gets older I want her to know about them. I want her to know they were her parents and that I'm her uncle who's nothing more than her caretaker."

Alli tried not to glare at him but felt herself doing so anyway. What he'd said sounded too detached and she knew that wasn't the case. Anyone could see how much he loved and adored his niece. Alison had been in his office when he had received the call regarding his brother's and sister-in-law's deaths and his being named as Erika's guardian. That had to have been a tailspin for any carefree bachelor.

She would never forget the day he had flown to California to bring his niece home. And it was obvious he was fiercely protective of Erika, otherwise Alli wouldn't be here.

Pursing her lips, Alli studied Erika's features then met Mark's gaze. "She favors you a lot. You both have identical hazel eyes, the same skin coloring, and her mouth is like yours, just a smaller version. She could be your daughter."

He stuck his hands in the pockets of his jeans and rocked on his heels. She had worked with him long enough to know the first signs of his anger. "But she's not. You saw the photograph. Matt and I looked alike but there was a lot about us that was different. We were both Nathaniel Hartman's sons so there were some things that couldn't be changed, but Matt inherited a lot of Mama's ways. Although the old man tried making him hard, Matt had a soft spot. And he always wanted to grow up and have children. I never did."

Mark's words surprised Alli. He was sharing more with her now than he had before. "But how could you not want kids? You were married."

Mark stared at her in silence for a moment, reached out and absently took Erika out of her arms. He moved to put space between them. Moments later he said, "Getting married had nothing to do with it. Patrice knew I never wanted kids, which was fine with her since, because of a medical condition, she couldn't have them."

Alli felt her pulse go still and she inhaled a deep breath. It appeared that this was a touchy subject with Mark but she wasn't ready to put it to rest. She crossed the room to join him and Erika. "Now that Erika has broken you in, what do you think about fatherhood?"

His head shot around and hazel eyes collided with hers. Too late she realized what she'd asked was a mistake. "I'm Erika's uncle, let's keep that clear, Alli. Matt entrusted her into my care and I will do the best that I can by her. She will never want for anything. And as far as me ever wanting kids of my own, nothing has changed. I still don't want any."

Alli's chest tightened as he placed Erika in her arms and she watched him walk out of the room.

Three

It was the most stunning room, Alli thought, as she followed Mark into the bedroom that was conveniently located across the hall from Erika's.

Besides the huge four-poster, cherry-oak bed that sat between two huge windows, the other furnishings included double nightstands, a mirror dresser, a chest and an accent bench. All in all the elegant-looking accessories, from the floral bedspread and matching window treatments to the massive brick fireplace, and she felt it was a room fit for a queen. What was even nicer was the fact that she had her own bath, a rather nice modern one that had a separate shower and a bathtub. It was apparent some renovations been done since the original house had been built.

"I hope you like this room."

She swung around and the swift movement made

Erika happily squeal loudly. "Oh, Mark, it's perfect. Did you hire a professional decorator to do this room as well?"

He nodded. "Yes, when I moved back I found the place needed a lot of repairs." He took Erika out of Alli's arms and continued saying, "After the repairs were taken care of I started doing renovations. I wanted to give the place a whole new look and I didn't want anything here to remind me of before."

A part of Alli wanted to reach out and throw her arms around him. She regretted he did not have memories of a happy childhood. Although her father had deserted them and her mother had eventually worked herself into an early grave, Mildred Lind had done the best she could to make sure her daughters had childhoods filled with many fond memories. There hadn't been a lot of money to spend but there had been a lot of love to go around. Too bad Mark had missed out on that.

"I'd better get your things out the car," Mark said, handing Erika back to her.

Alli chuckled as she held Erika against her shoulder. Mark lifted an eyebrow in confusion. "What's so funny?"

"Have you noticed what we've been doing? I bet Erika has never been passed back and forth before between two people so much in her life."

A smile touched the corners of Mark's lips. "You're probably right. I hadn't noticed."

Alli smiled at Erika before dropping a kiss on her cheek. "But you noticed didn't you, sweetheart, and you enjoyed every minute of going from arm to arm, right?"

"That's something else she isn't used to."

Alli switched her gaze to Mark. "What?"

"Being kissed. You've done it three times since you've been here."

Forcing her gaze back to Erika, Alli asked, "You're counting?"

He shrugged. "I can't help but notice. I didn't know you were such an affectionate person."

There's a lot you don't know about me, Mark Hartman. She looked at him, wanting to tell him that she had more than enough affection to share if he was interested, but she knew that saying that wouldn't be a good idea. "Well, when it comes to babies, I'm as affectionate as anyone can get."

"You want children one day?"

She grinned. "You would have done better just asking me how many."

After studying her thoughtfully for a brief moment, he said, "Okay, how many?"

"A houseful. I'll even make room in the barn if I have to."

Evidently the image of that played out in Mark's mind and he chuckled. "I hope your husband will be able to afford all your kids."

"I hope so, too." Automatically and without thought, she kissed Erika's cheek again, making the baby giggle with pleasure.

When Alli glanced up she saw that Mark's gaze was focused on her lips while he absently wet his own with his tongue. She became aware of the tension that suddenly filled the room and the pulsing heat that was forming between them. As if his lips were dry, he licked them again and at that moment she was dying to know how his kisses tasted.

Alli was mortified that such thoughts had entered her mind and knew she should dismiss them, but she couldn't. Even if she were to kiss him until the cows came home, he would never be out of her system...or out of her heart. He was still staring at her mouth the way she was staring at his. The beatings of their hearts could be heard as a throbbing tempo in the room and even Erika's babbling couldn't drown it out.

Heat flowed all through her when she could see the guarded expression that he always wore was gone and he was staring at her as if he finally was seeing her as a woman. At that very moment, whether it was his intent or not, he made her feel desired. She wanted more than anything to curl up in his arms while he kissed her in all the ways she had dreamed about.

Her breath caught in her throat when he took a step closer, leaned forward and came within inches of capturing her mouth in his.

"Da-da. Play."

As if snapping out of a daze, Mark straightened, took a quick step back and ran a hand down his face. "I better get your things out the car," he said, turning quickly.

Emotions tightened Alli's throat. He had almost kissed her. After two years, he had shown some sign that he was attracted to her.

"You do remember about my Cattleman's Club meeting tonight, right?"

His question jarred her from her thoughts. "Yes, I remember."

"And don't worry about dinner. Mrs. Sanders was here yesterday and prepared enough dinner for today as well."

"Mrs. Sanders?"

"She's my housekeeper and cook, and she usually comes a couple of times a week."

Evidently seeing the question in her eyes, he went on to say, "She cooks and cleans but is quick to inform you that she doesn't do babies. She's fifty-seven, has five kids of her own and doesn't relish the thought of taking care of another child. She's one of those grandmothers whose kids can't just drop the grandkids off and keep going. Her philosophy is, and I quote, 'I raised mine, now you raise yours.'"

"I'm looking forward to meeting her," Alli said as she continued to stare at Mark. She thought it was a darn shame for any man to look that good. He took her breath away. She needed him to leave so she could breathe normally again.

He smiled warmly. "And I have a feeling that she's looking forward to meeting you as well."

And then he was gone.

"I hear you've solved your babysitting problems, Mark," Logan Voss said as the two of them entered the bar of the Texas Cattleman's Club and proceeded to the private meeting room.

Out of habit, Mark's gaze went to the Leadership, Justice and Peace motto on a far wall before meeting his friend's eyes. "Then I'm also sure you've heard that Alli is Erika's nanny."

Logan chuckled. "Yes, I did hear that."

"What did you hear?" Jake Thorne asked curiously

as he greeted the two men and watched them settle into the leather chairs.

"That Alli is Erika's nanny," Logan responded.

Jake smiled. "Yes, and knowing what a responsible person Alli is, we can safely say that Erika will be in good hands."

Mark nodded. At the moment, he would have given anything to know just how good those hands were; just as he would have loved sampling that mouth of Alli's. Luckily for him, when he had returned to the room with her things, she hadn't been there. She had placed Erika in her stroller and had taken her outside for a walk. He was grateful for that time alone to pull himself together. Never in his life had he wanted to kiss a woman so badly.

He had spent a long time in the shower berating himself for his weakness of coming within inches of kissing Alli. By the time he had gotten dressed for the meeting, he had decided that hell, he was only human, and any man would have wanted to kiss her given the way her lips were made, not to mention how alluring her perfume was. The total package would have any man interested and he was definitely a man.

Damn, he had to stop thinking about her. Thoughts of her had consumed him on the drive to this meeting and they were consuming him now. He hoped like hell that she'd be asleep when he returned home. But just in case, it might be a good idea if he didn't return to the ranch immediately after the meeting. Maybe he could interest a couple of the guys in a game of poker.

He glanced around. He knew Thomas Devlin and Gavin O'Neal were standing outside talking. But where the hell was Connor Thorne? He was the one who had ribbed Mark the most whenever he had shown up late due to babysitting issues. Mark wondered if Connor also had heard that his problem was solved.

Mark glanced over at Jake. "Where's Connor?"

Jake smiled lazily, his blue eyes shining brightly. "I am my brother's brother, but I am not my brother's keeper," he replied jokingly. He then glanced at his watch. "We have seven minutes to go. He'll be here."

Mark nodded and then asked, "How's the campaign going?" Jake's opponent in the mayoral race was Gretchen Halifax. In her mid-thirties, Gretchen was intelligent, sophisticated and had a large circle of influence in town. But what she didn't have was a clue about what Royal needed. If Gretchen became mayor, there was no doubt in Mark's mind that, with her proposed tax plan, the town would lose businesses to other areas.

"I'm playing by the rules and sticking to the campaign issues," Jake said. "But it seems Gretchen doesn't want to play fair."

Logan, who had stood to remove his jacket, sat and chuckled as he leaned back in his chair. "Now why doesn't that surprise me?"

The three men glanced up when Connor Thorne, Tom Devlin and Gavin O'Neal walked in. They could tell by the look on Gavin's face that the news he had to share wouldn't be good. As a relatively new sheriff, he had his hands full trying to figure out a murder as well as a number of suspicious happenings around town.

"We might as well get started," Gavin said, dropping into one of the leather chairs. Connor and Tom, who had recently joined the club, did likewise.

When Gavin was certain he had everyone's attention,

he continued to speak. "We still don't have a clue who fired that shot at Melissa Mason," he said to everyone, although the guys knew he was really answering the question Logan hadn't asked yet. Melissa was Logan's fiancée and the attempt on her life had riled him to say the least.

"So we're still operating on the theory that since Melissa was driving one of Logan's vehicles, the sniper thought it was Logan and was trying to dissuade him from going to see Lucas Devlin?" Connor asked, leaning forward.

"Yes. In my opinion someone is trying like hell to keep the Devlin and Windcroft feud going," Gavin said somberly.

"Hmm, but who would benefit from such a thing and how does it all tie in to Jonathan's murder?" Jake asked, as if thinking out loud.

"That's what we need to find out," Gavin said, sighing deeply. He glanced over at Mark. "I need you to go talk to Nita Windcroft to see whether her allegations are founded or she's blowing things out of proportion to stir up trouble. I'm fairly new to the area but what I'm hearing is that she's pretty damn headstrong and if she thinks we're not taking her seriously, she might take matters into her own hands. Heaven help us all if she does that. My deputies claim she has one hell of a temper and is as stubborn as they come."

Mark nodded. "All right. I'll talk to Nita."

Gavin then glanced over at Jake and smiled. "I thought I'd better give you a heads-up. Rumor has it around town that Gretchen is trying like hell to tie you to the vandalism of the Halifax Exhibit. She claims you're running a negative campaign and that's one example of your unsavory tactics."

Jake shook his head and chuckled. "Thanks for letting me know but if anyone is using unsavory tactics, it's Gretchen. But she'll eventually hang herself since the people who know me won't believe a word of it."

"What about the woman captured on tape stealing the map? Any new leads?" Tom Devlin decided to ask, his silver-gray eyes alert. Since he was relatively new to town, he was quickly finding out about the feud that involved the family he only recently had discovered he had.

"No, there's nothing new," Gavin said. "I showed the video around and no one seems to recognize the woman, so it's still a mystery." He glanced down at his watch. "That's all I have to report tonight. I'm sure you're all aware that word has gotten around that Jonathan was murdered by some sort of lethal injection and everyone has an idea of who did it." He shook his head. "You wouldn't believe how many people stopped me today with the list of their own suspects."

Mark lifted an eyebrow in amusement. "Any particular name that's heading the list?"

Gavin sighed. "Yeah, Nita Windcroft's, but only because of the feud. But then everyone was quick to add that more than likely she didn't do it because she would not have let poor Jonathan linger. If he had made her mad enough, she would have taken a gun and shot him on the spot."

Connor grinned. "She doesn't sound like a woman I would want to tangle with."

Tom chuckled. "From what I'm hearing, no one would."

Gavin smiled. "Well, that ends tonight's meeting. We'll get together again next Wednesday. At that time, Mark, you can tell us what you've found out after talking with Nita."

"Sure thing," Mark said." When the men all stood, he asked, "Anyone interested in a game of poker tonight?"

Jake smiled and shook his head. "Sorry, I have a lady waiting for my return."

"And so do I," Logan said, grinning as he put back on his jacket. His gray-green eyes had the quiet, determined intent of a man who knew just where he was going and didn't plan on wasting time getting there.

Mark studied the two men who were rushing for the door. "Hmm, I can distinctively remember a time when there were no ladies in your lives."

Jake paused in the doorway and chuckled. "Well, you know how it is." After studying Mark for a brief moment he said, "Then again, my friend, maybe you don't. But I have a feeling that one day soon you will." Then he was gone with Logan right on his heels.

Mark frowned and turned to look at Tom, Connor and Gavin. "What the hell did he mean by that?"

Gavin shrugged. "I'm through figuring out things for the night. I'll leave that one for the three of you to ponder." His brown eyes seemed to smile when he added, "I'm headed over to the diner for a cup of coffee." And he rushed out the door as well.

Mark, Connor and Tom shared a knowing look between them. They knew of Gavin's fascination with a certain waitress at the Royal Diner.

"The least he could have done was invite us to come along," Connor said jokingly.

"Yes, he very well could have. However, since he didn't, we can only assume he felt that four was a crowd," Tom replied laughing.

Mark nodded, amused. "Maybe I better warn Gavin that he's not the only one who has the hots for Valerie Raines. I've notice Malcolm Durmorr giving her a lusty eye more than once when I happened to be in there."

Connor sat and folded his arms over his chest, rolling his blue eyes heavenward. "Malcolm? That low-life?" He glanced over at Tom. "Sorry. I forgot he's a distant relative of yours."

Tom shook his head. "From what I understand, the Devlins try to forget that fact as well."

Connor seemed to understand. He then gave Mark a sly grin. "If I were you, I wouldn't tell Gavin anything about Malcolm's interest in Valerie Raines. Competition is good for the soul and it will keep our sheriff on his toes."

Mark smiled. "Maybe you're right." He glanced at his watch. It wasn't nine o'clock and chances were Alli hadn't gone to bed yet. He looked at Connor and Tom. "A game of poker anyone?"

When the two men agreed, Mark's smile widened. Good. He'd been saved by a poker game.

Holding Erika in her arms, Alli walked over to the rocker-recliner and sat. She could not believe that it was almost nine o'clock and the little girl was still wide awake. She couldn't help but smile down at the big, beautiful hazel eyes in that round little face that was staring up at her. Her dark curly hair framed her face and a little pink ribbon sat on top of her head.

Alli smiled as she shook her head thinking that every

time she'd seen Erika her hair had been fixed the same way, which was probably a convenient style for Mark. She decided that she was going to introduce Erika to some cute new hairdos and thought a mass of braids would look rather nice on her.

"So, your uncle is short on affection and you still love him anyway, huh?" Alli said as she began rocking the chair. "Well, I know just how you feel, so welcome to the club."

When the baby gave her a grin that showed a few sprouting teeth, Alli returned the gesture. "I guess it's going to take the two of us to give him a lesson in love, wouldn't you say?"

As Alli continued to rock, she thought that, affection or no affection, Mark was evidently doing something right for his niece to adore him so much. She had noted earlier while feeding Erika a snack that even the slightest sound had Erika glancing toward the kitchen door as if anxious to see her uncle walk through it. And a couple of times she had wandered around the living room chanting "Da-da" as if saying it would make Mark appear.

Okay, so he didn't go for all that kissy stuff, but he was bestowing affection on Erika in ways that Mark himself probably didn't even realize.

Like this rocker-recliner chair for instance.

He had mentioned how he used to rock her in it. An affectionless person would not have bothered doing that.

Alli sighed deeply. After what had almost happened between her and Mark in the bedroom, she had needed distance and a chance to escape. Spotting the stroller in Erika's room, she had decided it would be a perfect time to go for a stroll around the Hartman property.

She had never imagined the ranch consisted of that much land. It seemed she had walked endlessly, enjoying the beauty of the landscape and wondering how Mark had ever moved away since every tree, shrub and patch of grass was so beautiful. And Erika seemed to have enjoyed being outside, breathing in the rich Texas air and appreciating the warmth of a sunny September day.

Alli glanced down at the little girl who was still fighting sleep, although it seemed she wasn't winning as much as she had been earlier. "You have your uncle's heart and he doesn't even know it. He's so slow. A typical man," she whispered as she continued to rock.

Moments later she glanced down and saw that Erika had fallen asleep, but Alli wasn't ready to put her down yet. So she kept rocking and slowly her own eyes closed as thoughts of a very slow, typical man by the name of Mark Hartman filled her unconsciousness.

It was close to eleven o'clock when Mark returned to the ranch. As habit, he went straight to Erika's room to check on her and was surprised to find the light still on in her bedroom. He was further surprised to see Alli holding Erika in the rocker-recliner and they were both asleep.

He had seen Erika sleeping many times but this was the first time he had ever seen his administrative assistant anything but wide awake and fully alert. For a moment he couldn't move, too mesmerized by the beauty of her sitting there with her eyes closed. So he took the time to study her.

His gaze first went to her hair—thick, shoulder-length and dark brown. A vision entered his mind of him running his fingers though the silky strands while he was kissing her. His gaze then shifted to her face and took in the creaminess of her brown skin, the perfection of her naturally shaped eyebrows and the faultless precision of her chin. But what his gaze zeroed in on was her mouth. Even from across the room it looked moist, tempting, inviting.

He swallowed. His own lips suddenly felt hot, dry, parched and he was convinced that the only way to bring relief to them was to mate them with hers. Without questioning the wisdom of what he was about to do, he slowly crossed the room to her.

He leaned over and softly whispered in Alli's ear. "I'm putting Erika in her bed, Alli."

He watched as Alli's eyes flew open the moment he scooped his niece out of her arms. "Mark, you're back," she whispered and the low, throaty sound, as well as the sigh that followed, sent a riveting sensation all the way to his gut. And the sensuously seductive scent of her wasn't helping matters.

Holding Erika, he straightened and met Alli's eyes. "Yes, I'm back. Let me put her in bed."

He turned quickly and crossed the room to lay his niece down. Covering her with the blanket, he watched her for a moment to make sure she was all right and checked the monitor that was attached to the crib before turning his attention back to Alli.

She was standing and his throat tightened when he saw she was no longer wearing slacks but had changed into shorts. His desire was instantaneous and his gaze moved over her. Their eyes connected and he studied the darkness of her brown eyes and felt the same intense heat that he was feeling radiating from them. The same heat that was burning his insides with desire.

"I had meant to put her down earlier but fell asleep rocking her," she whispered.

"Did you?" he asked softly.

"Yes."

He slowly began walking over toward her.

Alli's pulse raced. He was looking at her that way again. The way he had earlier, which is the way he always looked at her in her dreams, especially the one he had awakened her from moments earlier. She knew she should be happy, thrilled and elated that after two years he was finally noticing her, but a part of her questioned the wisdom of becoming involved with Mark, although she was hopelessly in love with him.

When he came to a stop in front of her, his eyes leveled on hers. He reached out and lifted her chin with his finger. "You are a very beautiful woman, Alli."

She blinked, startled. She hadn't expected him to say such a thing. At first she didn't know what to say, then she decided to say something flippant, although being flip wasn't the norm for her. But it seemed that tonight neither she nor Mark was acting normally.

She smiled and tilted her head to the side. "So, it took you two years to notice, Mark?" she asked jokingly.

His eyes seemed to darken when he said, "No. I noticed the first day I met you, which is the reason I came pretty damn close to not hiring you."

His words wiped that glib look off her face. She then nibbled nervously on her lower lip. "I didn't think you noticed me."

He tilted her chin up more. "Oh, trust me, you've

been a distraction, Alli. In fact, for two years I've been fighting my attraction to you. And that night at the Anniversary Ball was the hardest, I think. You looked so damn beautiful in that gown and more than once I started to ask you to dance but stopped myself. The last thing I wanted when I returned to Royal was to become seriously involved with anyone, especially an employee."

Alli nodded. She hadn't known he had paid her any attention at the ball and knowing that he had filled her with happiness. "And now?" she asked quietly.

"And now I want to kiss you so bad I ache."

"Oh."

That was the only word he gave her time to say before he embraced her as his mouth descended on hers, stealing her next breath. At the same time, he swept his tongue into her mouth. And she accepted it with the same ease that he gave it to her.

Alli had never been kissed this way. If the truth were known, at twenty-five she had never really been kissed at all and was puzzled by how effortless it was to follow Mark's lead. Taking care of Kara had been a full-time job and left no time for dating. But she'd figured she had not missed out on anything…until now. She seriously doubted that anyone would have been able to blow her away with a kiss the way Mark was doing. He had the ability to turn on all her buttons and was sending new sensations zinging all through her. She wondered if he knew how much of a novice she was at this.

He did.

Mark had detected it the moment his tongue had entered Alli's mouth and he had felt her body go tense at the invasion, as if she hadn't been expecting such intimacy. He had kissed a lot of women, some more experienced than others. He wouldn't go so far to say that Alli had never been kissed before, but evidently the other men hadn't done it right.

Not only did he intend to do it right, but he also planned on taking it to another level. He pulled back slightly and whispered against her moist lips. "Wrap your arms around my neck, Alli."

She did as he asked and, the moment she complied with his request, he captured her mouth again and deepened the kiss while one of his hands stroked through her hair and the other wrapped around her waist, bringing her closer to the fit of him. He heard her moan softly and felt the way her heart was racing with her chest pressed so tightly to his. He also felt the firm tips of her breasts, which made his pulse quicken.

He knew the moment she became aware of his erection and, when she deliberately rocked into him, he released a low groan and automatically thrust his hips against hers. He had asked her to place her arms around his neck but now she was clutching his shoulders, kneading her fingers deep into the muscles as if to keep her balance. The way she was returning his kiss was robbing him of any control he might have had. He lowered his arms from her waist to mold her curvy buttocks more intimately against him.

The sound of Erika whimpering in her sleep made Mark withdraw his mouth and inhale deeply. It also brought about a semblance of self-control. He took a step back and stared at Alli's swollen mouth, thinking this woman was all fire and danger. At the moment he didn't want to tangle with either. Kissing her had definitely been a mistake. Not only she was an affectionate person, but she was a passionate one as well. And it had been obvious from their kiss that her sensuality hadn't been tapped yet.

He dragged in another deep breath and with it came a whiff of her perfume. Seductive. Alluring. A total turn-on. Needing to put distance between them, he crossed the room to Erika's crib to check on her.

"Mark, we—"

"Made a mistake," he said briskly, finishing what he knew she was about to say. "Go on to bed, Alli. I'll see you in the morning," he all but snapped.

Out of the corner of his eyes, he saw how Alli's spine stiffened. He was tempted to go to her and start the kissing all over again. But he knew he couldn't do that.

Mark didn't turn around until he heard the sound of the door closing. It was then that he sat in the rocker-recliner and dropped his head into his hands, thinking that he finally had given into temptation. And as a result, he definitely had made a mess of things.

Four

He owed Alli an apology.

Mark awakened with that thought and quickly glanced at the clock on the nightstand beside his bed. It was still early, barely five in the morning. Chances were she was still sleep so, for the time being, there was nothing he could do.

He rubbed his hand down his face when the memory of kissing her seeped into his mind. Damn, she hadn't been in his house for a full night and he had acted like a stallion in heat. That had been unfair to her.

She was here to take care of his niece, something he appreciated her doing. But he had shown his gratitude by pouncing on her the first chance he'd gotten and would have continued kissing her if they hadn't been interrupted by the sounds Erika had made in her sleep.

Although he didn't want to, he found himself again

thinking about the kiss they had shared. He had wanted to taste Alli, and had gotten more than he'd bargained for. Her lips had fit perfectly to his, as if they had been made just for him, and they had felt soft and had had such a seductive flavor. And when he had deepened the kiss, he had wanted more than anything to pick her up, take her into his bedroom, place her on his bed, undress her and then slide inside of her, between her long shapely legs…

Mark muttered a curse as he threw back the covers to sit on the side of the bed. Since it seemed that going back to sleep was out of the question, he decided to get up. Although it was early, there were a number of things he could do before leaving for the studio. And no matter how many appointments he had on his calendar, he intended to give Nita Windcroft a call to determine the best time he could drive over to the Windcroft horse farm to talk to her.

But first thing this morning, as soon as he saw Alli, he intended to apologize for his actions last night.

Sitting on the accent bench in her bedroom, Alli closed her eyes when she found herself still shivering from the sensations that had gripped her the night before. She barely had been able to sleep, so instead she had decided to get up and think. However, she found that all she could do was mentally replay every single detail of being in Mark's arms.

An undefined ache still throbbed between her legs, and all during the night while trying to sleep she had shifted positions in an attempt to ease it. Whenever she had closed her eyes she had felt the pulsing heat from his erection pressed so intimately against her while he kissed her in a way that had melted her insides.

"This isn't good," she said softly with a sigh as she leaned back on the bench. She loved Mark but she wasn't sure she was ready for the degree of passion that he invoked.

Like his toe-curling kiss, for instance.

And although he had definitely left a lasting impression on her, she was convinced that she hadn't left any on him except possibly the question why a twenty-five-year-old woman knew absolutely nothing about the pleasures that men and women shared. He had even gone so far to admit that kissing her had been a mistake. But she didn't see things that way. What had been a mistake to him had been pure enjoyment to her.

Did he also see her being here as a mistake? Did he feel there was no way she could stay on as Erika's nanny since it was obvious that her presence was causing problems? What if he intended to take it further and ask her to quit her job as his assistant as well, since their employer-employee relationship had been breached? Panic tightened her throat. She couldn't lose her job now when Kara was depending so much on her.

Heaving a troubled sigh, she rose and walked back over to the bed. Feeling exhausted from lack of sleep, she decided to close her eyes and try to rest a while before Erika awakened for breakfast.

The last thing Alli wanted was to see Mark this morning, but she knew that was something she would not be able to avoid.

* * *

"Da-da. Eat."

Alli snapped her eyes open when the sound of Erika's voice seemed so close to her ear. She quickly turned over and remembered the monitor that Mark had installed in her room the day before. She smiled. Evidently Erika was awake and hungry.

Quickly getting out of bed, Alli slipped into her robe and, after tightening the belt securely around her waist, she opened her bedroom door only to collide with the solid wall of a male's chest.

"Oops."

"Sorry."

Mark caught her when she nearly lost her balance and the sensations she had been fighting all night intensified with his touch. As soon as he released her, she took a step back. "Thanks. I heard Erika."

He nodded. "So did I."

Alli noticed that his chin was covered with shaving cream, which meant he had been about to shave. She also noticed—although she wished she hadn't, but there was no way to avoid it—that he was bare-chested. The only thing covering his body was a pair of jeans and the towel wrapped around his neck. The top button of his jeans was undone and the dark mass of hair on his chest went down toward his abdomen and disappeared beneath the waist of his jeans. The one word that immediately came to Alli's mind was *sexy*.

When he leaned back against the wall and grinned, she frowned in confusion and wondered if he knew what she'd been thinking. "What's so funny?" she asked when he continued to grin.

"This," he said before reaching out and touching her cheek. He held up his finger.

"Oh," she said when she saw the shaving cream. She lifted a corner of her robe to wipe it off but he stopped her.

"No, let me."

Before she could stop him, he used his towel to wipe off her cheek. His touch was gentle and soft and the towel held his manly scent. She tried averting her gaze but found herself meeting his anyway. When she locked on the hazel eyes staring at her, she gulped, almost losing her breath. The heat that flared between them was instantaneous, absolute, blinding. And when he slid his gaze to her mouth, she had enough sense to know that she was in big trouble.

Deciding to head it off, she took another step back. "I need to go check on Erika."

He nodded and took a step back as well while placing the towel back around his neck. "We need to talk later, Alli."

She sighed deeply. "Yes…I know."

"But first I need to apologize about last night."

Stunned that he was placing the blame all on himself, she could only stare at him for a moment before finding her voice to say, "And I need to apologize as well."

He lifted an eyebrow. "For what?"

She shrugged. "For whatever you're apologizing for and for the fact that you evidently found me lacking."

Mark frowned. Apparently exhaustion was impairing his hearing. There was no way she could have said anything about him finding her lacking…was there? He leaned forward. "Lacking?"

"Yes." And without saying another word, she spun around and quickly entered the baby's room.

Totally stunned, he watched as Erika's door closed behind Alli. Seconds later he threw up his hand. *He found her lacking?* Where in the hell did she get a crazy idea like that? The last thing he thought was that she was lacking in anything. If the truth was known, he was convinced that she had an overabundance of everything, especially sensuality and passion. And he had a good mind to follow her into Erika's room to tell her that.

Okay, he quickly decided, now was not a good time to have that sort of a discussion with her. He needed time to think and he'd already told her that they needed to talk. He realized that they needed to do more than just talk. He definitely needed to straighten her out on a few things.

"Ah, just look at you," Alli whispered to Erika after putting the finishing touches on her hair. "Your uncle won't even recognize you."

Alli sighed. She'd had a lot of time to think while getting Erika dressed. Mark was right, they needed to talk. After what had happened last night and if he was uncomfortable with her being here, then she definitely would leave once he found someone to take her place. The same held true with the studio. If he felt their kiss had left it impossible for them to work together, then she would resign. It would be that simple.

She shook her head. She was fooling herself if she thought anything involving Mark Hartman was simple. But then she had known that living under the same roof with him wouldn't be easy given her feelings for him.

She inhaled a calming breath. Maybe it was time that she realized that nothing could, or would, ever develop between her and Mark. She could now admit that for the past two years she'd been waiting for a fairy tale to happen to her. A part of her had actually wanted to believe that one day she would walk into Hartman's Self-Defense Studio and Mark would see her with different eyes and realize she was capable of being more than just his dependable and efficient administrative assistant.

Well, okay, he had admitted that he thought she was beautiful. But she'd heard from several sources that men thought most women were beautiful; especially women they were interested in sleeping with. But now that Mark realized she couldn't kiss worth a damn and lacked the skills to pleasure a man, she was quite certain that any interest he might have had had died a sudden death.

And maybe it was for the best. If nothing else, her father's actions should have taught her that most men didn't deserve a woman's heart. All she had to do was remember the pain Arthur Lind had caused her mother to know that was true. In addition to that, Mark had told her yesterday he didn't want children. She, on the other hand, had made it pretty clear that she wanted several, which meant the things they wanted or didn't want out of life were vastly different.

At least with things ending this way she saved the humiliation of him finding out that she was in love with him. This way she could move on, concentrate on helping Kara finish college and then continue to live a peaceful existence for the rest of her life. It was time she began being practical and levelheaded.

Picking Erika up off the dressing table, Alli left the bedroom accepting the fact that handsome millionaires didn't fall in love with plain old regular folk like herself and it was time she got rid of any foolish romantic notions that such a thing was possible.

Mark could not stop staring the moment he walked into the kitchen. Both Erika and Alli looked different. It was quite obvious that Alli had taken the time to fix Erika's hair another way but the difference in Alli's appearance was a bit more startling.

She was wearing jeans.

Forget about the western shirt she also had on; his concentration was on her jeans and just how good she looked in them. He always thought she looked good wearing pants, but nothing—and he meant nothing— compared to her wearing jeans. Maybe it would not have been obvious if, when he had walked in the room, she hadn't been leaning over while searching inside the refrigerator.

Transfixed, he watched her move around his kitchen, unaware that he was watching her. Everything was shapely about her, lushly so, and the way the jeans fit her butt had him swallowing hard. And that wasn't the only thing that was feeling hard. He could actually feel his blood heat up, shooting hot fluid through all parts of his body, especially one particular stop. He shifted his position when he felt his erection strain against the zipper of his own jeans.

He couldn't help wondering how on earth he and Alli would maintain an employer-employee relationship now. Kissing her was bad enough, but having lustful thoughts about her was worse. Oh, as he had told her last night, he had wanted her for two years, yet had managed to keep his desire in check. But that was before he had tasted her and knew just how sweet and delicious she was. Now he would be hard-pressed to call her into his office without wanting to have his way with her on his desk.

"Da-da!"

Erika's outburst made Alli swing around, her gaze meeting his. Damn. He'd been caught staring. And when she reached up to get something out of his kitchen cabinet, causing the cotton shirt she was wearing to stretch tight across her breasts, he almost swallowed his tongue.

"I didn't hear you come in," Alli said in a breathless whisper that didn't help the erotic thoughts flowing through his head.

"Sorry, didn't mean to startle you," he said and walked over to where Erika was sitting in the high chair. The little girl automatically reached for him. "Da-da."

"Mark," he tried correcting her as he picked her up. He looked forward to the day when she would understand who he was and his role in her life. When she merely giggled and said, "Da-da," again, he shook his head. He studied the way her hair was styled and smiled. He liked it.

He glanced up to find Alli watching him, evidently waiting to hear his opinion. "I guess braiding her hair is better since it was getting all tangled. She was beginning to make a fuss whenever I combed it."

Alli nodded. "Yes, it will be more manageable this way." She turned back around to the stove. "Would you like something for breakfast? I'm fixing pancakes, eggs and bacon."

Mark wished she hadn't turned around, giving him

a view of her delectable backside. Her curves were out of this world and he couldn't help but appreciate just how snugly her jeans fit.

"Mark."

He blinked when she turned back and met his gaze. He had been caught staring again. "Ah, thanks for the offer but I have several appointments this morning. I had planned to come back here for lunch but I need to go out to the Windcroft horse ranch and talk to Nita."

Alli nodded. "The Texas Cattlemen are finally taking her seriously?"

Mark placed Erika on his shoulder while he leaned against the counter. He lifted an eyebrow. "You know about what she claims is going on over there at her farm?"

Alli shrugged. "I know what she's told me, and I have no reason not to believe her. I've known Nita a long time, every since Kara was small and Nita gave her riding lessons. There's no way she would make that stuff up."

Mark nodded as he returned Erika to the high chair. It was apparent that Alli had an idea that the Texas Cattleman's Club did more for the community than hosting fund-raisers, but he wasn't at liberty to disclose everything they did and felt the best thing to do would be to change the subject.

"How is your sister doing at college?" He watched as a frown puckered Alli's forehead.

"She was doing just fine until a few days ago when she met this guy at the library.

Mark heard the concern in her voice. "Is something wrong with her meeting guys?"

Alli's gaze narrowed. "She's at college to get a higher education, Mark, not to meet boys. She'll have plenty of time for a social life after she finishes school. Right now that's the main thing I want her to focus on. She's been making the dean's list every semester and I want her to continue to do so."

Mark nodded, wondering if perhaps Alli was expecting too much from her sister, but he decided it wasn't his business to mention that fact. Alli had begun working for him the summer before Kara had started college and he had met Kara several times when she had dropped by the studio to visit with Alli. Kara was a beautiful teenager who, in his book, was a younger version of Alli. Kara had been valedictorian of her senior class and her manners had been exemplary, which was a pretty darn good indication that Alli had done a great job raising her.

One of the reasons he had offered Alli so much money to work for him was that he'd heard about the extra expenses she would be putting out to assist her sister.

"I'll be at the studio if you need to reach me," he said, grabbing his hat off the rack. "You also know my mobile number."

"You haven't forgotten that I have class tonight have you, Mark?"

He dug into his pocket for the keys to his truck. "No, I haven't forgotten. I'll be home for dinner. Mrs. Sanders should be here around noon. If she asks, please tell her that I'd like to have some of her fried chicken, mash potatoes and gravy. She makes the best."

Alli smiled. "All right, I'll tell her."

Mark looked down at Erika and lightly pinched her cheek, making her squeal with laughter. "See you later, kid." He then looked at Alli and forced the thought from his mind of how much he wanted to walk across the room and kiss her goodbye. "I'll see you later, too," he said then headed for the door."

"Will we have our talk when you come home later?"

He stopped, turned around and met her gaze. "Yes, we'll talk then."

"So you're the new nanny?"

Alli smiled at the older woman who had shown up precisely at noon just as Mark had said she would. Erika had been fed lunch and was taking a nap, and Alli decided to take that time to do the baby's laundry. She was sitting at the kitchen table folding clothes while keeping the older woman company.

"Yes, but only on a temporary basis. I work as Mark's administrative assistant at the studio. He needed someone to fill in here and asked me to do it for a while."

The older woman shook her head as she tossed chicken in the bag to be floured. "I'm glad. Someone needed to help that boy with the baby."

Alli lifted an eyebrow, remembering what Mark had told her. "But you wouldn't," she decided to point out to the older woman.

Still shaking her head, Mrs. Sanders smiled over at her. "No. I had my reasons and they went deeper than what I told Mark. I felt he needed time to bond with his niece. When he brought her home he was a nervous wreck. Had I pitched in and helped, he would have depended on me and would have practically ignored that child. But I saw what was needed."

Alli leaned back in her chair. "And what was needed?"

"Time for him to get to know the baby, to remember

who she was and why she was here, to figure out things about her care on his own."

The older woman paused to peer into a pot that was cooking on the stove. In addition to making the dishes Mark had requested, she had decided to cook a huge pot of vegetable soup. She turned and met Alli's gaze. "Erika was such a precious thing when she first got here, but like most babies she was a little fidgety, crying all the time and whimpering. Mark didn't know how to do anything, not even change a diaper. I taught him the basics and told him the rest would come naturally. He'd learn as he went along. He caught on quick and is doing a wonderful job with her."

Alli nodded. She had to agree with that. "Have you known Mark long?" she asked as the woman began peeling potatoes.

"Practically all his life. I came to work for his pa off and on after his mother died. Mark was only seven at the time and Matt was five. Losing their mother was like losing their best friend. Carolina Hartman was a fine woman and to this day I never knew what she saw in Nathaniel. He was cold and heartless. All he ever cared about was this land and the oil that was on it. He wouldn't show affection of any kind, claimed it was a sign of weakness and punished his sons if they ever slipped and showed such an emotion in front of others. I remember Mark and Matt going to bed plenty of nights without supper after their mother died."

She joined Alli at the table. "Matt got punished all the time since he was so much like his mother he couldn't help it. Mark, on the other hand, learned to roll with the flow and did what the old man wanted so he wouldn't get into trouble. Hell knew no fury like Nathaniel Hartman's temper. That's the reason both Mark and Matt got the hell out of here as soon as they finished school. Mark left for the marines and two years later Matt left to attend college out west. Both swore they would never return to Royal while the old man was living and they kept their word. The only time they came back was for the funeral to see their pa laid to rest. I was so happy for Mark when he told me that he had met someone and planned to marry. Then I was so sad when I heard what had happened to his wife and he was left all alone. Too bad they never had any children. Mark had told me at his father's funeral that he didn't ever plan to have any. And he was pretty adamant about it, too."

Alli who had just folded one of Erika's shirts, glanced up and met Mrs. Sanders's gaze. "Why do you think he is so unyielding about it?"

The woman shook her head sadly. "Mark thinks he will grow up to be cold and heartless like his pa. Of course I don't believe it, which is why I wanted him to play a big part in Erika's care, just to prove him wrong. He needs to see that he's nothing like his old man. I'd watched him with that baby and he's given her so much love, affection and attention that at times I don't think he realizes that he's doing it."

Alli had to agree, thinking of him playfully tweaking Erika's cheek before he left. "It's sad that Mr. Hartman treated his sons that way. I remember hearing about it from my mom when I was younger and—"

"Your mom?" Mrs. Sanders asked with her bushy eyebrows arched.

"Yes, my mother used to do the ironing for Mr. Hartman years ago."

Rearing back, Mrs. Sanders sat in silence for a moment while staring at Alli, as if she were trying to make a connection to her last name as well as to her features. Then Mrs. Sanders's eyes lit up. "You're Mildred Lind's daughter?"

"Yes." Alli was surprised the woman would remember her mother.

The older woman laughed as she stood and walked over to the sink. "Well, I'll be. Now isn't it a small world? I knew your mother. We attended the same church for a while when she first married your father. My husband and I moved away for a few years. When we returned, instead of moving back to the city, we bought us a piece of property in the country since we needed a bigger spread to raise our kids."

She met Alli's gaze and regretfully shook her head. "I heard your mother had passed some years ago and I was sorry to hear about it. She was a good woman and a hard worker."

"Thank you." Alli paused, feeling a moment of unease when she wondered if Mrs. Sanders would bring up the incident involving her father at the time of her mother's death. News had gotten around about it when it had occurred eight years ago. It wasn't something most people would forget; at least she knew she never would.

Arthur Lind, who had deserted his wife and daughters years before, had shown up on the day of the funeral anticipating that he would inherit the house his wife had purchased without him. He actually had gotten ticked when he'd discovered she had willed it to her daughters.

He had filed a lawsuit claiming since he and his wife had never divorced, he deserved at least half of whatever assets she had accumulated.

Luckily for Alli and Kara, by the time the judge ordered her father to pay the back child-support payments he owed her and Kara, the amount was well over the equity he felt he was due from the house. In fact, he was ordered to pay an additional five thousand dollars, which he never did, and neither Alli nor Kara had heard from him again.

"You have no reason to thank me since I'm speaking the truth," Mrs. Sanders said as she resumed peeling the potatoes and glanced up for only a second. "How's your baby sister doing?"

Since it seemed that the older woman already had had a glimpse into her past, Alli spent the next ten minutes telling her how Kara had adjusted over the years and how well she was doing with her studies at college. Inwardly, she hoped her sister continued to do so. They hadn't talked since Kara had told her about her upcoming date for this weekend. Kara had dated some in high school but had never taken any of the guys seriously. But there had been something in her voice when she'd told Alli about the library guy that Alli had never heard before whenever the two of them had any discussions about the opposite sex.

"Something smells good in here."

Upon hearing Mark's voice, Alli whipped her head around and stared at him in surprise. She hadn't expected to see him until dinnertime. She took a deep breath and slowly exhaled. Seeing him again was turning her insides to mush. She may not have experienced the pleasures a man and a woman shared but being around Mark had her body yearning to do so. The memory of their kiss just wouldn't leave her alone.

He must have read the questions lodged in her eyes and said, "My last appointment canceled so I thought I'd drop by to see how things were going."

Before Alli could open her mouth to respond, Mrs. Sanders replied as she checked on the food she was cooking, "Things are going fine. Erika is sleeping, and Alli and I were taking the time to get to know each other."

"Hmm, you don't say?"

Alli decided not to say anything. Instead, she went about folding the last piece of Erika's laundry. She glanced up, however, when Mark came to stand beside the table.

"Do you think Erika will be sleeping for a while?" he asked.

Alli shrugged as she held his gaze. "It's hard to say. She's been sleeping for half an hour. I'd think she'll have another hour or so to go. Why?"

"I came by to see if the two of you wanted to take the ride with me over to Nita Windcroft's place."

"Oh."

"You two can go on. I'll keep an eye on Erika."

Alli stared at the older woman, surprised at her offer. Evidently Mark was surprised as well and said, "I thought you didn't take care of babies."

Mrs. Sanders flapped her hand before she lifted the lid of her pot. "I don't. But Erika is sleeping and chances are she'll stay that way for a while and if not, then I'll make an exception and handle things. No big deal."

"B-but, I—I'm sure he wanted Erika to go, too. This would have been a good outing for her," Alli sputtered, not sure she was ready to be alone with Mark. That would give them the perfect time for the talk they needed to have; something she wasn't looking forward to.

Leaning against the sink, Mrs. Sanders gazed at both her and Mark. "Well, Erika can't go because she's sleeping and I doubt you'd want to wake her. She's a fuss box if she doesn't get her rest." Frowning, the woman then dipped her chin as she stared at Mark. "Besides, I got the feeling that Mark just wanted some company."

Alli stole a quick glance at Mark. He was shaking his head, smiling while holding Mrs. Sanders's gaze, as if he knew what she was up to. Evidently there was a private joke going on that Alli wasn't privy to.

Mark then turned and met Alli's gaze. "Yes, I'd love the company if you'd like to go with me, Alli."

Inhaling a calming breath, Alli silently told herself that Mark was just being kind in asking her to go. The smart thing to do would be to turn down his offer. But then, as much as she wasn't looking forward to it, they needed to talk, and putting things off wouldn't help matters.

"Okay, I just need to put these things away and grab my jacket." She stood and, without looking at either him or Mrs. Sanders, walked out of the kitchen.

Alli took the time to do more than grab her jacket. She brushed her hair and applied some lip gloss. She also changed blouses since Erika accidentally had spilled some syrup on it at breakfast.

Moments later, she stared at her reflection in the mirror, deciding that she looked decent. She sucked in a deep breath as she left the bedroom and decided to quickly check on Erika. Alli stopped dead in her tracks when she found Mark in the room standing over the crib staring down at the sleeping baby.

Alli wanted to give him a private moment with his niece. She was quietly backing out of the room, more than certain he hadn't heard her, when he turned his head and met her gaze.

She opened her mouth to apologize for the untimely intrusion when he placed a finger to his lips and beckoned for them to step outside the room. After following her into the hall, he closed the door behind them.

"Sorry, I thought I'd check on her before we left," Alli said softly, trying not to notice how close together they were standing. She could see the irises of his hazel eyes as well as smell the masculine scent of the cologne he wore.

He smiled in understanding. "I thought I'd check on her, too. For some reason I like watching her sleep. She seems so at peace," he murmured.

Alli returned his smile. Earlier today she had thought the same thing. "She's that way when she's awake as well. Erika is a happy baby."

Mark lifted an eyebrow. "You really think so?"

Alli chuckled. "Yes. She has such a good temperament and is a joy to take care of."

Mark couldn't help but be pleased at what Alli had said. "Her father was that way. No matter how bad things were around here, nothing could break Matt's spirit, although the old man tried. My brother was always able to look on the bright side."

Alli felt a tugging at her heart. She couldn't help but recall the conversation she'd had with Mrs. Sanders and could only imagine Mark and his brother as young boys dealing with a father who thought it was wrong for him or his sons to show emotions.

"Ready to go?"

Mark's question jarred her out of her reverie. She stared at him for a moment and then asked, "I know you're visiting Nita on Texas Cattleman's Club business. Are you sure you want me to come along?"

He nodded his head. "Yes, I'm sure. Besides, this will give us time to talk."

Alli nodded. That's what she'd been afraid of.

Five

Mark glanced over at Alli as they walked out to his truck, not able to suppress his full awareness of her. He could feel her nervous tension and wondered if it was because of him.

He knew that kissing her had been a mistake, although, heaven help him, he wanted to do it again. The desire for her wouldn't go away. It was as if the lust that had been building and accumulating for two years was demanding to break free. They had crossed the boundary of what was acceptable between an employer and his employee and he couldn't help wondering what she thought about it. His actions last night had put him at risk of losing the best assistant he'd ever had.

But as much as he tried, he could not ignore her presence. He had dated some since his return to Royal but never had he let any woman get close to him. In fact, other than Erika, Mrs. Sanders, Christine Travers, the interior decorator and the other piss-poor nannies he'd hired, no other female had been allowed across the threshold in his home.

He was suddenly pulled from his thoughts when, to avoid coming into contact with the branch of a shrub, Alli moved closer to him and innocently touched her arm to his. He stiffened when a jolt of awareness shot through him. Just being around her was murder on his self-control.

How in the world could she think that she was lacking in anything? he wondered again. Although he could tell she wasn't an experienced kisser, that hadn't had any bearing on how she had made him feel. In fact, he had found her inexperience totally refreshing and unique. There weren't too many twenty-five-year-olds who hadn't been in and out of numerous affairs. After thinking about it most of the day, he realized that during the two years Alli had worked for him, he'd never known her to go out on a date, not that he was privy to everything there was to know about her personal life and how she spent her free time.

Hell, for all he knew she could have had a boyfriend, several of them. How did he know for sure that she didn't have one now? She was a beautiful woman, a real head-turner no matter where she went, so it was possible she *was* seeing someone. For some reason, he was disturbed at the thought that there might be a special man in her life, although he had no right to feel that way.

He sighed deeply. Instead of his mind being focused on Alli and whether or not she was involved with someone, he should be concentrating on his meeting with Nita Windcroft.

But he knew he couldn't put it off any longer. He and Alli needed to talk.

Mark and Alli rode for about four miles before either one of them spoke.

"It won't be much farther now," Mark said, glancing over at her.

"Yes, I know." Alli turned from looking out the window and glanced over at him, barely seeing his eyes because of the wide brim of his Stetson. "You said that we would talk." She had decided that if she needed to look for other employment, the sooner she did so, the better.

"Yes, I did." He glanced back over at her again. "About last night. I think you misunderstood the reason I was apologizing."

She lifted an eyebrow. "Did I?"

He gave her a lazy smile. "Yes, I think you did."

She took a deep breath, reminding herself that lately she and Mark weren't on the same wavelength, so she decided to let him do the explaining. "I don't understand what you're saying, Mark."

She blinked when she saw he was pulling to the side of the road, and once they were stopped, he turned off the engine of his truck. He turned in his seat to face her, tipping his hat back. In a way, Alli wished that he hadn't done that. Now she could see his eyes and the intensity she saw in them made her breath catch.

"The reason I apologized, Alli, was because I'm the one who initiated the kiss and I was out of line to do so. When I said that we made a mistake, what I meant was that the kiss should not have happened. I told you that I wasn't ready to become involved with anyone. But last night I gave into a weakness I've been fighting for two years."

Alli blinked in surprise. "Two years?"

He smiled warmly. "Yes, for two years. I've wanted to kiss you for a very long time and my apology had nothing to do with your lack of experience."

Alli wanted to believe what he was saying. "I wasn't sure since I haven't dated much. Over the years, even while I was in high school, taking care of Kara occupied most of my time and there wasn't time for dates."

There was no way she was going to tell him that once Kara had left for school she could have started dating, but by that time she had fallen in love with him and no other man had interested her.

"I don't want to become involved with you, Alli."

She pursed her lips and raised her chin. "And I don't want to become involved with you, either."

"Good. I'm glad we agree on that. Another kiss would be asking for trouble."

"I totally agree."

He leaned back in his seat. "If we were to kiss again it will be hard for us to go back to having a strictly professional relationship."

"I concur with that as well."

"We will be living together for a while and since we know what's the most sensible thing to do, which is the only thing that we can do, what do you suggest?" His gaze slid to her mouth. She saw it happen and her pulse quickened.

"I could leave here today and, if you want, I'll even quit my job at the studio."

"No. That's not what I want, Alli." Mark rubbed his hand down his face. He needed to rid her of the notion that he preferred she leave.

"I need you here, Alli, and when I find a nanny who I can depend on, I'll need you back at the studio. In no way am I suggesting that you stop working for me."

"Then what are you saying?"

His muscles tightened at the memory of what had happened to Patrice and the months of endless guilt he endured following her death. Never again would he set himself up for such heartbreak. The quicker he established some distance between Alison and him, the better things would be for both of them.

His eyes met hers. "What I'm trying to say is that I need to practice more self-control when it comes to you. But it won't be easy. I need your help. We both need to accept that we're attracted to each other. It's an attraction that will lead nowhere, since I don't ever intend to get serious about a woman again." He held her gaze intensely. "Do you understand what I'm trying to say, Alli?"

She nodded, fighting the tightness in her throat. He was telling her in a nice way that he didn't want her. Ever. "You want to keep things as they have been between us for the past two years, a strictly professional relationship. Is that what you want?"

Mark nodded. "Yes, that is exactly what I want."

"We're here," Mark said, glancing over at Alli. She hadn't said more than two words to him since they'd had their talk. More than once he had tried to strike up a conversation with her but in a polite yet distant way she had let him know she wasn't prone to chitchat. In fact, she was doing exactly what he'd asked her to do—establish a strictly professional relationship between them.

And already he didn't like it.

He glanced out of his truck's windshield and stared at the main house of the Windcrofts' Horse farm. The structure was very modern with a lot of tall windows and a stone facade. The primary stable was located close to the house and an older farmhouse—probably the original family dwelling—was set back in the distance. There were also four corrals, stallion pens as well as a training pen.

From his early days of living in Royal, Mark recalled that Will Windcroft's wife had died when his two daughters, Nita and Rose, were small children. The Windcroft girls were as different as day and night. It had always been Rose's dream to leave Royal and pursue a career in the big city. Nita never wanted to leave and had looked forward to continuing her father's horse-breeding farm. In recent years, as business had increased, she'd begun assuming a greater role in running things.

"I've always liked this place."

Mark jerked his head around. Alli had spoken without being prompted. It suddenly occurred to him how much he liked hearing her voice. Even while at the studio when she was going over reports, he would be more in tune to listening to her voice than concentrating on the subject they were discussing.

"My dad used to purchase his horses from Mr. Windcroft and I've always liked it here, too," he said. "You come here often?" he asked, wanting to keep her talk-

ing. Just because they had agreed to have a strictly business relationship was no reason they had to act like total
strangers.

"Not as often as I'd like to. When I was a little girl,
Mr. Windcroft taught me how to ride my first horse, and
later when Nita took over the running of things, she
taught Kara. Even now there are days on the weekend
when I'll come and get one of their horses and ride for
hours, although not as often as I used to."

Mark gave her an incredulous look. Though he knew
most people in Royal could ride, he never gave it much
thought that she could. For some reason, he could not
imagine her sitting on the back of a horse. She seemed
too prim and proper for that. "I have horses at my ranch.
You're welcome to take one out whenever you want.
John Collier is my foreman. He'll be glad to saddle one
up for you."

She glanced at him as she brushed her hair back from
her face. "Thanks."

Before he could say anything, she opened the truck's
door and hopped out. He figured she was putting distance between them again. He inhaled deeply as he
opened his own door. And for the second time he had
to remind himself that he was getting just what he'd
asked for.

She wasn't trying to be difficult, Alli tried convincing
herself. What she was doing was trying to make the best
of a difficult situation. Mark had made things pretty
clear. In order to keep her job, she needed to keep her
distance and he would keep his. Although it would be

challenging with them living under the same roof, she intended to do it.

She smiled when she saw Jimmy, the Windcrofts' foreman, approaching. However, she tensed when she felt Mark's presence beside her. She hadn't wasted any time getting out of the truck because of the desperate need to catch her breath and gather her composure. She was sure Mark wasn't aware of it, but each and every time he looked at her for too long or got too close to her, her insides filled with heat. She walked away from him to meet Jimmy, needing desperately to escape his presence.

"Ms. Lind, how are you?" Jimmy greeted her, smiling brightly. "It's been a while since you've come out for a ride."

She returned the man's smile. "Yes, I've been pretty busy lately. How is everything going?"

Before Jimmy could respond, his gaze moved to Mark, who had joined them. "Jimmy, do you know Mark Hartman?" Alli asked. "He's here to talk to Nita."

The two men regarded each other as introductions were made and handshakes exchanged. "I don't think we've ever met, since I was hired on here after you left Royal years ago," Jimmy was saying. "You own the Hartman place, right?"

Mark smiled. "Yes, that's right."

"You have a mighty fine spread."

"Thanks. Is Nita around?"

"Yeah, she's out back near the stables with a few of the hands. I'll be glad to take you to her," Jimmy said. He then glanced over at Alli. "Are you coming, too, Ms. Lind?"

Alli shook her head. "No, I think I'll go inside and visit with Will and Jane. Is she in?"

Jimmy chuckled. "Now you know Jane isn't going any-place," he said of the Windcrofts' housekeeper. "In fact, there's a rumor floating around the farm that she's baking a ton of pies today, so you came to visit right in time."

"That's wonderful. I love Jane's pies," Alli said chuck-ling. She made a move to step past Mark and he reached out and touched her arm. Although she tried to remain unaffected, every part of her tingled from the contact.

"I'll see you again in a little while," he said huskily, the depth of his gaze holding hers.

She gave him a strained smile. "All right." And then she quickly walked off toward the main house.

When they reached the stables, Mark looked around. Several ranch hands were crowded around the training pen watching one of the hands break in a horse. The an-imal was a beauty. He was also mean and it was obvi-ous that he intended to throw the rider. However, the rider was showing the animal that he wasn't going any-where. There was nothing like seeing man tame beast… or vice versa.

Fascinated, Mark walked to the corral and joined the onlookers. Everyone was cheering the rider on and, from the way the man was handling the horse, it ap-peared he was definitely up to the challenge, even with the horse not making it easy for him bucking all over the place.

The longer Mark watched, the more fascinated he be-came with the rider's skills. Moments later when it be-came evident the cowboy was the victorious one, a loud cheer went up. "What a way to go, Nita!" the crowd called out.

Mark blinked. "Nita?"

He stared at the rider who was getting off the horse and, when her feet touched the ground, she pulled off her hat, spilling a mass of black hair that she'd tucked underneath. She smiled and waved to the crowd.

"Damn." That was the only word Mark could think to say at that moment. How could he have forgotten that Nita Windcroft could outrace, out rope and outride just about any male?

He watched as the slim woman glanced his way after Jimmy said something to her. Without a hint of any smile on her face, she walked toward Mark. When she reached him, instinctively he held out his hand. She took it, although a deep, dark frown had settled on her face.

She met his gaze. "Hi, Mark. It's about time one of you guys decided to pay a visit."

Mark nodded. He knew she had expected them to drop everything and come running the first time she'd come to them claiming that the Devlins were causing mischief. "Any new developments, Nita?" he asked.

She placed her hands on her hips and glared at him. "Like poisoned feed, broken fences, cut lines, spooked horses and threatening notes aren't enough?"

Mark sighed deeply. The Texas Cattleman Club had seen the so-called threatening notes and thought they were too vague to actually take seriously, and although Nita had disagreed, there was no evidence that indicated the Devlins were involved. "Have you received another threatening note?"

"No."

"Then things have gotten back to calm around here?"

Nita narrowed her eyes. "For now but I'm not going to hold my breath it will last."

Mark nodded. "I'd like to take a look around."

"That's fine. I'm just glad to see you guys are finally taking me serious."

Mark sighed, choosing not to tell her it hadn't been decided if they were taking her seriously or not. "It might be a good idea if we have a list of names of anyone and everyone you do business with. It could come in handy later."

Nita nodded. "All right. It will take me a few moments to print it off the computer."

After Nita left, Mark checked out the other areas of her property, looking for anything that could give him a hint of who might be responsible for the activities going on at her place.

Mark had circled around the back of the stable when suddenly something lying on the ground near the barn caught his attention. He kneeled down for a closer look. Lying in the grass near a shrub was a syringe, the kind typically used in hospitals to give injections.

He sighed deeply. It was probably the same kind, or pretty similar, to the one used to kill Jonathan Devlin.

Six

"I'm leaving for class now, Mark."

Mark glanced up from the printout of names he'd gotten from Nita Windcroft to Alli as she walked into the room. Ever since their talk earlier that day, things had been strained between them. They had barely said two words to each other on the ride back from the Windcroft farm.

He glanced out the window. It was already dark and the thought of her going out alone at night bothered him. He remembered the incident with her car breaking down and stood to fish his car keys out of the pocket of his jeans. "Here, use my car."

Alli stared at the keys he held out to her. She then looked up with a puzzled expression on her face. "Why?"

"Because I rarely drive it since I mostly use the truck and it's in a lot better shape than yours."

Alli frowned. Well, of course his car was in better shape, for heaven's sake. Her car was eight years old and his brand new Maxima probably hadn't hit one hundred miles yet. Although what he said was true, she didn't appreciate him pointing out that fact. "Thanks for the offer but I prefer driving my own car."

From the expression on his face, she could tell he didn't like her response. "Why?" he asked.

She managed a smile when she said, "Because I just do."

Immediately she could tell he liked that response even worse. He crossed his arms over his chest. "I prefer that you take mine."

Her frown deepened. "Again thanks for the offer, Mark, but I prefer driving my own car."

She watched as he took a deep breath and glared at her. "You need a new car."

Again what he said was true but she resented him telling her that. "I plan to get a new one this weekend when Jake has the time to go with me to the dealership."

His dark eyebrows arched. "Jake?"

"Yes, Jake. Christine thought a man should go with me when I pick out a car since some salesmen have a tendency of taking advantage of female customers." She turned to leave.

"You could have asked me to go with you," Mark snapped angrily.

Alli stopped and turned around. She met his glare as calmly as she could and wondered just what his problem was. "No, I could not have asked you to go with me, Mark."

A confused look covered his face. "Why not?"

"It would not have been ethical. Jake is a friend. You're my employer. Good night." She then paused long enough to bend down to give Erika a kiss on the cheek before walking out the room.

With an agitation that he felt all the way down to his toes, Mark sat on the sofa across from the television as he flipped though several channels before muttering a curse and tossing the remote aside. He stood and began pacing the floor.

It was one of those rare nights that Erika had fallen asleep early, and although there were a number of things he could be doing, he could barely concentrate.

Alli had really ticked him off. The nerve of her asking Jake instead of him to go with her to pick out a car. Mark would have been glad to assist her in making a selection. Then for her to say she hadn't asked since he was her employer really grated on his nerves.

He was about to go into the kitchen for a beer when he heard a knock at the door. He glanced at the clock on the wall. Alli's class wouldn't be over for another hour and she had her own key. Fear gripped his gut. Was someone at the door to tell him something had happened to her? Had her car broken down by the side of the road and...

He inhaled deeply as he rushed to the window and looked out. He quickly let out a deep breath of relief when he saw it was Gavin's SUV out front. He had totally forgotten that he had called Gavin earlier and asked him to stop by.

He walked over to the door and opened it. "Evening, Sheriff." Mark was tall but Gavin O'Neal was taller, which was something Mark couldn't help but notice when the man walked into the house.

"Mark. Sorry it took so long for me to get here but I had to transport a prisoner to Midland. You indicated when you called that you may have found something out at the Windcrofts' place today."

"Yes," Mark said as he crossed the room to retrieve the bag he had placed in his desk drawer. "Like I told you, it's a syringe. I know syringes are used in the breeding of horses but this one is the kind used in hospitals for human injections."

Gavin took the clear plastic bag Mark handed him and studied the syringe inside of it. "Did you mention you had found this to Nita?"

Mark shook his head. "No, I didn't mention it to anyone. Luckily I was alone when I found it."

Gavin nodded. "Good. The last thing we need is word getting out and people speculating whether or not it's connected to Jonathan's murder since it's all around town that he was killed with some sort of lethal injection. The lab is closed tonight but I'll have it to them first thing in the morning. It shouldn't take long for them to analyze it and get back to us. I hope to have their report at our club meeting on Wednesday night."

"Here's a list of names of Nita's entire clientele, which includes anyone using her breeding services, those she's giving riding lessons to, as well as everyone who boards their horses in her stables."

Gavin let out a whistle as he accepted the pages from Mark. "It seems she does a lot of business."

"Yes, which is the main reason she wants us to do

something to stop what's going on. If word gets out that she's being harassed, she can start losing business. People will be afraid to patronize her."

"You have a point there," Gavin said, glancing down at his watch. "I hate to run but I need to get by the Royal Diner for a cup of coffee before they close."

Mark lifted an eyebrow knowing that a cup of coffee wasn't the only interest Gavin had at the diner. He tried hiding his smile when he said, "You're in luck, Sheriff. I just made a fresh pot and you're welcome to a cup if you like."

Gavin shot him a quick apologetic look, and then said, "Ah, sorry, no offense, I'm sure your coffee is decent but I like the diner's coffee better. Thanks for the offer though." He quickly headed for the door.

Mark chuckled as he locked the door behind Gavin, thinking that, whether or not Gavin realized it, he was definitely acting like a man smitten.

Alli opened the door and breezed through it still feeling elated. She had gotten an A on her paper tonight and she was thrilled. Professor Jones was a stickler for grades and she was trying hard to make it through the end of the semester without getting on his bad side the way a lot of the other students were doing.

Taking classes part-time was bad enough and she didn't envy her sister one bit with her full load, which was one of the main reasons she didn't want Kara to lose focus on her studies. The only good thing, Alli thought, about her own personal situation was that she could finally see a light at the end of the tunnel. Taking two classes for the next four semesters—even though it meant going to school year-round—and she could be graduating in December of next year.

"You're back."

Alli whirled around clutching her chest. Mark had practically scared the living daylights out of her. She watched as he straightened away from the wall and emerged out of the shadows to stand in front of her.

She met his gaze as she forced her heartbeat back to normal. "Yes, I'm back."

She stared at him. He was wearing a pair of blue silk pajamas and a matching bathrobe. "I didn't expect to see you," she said quickly as she tried not to stare, but she'd always thought that blue was his color. "I thought you'd be in bed."

"I was but my throat got dry and I decided to get up for a glass of water."

"Oh."

"And how was class?"

She wanted to say that her class was none of his business. But since Hartman's Self-Defense Studio's tuition-aid policy was paying a percentage of her college expenses, he did have a right to know how the investment was paying off. "Class was great tonight and I got an A on my paper," she said excitedly.

He smiled. "That's great."

"Thanks."

"You, Erika and I will have to celebrate."

Alli lifted an eyebrow. "Celebrate?"

"Yes. I think it's something worth celebrating. It's not easy to get an A on a paper in college these days."

"Yes, but—"

"Then it's settled. Erika and I usually eat at the

Royal Diner on Friday evenings and we invite you to join us."

Alli stared down at the floor as she thought about his invitation. She looked up and met his gaze. Her mouth tightened briefly. "How does dinner with you and Erika fall under the category of an employer-employee relationship?"

A smile touched the corners of Mark's lips. "That's easy enough to define," he said simply. "I've hired you to take care of my niece and as her nanny you'll be there enjoying a meal with us." He held her gaze for a moment, then he asked, "Does that suit you?"

Alli inhaled deeply. No, that didn't suit her, not after he had made it absolutely clear that he wanted distance between them. Having dinner with him tomorrow night was not keeping distance. "If I remember correctly we agreed that I would have Friday and Saturday evenings off," she said, reminding him of that fact.

He slanted her a glance that looked as if he might argue the point. Then he said, "You're right. I had forgotten about that. The three of us will have to celebrate some other time, perhaps."

"Perhaps. Now if you'll excuse me, I want to check on Erika before I go to bed."

Without giving him a chance to say anything else, she quickly walked out of the room.

Mark lay in bed and sucked in a sharp breath as soon as he heard the shower come on in the bedroom next to his. It didn't take much to visualize Alli undressing—first, taking off the dress she had worn to school, followed by her slip, bra and panties. Then stepping beneath the pounding spray of warm water as it cascaded over her body, soaking her face and running rivulets down her neck to flow over her breasts.

He further imagined that at some point she would grab hold of one of those bottles of shower gel that he had seen her unpack yesterday and dab an ample amount in the palms of her hands to rub generously over her body, starting with her flat stomach, then moving upward to her breasts, making circles around her nipples, coming back lower to massage her curves, before reaching down to her thighs and then the area between her legs and…

He bolted up, unable to handle the vision any longer. Why couldn't he follow her lead and accept what he himself had decreed regarding their relationship? *Strictly professional.* She had accepted his dictate and moved on. It seemed that he was the one who had issues. Such as with Jake going to the dealership with her to purchase a new car instead of Mark.

He dropped back down in bed thinking, *Fat chance of that happening!* She was his employee. He was the one who had given her the bonus for the down payment on the car. If anyone deserved to be there when she purchased a new vehicle, it was him. Satisfied he had reached that conclusion, he decided he would contact Jake tomorrow…on behalf of his employee. And what was the problem if she considered him a friend as well? A lot of bosses had friendly yet professional relationships with their staff.

Mark lay down, wondering why that thought hadn't occurred to him before. Probably because over the past two years he had been too busy fighting his attraction to her. What he should have been doing was getting to know her as a friend on a professional level. There was no law that said she couldn't be his assistant as well as his friend. It would definitely relieve some of the tension he felt when they worked together, and it would contribute to a more comfortable environment regardless of whether it was at his home or at the studio.

So, as far as he was concerned, there was no reason the two of them couldn't get better acquainted while she was staying in his house, as long as they established boundaries. And the first thing he had to do was get rid of any and all lustful thoughts about Alli that were plaguing him.

With that decision made, he felt a lot better and snuggled under the covers, pulling the pillow over his head. As sleep came down upon him, his earlier imaginings returned and invaded his unconscious mind.

It was the vision of Alli in the shower.

Alli stepped out of the shower and grabbed a towel to dry herself. She had been excited about her grade from Professor Jones until Mark had made the suggestion that she join him and Erika for dinner tomorrow night. There was no way she could do that and have people speculating that she had designs on her boss. She had loved him secretly for two years without anyone having a clue and she intended to keep things that way.

She knew after what he'd said on their way over to the Windcrofts' place that nothing would ever develop between them. He saw her as his employee and nothing more. At least she would have memories of the one and only time they'd kissed—how he'd held her in his arms, how his mouth had moved over hers and how her mouth had parted instinctively when he had inserted his tongue. And when he had deepened the kiss, taken her mouth with a skill and a mastery she hadn't known existed, she had felt sensations and emotions unlike any she'd had before. And now, although she was still damp from her shower, she could feel heat flow through her belly and settle right smack between her thighs.

She sighed so deeply it was almost a moan deep in her throat. She would always remember the taste of him, a taste she was dying to sample again, but knew there was no way that she ever would.

She would have to be satisfied with her memories.

Seven

Mark walked into the kitchen the next morning in a much better mood than he'd been in the night before. Immediately his eyes lit on Alli. She was standing in front of the high chair, showing Erika how to hold her spoon properly, and was dressed in a T-shirt that advertised Hartman's Self-Defense Studio and a pair of black walking shorts.

He shook his head and smiled. Even now, she was trying to keep her attire modest and professional. He had discovered a long time ago that it didn't matter what type of clothing Alison Lind placed on her body—she would still look delectable. The red-and-white T-shirt was tucked inside her shorts and emphasized her small waist and curvy hips. And her shorts showed enough of her long, slender legs to remind him of the visions that had taken over his dreams last night. In all his twenty-eight years, he had never dreamed about a woman taking a bath.

His dream had alternated with visions of her bath and of him kissing her. He had kissed her so much that she had begged him to make love to her. And he'd been about to do just that when his alarm had gone off.

Sighing deeply, he forced his gaze from Alli to his niece. Erika seemed to be enjoying Alli's instructions. He couldn't help but notice how his niece was dressed. Since Alli's arrival two days ago, Erika's hair was combed differently, in a cute little style, and she wore ribbons and bows to coordinate with whatever outfit she had on that day, not to mention the matching stocks.

As he leaned against the wall, he had to admit that the way Erika was dressed was just one of many noticeable changes Alli had made in less than seventy-two hours. His niece seemed to smile even more. She ate home-cooked oatmeal instead of the instant kind, and Alli had no problems cooking a full-course breakfast whenever his niece muttered the word *egg*.

Then there was the scent that always emitted from Alli's bedroom whenever he passed it. It was a feminine scent. A woman's scent. More than once he had paused in the hallway outside her door to get his bearings and to remind himself that a woman was now in residence…as if he really needed reminding. There was no way he could forget that Alli was in his house.

"Da-da!"

He couldn't help but smile when two pairs of eyes lit on him. From Alli's expression it was plain that she was surprised to see him. Had she forgotten that he lived here? "Good morning," he said coming into the room.

"Good morning. I thought you were gone," Alli said still eyeing him strangely. "When I got up and looked out the window I saw your truck driving away."

He nodded, now understanding her confusion. "John is using my truck to pick up supplies. His is in the shop getting repaired."

"Oh." She then turned her attention back to Erika. He felt dismissed and ignored when she began talking to Erika and telling her how good oatmeal was for her.

He walked across the room and his niece's attention switched from Alli to him and she extended her arms for him to pick her up. "Da-da."

He gently tweaked her cheek, then said, "No, sweetheart, I'm Mark. And Alli needs to feed you so you can grow up to be big, strong and healthy like your daddy was."

"She won't understand the name thing until she gets a little older, Mark," Alli said, standing beside him. He glanced at her. Instead of looking back at him, she kept her gaze focused on Erika, but he didn't miss the guarded look on Alli's face, as if she were protecting herself from something. He couldn't help wondering just what that something was.

She walked toward the sink. "I'm taking Erika with me on an outing today," she said over her shoulder.

"Oh? Where are you ladies going?"

She turned around. The guarded look had been replaced with a bright smile. "Car shopping. I thought I'd take the time to look around today so that when Jake meets with me tomorrow I'll have an idea of the type of vehicle I want."

He nodded. "That's a good idea, however there's a problem with that."

She lifted an eyebrow. "What?"

"I spoke to Jake earlier this morning about TCC business, and he mentioned all the things he has going on this weekend. It seems that someone has pulled up his campaign signs and he and his workers are going to be busy tomorrow going around town replacing them."

Seeing her disappointed look, he added, "I told him you would understand and that since I was free tomorrow I'd be glad to go with you."

"But, but I thought that—"

"For me to go car shopping with you is perfectly fine," he rushed on to assure her. "No matter what, we still need to maintain a friendly working relationship, right?"

"Yes, but—"

"Then it's settled. I'll go with you tomorrow and I don't want you to worry about a thing. All right?"

Reluctantly she nodded.

"Good. Now I hope you ladies enjoy your day."

He smiled as he quickly walked out of the kitchen, not giving her the chance to say anything.

Mark looked at the sporty SUV and then at Alli. He raised an eyebrow. "Are you sure this is the vehicle you want?"

She smiled brightly. "Yes, I'm sure. Erika and I saw it yesterday and the man was nice enough to let me give it a test drive and I love it. I know it doesn't look like me but this is what I want."

She was right. It didn't look like her. He hadn't pegged her as the sports-utility-vehicle type. She looked like someone who would drive a car similar to the one she had now—a low-key four-door sedan. The vehicle she had selected, with its leather seats, sunroof, state-of-the-art sound system, just to name a few of the features, was definitely sporty.

Sighing, he turned to the salesman who'd been waiting patiently. "This is the one she'll take. And I want you to work up the best deal along with the best payment terms. Understand?"

The man smiled eagerly. "Yes, Mr. Hartman. Mr. Cross said you were a personal friend of his and to make sure we take care of you right."

Mark nodded. He and Stan Cross had gone to high school together and Mark had been glad when Alli had mentioned the vehicle she wanted was at this particular dealership. "Now we have two reasons to celebrate and I would like to invite you to dine with me and Erika at the Royal Diner."

"I thought you and Erika ate at the Royal Diner yesterday," she said, placing Erika back into the stroller. Alli had stayed at her own house last night to do some more packing, and had been glad to see Erika when she had arrived at the ranch this morning. And although she didn't want to admit it, she had been glad to see Mark as well.

"No matter how often you eat there, the food is always good," Mark said grinning. "So how about it? After spending so much fun time with you, I believe Erika is beginning to peg me as a bore. Whenever I look after her, she goes to bed early."

Alli held his gaze and her pulse quickened at the teasing warmth she saw in his hazel eyes. She would love go to out to eat with him and Erika but she didn't

want to cause problems regarding their working relationship. "Are you sure it will be okay if we were to go
to dinner together?"

Mark nodded. A part of him regretted he'd ever had
that conversation with her. "Yes, I'm sure. So how about
if we finalize the paperwork for your new vehicle and
then we can meet up at the diner?"

Alli smiled. "All right."

The tinkle of the little gold bell that hung over the
entrance door of the Royal Diner signaled Alli's arrival.
The diner was your typical family café that didn't serve
alcoholic beverages. The waitresses wore pink short-
sleeve polyester dresses with well-above-the-knee hems
and tailored collars and small white aprons.

The diner wasn't the best-looking place in town, with
its worn and cracked dull-gray linoleum floor and the
faded red plastic booth seats, as well as the scratched
chrome strips that edged the tabletops, but the food—
thanks to a cook by the name of Manny Reno—was
mouthwateringly delicious.

Alli could almost smell his famous coconut-cream
pie the moment she walked through the door. She
glanced around and saw Mark waving to get her attention. She couldn't help but grin when she saw Erika following her uncle's lead and waving as well. Alli made
her way around the long Formica counter toward the
booth in the back.

The jukebox was playing a Ray Charles tune and, as
expected, the diner was packed. It seemed that regardless of whether you were rich or poor, the Royal Diner
was the place to be on Saturday evening and Manny's

sinfully juicy hamburgers and coconut-cream pie were the hot items on the menu.

As Alli glanced across the room at Mark, she thought he was hot off the menu. She may not know a lot about the intimacies men and women shared, but she could recognize sexual tension and it seemed that whenever the two of them were together the air was full of it.

Every time she saw him, no matter the time or the place, she was reminded of their kiss, the feel of his mouth on hers, and how she had returned the kiss with everything she had, becoming rocked by sensations that still flooded her.

And she was frightened by them.

She didn't want to think about what might happen if those sensations continued to consume her. Now that she and Mark had had their talk, she wanted to do the right thing, which meant she needed to stop thinking about the one time they had made a mistake, as he'd put it, and crossed over boundaries that they shouldn't have.

Mark stood when she reached the booth. "Sorry, I'm late but I wanted to cruise awhile and try out everything," she said taking the seat across from him. Erika was sitting in a toddler seat next to Mark.

Mark sat back down and grinned. "And how does it drive?"

She gave him a cheeky smile. "Like a charm. I love it and it's so easy to maneuver. I can't wait for Kara to see it."

He smiled at her. "When will she be home?"

"I'm hoping next weekend. She's carrying a full load this semester and has a lot of studying to do." A few moments later she said, "I miss her."

Mark leaned back in his seat. He knew how close Alli and her sister were. "I may not have ever told you this, Alli, but I think you did a remarkable job raising her. I'm sure it wasn't easy."

"No," she agreed, "it wasn't. But if I had it to do all over again, I would. Kara was such a swell kid, but that didn't mean we didn't have our moments," she said grinning. "I thought I would never talk her out of getting her nose pierced." Alli didn't want to think of what could turn out to be her next crisis with Kara. Alli couldn't wait until she talked to Kara tomorrow to see how her date with the hottie had gone. "But I can't see Erika ever getting her nose pierced, do you?" she asked teasingly as she put thoughts of Kara from her mind.

Mark's eyes flashed with amusement as he glanced over at Erika, who was busy playing with a toy one of the waitresses had given her. "No, but I wonder what the fad is going to be when Erika reaches her teen years."

"Trust me, you don't want to know," Alli said chuckling.

Mark laughed. "You're probably right. We'll just have to wait and see."

Alli's heartbeat quickened. He had said it as though he expected her to be around during that time. Did he think she would still be working for him then? She didn't have time to ponder that question when a waitress walked up to take their order.

"Good afternoon, everyone."

Alli looked at the attractive waitress with the golden-blond hair and periwinkle-blue eyes who handed them plastic-coated menus. "Hello."

When the woman leaned over to fill their glasses

with water, Alli noticed that a pendant that had been tucked inside her dress slipped out. Alli thought the piece of jewelry, a heart that was etched with two intertwining roses, was simply beautiful. When the waitress walked off, Alli couldn't help wondering if the pendant had sentimental value like the one she was wearing, which had belonged to her mother.

"Gavin has a thing for her."

Mark's words jarred her attention. "For who?"

He smiled. "Our waitress. Her name is Valerie Raines and she arrived in town a few months ago. Gavin has a thing for her."

Alli lifted an arched eyebrow. "Sheriff Gavin O'Neal?"

Mark chuckled. "Yes. He makes sure he comes here every night for coffee. Before she arrived in town he didn't consume it as much as he does now." He chuckled again. "If he's not careful he might be headed for an addiction of another kind."

Alli nodded. She wondered if there was a particular woman out there that Mark had a *thing* for. She was well aware that he dated occasionally since she often screened the phone calls he received at the studio. He'd been known to date a number of gorgeous women and just last year his name had been linked to a senator's daughter. But all that had changed after he'd gotten Erika. His social life had practically become nonexistent.

"Do you have any idea what you want to order?"

She looked up from the menu. "I think I'll get a hamburger, a peach milkshake and for dessert, a slice of Manny's coconut-cream pie."

Mark set aside his menu. "I think I'm going to have the same."

* * *

"I think we wore her out," Mark said as he entered his home with a sleeping Erika in his arms.

"Hmm, it seems that way doesn't it? I think the circus did it."

As they were leaving the diner, Manny had called Mark over and given him tickets to the circus that was in Midland. Since Midland wasn't too far away, Mark thought it would be the perfect opportunity to put Alli's SUV on the road to break it in.

Instead of leaving his truck at the diner, he had left it in the Cattleman's Club parking lot. It was the first time Mark had been a passenger while Alli was a driver. On the way back, he had done the driving and had made a number of positive comments on how impressed he was with the way she had handled her new vehicle.

"Let me get her ready for bed," Alli said, taking Erika out of his arms. They touched in the process and the sexual tension that had been humming between them all evening increased.

"Do you need help with her?" Mark asked throatily, hoping Alli would say no. He needed to put distance between them to get his bearings. The conversation during the drive to and from Midland had been enjoyable, but he had been fully aware of the chemistry that stirred whenever they were together, and being in such close quarters hadn't helped. The spark he'd felt just now when she had taken Erika from him was almost too much.

"No, I can handle her all by myself," Alli said, cradling the sleeping baby in her arms. "Thanks for going with me to pick up my truck and thanks, too, for dinner and the circus. I had a wonderful time."

He nodded. "And I had a good time, too."

He wouldn't admit that he had spent most of his time watching her. As usual, she looked good and the skirt and blouse she was wearing emphasized her curves to perfection. The hem of the skirt was short enough to show off what he considered the best-looking legs he'd ever seen on a woman. He hated admitting it, but during the entire evening his mind had been filled with erotic fantasies of those legs wrapped around him while they made love. To his chagrin and dismay, he had been thinking about that a lot lately. Despite his effort, the fact that she was his employee was slowly fading to the background.

"Good night, Mark. I'll see you in the morning."

"Good night, Alli. I'll see you in the morning as well. "

As soon as she entered Erika's bedroom and closed the door, he quickly moved down the hallway, desperately needing the privacy and seclusion that he would find in his own bedroom.

Mark couldn't sleep. He had tried counting sheep, pigs, cattle and even little lambs, and nothing did the trick. It didn't help matters that earlier he had heard the sound of the shower in Alli's room again, and those visions that had played havoc on his mind two nights ago came storming back. At least the house was quiet, which meant she had settled down and one of them was getting some sleep.

But it seemed that sleep wasn't coming his way. He was sentenced to lie in bed wide awake and fight this overpowering physical attraction that he felt for her.

Physical attraction, hell! What he was beginning to feel was need, deep-in-the-gut need that a man felt for a woman he wanted. Alli was intensely woman, seductively female. No matter how much he tried, he couldn't ignore the way his body, his entire being, was craving another taste of her. It didn't take much to remember the feel of her mouth beneath his, soft, hot, delicious, and the texture of her skin, smooth and creamy, whenever he touched her. Then there had been the feel of her breasts, lush and firm, when they had pressed up against his chest. And last but not least, there was something about her smile. He was inherently drawn to it. The one she gave Erika was different than the one she gave him, which wasn't as easy and open, but nevertheless, it did things to him.

He changed positions and tried rearranging his pillows. Tomorrow was Sunday and with Alli in the house to take care of Erika, he would get to sleep late. But a part of him didn't want to sleep late. He wanted to get up and see Erika and Alli, have breakfast with them and spend time with them.

He didn't want to admit it but he had enjoyed their company today, and Alli's presence had been like a breath of fresh air. Unlike other women he'd dated, she didn't try to impress him. She had been able to make an impact by merely being herself.

Seeing that sleep was impossible, he got out of bed, slipped into his pajama bottoms and decided to go into the kitchen to get something to drink.

Alli couldn't sleep and decided to get up to check on Erika. She was easing out of the baby's room, closing the door behind herself, when she stopped, the cool wood floor beneath her bare feet suddenly feeling warm. She tensed, abruptly turned and her gaze collided with Mark's as he walked out of his bedroom.

For a long moment their gazes held, connected, interlocked with a fierce tension. Even from the few feet that separated them, she could smell his scent, and seeing him dressed in a pair of low-slung gray pajama bottoms wasn't helping matters. Not when his bare chest reminded her of when they had collided that morning he'd been about to shave.

And now, like then, her body tingled with full awareness of him as a man.

"I thought you were in bed asleep," Mark said, almost in a whisper.

She swallowed, trying to get both her brain and her mouth to function, and knew she needed to stop staring at his chest, especially the way a thin, hairy line made a path downward to disappear in the waistband of his pajamas. "I decided to check on Erika," she somehow managed to say.

Concern touched his features and he covered the distance to stand in front of her. "Why? Was something wrong? Is she okay?"

Erika is fine. I'm the one about to go up in flames, she wanted to say, meeting his gaze. "No, she's okay. I couldn't sleep and decided to check on her."

"Oh, I see."

Alli doubted that he did, but that was okay. Right now she needed to escape to her bedroom and fast. "Well, I'd better go back to bed. Good night."

"Good night, Alli." He stepped back to let her pass

but then, driven by a need he didn't understand, he reached out and touched her arm.

Mark felt it the moment their flesh connected, that spark. He heard the quick intake of her breath and knew she had felt it, too. And if that wasn't bad enough, the air around them seemed to change. It got thicker, overpowering, and pulsated with sexual energy of the most potent kind. He could breathe it, smell it, almost taste it.

The same way he desperately wanted to taste her.

Acting on something greater than instinct and driven by a need that suddenly took control of his entire body, he leaned down and captured her lips, urging and coaxing them to part under his, then tempting her tongue with his own. His fingers tangled in her hair as he held her immobile, determined to get his fill of what had been the cause of his sleepless nights.

His tongue took hers in firm strokes and when he heard a whimper from deep within her throat, he deepened the kiss, pulled her closer to the fit of him, flexed his hips and rocked hard against her, wanting her to know just what she was doing to him.

He refused to ease the pressure he was placing on her mouth and with each fragmented moan she released, he deepened the kiss more, fighting the thought that although this kiss was as good as it got, there was something else here, something he was feeling that went beyond sexual.

The sudden need to breathe overrode his urgency to continue tasting her and he slowly let go, but he didn't pull back, nor did he stop kissing her completely. His tongue made slow, teasing strokes to each corner of her mouth and he felt the deep shudder that passed through her.

"We broke the rules again, didn't we?" she said softly, releasing a shaky breath and burying her face in his chest.

He inhaled deeply as his arms tightened around her. She sounded so disappointed, so sad, and her entire body was trembling.

"I'm sorry, Mark. I allowed things to get out of hand again. I'll pack my things and leave in the morning."

Her words infiltrated his heat-infested mind and the beating of his heart almost stopped. Did she actually blame herself for this?

He sighed deeply and pulled her closer. No one was to blame, especially not her. Yes, they had broken the rules again, but at this point it didn't matter because he intended for them to keep breaking them. He didn't care about the strictly professional relationship they were supposed to have anymore. He knew that he might be making one of the biggest mistakes of his life, but he wanted her, this woman, in his arms, his bed. He wanted her to have an in-depth, intimate knowledge of him and he wanted an in-depth, intimate knowledge of her.

"Alli, look at me," he whispered softly.

It took a while but she finally lifted her head and met his gaze. "Now tell me, what do you see?"

Alli silently searched his face. What she saw was a very handsome man; a man with a big heart and a lot of love to share. But he was trying desperately to keep that love shut up inside. He was a man who could love with a passion if only he allowed himself to let go. He was also a man who cared but was determined to keep his emotions buried and unexposed. But what she saw more than anything was the man she had fallen in love with two years ago. A part of her wanted to expose those hidden emotions within him, bring them out in the open and destroy the heart-wrenching pain that engulfed his world. Then it hit her. She felt it and couldn't ignore it. Absurd as it might seem, for the moment, she believed it.

Mark needed her.

She inhaled deeply and finally responded by making him think about his own question. "You tell me what I *should* see, Mark."

Time stood still as he gazed at her, saying nothing, then after drawing in a ragged breath, he said, "You should see a man who doesn't give a damn about rules right now. A man who will have no regrets tomorrow. What you should see is a man who desperately wants you, who has wanted you for a long time and at this moment he can't breathe another breath unless he has you, in his arms, in his bed."

Knowing he had to be completely honest with her, he continued to speak. "I can't make you promises and I won't. I don't want, nor am I looking for, a serious, lasting relationship, which is the main reason I never wanted to become involved with you. But if you allow me, I'll introduce you to all the pleasures that a man and a woman can share. Pleasures you've denied yourself and pleasures I've denied myself as well. I haven't been with anyone for over a year, Alli, because every woman I dated I wanted to be you. I've wanted you that much."

Emotions clogged Alli's throat. In no way was he saying that he cared anything about her. In fact, he was letting her know that commitment of any kind was out of the question. But what he'd said touched her. He wanted her, and although there weren't promises of forever, she felt drawn to him nonetheless.

·"I know that considering everything I've just said, I don't have any rights to ask anything of you, so I won't," he said, reclaiming her thoughts. "I'm going back to my room so you can think about what I'm offering. If you decide to accept my terms, then come to me. You don't have to knock, just open the door and walk on in."

He swallowed deeply and then said, "If you decide not to come, I'll understand. The decision is yours."

Before Alli could say anything, he had turned, reentered his bedroom and softly closed the door behind himself.

Alli breathed deeply. Mark was wrong. The decision wasn't hers. It belonged to her heart.

Eight

She wasn't coming.

Mark blinked, realizing that his gaze had been riveted on his bedroom door ever since he had left Alli standing in the hall. He glanced at the clock on the nightstand. Twenty minutes had passed.

His stomach tumbled in disappointment, but he accepted her decision. After all, he wasn't offering her anything except pleasure and for her that might not be enough.

But that was all he could give her.

He had made sure he thoroughly explained that, not wanting to take a chance on there being any misunderstandings. A misunderstanding would not be a good situation for either of them. He had wanted her to know the score.

Knowing sleep was impossible, he threw back the

covers and got out of bed to walk over to the window that overlooked the back of his property. From the moon's satiny glow, he could see the outlines of the meadows and valleys that were Hartman land. As a child he had loved it here, but as a teenager he had counted the days before he could leave. Both he and Matt had sworn never to return as long as their old man had lived. And they never had.

Mark's body jolted to attention when he heard his bedroom door opening and he held his breath, too afraid to turn around for fear he had just imagined the sound. But moments later when he heard the soft sound of bare footsteps touching the wood floor, and inhaled the scent that was distinctively Alli, he knew he wasn't imagining things.

With his pulse racing a mile a minute, he forced back the surge of desire that rammed his body as he slowly turned around. His gaze went to her face and watched as a nervous smile touched her lips.

"I'm here," she whispered softly, and the seductively quiet voice sent his pulse racing even more.

His breath hitched and the only words he could manage to say while his brain seemed not to be functioning were, "Thank you for coming."

His gaze then took in what she was wearing. She had changed from the tea-length nightgown and matching robe she'd had on earlier to a more seductive outfit. Now she was wearing a very short, red silk sleep shirt that did more than just complement her chocolate-brown skin. And with her five-eight height and long, gorgeous legs, the outfit looked both feminine and sexy on her.

"I didn't think you were coming," he said huskily, abruptly aware that the room was filled with the sound of their uneven breathing.

She smiled wryly and he saw the nervousness begin to ease from her features. "I wanted to put on something that I thought would be more appropriate."

Doesn't matter since I plan to remove every stitch from you, he thought, slowly dropping his gaze to rake it over her. Moments later he was staring back into the beautiful face that had haunted his dreams for nearly two years; whether he had wanted it to or not.

Is she sure about this? he wondered, as he swallowed the lump that suddenly appeared in his throat. He had to be certain. "Are you positive this is what you want?" he asked in a slightly hoarse voice.

"Yes, I'm positive." She lifted her chin and what he saw almost took his breath away. The same desire that he knew was lining his features was also lining hers. Tonight she had more to lose than he did, since he was fairly certain, could probably bet his ranch on it, that the woman standing before him was still a virgin. It all made sense. The way she always seemed unsure of herself when they kissed and how she would let him take the lead and eagerly followed. But then he had to admit, tonight would mean a lot to him as well. He had never introduced sexual pleasures to a virgin and hoped that he went above and beyond her expectations.

He decided to set the tone for what was about to follow. "If you're absolutely certain, come here."

With her gaze still holding his, she padded over to him. "Closer," he whispered as her soft feminine scent filtered into his nostrils. He watched her swallow, saw the thickness in her throat when she took another couple of steps, bringing her nearly face-to-face with him. But as far as he was concerned, that wasn't close enough.

"Closer," he whispered lower still.

She lifted an eyebrow, obviously confused. If she took another step, she would be all on top of him. A smile touched the corners of his mouth. That was the idea.

Mark watched as she drew a quivering breath and when she took another step, he automatically widened his stance and, as he'd known, she fit perfectly, positioning herself between his legs. He wanted her to feel the size of his erection and this way she couldn't miss it. And from the sudden look that appeared on her face, she hadn't.

The feel of Mark's erection pressed large, hard and throbbing against her middle sent a deep ache through Alli's body. It was an ache for something she couldn't name but wanted just the same. When she had eased between his open legs, her nightshirt had risen up past her thighs, beyond what was decent, and provided a provocative glimpse of her matching bikini panties. A surge of heat ripped through her and all she could think about was the degree of passion he was making her feel. To want him this much and be this close to having him were things she had only experienced in her dreams. Now she had to concede that reality was a whole lot better.

She had decided to do this, to become his lover for tonight, tomorrow, for however long he wanted. He might think of it as animal attraction, lust, an uncontrollable yearning or overwhelming desire, but for her she knew it was love. She loved this man with every ounce of her being and if this would be all they would ever share, then she was willing to make do. But just as he had given her a choice tonight, when it was time for her to leave she would give him the chance to make a choice as well. She believed that behind the stone wall surrounding his heart was the loving kindness of the man she knew he was.

"Feel it?"

His question jolted her to attention. She met his gaze. It was intense, hypnotic, arousing. She didn't doubt for an instant just what he was asking. "Yes, I feel it."

"Would you like to have it?"

She hesitated a second; not that she wasn't sure that she wanted it, but because she was surprised he would ask. She sucked in a deep breath when it seemed the throbbing tempo of the erection pressed against her increased and the size of it got larger. She tilted her head. "Yes, most definitely."

She watched as a smile touched his lips. "I hope you know what you're getting into because I plan to get all into you," he whispered huskily, before leaning down and kissing her with an urgency that almost made her swoon.

The way his tongue was taking her had desire—as potent as it could get—seeping into her pores, making her want things she never had before. And not knowing how it was possible, he pulled her closer to the fit of him as silk rubbed against silk, flesh against flesh, heat against heat. She felt it the instant he slid his hands up her thighs while deepening the kiss at the same time. She felt his fingers work their way beneath her shirt then inch toward the edge of her panties.

While changing clothes, she had been tempted to leave them off, which would have had her completely bare to his hands at this point. But it seemed nothing was going to stop him and he intended to have her bare anyway. And when his fingers eased past the waistband on her panties and he touched her intimately, she knew how it felt to place oneself in a man's hands.

She was wet, drenched, Mark thought as his fingers found their mark and gently eased inside of her. He shifted positions, widening his legs, as well as hers. He fought for control, clung to his last ounce of willpower when the moans she began making filled the room. The scent of her aroused body was permeating the air and it was like an aphrodisiac, stimulating every cell within him and amplifying his libido.

And then she did something he hadn't expected and wasn't prepared for. She shifted her body, reached out and wiggled her small hand into the opening of his silk pajama bottoms and grabbed hold of him. He could tell she was just as surprised by her actions as he was. But in no way did he intend to discourage her. Unlike her, he didn't have on a stitch of clothing beneath and all he could think about was the feel of her soft hand on his hard shaft. When she began running her fingers down the length of him, as if she needed to find out for herself what his erection was all about, he almost lost it.

With an animal groan that erupted deep from within his throat, he swept her into his arms. Never in his life had he ached so much for a woman and, clinging to his last shred of self-control, he carried her over to his bed.

Alli buried her face into Mark's hair-covered chest, now fully understanding how if felt to be swept off her feet. From the moment she had walked into his room, he had made her feel like the most desired woman in the world. Now being engulfed in his strong arms, she felt doubly so.

When he placed her on the bed and joined her there, she knew her endurance was about to be tested. He reached out and began unbuttoning her shirt and then removed it from her body, leaving her clad only in her panties. She wondered if he realized that he was staggering her senses.

He raised high above her, after letting his gaze roam over her near-naked body, his hazel eyes locked on her face. "If I do or suggest doing anything you aren't comfortable with, promise that you'll let me know," he whispered huskily as he brushed her hair aside and moved his lips closer to her ear.

"I promise."

Her body began shuddering when the palm of his hand moved slowly down her bare arms at the same time his warm breath trailed over her neck. "And I want you to promise if I tell you *not* to stop that you won't," she whispered, feeling herself lose what little control she'd been holding on to.

She felt the imprint of his smile against her neck. "You sure about that?"

"Positive."

"I don't think you know what you'll be asking for," he said, swathing her neck with a series of wet butterfly kisses.

"Yes, I do," she whispered when his mouth started moving lower. "I'll be asking for more of you."

He lifted his head, met her eyes and penetrated them

with a deep intensity. "I promise," he whispered. And then, as if in slow motion, he connected his mouth to hers.

In Alli's mind this kiss was different. Using the tip of his tongue, he invaded, teased and explored every corner, nook and crevice of her mouth, especially those areas she hadn't been aware were insanely sensitive until now. And with every movement of his tongue, he elicited her reaction; he seemed to feed on it and, in no time at all, he had her moaning out sounds she wasn't aware she was capable of making.

The multitude of what she was feeling stunned her, captivated her and filled her with a need that was all consuming.

As slowly as he had entered her mouth, he was pulling out, but didn't go far. He trailed kisses down her neck, easing down her chest and, when his lips came to her breasts, he pulled her close and took one into this mouth, licking, sucking and nibbling, one then the other.

No man had ever touched her there, let alone kissed her, and the feel of Mark's mouth on her nipples—as well as what he was doing to them—had her sucking in deep breaths. Winding her arms around his neck, he intensified his mouth tugging on her, making her feel erotic sensations all the way to her toes. He had a very talented mouth, she quickly concluded, and when he finally pulled back, she suddenly felt a deep sense of loss.

"You taste good," he whispered, the intensity in her eyes making her even hotter. "And I want to get inside of you, Alli."

The heat of his words, uttered so close to her ear, made her skin vibrate and her stomach quicken in anticipation. "And I want you, Mark," she whispered back, still swooning from the drugging sensations of his kisses to her mouth and breasts.

"I want to make sure you're completely ready for me, baby."

She met his gaze, wondering why he would do that when her body was already overheated. "Remember, your promise," he whispered softly as he leaned down and his lips began skimming softly, gently, heated over her bare flesh. He stopped when he reached her navel and plied it with wet kisses that brought her to complete awareness.

While Mark had her full attention, Alli was aware that he was removing her panties, and he pulled back slightly to ease them down her legs. Then he stood and she watched as he eased his pajama bottoms from his body, and they became a puddle at the foot of the bed. The lamp in the room gave her enough light to see him and she began breathing hard. Never had she thought that a male's body could be so beautiful, so well defined and so masculine. She had thought he was built before, but now, seeing him completely naked sent a delicious shiver all the way through her.

She wanted to reach out and touch him, run her hands down the expanse of his hairy chest, along the muscles of his shoulders, and as her gaze moved lower to that part of him that she had brazenly touched earlier, she inhaled deeply at the size, wondering how on earth…

She blinked when he moved and reached over to the nightstand, opened the drawer and pulled out a condom packet. Anticipation ran rampant through her as he put it on.

Then he lifted his head and their eyes met. The way

he looked at her made erotic sensations engulf her. He joined her on the bed again. Leaning back on his haunches, he continued to look at her. Instead of making her nervous and embarrassed about not having on a stitch of clothing, she was eagerly anticipating his next move.

He made it.

He leaned down and slipped his hand between her thighs, touching her intimately. She sucked in a deep breath when he gently inserted a finger inside of her, and instinctively her hips moved, her thighs opened to accommodate him.

If she thought he had a talented mouth, then his fingers were a close second. She began feeling dazed at the way he was making her feel with each movement. The feelings it was evoking within her were beyond belief and, when he drove a little deeper and touched an area inside of her that had to be some type of pleasure point to make her body feel this way, she felt a gush of blood rush through all parts of her, centering right where his finger was located. The intensity of it caused her moan almost to become a sob. Never had she been so unreservedly aroused before.

"I think you're ready for me now."

She met the intensity of his gaze, thinking that she'd been ready…for nearly two years. Long ago she had made up her mind to have him if he ever made the move. She was tired of living a lonely unexciting life. She wanted to share this most intimate and personal act with the man she loved. And although he might not love her, tonight he was making her feel wanted, desired and beautiful.

Before she could think another thing, he eased over

her, positioning himself between her open thighs, supporting his weight on his elbows. The heady thought of what they were about to do sent shivers racing through her. He must have felt them and looked down to meet her gaze.

She closed her eyes, but he whispered, "Open them. I want to be looking at you the entire time. I want to see your reaction, your response to my loving you this way, Alli."

She opened her eyes and wound her arms around his neck. Then she felt it, his attempt to ease inside of her, but struggling to do so because her body was too tight. He eased out a little and then tried again, the huge tip of him hot and eager at her entrance.

Alli watched perspiration forming on his forehead, his gaze still holding hers. "We're going to try this again. Hold on, baby."

She did.

And she breathed deeply as she felt him entering her once more, this time not letting the barrier get in his way. Inch by sensual inch, he continued going deeper, breaking through, overwhelming her with his size as well as his possession. She felt the pain and tried not to show it on her face but knew she did anyway. And when a tear she couldn't control eased from the corner of her eye, he paused.

Apprehension about what she knew he was thinking about doing ruled her mind. Still holding his gaze she whispered, "Don't stop." And when he still hesitated, she added, "Remember your promise."

She watched as he breathed in deeply, and then he

was slowly penetrating her again, moving deeper, painfully so, until he was completely sheathed inside of her.

"Are you okay?"

Looking into his eyes, she nodded, seeing the concern and the caring there. She noticed the pain was going away and what she was beginning to feel was a deep driving need right in the place where their bodies were joined. He must have felt it, too, because she felt him move, slowly at first, gentle, long, even strokes that started a heated flame escalating through her, as if feeding on what she needed. Feeding on it as well as intensifying it.

Her body began writhing at the sensations she was feeling and all she could think of was having more of him, him going deeper inside of her, touching every part of her that existed. He increased the tempo, the intensity of it took her breath away. He stroked deeper, thrusting back and forth. She cried out at the tension she felt building inside of her and the only thing she could think about was how much she loved him and how he was making her feel. Mark had captured her heart and was initiating her into the throes of womanhood in its truest form.

Then something happened. Something snapped inside of her and her first instinct was to scream but she knew doing so would wake the baby. Instead she groaned and moaned out loud as sensations racked through her and she muttered his name from deep within her throat.

"Mark!"

"That's it, baby, let go. I'm here with you all the way."

And he was.

He grabbed her hips as he continued to thrust inside of her, over and over again, completely filling her with him and taking everything she was offering. He shuddered one, twice, a third time then called her name, the sound a deep wrenching moan from his lips. She felt his body jerk, the same way hers was, and knew that what they were experiencing was an orgasm of the highest magnitude, the most explosive kind.

Their moans of pleasure filled the room and when he lowered his mouth to hers, the joy of what they were sharing brought more tears to her eyes. She knew that she would love Mark Hartman forever, no matter what.

Some time during the night, Mark woke up and glanced down at the woman snuggled against him. After making love to her that first time, he had picked her up and carried her into the bathroom where he'd run bathwater for both of them. In his huge whirlpool tub, he'd washed the soreness from her body, glorying in them sharing such an intimate act as bathing together.

Then he had wrapped her in a huge towel and taken her back to his room to dry her and had slipped her nightshirt on her. Evidently assuming she was being dismissed, he had reached out to capture her wrist when she had headed for the door. After kissing her deeply, to show her how wrong that assumption was, he had picked her up in his arms and taken her to bed with him, cuddling her gently beside him until they had gone to sleep. He could even admit that he had gotten the best sleep he'd had in years.

He would never forget the expression on Alli's face when she had experienced her first orgasm. That sight would remain in his brain forever. She had come apart in his arms the same way she did everything else, with breathtaking enthusiasm.

They had broken the rule of maintaining a strictly professional relationship, but that didn't bother him. In fact, he was waiting for her to wake up so they could break the rules again. He smiled, not ever remembering wanting a woman so much.

He closed his eyes and pinched the bridge of his nose, refusing to think where all this could lead…and where it couldn't lead. How would they go back to spending hours in the office together without him needing to touch her, spread her out on his desk and enjoy a little afternoon delight? How in the hell was he going to control his deep craving for her? It was different when he just had his fantasies, but now he had sampled what he considered the most delicious morsel he'd ever had the pleasure of tasting.

And that included Patrice.

Patrice had never really enjoyed making love and only did so because she felt it was her duty. But Alli was totally different. She had to be the most passionate woman he knew and he could tell she thoroughly enjoyed making love with him. He was going to enjoy tapping into her passion.

A sudden thought unnerved him. What if now that he had unleashed her sensual side, she decided that making love with him wasn't enough? What if she decided that since he wouldn't commit to her, dating other men was the thing to do? His jaw tightened at the thought of her in bed with another man, another man holding her in his arms this way, another man making her scream out his name.

Mark inhaled in a deep breath. He would have to make sure that while Alli lived under his roof and worked at the studio, he was the only man she needed. The only man she wanted.

Satisfied with that decision, he shifted positions, reached out and held her in his arms as he drifted off to sleep.

Alli slowly opened her eyes and glanced up. Mark was lying beside her and had been resting on his elbows looking at her, evidently watching her sleep…or waiting for her to wake up.

"Good morning, Alli."

The sound of his voice, deep, rich and ultra sexy, sent shivers through her. She tilted her head and glanced at the clock on his nightstand. She guessed that technically it was morning although it was just five o'clock. "Good morning," she said, trying to rid her voice of that drowsy sound.

"I've been waiting for you to wake up," he said, leaning down, close to her lips.

"You have?" Her pulse began racing, especially when he shifted positions slightly and placed his leg over hers. The contact of flesh on flesh sent more shivers escalating through her.

"Yes. I want to make love to you again."

She swallowed. "You do?"

He chuckled. "Oh yes, I do." And then he was kissing her and she forgot everything except how he was making her feel.

The only thing she remembered after that was him pulling back long enough to remove her nightshirt and his pajama bottoms and put on a condom, then him using his hands to drive her to what had to be the highest sexual peak. It was at that moment that he eased his body over hers and slowly entered her, not finding the impediment he had the night before.

As he continued to kiss her and thrust back and forth inside her body, his tongue did likewise, moving back and forth between her parted lips. She felt emotions in every part of her as he deliberately drove her over the edge. When she lost control and exploded in what seemed like a thousand pieces, she cried out his name. With a deep animal groan, he followed her and she felt the tremors that slammed into him ram into her as well.

And when he pulled her closer as he continued to pump into her as they groaned out their pleasures, she had a feeling that Mark Hartman wasn't through with her yet.

And wouldn't be for a long time.

Nine

Mark walked into Erika's bedroom and saw Alli and Erika sitting on the floor going through his niece's toy box.

The sheer beauty of everything they had shared left him breathless when he thought about it. After making love to her again that morning, once, twice, he had been driven to make love to her over and over again until they had both succumbed to total exhaustion. And when they heard the sound of Erika's voice coming over the monitor, exclaiming she wanted to eat, he had encouraged Alli to sleep a little longer while he took care of his niece. It was halfway through breakfast when Alli had walked into the kitchen, looking utterly gorgeous and apologizing for having overslept. He had taken great pleasure in pulling her into his arms and kissing the apology right off her lips.

"Da-da!"

Automatically, as if it were the most natural thing in the world to do, he crossed the room to them and crouched down to place a kiss on Alli's lips.

"Kiss me, Da-da," Erika said, wrapping her arms around his neck so he could pick her up. Her request caught him up short. He had never gone far in showing that sort of affection to his niece. "Kiss me, Da-da," she said again. A little more adamant this time.

Not wanting to disappoint her, he placed a kiss on her cheek and she let out a shriek of happiness. He quickly handed her to Alli. "I just wanted to let you know I need to go to the studio for a second. I'll be back in an hour."

Alli nodded. "How is the temporary help working out?"

He shrugged, deciding not to mention the mix up in appointments the woman had made on Friday. "She'll do until you get back. I'm hoping to hear something from Mrs. Tucker in a couple of weeks whether or not she'll be returning to Royal."

"Do you think that she will?"

"I'm hoping that she does. That would be the best thing that could happen."

To Alli, the best thing that could happen was for Mark to fall in love with her and want to keep her around, but she knew that was really reaching for the stars. "What do you think about grilling something for dinner?"

Mark raised his eyebrow. "We usually eat whatever Mrs. Sanders prepares on Friday."

Alli smiled. "I thought it would be nice if you grilled hamburgers or hot dogs. Something simple. I'd be glad to prepare all the trimmings."

"Trimmings like what?"

"Potato salad, corn on the cob, bake beans."

Mark smiled. "Sounds delicious."

Alli returned his smile. "Then it's settled. I'll have everything set up when you get back."

"Okay." Then he leaned over and kissed her before turning and walking out the door.

"So how was your date last night, Kara?"

"Do you really want to know, Alli, or are you calling to lecture me again like I've never gone out on a date before? I know more about dating than you do."

Alli opened her mouth to say something then changed her mind and closed it. In a way Kara was right. How could someone who'd never dated give anyone advice about it? And spending a night in Mark's arms didn't really count.

"I'm sorry, Alli. That was tacky of me to say such a thing. Tacky and thoughtless especially when you sacrificed your social life for me."

Hearing Kara's apology she said, "Hey, it's okay and you're right, I'm no expert. So how was the date?"

She spent the next few minutes listening to Kara tell her how the hottie named Cameron took her to a fraternity party on campus and what a perfect gentleman he'd been. Kara also mentioned that they had another date this weekend and would be going to the movies.

"Look, this might not be the best time to remind you, but you were coming home this weekend," Alli decided to say.

"Oh my gosh, I forgot all about that." Moments later she asked. "Do I really need to come home?"

Alli sighed deeply. This would be Kara's first visit

back since school had started and Alli wanted to see her. Besides, she hoped to have a surprise for her. The extra money she was making as Erika's nanny meant that she could swing the payments for a used car for Kara and had wanted to surprise her with it . "No, not if you don't want to."

"It's not that I don't want to come home, Alli, but I forgot and told Cameron I'd go to the movies with him this weekend. Please don't get upset with me about it."

Alli considered Kara's words. She knew that she and her sister loved each other but even the strongest loving relationships could suffer from the strain of opposing opinions about things. "I'm not upset and I understand you wanting to stay there and go out with your new friend."

"Thanks for understanding, Alli. You're the greatest and I love you."

Alli smiled, not really understanding. "And I love you, too, kiddo."

After hanging up the phone, Alli walked over to the window and looked out. Was she being unfair to Kara by expecting more of her than she should? It was natural for girls to be interested in boys and vice versa. Although Kara had dated while in high school, she'd never let anything, especially boys, interfere with her studies.

Alli turned when she heard the gentle knock on her bedroom door. "Come in."

Mark entered the room looking as gorgeous as usual. "I finally got Erika off to sleep. She was determined to play all night." He grinned. "If I didn't know better, I'd think that applesauce you gave her was laced with some sort of energy booster. She's been a live wire all afternoon.

Alli couldn't help but agree. When Mark had returned from the studio, she'd been busy in the kitchen preparing the trimmings. It hadn't taken him any time to put the hot dogs and hamburgers on the grill. He'd even cooked a couple of steaks. Afterward, they had sat outside on the patio. For a handful of seconds while sitting across from him, it had run through her mind just how much of a real family they seemed to be. When he'd mentioned something about Gavin calling a Cattleman's Club meeting for tomorrow night, she had been reminded of just how outside of his world she really was.

She watched as he stepped farther into the room. "I was wondering if you wanted to eat a slice of apple pie with me," he said. "And I know I've already told you, but I have to tell you again how good the pie was."

She smiled at the compliment. "Thanks. And thanks for inviting me to have another slice of pie but I don't think I can eat anything else." She tilted her head and looked at him. "I'm wondering how you can."

He chuckled. "Well, it was just that good. You knew apple pie is my favorite, didn't you?"

"Yes."

He leaned against her bedpost. "And how did you know that?"

She chuckled. "Mark, I'm your assistant. I'm supposed to know these things. Besides, I asked you once when Mrs. Gallant wanted to bake you that pie for giving those self-defense classes to the ladies at that senior-citizens center the first of the year. Don't you remember me asking you about it?"

He shook his head. "No." Evidently, that had to be one of those times when he'd been concentrating on her and not on what she'd been saying, he thought.

"Will you be available Tuesday for Erika's doctor's appointment?"

Her question jarred his attention to her. He raised his eyebrow. "Erika has a doctor's appointment?"

"Yes, the doctor's office called last week as a reminder. It's for her routine checkup." Alli smiled. "She'll be celebrating her first birthday next month."

Mark sighed. Had it been nearly three months already? Erika had been a bouncing eight-month-old baby when he had flown to California to get her. "I've never gone to her doctor appointments. Mrs. Tucker always took her and afterwards told me what the doctor said. I prefer doing things that way."

Alli nodded. She knew it was another technique he was using to keep a semblance of distance between him and his niece. "I would think you'd want to meet her pediatrician and hear what he has to say about Erika's health."

Mark frowned. "Why? You think there might be something wrong with her?"

Alli heard the panic in his voice. She wondered if he was hearing it. "No. Like I said it's a routine checkup. She'll probably get a vaccination of some sort."

Mark nodded. "Then there's no reason for me to be there. I'm sure you can handle things."

She opened her mouth to push the issue, then decided not to push now. She would push later. If nothing else, she was determined to make him see just how deeply he cared for his niece.

Mark continued to gaze at Alli, getting turned on by the minute just looking at her. She was wearing the tank top and cutoff jeans she'd had on earlier, which meant she hadn't taken her bath yet.

Deciding that he was a man of action, he walked across the room to stand in front of her. "If I can't interest you in eating a slice of pie with me, can I interest you in something else?"

He could tell that her curiosity was piqued when she lifted an arched eyebrow. "Something else like what?"

"A bath."

She chuckled as she slumped back against the windowsill. "Are you suggesting that I need one?"

"No," he said, taking a closer step to her. "I was suggesting that you take a bath. With me."

A smile curved her lips. "And just what will I get out of such a venture?"

He shook his head, chuckling, remembering. "Do you have to ask after last night and this morning?"

Mark saw an intense look appear on her face and he knew she was reliving the memories just as he was. "So, are you game?"

Alli knew she was more than game. She was becoming putty in his hands and she didn't have any regrets. "You're going to have to convince me it's something that I should do," she said, knowing she was giving him a challenge—a challenge he wouldn't hesitate in meeting.

"Convincing you is no problem, Alli," he whispered softly, reaching out, taking hold of her wrist and pulling her closer to him. His hands slid under her tank top, finding her bare, just as he thought. He hadn't been able to take his eyes off her chest while eating, seeing how the tips of her nipples were pressing against her top. He'd known that she was braless.

He watched her eyes as he caressed those same nipples, rubbing his fingers over the protruding tips, feeling them harden. "Remember how my mouth was on them last night, Alli, and how my tongue teased and tasted them?" He continued to let his hand fondle her, making her feel what he was feeling, getting her as aroused as he was. "Do you remember?"

"Yes, I remember," she answered in a raspy voice.

He liked the sound of it. "And do you remember how I kissed you and the number of times I kissed you?"

"Yes."

"Good, because I want to kiss you now. Part your lips for me, Alli, and let me in."

The moment she parted her lips, he leaned closer and his tongue slid heatedly over hers and the moment she released a deep moan, he went inside her mouth, kissing her with a hunger that she felt all the way to her toes. Pulling her closer to him, she couldn't help but cradle her thighs against the hardness of his aroused body.

She shuddered when sensations seeped through her pores, blood gushed through her veins and her pulse escalated to a point that had her sighing in pleasure. He kept kissing her until she was almost weak in the knees. It was only then that he pulled back.

He dropped his hands to his side. "Now will you take that bath with me?"

They stared at each other. Alli knew what her response would be, but she decided to show him rather than tell him. She leaned closer, framed his face with her hands, then kissed him with the same intensity that he had kissed her earlier.

Suddenly he broke off the kiss and he led her by the hand out of her bedroom into his. The first thing she noticed was the wood blazing in the fireplace. It had been warm earlier that day but the night had brought in cooler air.

He didn't stop until they reached his bathroom. She watched as he began running the bathwater in the tub that could fit two people easily. He turned to her, and without saying a word, began removing her clothes. When she was completely naked, she eased up to him to get some of his heated warmth. He gently lifted her and placed her in the tub.

She watched him remove his own clothing as his gaze locked on her with restrained hunger. She eased into the bubbles, thinking they might offer relief for her overheated body. She raised an eyebrow when he placed several condom packets on the edge of the tub.

"Lesson number two," he said, as his smile widened. "We have the freedom of making love at any time and any place on this ranch as long as we're protected from prying eyes." He joined her in the tub, grabbing the scented soap and lathering up his hands.

When he pulled her to face him, curving her legs around his waist and began rubbing the bubbles all over her, she let out a sigh. "We do?" Her breathing escalated at the way he was rubbing his soapy hands over her stomach, arms and breasts.

"Yes, we do," he whispered. His gaze held hers so she could see the intense desire in his eyes. "Now let me prove it."

And it didn't take long for him to do so.

Sheriff Gavin O'Neal glanced around the table, meeting the gazes of all the men present. Their Texas Cattleman's Club meeting was scheduled for Wednesday, but he thought he should share the lab's report with everyone as soon as possible.

"As all of you know, Mark found a syringe on the Windcrofts' ranch. The lab report came in today and their findings indicate it contains traces of potassium chloride, the same drug used to kill Jonathan."

It was Jake who spoke. "That makes Nita Windcroft a prime suspect."

Gavin nodded. "Yes, but I'm also looking at the possibility that someone might be framing her."

Logan leaned in. "Who?"

"Whoever is responsible for killing Jonathan. What could be better than to plant evidence on a major suspect? And if that's the case, then the person who put it there expects us to fall for it."

"And when we don't?" Connor Thorne asked.

Gavin met his gaze. "Then there's the likelihood they'll try again to make it seem like Nita did it."

Mark sat back in his chair. "Shouldn't we tell Nita so she'll know what to expect?"

Gavin shook his head. "No, because for now there's still a chance she might be guilty and want us to think she's being framed."

Mark sighed deeply. "Just so you'll know, last night Alli asked me about the rumors that are going around that Nita might be responsible for Jonathan's death. Alli went with me out to the Windcroft ranch and got to talk to Nita. According to Alli, Nita has heard the rumors and maintains she is innocent. Alli knows her better than I do and she believes her. She says there is no way Nita could have done it."

Gavin nodded again. "Then it is up to us to catch the

right person and prove Nita Windcroft's innocence. This is a listing of all Nita's clients," he said, passing copies of the list around the table. As you can see she has plenty of them. I want all of you to take a look at it and at our next meeting we'll discuss anyone who we might want to add to the suspect list."

"Hey, Jake, I see your opponent's name on the list. Can you believe Gretchen Halifax owns a horse that she keeps boarded at the Windcrofts' farm?" Connor said, chuckling. "I thought the lady-who-wants-to-be-mayor was too dignified to mount a horse."

"Yeah," Logan said, joining in. "And can you believe her horse is named Silver Dollar?"

Mark shook his head, smiling. "Figures."

Gavin shifted in his chair, deciding to bring the meeting back to order. "There's another reason I called this meeting tonight. The map has been returned."

"What?" The exclamation was uttered by five men.

"Yes, I got a call from Aaron Hill, the director of the Royal Museum. Hill says the map mysteriously returned today with a note."

"What note?" Thomas Devlin asked.

"A handwritten note of apology."

"Did the person say why they stole it in the first place?" Jake asked, shaking his head.

"Yes, the reason given was to keep it out of the hands of the real thieves," Gavin replied, placing the note in the middle of the table.

Logan chuckled. "At least we know for certain the person who stole it was really a woman. Only a female would see the logic in that."

The other five men at the table nodded in agreement.

"I had the handwriting on this note compared to those threatening notes that have been sent to Nita Windcroft. According to the lab, this note was definitely written by a woman and the notes Nita received were written by a man."

"Is there anything you need for us to do, Gavin?" Mark asked, checking his watch. He was looking forward to spending time with Alli again. He was still having memories of the bath they had shared last night and the lovemaking that had followed.

"No, that's about it other than to keep both your eyes and ears open and report anything. I won't rest until the person responsible for Jonathan's death is brought to justice."

"And just so you guys will know," Connor said, looking around the table. "I'm leaving to go out of town for a while. I have business to take care of in Virginia, but I hope to be back in a few weeks."

Gavin rose. "Well, that ends tonight's meeting." No sooner had he said those words, Mark was out of his chair headed for the door.

"You're in a hurry tonight, aren't you, Mark?" Jake called out.

"Yes, I guess you can say that," Mark replied over his shoulder without stopping or looking back.

Mark swung around and faced Alli, his eyes locked on hers. "What do you mean you can't take Erika to her doctor's appointment this morning?"

He tried not to notice how much of her thigh he saw when she crawled out of his bed and how her hair was tumbled around her face. When he had gotten in from the meeting last night, Erika had been asleep and Alli had been awake waiting for him…in his bed. And this was the first opportunity she'd had to get out of it.

"I know this is last minute and I do apologize, but I got a call from the bank yesterday reminding me that I needed to be there first thing this morning to sign those loan papers."

He lifted an eyebrow as she passed him on her way to the bathroom. He hurried after her. "What loan papers?"

She stared at him before walking into the bathroom where she intended to have a few private moments. "I'm getting Kara a used car. She could use one to get around on campus. Nothing fancy and definitely something I can afford since the payments on my new one will be low thanks to your friendship with that car dealer."

"I would have loaned you the money for that," he said as if he were in the habit of making car loans.

"Yes, well, I thought it best if I went to a financial institution, Mark, considering everything."

"Everything like what?"

"Our relationship. When Mrs. Tucker returns or when you find a permanent babysitter things between us will go back as they used to be. Besides, all I'm asking is for you to take Erika over to the doctor's office. Once I sign those papers I will join you there and take over. Now if you'll excuse me, I need to use the bathroom." She closed the bathroom door behind herself.

Mark's jaw tightened and his hands balled into fists at his side. He knew he was handling this badly, but he couldn't help it. First of all, he didn't want Alli reminding him that their relationship would be changing in a month or so. Secondly, he didn't want to take Erika to the doctor's office. He didn't want to sit in the waiting room with all those other people who would be parents and have them assume Erika was his daughter when he didn't know the first thing about being a dad. What if they tried making small talk about stuff he was supposed to know?

Damn, he wasn't looking forward to this particular assignment.

Mark sat in the doctor's office holding Erika in his lap. There were only a few people there and so far no one had been talkative. One woman had commented on how cute Erika looked. He had glanced down and noticed her pink coveralls, pink socks, white sneakers and the pink bows in her hair and had smiled proudly. She did look cute.

He glanced at his watch. Alli had said that she would be arriving around ten and it was almost that time. He hoped she got there before Erika's name was called.

"Erika Hartman."

"No such luck," Mark muttered quietly, glancing at the door beside the reception station and seeing a nurse standing there holding a patient's chart. "Looks like we're up, kid," he whispered softly, standing and holding Erika tightly as he maneuvered the diaper bag onto his shoulder.

"We're here," he decided to call out so the nurse wouldn't think they had disappeared.

The woman smiled when she saw Erika. "Well, hello little Miss Hartman. How have you been?" She then offered Mark her hand. "Hi, I'm Laurie, Dr. Covert's nurse. I don't think we've met."

And we wouldn't be meeting now if I'd had my way, Mark thought, accepting the woman's handshake. "No, we haven't. I won't be here with her long today. Her nanny is on the way."

Laurie nodded as she took Erika from Mark. "All right, but we can go ahead and get started. Follow me to an examination room."

Moments later, Mark stood on the sideline as Laurie undressed Erika. "She's such a happy baby," the nurse commented. "I remember the first time Mrs. Tucker brought her in here. The poor thing was crying so much we had to calm her down before we could check her and that was only a few months ago. You've done well in helping her to adjust."

"Thank you."

Mark turned around when the examination-room door opened, hoping it was Alli, but instead an older man he knew to be the doctor walked in. "Good morning, I'm Dr. Covert, and I understand it's time for this little lady's physical."

Mark continued to stand to the side and watched Erika get placed on a scale to be weighed, get her lungs checked and her head measured. "She seems to be developing nicely," the doctor said smiling.

The only bad moment was when the nurse had to give Erika a measles vaccination. She let out a loud wail but her tears quickly dried up when Laurie gave her a rubber ball to play with.

"Hmm, let's see," Dr. Covert was saying. "She's eleven months old so she should be standing alone—or at least trying to—responding to simple instructions, taking a few steps and saying mama and dada to the correct parent."

"She's not doing that," Mark decided to say.

The doctor lifted his gaze from Erika's chart and met Mark's eyes. "She's not doing what?"

"Saying those things correctly."

"She's not?"

"No."

The older man lifted a bushy eyebrow. "She's calling you mama and your wife dada?"

"No, I don't have a wife, just a nanny. And Erika's calling me dada but I'm not her daddy, I'm her uncle."

The doctor smiled. "That's natural. She sees you as a father figure, the one person who is constant in her life. Whenever she calls you dada just tell her your name, or the name you want her to call you."

"I've been doing that," Mark said, glancing at his watch again.

"Then just continue. She'll eventually catch on. Within the next month she'll start forming other sounds and I'm sure she'll start calling you by your name or at least she'll make attempts to do so. Just be patient with her."

Mark nodded. "What else will she try to do?"

"She'll try responding to simple instructions."

Mark chuckled. "Hey, she's doing that now."

"Then you have a very smart girl on your hands."

Mark beamed proudly. "Yes, she sure is that. What about walking? She's standing alone and has even tried taking a couple of steps while holding on to something. Is there anything I can do to motivate the process?"

Dr. Covert chuckled. "Try not carrying her wherever she wants to go, that will usually work."

Mark nodded. "All right. Is there anything else?"

"No, that's it. Your niece seems to be in good health

and after her visit next month we'll only need to see her every six months."

"What about foods? Is there anything she shouldn't have?"

The doctor spent the next few minutes explaining what foods were the best for Erika to eat and how they aided in her body's development, as well as those foods Mark should avoid giving her.

The examination-room door suddenly opened and Alli breezed in. "Sorry I'm late."

Mark waved away her apology and smiled. "That's fine. Things weren't so bad and Dr. Covert and I were having a little chat."

"Did you know we shouldn't give Erika honey until after her first birthday, and that honey can contain spores that cause botulism poisoning in babies?" Mark switched positions in bed to ask Alli.

Alli couldn't help but smile. It didn't take a Ph.D. to figure out that taking his niece to the doctor had certainly been an adventure for Mark. He hadn't stopped talking about it…at least he hadn't brought it up during the time they had made love. Now she didn't feel so bad about manipulating her time at the bank so he'd be the one to take Erika to the doctor once she'd discovered his calendar had been clear that morning.

"Yes, I knew it," Alli replied. "However, such a situation happening is rare."

Mark's expression turned serious. "Yeah, but it can happen. I'm going to have to remember that."

Alli shook her head smiling. She hoped he wasn't thinking of getting rid of all the honey in the house.

"Erika is almost a year old now. She'll be able to have honey pretty soon."

"Hmm, I don't know," Mark said. "Just because she'll be a little older how do we know for certain she won't get that botulism stuff?"

"We won't. We just have to believe that the doctor knows what he's talking about."

"Yeah, I guess you're right." He reached out and pulled Alli into his arms, tight against his body. "I'm tired of talking. I want to do something else," he said, leaning over and placing small kisses along her ear and neck.

"Again?"

Mark pulled back slightly, his expression turning serious again. "Do you think I want to make love to you too often?"

Alli smiled. "No, I was just kidding." When he didn't move but continued to stare at her as if he hadn't believed her, she said, "Honest, Mark, I was just kidding. I want you as much as you want me and every time you want to make love I'm right there with you. Why would you think you want to do it too often?"

He sighed deeply and met her gaze. "Patrice always said I did. She didn't like making love with me."

His words stunned Alli. She couldn't imagine any woman not wanting to make love with Mark, especially the woman who'd been his wife. "But why?"

He shrugged. "She didn't like sex."

Alli reached out and wrapped her arms around his neck. "Well, I happen to like it, but only with you." She could tell her words pleased him.

"No kidding?"

"No kidding. Can I prove it?"

She could tell her question caught him by surprise. "Well, uh, yes, I suppose so."

"Good, then lay back and enjoy. Keep in mind that I still lack a lot of expertise in this, but I'm finding that I have an excellent teacher."

Mark didn't get a chance to say anything. Her mouth captured his as she got on top of him. Incredible, he thought, loving her taste and thinking that he would never get tired of kissing her, but evidently she had other ideas and slowly pulled her mouth from his.

And then she was kissing the area around his ear, taking her tongue and licking it while whispering just what she wanted to do to him, what she planned to do to him. Her words and the feverish pitch of her voice inflamed him and he felt himself getting harder. She must have felt it, too, and adjusted her thighs to cradle his, while at the same time thrusting her hips against him so he could feel the contact of flesh touching flesh.

"I remember the first time I got on a horse," she whispered. "Do you remember your first time?"

He was trying to maintain his control but the feel of the tip of her tongue sliding alongside his ear was driving him crazy, and the way her naked body was fitting intimately to his wasn't helping matters. "Yes, I remember."

"Do you also remember how it felt to have such a huge animal beneath you?"

When her soft hand slid down his body and she took hold of his aroused staff, he gasped, then said huskily. "Yes."

"I do, too, and being on top of you this way reminds me what it felt like and it makes me want to do something."

She was rubbing her fingers up and down him, as if

she needed to know the shape, the texture and the degree of his heat. Her curiosity was pushing him over the edge. "Do something like what?"

"Ride you."

She reached over and took a condom pack off the nightstand and within minutes she had slipped it on him, almost driving him crazy in the process. "Now where were we?" she asked, shifting her body until she was over him again, locking his hips between her thighs. She braced herself above him and opened her legs wider.

Holding his gaze, she slowly eased her body down, taking him inside of her while listening to his labored breathing. Impatient, he thrust his hips upward, trying to hurry the connection, and since she was wet and slick, he drove easily into her to the hilt.

"I don't think you can go any farther," she panted, still looking at him. Their bodies were connected tight. But that didn't stop her from clenching her muscles around him, making him groan her name out loud.

"I'm dying," he whispered brokenly, not thinking he could last another minute. "I'm going to lose control."

"Not before I get a chance to ride."

It began. She withdrew partially, then plunged back on him again, taking him deeply inside of her. Over and over, thrusting her hips, rocking her bottom, slapping flesh against flesh, drawing up her knees and arching her body to ride harder. Each time she took him back inside of her, he seemed to go deeper still.

Mark grasped her hips, trying to hold himself inside of her but it wasn't working. She was determined to ride him and all he could do was give in and meet her movement for movement, thrust for thrust, stroke for stroke.

His gaze locked on hers and what he saw in their dark depths sent even more heat rushing through his body.

He released her hips to curl his fingers in Alli's hair and gritted his teeth against the intense pleasure that was overtaking his body. He needed to kiss her, join her mouth with his but, before he could do so, she cried out his name. It was then that he let himself go and was thrown into a climax the depths of which he had never experienced before. His release kept coming and coming and she kept riding and riding.

She cried out his name again and threw her head back. Then after thrusting hard one final time, she collapsed on his chest. After a few moments, he felt her body go slack and could tell she was about to drift off to sleep. He wrapped his arms around her while trying to recover from what had to be the most exquisite experience of his life. He wanted to hold her in his arms for the rest of the night.

"How did I do?"

Mark groaned as a chuckle escaped his lips. "Sweetheart, if you would have done any better, I'd be a dead man."

All he could think about was the way she'd looked on top of him, riding him to her heart's content with the potency of her scent tantalizing his senses, her head thrown back, her firm and perfect breasts jutting forward, her hair tumbling wildly and swaying with every motion of her body as it moved up and down over his.

He took a deep breath as an overwhelming sense he'd never felt before caused his body to go taut and something inside of him came close to shattering. Closing his eyes and tightening his jaw, he forced the foreign feeling aside.

With a confused groan, he buried his face in Alli's throat as he fought to stop his control from slipping any further. He reminded himself that this was all he and Alli could ever share.

No matter what, he could not let her get past his defenses.

Ten

A week later, Alli stood on the sidelines and watched Mark instruct a class of women on the art of self-defense. Her throat felt tight and her pulse escalated as she watched how he moved with precision, causing his broad shoulders to flex under his T-shirt. His firmly muscled thighs encased in a pair of sweats demonstrated incredible energy whenever he hunched down or let out a kick with lightning speed.

She swallowed thickly, amazed at how much Mark continued to appeal to her on a primal level. Intense heat rushed to pool between her thighs and she shifted positions to find relief. The cool air blasting from a vent overhead wasn't much help.

As she continued to watch him, she couldn't help but think of how things were between them. A smile tugged at the corner of her mouth when she remembered the picnic they'd had a few days ago. Mrs. Sanders had urged them to get out of the house and enjoy themselves while Erika was taking a nap and had gone so far as to pack a lunch for them.

Mark had driven them to a section of Hartman land near a huge lake, and after spreading a blanket on the ground under an oak tree, they had sat down. She had enjoyed eating the sandwiches while listening to him share his days of being in the marines and the close relationship he and his brother had with her. He even had talked about his mother and what a loving and thoughtful woman she had been. Alli noted that he avoided any conversation about his father or his deceased wife. But what she remembered most of all was them making love beneath the low hanging branches of that oak tree.

Alli's thoughts shifted to how she and Mark had gotten into the habit of sharing a bed every night. But a tinge of disappointment touched her heart when she thought of the shield he continued to keep not only with her but also with Erika. It seemed as though this boundary was elementally necessary for him to maintain a detached persona. But she had seen him let his guard down a few times, but quickly he would resurrect it.

"Da-da."

She glanced down at Erika who was sitting in her stroller getting excited at seeing Mark. No matter how many times Mark corrected his niece, Erika was intent on calling him daddy.

Alli hunched down to Erika. "He's busy now, sweetheart, but he knows you're here and will come over as soon he's finished." Alli had taken Erika shopping that morning for some winter clothes and while in town she'd decided to drop by the studio.

A few minutes later when class was over, Mark glanced over in their direction and smiled. The expression on his face indicated he was glad to see them. He ducked under the rope that kept the observers off the gym floor and walked over to them.

"Hello, ladies."

Alli smiled. "Hi, yourself." She felt her pulse go haywire again. God, but he smelled good. Only with him did sweat mix with a magnetic male force to produce a scent that was physically overpowering. She wished that for once he would defy proper etiquette and pull her into his arms—something he would do if they were behind closed doors.

"Erika and I were wondering if we could tempt you to have lunch with us at the Royal Diner," Alli said, forcing her brain to function normally.

He glanced at his watch. "I wish I could but I have a few things I need to do around here. Maybe some other time."

She caught her bottom lip between her teeth and glanced down at Erika to hide her disappointment. "Sure."

She glanced up to see him looking at Erika. That's when Alli saw it, a deep longing to pick up his niece, plant a kiss on her cheek and cuddle her close. But Alli knew that he wouldn't. To do so would show emotions and he had been taught as a child that to expose himself that way was a taboo.

He met her gaze, and at that moment, although she knew that he didn't feel anything for her, she felt all the love she had for him. The degree shook her to the core.

Realizing that they were standing staring at each other, she broke eye contact and returned her attention to Erika. "Well, I guess we'll be going."

"All right. Thanks for dropping by."

Alli glanced around. "Things seem to be running pretty smooth here without me."

He hesitated only the barest second and then said, "Don't ever think you aren't needed, Alli."

His words sounded breathy and Alli had to force herself not to put much stock in them. However, she couldn't resist cocking her head to the side and asking, "You sure?"

He nodded and said, "I'm positive."

Her heart suddenly lodged tightly in her throat. "We better be going. It will be time for Erika's nap pretty soon."

"All right."

"Da-da."

Alli couldn't help but smile. It seemed that Erika didn't intend to be ignored.

Mark hunched down. "You're ready for lunch, little lady? Uncle Mark can't go this time, but maybe next time."

Alli shook her head. Now it had gone from just *Mark* to *Uncle Mark*. "We'll see you at dinner, Mark."

He straightened and met her gaze again. "All right. Enjoy lunch."

"We will." She pushed Erika past him and kept walking without looking back.

Later that evening while Alli was giving Erika her bath, Mark came home. He had called to let Alli know that he would miss dinner. Nita Windcroft had contacted him. She had received another threatening letter and the Texas Cattleman's Club had met to discuss it.

"I can't believe someone is still harassing Nita," Alli said as she leaned over to take Erika out of the tub. Squealing at the fun she'd been having, Erika kicked up her legs and splashed water on both Alli and Mark.

Laughing, Alli wrapped Erika in a thick towel and handed her to Mark. "I washed now you can dry." She ignored the surprised look on his face.

"So what did the note say this time?" she asked, walking out of the bathroom to go to Erika's bedroom with him following behind.

"More of the same. The message is always vague. This one said, *Get out or else.*"

Alli turned and raised an eyebrow. "If someone thinks a few notes and a little mischief will force Nita to leave her land, then they are crazy. I just hope you guys do something before Nita has a mind to take matters into her own hands."

Mark nodded as he continued to dry Erika. "I'm going to turn the note over to Gavin to see if the person who wrote this is the same one who wrote all the others."

He handed his niece back over to Alli. She'd noticed that lately Mark avoided any physical contact with Erika whenever he could, yet he had confided in her once that, when he had first gotten Erika, he would spend time rocking her in the rocking chair. It seemed to Alli that he had a tendency to put up a boundary when he found himself getting too close or when he felt his emotions were becoming involved.

"I left dinner warming for you in the oven."

"Thanks."

"Once I get Erika dressed for bed, I'm going to rock her for a while. You can join us if you'd like."

"Why?"

She shrugged. "I thought that perhaps you'd want to spend some time with her before she goes to sleep."

He looked at her for a moment, then at Erika and said, "No, that's not necessary." Without saying anything else he walked out of the room.

Alli walked through the French doors that led out onto the patio where the pool was located. She had put Erika to bed and had gone looking for Mark only to discover he had eaten and was in his office going over the ranch's accounting books. Deciding not to disturb him, she had gone to her bedroom to change into her bathing suit. She felt tense and thought a little swim might help.

She'd swum a dozen or so laps when she decided she'd done enough. Releasing a contented sigh, she climbed out of the pool and began drying herself with the huge velour towel when she glanced over and saw Mark standing in the doorway.

She met his gaze. "How long have you been standing there?"

"Long enough."

"Long enough for what?" she asked.

"Long enough for me to realize how much I want you."

Alli found herself melting under Mark's intense stare. There he stood, leaning in the doorway wearing a pair of stonewashed jeans and a T-shirt. She wondered if he knew he had a patent on the word *sexy*. Without batting an eye she asked, "So what do you plan to do about it?"

The wantonness of her invitation was so unlike her, but so were a number of her actions since she had moved into this house with him to become Erika's nanny. There was something about Mark that brought out something within her that she hadn't known existed. It was as though beneath the layers of flesh that covered her lived a passionate, insatiable being.

"Haven't you learned by now never to tempt me?" he asked, beginning to walk toward her.

As soon as he came closer into the light, she saw just how much he wanted her. She could barely draw breath into her lungs. The lower part of his body that she knew would soon be connected with hers looked bigger than she'd ever seen it before. All from watching her swim?

He stood directly in front of her and reached out to take the towel from her hand and toss it aside. "I want you so bad I actually ache, baby," he whispered in her ear.

She was beginning to ache, too. The sexy sound of his voice, his breath hot against her skin wasn't helping matters. "Then I think I better help you find relief."

She lifted up his T-shirt, then smoothed her finger-tips against the bare portion of his waist before easing them lower to the fastener of his jeans. She began un-doing the zipper, and when that was done, she worked her fingers inside the waistband of his jeans. Her pulse increased at the feel of his hot, turgid flesh.

She caressed him, remembering the first time she'd done so and how aroused he'd gotten because of it. She moved her fingers back and forth, thinking there was something deliciously naughty and decadent about hav-ing him in her hands this way. She might be putty in his hands, but right now, at this very moment, he was the opposite of putty in hers. He was as solid as a rock.

"Your touch is driving me crazy," he whispered and

seemed to grow larger in her hand. "I got to have you. Now!" he growled as if in pain.

Before she could draw her next breath, he had pushed her hand aside and snatched down the top of her bathing suit, freeing her breasts. But he didn't stop there. Determined to see her completely naked, he lowered his body to remove the suit entirely. Then he stepped back, ripped off his T-shirt, followed by the quick removal of his jeans and briefs. The sound of foil being torn rent the silence and she watched as he prepared himself, not for the first time wondering how such a small condom could fit over anything so big.

Heat of the highest intensity rushed to pool between her thighs when his hand suddenly reached out and went there, at the same time that he pulled her close to him and began sucking on her breasts. She shuddered, already so close to climax with the feel of his fingers stroking her between her legs and his mouth making a treat of her breasts. Her shivers became so intense that it was becoming hard for her to stand upright.

"Mark!"

"Not yet, baby, just hold on for a little while longer."

That was easy for him to say, she thought as his assault on her became more intense, more pleasurable. The feelings he was causing to flow through her were too great and she didn't know how long she would be able to hold on.

"Can't last until we get to the bedroom," he growled in her ear as he walked her backward until the backs of her legs touched the daybed and they tumbled on it together. She reached out to touch him but he shook his head. "No, not yet. There's something I have to do. It's something I've dreamed of doing to you for a long time."

Before she could ask what that something was, he dropped to his knees in front of her and curved her legs around his shoulders. He looked at her and she saw how his hazel eyes darkened and heard how deeply he was breathing just moments before he dipped his head between her legs, pressing an open-mouth kiss to her womanly core.

When the tip of his tongue touched her, she thought she was going to moan her throat raw, and when his tongue began twirling around inside of her, then licking and flicking out torture of the most sensuous kind, she threw her head against a huge fluffy pillow and instinctively raised her hips against his mouth. "Yes…oh yes."

What words she muttered after that she couldn't remember, but she was sure she said, *Please, don't stop, go deeper,* and *Yes, right there.* The intimate kiss grew more intense. It was as if he were hungry and planned to feast on her all night. She had heard about men and women engaging in this special form of lovemaking, but had never in her wildest dreams thought she would ever indulge in anything like this. Mark was proving her wrong. And when the swift signs of an orgasm began taking over her, she couldn't help but scream, grateful that Erika's bedroom was on the other side of the house.

"Mark!"

And then he was moving over her, parting the slick flesh that he had kissed greedily just seconds before. He entered her, sinking inside of her to the hilt and filling her completely.

"Hold on, baby. We're about to test this daybed's endurance," he said, pinning her arms above her head and smiling when her breasts jutted out. He began feasting on them at the same time the thrusts began. He pumped his throbbing arousal into her and pulled it back out again, over and over. And each time he filled her, he absorbed the shivers that hit her body with the impact. It seemed her womb was contracting with every stroke of his manhood.

Each time he withdrew, her hips followed him, almost coming off the bed, refusing to be disconnected from him, only to have him thrust back inside of her. When she heard him growl out her name, he let go of her arms and grasped her hips.

"Alli!"

She watched how he gritted his teeth, stretched his neck and threw his head back as an orgasm rammed through him. He pulled out slightly but was thrusting back inside of her again, gripping her hips, refusing to sever the connection and she knew he was having yet another climax.

Watching his intense pleasure spurred her into another one and her fingers dug into the muscles of his shoulders and almost instantly she cried out. Words she had held back for two years found their way out of her throat and she heard herself saying, "I love you, Mark," just moments before another shudder worked its way through her body and she was entrenched in the throes of total fulfillment.

She had literally driven him wild and the shock of it jolted right through Mark. But what was even more detrimental were the words she had whispered while having an orgasm…*I love you, Mark.*

The sheer shock of her words had sent him into a

panic. He didn't want her to love him. Want him, yes. Need him, yes. But love him, no.

Alli was the kind of woman a man could, and should, love but Mark wasn't the one to do it. He had issues to deal with and they were issues that the rest of his life wouldn't resolve. He looked down at her. So that both of them could fit in the daybed, her body was spooned intimately against his. She had drifted off to sleep. He studied her features and wondered how a sleeping woman could look as if she were ready for the next round of making love.

He sighed deeply. She was not supposed to fall in love with him. There was no place for love in his life, which meant there was no place for her in his life, either. He should have known, should have expected. Alli wasn't the type of woman who would give her body to a man without believing that her heart was involved. He had made a humongous mistake in letting his desire for her get in the way of his better judgment.

Long moments later, he listened to her even breathing and he knew what had to be done. Picking her up into his arms, he carried her into her bedroom and placed her in her own bed. After placing the covers over her, he stood back, deciding since she'd slept in the nude before, he wouldn't wake her to put on a nightgown.

Mark knew that the intimacy the two of them had shared during the past three weeks would always be a part of him. The thought that he was the first man ever to make love to her was truly special and at no time would he ever regret what they had shared. But there could never be anything lasting between them. He was a man who understood duty and not love.

After Patrice's death he had made a vow never again to let a woman matter to him and he meant to keep it.

The bedroom shone in the brightness of the morning sun by the time Alli awoke the next morning. She sat up and glanced around.

She was in her bed.

She lay back and drew in a ragged breath as she recalled in vivid detail what she and Mark had done just moments before she'd fallen asleep. She didn't need the fact that she'd slept in the nude to remind her. Ever since they had made love that first time, she had shared his bed so why had he brought her in here? She stared up at the ceiling trying to remember anything that could have happened to make him…

Then she remembered. She closed her eyes as she recalled the words she'd whispered to him while coming apart in his arms. She opened her eyes and pushed herself back up in a sitting position. Was this going to be his way of denying what she'd said? Did he think just because he wasn't one who was prone to show his emotions that she shouldn't show hers, either?

Alli winced at the thought that yes, that's exactly what he believed. He was no more interested in the fact that she loved him than he was in whatever was going on in Midland. And why should he when he had conveniently closed his heart ever to loving anyone again?

"Eat."

Alli forced her thoughts aside when she heard the sound of Erika on the monitor. Moving quickly, she got out of bed and headed for the bathroom. She and Mark would have a lot to talk about when she saw him.

* * *

She didn't see Mark at all that day and she was trying hard not to think that he was avoiding her, although deep down she knew that he was. Before, even when he would be away from the ranch for long periods during the day, he would call and tell her his schedule, and more than once he had surprised her and Erika by dropping by for lunch. But today he did neither.

The only highlight of her day had been a call she had gotten from Kara. Kara had told her all about her date at the movies. Alli had heard all the happiness and excitement in Kara's voice and it hadn't taken a rocket scientist to know that Kara was really taken with this guy.

Over the past couple of days, Alli had decided to let her sister live her own life and learn from her own mistakes. Alli was certainly learning from hers. It was true what everybody said about experience being the best teacher. And deep down she knew that Kara had a good head on her shoulders.

That night, Alli was in bed but not asleep when she heard Mark walk past her bedroom door going to his room after checking on Erika. At the sound of his bedroom door closing, she got out of bed and quickly slipped into her bathrobe. Leaving her room, she walked purposefully down the hall to knock softly on his door. When moments passed and he didn't answer, she knocked again, knowing he was there.

When he didn't answer after her second knock, she opened the door, stuck her head in and called his name. "Mark." She heard the sound of the shower running, figured he was in the shower and made the decision to wait.

He walked out the bathroom stripped down to his

jeans at the same moment she walked into his room and closed the door. She tried not to notice the fact that his jeans were unsnapped.

"What are you doing in here, Alli?" he snarled.

She winced. In all her years of knowing him, this was the first time he had used that tone of voice with her. "I need to talk with you about something. I knocked twice and when you didn't answer, I thought I'd just come in and wait for you to finish your shower."

He leaned in the doorway of the bathroom. "Does what you want to talk to me about concern Erika?"

"No."

"Then whatever it is will have to wait until morning. I had a rather tiring day today and—"

"Why are you doing this, Mark?"

He tilted his head and looked at her. "Why am I doing what?"

"Casting me aside."

He crossed the room in a second flat, grabbed her wrist and stood looming before her. Anger was etched in his features. "Do you think that's what I'm doing? Casting you aside? Don't you know that I'm trying to be considerate of your feelings, Alli? I heard what you whispered to me last night, and knowing how you feel, how can you expect me to continue when I can't reciprocate those feelings? I want you, but I don't love you. As for Erika, what I feel for her is a sense of duty which I intend to carry out as long as there is breath in my body. I owe it to Matt. I care for both you and Erika but love has nothing to do with it."

Alli took a deep breath. No matter what Mark was saying, he loved Erika. He did more than care. Since living in his home, Alli had observed him with his niece and, although he wasn't quick with the kisses and cuddles, he'd always been there, helping her with Erika's feedings, baths. Why couldn't he see what was so obvious? And why couldn't he believe that over time he could love her as well? She knew loving didn't come easy for him but she refused to believe he couldn't find it in his heart ever to care anything about her. There wasn't a time when they'd made love that he hadn't made her feel loved, whether he knew he was doing so or not.

"You can love someone if you let yourself do so, Mark," she said, believing her words as she said them.

He stiffened, then let go of her hand and stared at her for a long moment. "Is this what you've been about all this time? Did you take the job as Erika's nanny because you thought doing so would be a way to get next to me? And that eventually I'd think differently about how I feel about love?"

When she didn't say anything but continued to look at him, he said in a sharp tone, "Answer me, dammit. Did you?"

Unable to believe he would ask such a thing, pain ripped through Alli. She glanced at the bed, where they had shared numerous passionate nights, before meeting his gaze. She swallowed, fighting back the emotions that were thick in her throat. "The reason I'm here as Erika's nanny is because you said you needed me, Mark."

She quickly looked away. "I guess I heard you wrong." She met his gaze again and then said, "There is no reason for me being here other than that. Good night."

Without giving him a chance to say anything, she brushed past him and swiftly walked out of the room.

Eleven

"**A**re you all right, Mr. Hartman?"

Mark opened his eyes and released his hand from the bridge of his nose, glancing across his desk at his temporary secretary. He had been in the middle of reciting a list of things he needed for her to do next week when thoughts of Alli suddenly had consumed his mind.

It had been almost a week since their argument, which was the last time he had seen her. He deliberately was gone from the ranch by the time she got up in the mornings and he didn't return until way past her bedtime. He would check on Erika every night when he got in, and a couple of times he had paused outside of Alli's door. But knowing the way things were between them was for the best, he had quickly moved on.

"Mr. Hartman?"

The woman was staring at him strangely. "Yes, Mrs.

Roundtree, I'm fine. I just had a tension headache. Let's finish this later, all right?"

She nodded as she stood. "Yes, sir. Buzz me when you're ready to get started again."

Mark heaved a deep sigh and leaned back in his chair when Mrs. Roundtree closed the door behind herself. He knew that his accusations had hurt Alli and he wanted to kick himself in the rear end every time he thought of what he'd said. But at the time, he still had been in shock at the thought that she could be in love with him.

Although he believed that letting her know how he felt had been the right thing, he owed her an apology for some of the other things he'd said. He had been wrong to suggest she'd had an ulterior motive for taking the job as Erika's nanny. He knew the only reason she was there was that he had asked her to help him out. He had told her that he needed her and he still did.

When he saw Alli again, he would give her the apology that she deserved. She was the type of woman he should be running away from. She had been pretty clear that whenever she married she would want kids and he'd been adamant about not wanting any. She always would be the type of woman who would expect her husband to love her and Mark was incapable of loving anyone. With Erika, he was there to meet her physical needs, be her caretaker and nothing more. Why was it so hard for Alli to accept things?

His thoughts were jarred with the ringing of his telephone. He quickly picked it up. "Yes, Mrs. Roundtree?"

"Jake Thorne is on line one, sir."

"Thanks. Please put him through."

As soon as the connection was made, Mark said.

"Jake? What's up man?" He wondered if Jake's call had anything to do with them getting a possible lead on the Jonathan Devlin murder.

"I just left campaign headquarters and passed by the studio, saw your truck and wondered if you wanted to join me for lunch at the Royal Diner since Alli and Erika won't be at home."

Mark lifted an eyebrow. "They won't?"

"No, they're out shopping with Chrissie."

"Oh."

Jake chuckled. "Can't you keep up with your womenfolk?"

"No, I guess I can't."

"Trust me, it'll get easier."

Mark doubted it. He checked his watch. "I can join you in half an hour."

"That's good timing. I'll stop by the sheriff's office and talk to Gavin to see if there's news on anything."

"Okay, I'll see you there."

"Oh, look Erika, this is such a pretty playsuit and it's going to look so nice on you. I can even see you wearing it on Christmas Day," Alli said as she folded the newly purchased item to place in the drawer in the little girl's room.

Too bad I won't be here to see you in it, she thought as a pain settled around her heart. She had made her decision and it was final. During the past week, Mark had withdrawn so much, retreated into a shell, that not only was he trying to avoid her, but in doing so he was avoiding Erika as well. Alli couldn't let it continue.

As painful as it had been, she had gone to the Royal

newspaper office and placed an ad for someone to replace her as Erika's nanny. Once she felt comfortable
the person Mark hired would work out, she would give
him her resignation as both Erika's nanny and his administrative assistant.

She had decided that leaving Royal would be for the
best. She had contacted a real-estate agent in Austin and,
although she hadn't mentioned anything to Kara when
she'd called yesterday, she was seriously considering
moving there. With Alli's secretarial experience and
good work record, it shouldn't be hard to find a job in
Texas's capital. She had never lived anywhere other
than Royal but felt that now it was time for a change.
She hadn't told anyone about her plans other than Christine. Alli would tell Kara when she came home next
weekend to get the car Alli had gotten for her.

The only thing Alli had to keep her going were the
memories of the time she and Mark had spent together,
alone and with Erika. Like the fuel she needed, she constantly replayed those special moments in her mind.
And she believed that no matter what Mark thought, he
was wrong. There was room in his heart for love but he
was just too bullheaded to see it.

"Da-da."

Closing the drawer, Alli crossed the room and picked
up Erika. "Your da-da hasn't forgotten you, little one. I
know for a fact that he checks on you every night when
he gets in. It's me he's trying to avoid, not you." She
pulled Erika to her and hugged her tight. This little girl
had come to mean a lot to her during the past three
weeks and she would miss her dearly when she left.

But she had to do what she had to do.

* * *

Mark walked into the Royal Diner and glanced across the room. He saw Jake and quickly moved in that direction. Jake stood, stuck out his hand and Mark took it in a handshake.

"I was beginning to think you weren't coming, Mark," Jake said smiling. "I just finished talking with Chrissie and she says that Erika and Alli are back at your place. I might as well warn you that they spent a lot of your money."

"It was for a good cause I'm sure," Mark said pulling out a chair and sitting. Not wanting to discuss Alli and Erika any longer, he asked, "Did Gavin have any other news?"

A frown appeared in Jake's rugged face. "No, but he did mention that last note that Nita received was written by the same person who wrote the others."

Mark nodded. He was afraid of that.

"Excuse me, Mr. Hartman."

Both Mark and Jake looked up to see a young woman standing beside their table. She was not someone Mark recognized, and since she wasn't wearing a uniform, he knew she wasn't one of the waitresses. "Yes?" Mark said, rising from his chair.

"I was wondering about that ad in today's newspaper. Is the position still open?"

Mark's eyes widened in surprise. He knew nothing about an ad in the newspaper. "What position are you talking about?"

The woman looked at him strangely, then replied, "The one for a nanny. The ad said you were looking for someone and I've got a lot of exper—"

"There must be some mistake. I'm not looking for a nanny and I didn't place an ad in today's paper for one."

"Oh. The paper must have run an old ad by mistake then. Sorry to have bothered you."

Mark watched the woman walk off. Instead of taking his seat, he turned to Jake and said, "Excuse me for a minute. I need to snag Manny's newspaper to check out something." He returned a few minutes later with a deep frown on his face.

"Well?" Jake asked, leaning back in the chair. "Was it a mistake?"

Mark sighed deeply. "Evidently not. There is an ad in today's paper. I called the newspaper and they said Alli came in and placed the ad a couple of days ago."

Jake lifted an eyebrow. "She's quitting?"

"Apparently."

Jake tipped back his hat. "You really don't know what's going on with your womenfolk, do you? I found out the hard way that's the worst mistake a man can make."

Mark sighed deeply thinking that no, that wasn't the worst mistake a man could make. Being a total fool was. "I have to go, Jake," he said, already crossing the diner and heading for the door. The newspaper had to be wrong. Alli could not be leaving him.

"Where do you think you're going?"

Alli's hand flew to her chest. She had just walked out of Erika's room after placing her down for her nap, only to find Mark standing in the hall with an intense look on his face. "Mark, you scared me. I didn't know you were home."

"Answer my question, Alli," he said, struggling to control his temper.

Alli inhaled deeply. "Okay, we can talk in the kitchen."

He walked ahead of her and was pacing the kitchen by the time she got there. He stopped and glared at her. "All right, now where do you think you're going? We had a deal."

"Yes, and it's one I plan to honor so I'm not going anywhere, at least not until you find my replacement. Then I will be leaving. And just so you'll know, I'll be turning in my resignation as your administrative assistant as well. I've made a decision to leave Royal and move to Austin."

Her words were like a punch in the gut. He leaned against the kitchen counter to get his bearings. *She wasn't just leaving him, but was actually planning on leaving Royal?* "Why are you doing this, Alli?"

She took a deep breath as he continued to look at her. "To me it's simple. For two solid years I've loved you, Mark, and worked hard not to ever let you know it. It was my secret and my secret alone. I'd heard about what happened to your wife and knew there was a chance you might not ever get over her and it didn't matter to me if you didn't love me because I loved you and that's all that mattered."

She walked across the floor and sat at the kitchen table. "But that's no longer true. My feelings do matter to me. I came here to be Erika's nanny and it hurt that you thought I was manipulating the situation to be your lover. That wasn't the case, Mark."

He crossed the room to join her. "I know that, Alli,

and I want to apologize for insinuating such a thing to you. I was still shocked at what you'd said the night before, although that's no excuse."

She met his gaze. "No, it's not an excuse and as far as my emotions are concerned, my feelings are my feelings, Mark, and nothing you do or say will make me change them. However, I respect and appreciate your honesty about how you feel. Therefore, I think the best thing for me to do is to leave Royal."

When he started to say something, she held up her hand. "No, Mark. You need to understand something. I've spent a large portion of my life taking care of Kara. When you came to town I fell in love with you, and I honestly thought that loving you secretly would be enough. Until I moved in here and became your lover, it was. I was even willing to sentence my sister to the same type of life I had, all work and no play. That would have been wrong. There's beauty in loving someone, sharing your time and life with that person."

She paused briefly before continuing. "Now that I know how wonderful it is to love someone openly with no boundaries, I've decided that's what I want. My only problem is the man I love doesn't want me or love me back. So the only thing left is to pick up my pride and move on. I'm not a woman who can be a man's lover and not want something in return. I have to have love. I can't change the way I feel no more than you can change the way you feel. That's why it is best for me to leave Royal and start a new life someplace else."

She took a deep breath and slowly released it as she

stood. "Now if you don't mind, I want to get some rest while Erika is sleeping."

Not giving him a chance to say anything, she hurried out of the room.

Mark remained sitting in the chair long after Alli had left. Maybe leaving Royal would be the best thing for Alli since she deserved better. But why did the thought of her leaving cause a colossal pain to settle deep in his heart? The thought of never seeing her again was something he just couldn't bear. He thought about how his relationship with Patrice had been and knew what he'd shared with Alli had been so different. Was he going to go around blaming himself for the rest of his life for Patrice's death, knowing things might not have been any different had he been in the States? He and Patrice had begun living separate lives even while residing under the same roof. He had offered to teach her self-defense many times but she had refused his offer.

He thought of all the things he and Alli had shared. There was such a goodness about her that went beyond how she took care of Erika. It went beyond how she'd taken care of her sister and, more importantly, it went beyond how she had taken care of him.

And she had taken care of him. Since she had moved to the ranch, he had experienced some of the happiest and most joyous moments of his life. Suddenly he was struck with the reason why.

He loved her.

There was no sense denying it. As much as he hadn't wanted to fall in love with her, he had, and he could be honest enough with himself to admit he had probably loved her for as long as she had loved him. But since coming to live in his home, she had shown him love and how to express it, with her and with Erika. And he wanted to continue what they shared. It no longer bothered him that Erika referred to him as her father. When she got older, he and Alli would tell her all about her parents and how much they had loved her and that Matt had entrusted her in Mark's care because deep down his brother had known that eventually he would show her love and not expose her to the loveless child-hood they had endured.

He stood, knowing what he had to do. He had to convince Alli that he loved her and wanted her as part of his life.

Alli had sworn she wouldn't cry but was doing so anyway, she thought as she wiped tears from her eyes. Moving away from Royal wouldn't be so bad. Austin was a big city with a lot of opportunities. She would make new friends and, who knew, she might even meet someone whom she could learn to love.

Fat chance! Her heart would always belong to Mark.

She lifted her head off the pillow when she heard a knock at her bedroom door. Knowing it could only be Mark, she ignored it. There was nothing left to be said. When she heard the knock again, she decided to see what he wanted. Definitely not her, she thought.

With a heartrending sigh, she crossed the room to open the door. "Yes?"

"I listened to what you said in the kitchen and now I'm asking that you listen to what I have to say."

Alli glanced down at the floor, not wanting him to

see her red-rimmed eyes. Besides, she couldn't look into his face without seeing the man she loved more than anything. Feeling somewhat composed, she finally looked up. "I'm sure your message will be the same, Mark, so why bother?"

"Please hear me out, Alli."

Instead of saying anything, she backed up to let him in. He walked over to the window and looked out a long moment before turning around to face her. "The one special memory I have of my mom that I'll always hold dear to my heart was the day she took me and Matt for a walk. I believe it was the same day the doctor had given her the news that she only had a short time to live."

He looked out the window for a moment again and then his gaze returned to Alli. "She told us the story we'd heard so many times before about how our grandparents found oil making them rich. She also said that it was her dream that that legacy would continue with our kids. It wasn't until years later after she'd died and I was raised by a father who didn't know the meaning of expressing love that I decided I would never marry nor would I have children."

He walked across the room to lean against her dresser. "While serving in the marines, I met Patrice through a friend. Her childhood had been just as rough and unloving as mine, and because of a medical condition that had left her sterile, she couldn't have children. What we entered into was more of a partnership than a real marriage. Neither of us knew how to express our emotions and we were fine with it."

He looked down at the floor a moment then back at Alli. "I'd been satisfied until Erika came into my life. I kept wanting to give her more of myself but didn't think that I could. The one thing I didn't want was for her childhood here with me to resemble the type Matt and I had with our father. But it was only until you came to live here that I could see how much distance I'd put between me and my niece, even when I hadn't meant to do so."

He crossed the room to stand before Alli. "I'd never been my happiest, Alli, until you came to live here with us. I thought I could go the rest of my life without love but I see I can't. Knowing you might be leaving Royal has knocked some sense into me. I love you, Alli. I love both you and Erika, and I don't think I could handle it if you were to leave. Stay here, marry me and make this place a home for us. I want the three of us to become a family. I told you once that I needed you. At the time I didn't know how much. Now I do. If you will have me, I will never give you a reason to want to ever leave again."

Alli's mouth trembled and she swallowed a lump caught deep in her throat. She was speechless after Mark's declaration of love.

"I'll be good to you and our daughter. I promise."

Alli blinked back her tears. "Our daughter?"

"Yes, I want us to adopt Erika and when she gets older we will tell her all about Matt and Candice. I think they would have wanted things that way."

"What about other children? I want them but you don't, Mark."

"I do now," he said softly, meaning every word. "I want to give you my babies, Alli. As many as you want. I want to be a father to our kids, a good and loving father who won't be afraid to show them how much I love them every day of my life."

Alli squeezed her eyes shut to stop the flow of her tears and dipped her head. Mark's words were making her dream come true. He reached out and tilted her chin up with the tip of his finger. "I love you, Alli. Will you marry me and continue to show me love in its purest form?"

She met his gaze, saw the hopeful look in his eyes. "Yes," she said tearfully. "I love you, too, and I want to marry you so you, Erika and I can be a family."

He pulled her into his arms and held her close to his heart. "I love you, Alli," he said for the third time that day. "Everything will work out between us and we will be a family."

She smiled up at him. "Yes, we will be a family."

He pulled her into his arms, tasting the tears on her lips. And this time he put all the emotions he'd ever held back into this kiss, wanting her to feel the love that was flowing through every vein in his body. Desire ran rampant through his blood and he needed to make love to her, claim her as his, connect with her, and let her know just how much she was loved.

He picked her up in his arms, sweeping her off her feet, and carried her over to the bed. Without uttering a word, they undressed each other and, when they were both naked, he placed her against the pillows. He thought she was the most beautiful woman in the world lying nude before him with her hair spilled over the aqua bedspread.

She reached out for him. "Make love to me, Mark."

He came to her, drew her tongue deep into his mouth, sucking on it until she groaned out. His hand went lower down her body, past her stomach to settle between her legs and found her wet, ready, hot. Pulling back, he quickly sheathed himself with a condom and then moved his body in position over hers.

He met her gaze. Held it. And when he began entering her, he knew he had come home. When he'd gone as deep as he could, he kept his body motionless, needing to feel her around him, clutching him, loving him. Then with a loud animalistic growl, he withdrew, then thrust back into her again, feeling her body shiver and shudder at his onslaught. Over and over, he withdrew and went back in, knowing this would be his home for the rest of his days. And that she was his woman.

He spread her thighs some more, grasped her hips to part her farther, then threw his head back as flesh slapped against flesh, the sound heating up their desires and passion even more.

"Mark!"

She screamed his name, once, twice, three times and he continued to move within her. Then he gritted this teeth as a howl burst from his lips and he frantically rocked his body into hers, needing to go as deep as he could with the woman that he loved.

And he did.

Mark rolled off Alli to stare at the ceiling as he fought for breath. They had made love several times before, but never with this intensity. He pulled her into his arms. "I love you."

She looked over at him and smiled, fighting for breath as he was. "I love you, too."

"I want to get married next weekend, Alli."

She let out a soft chuckle. "Rushing things, aren't you?"

He grinned. "Yes, I suppose I am. Do you think it can be arranged?"

She sighed upon seeing he was dead serious. "I'll call Kara. She was coming home next weekend anyway to get her car so that time might be perfect."

"Good, and when Erika wakes up we'll go to the jeweler so you can pick out a ring. We're going to make it a family affair."

Alli smiled. "That sounds wonderful to me."

"Da-da. " Erika's voice could be heard through the monitor.

Alli smiled sheepishly. "Oops. My screams may have wakened her."

Mark chuckled. "Or it could have been the sound of this bed knocking against the wall."

"Mark!"

"Well, it's the truth," he said laughing.

"Da-da."

Mark leaned over and flipped on the speaker that was connected to Erika's room. "Your daddy is coming, sweetheart," he said with all the love in his heart.

He glanced over at a smiling Alli. An expression of love and tenderness consumed his features when he said, "And so is your mommy."

Four days later, a smiling Mark walked into the Texas Cattleman's Club to attend a meeting that had been called by Gavin. It was a perfect Texas night and back home waiting for him were two perfect young ladies. Everything was set. He and Alli would be getting married this coming weekend. Her sister would be there as well as all of their friends. Mrs. Tucker had called two days ago to let them know she would be returning to Royal and would love to have her old job back as Erika's nanny.

Mark and Alli had jumped for joy and, since Mrs. Roundtree was working out just fine at the studio, he suggested that Alli attend school full-time to obtain her degree. When she finished, he wanted her to use the vacant space in the studio as her computer-engineering business office.

"Hartman, wipe that silly grin off your face so we can get down to business," Logan said when Mark took a seat at the table.

"Hey, don't get testy because I decided not to have a long engagement and move ahead and marry my woman. I expect all of you to be at the wedding on Saturday."

"We'll be there," Gavin said grinning. "Now let's get down to business. With this last threatening note to Nita Windcroft if things continue to escalate, one of us may need to start watching the Windcroft farm. I think Connor would be the logical choice. With his army ranger experience he will be the perfect person for the job."

Jake leaned back in his chair. "Have you broken this news to Connor yet?" he asked, thinking that his brother would have his hands full taking on Nita Windcroft. He wouldn't wish that nightmare on his worst enemy.

"No, and I don't plan to do so, either, until he returns from Virginia. This is something he needs to hear in person."

Everyone nodded in full agreement.

"Connor did indicate he wanted me to call him tonight and place him on speaker phone so he can personally congratulate you, Mark, since he won't be attending the wedding. He's still tying up loose ends."

Mark nodded, understanding.

"And we all decided," Jake said, standing, "Since all of us are here and Connor will be shortly by way of speaker phone, we'd end this meeting and turn it into a bachelor party. Everything has been set up downstairs."

Mark laughed. "Thanks, guys."

Gavin leaned back in his chair. "Any advice for die-hard bachelors?"

Mark grinned. "If you find the woman you want, don't let anything stand in your way of getting her."

Both Jake and Logan, who also were engaged, nodded in full agreement.

Gavin rubbed his chin and said, "Hmm, that's interesting advice."

Tom smiled. "It sounds pretty damn debatable if you ask me."

But all the men later agreed that a woman was something none of them could live without.

Epilogue

All eyes were on the couple on the dance floor sharing their first dance as man and wife. The wedding reception at the Hartman Ranch had been in full swing for almost an hour and everyone present had to agree it had been a beautiful wedding for such a gorgeous couple. The bride was wearing a long white bridal gown and the groom was wearing a black tux. Alli's sister, Kara, had been her maid of honor and Christine had been her bridesmaid. Jake had been Mark's best man.

Mark and Alli would be leaving later that night for a flight that would take them to Dallas and from there to Hawaii, where they would spend the next week. They couldn't imagine being away from Erika any longer than that. They were thankful that Mrs. Tucker had arrived and would be taking care of their precious darling.

Mark tightened his arms around Alli. He felt as if he

were the luckiest man alive and looked forward to being a good husband to Alli and a wonderful father to Erika. He intended to spend the rest of his life showing both of his ladies just how much he loved them.

"Nita looks nice doesn't she?" Alli asked.

Following her gaze, Mark saw Nita Windcroft talking to Mrs. Tucker. She was wearing a light blue pantsuit. "Yes, she does and this is the first time I've seen her in anything other than a pair of jeans."

Alli nodded. This was the first time she had seen Nita wearing anything but jeans, too. Alli thought the pantsuit looked really good on Nita and couldn't wait for the day she got to see Nita wearing a dress—if that day ever came. "So, Mr. Hartman, are you ready to take time away from Royal for a while?"

"As long as I am with you, Mrs. Hartman, I am ready for anything." He leaned closer and kissed her, ignoring the catcalls and applause.

When he released her, Alli glanced across the yard at her sister, who was smiling happily at her. Alli smiled back. Cameron, who had arrived in town with Kara to help her drive her new car back to Houston, was indeed a hottie. But after talking with him, Alli concluded that he was also a really nice guy. He had come from a family of attorneys and had plans to go to law school. She could tell he cared a lot for Kara and he told her that he and Kara had talked about it and had decided not to let their dates interfere with their schoolwork. Alli liked that decision. Even Mark had said he liked Cameron since he seemed to be a pretty decent and mature guy with a good head on his shoulders.

Moments later, when Mark escorted her back to their

table where Erika was sitting in her high chair, he leaned over and kissed his niece. Love ran swiftly through Alli's veins as she watched her husband. He was no longer afraid to show his emotions and for that she was thankful.

Hand in hand, they began walking around thanking their guests for coming and sharing in their special day. Happiness shone on their faces in knowing this was the beginning of their lives together and they intended to make every day exceptional.

"How about another dance, sweetheart?" Mark asked, pulling her into his arms and leading her toward the dance floor.

"I'd loved to," she said, smiling up at him.

He leaned down and brushed a kiss across her mouth. "And I love you," he said softly, thinking he could never say it enough. Never had he dreamed someone so beautiful would come into his life and help him to overcome his past, and give him the love and the passion he'd always yearned for. He gathered her closer into his arms and couldn't wait for later that night when they would be alone.

"What are you thinking about, Mark?" Alli asked, leaning back slightly to look into his eyes.

His eyes—no doubt full of love—held hers. Deciding that what he was thinking about was for her ears only, he leaned closer and whispered to her.

What he said nearly took her breath away. He smiled and hugged her closer, burying his face in the curve of her neck and inhaling the scent that was so much a part of her. "You did ask."

A smile touched the corners of Alli's lips. He had just

whispered some very naughty things that he had planned for her later. "Yes, I did, didn't I?"

"Yes, you did," he murmured softly. And then he was kissing her again.

* * * * *